SIGNALS FROM SAIPAN

SIGNALS FROM SAIPAN

REGINALD NELSON

Signals from Saipan

Copyright © 2022 by Reginald Nelson. All rights reserved.

No part of this publication may be reproduced, stored in a retrieval system or transmitted in any way by any means, electronic, mechanical, photocopy, recording or otherwise without the prior permission of the author except as provided by USA copyright law.

The opinions expressed by the author are not necessarily those of URLink Print and Media.

1603 Capitol Ave., Suite 310 Cheyenne, Wyoming USA 82001
1-888-980-6523 | admin@urlinkpublishing.com

URLink Print and Media is committed to excellence in the publishing industry.

Book design copyright © 2022 by URLink Print and Media. All rights reserved.

Published in the United States of America

Library of Congress Control Number: 2022905180
ISBN 978-1-68486-146-0 (Paperback)
ISBN 978-1-68486-147-7 (Hardback)
ISBN 978-1-68486-148-4 (Digital)

15.03.22

A PRAYER

Thank You, Lord.
Thank You for this day.
Thank You for making me a part of Your glorious creation.
Thank You for Donna.
Thank You for Neal and Stephanie, Shaun and Jarod and their families.
Thank You for Steve and Jeff and their families.
Thank You for Spenser, Sully, Scooter, Stella, Sophie and Stormy.
I ask only for knowledge of Your will for me and the power to carry it out.
I ask this in Your Son, Jesus' name.
Amen

(My daily prayer)

PROLOGUE

Sergeant José Camacho finished loading his last clip with the ammunition from the open metal ammo box that he and some of the others in his platoon were reaching into. He placed the clip into his utility belt and looked into the faces of the men around him and slowly shook his head in awe. They were all here to fight and maybe die to liberate his beloved Chamorro people from Japanese control.

José had gone through basic training with the marines and with his training he had become intimate with his .30-06 Springfield rifle. He could disassemble the weapon with his eyes closed and reassemble the rifle in record time. He was taught that his weapon was an important extension of his body. He thought of his rifle as an additional body part. A part of his being.

Most of the men in José s unit had been issued the M-1 carbine. This rifle was newer and lighter, but lacked the stopping power of the .30-06 Springfield. These men were loading their magazines from a different ammunition box on the rolling deck of the ship that had carried them to the small island off in the distance that they could see inside of the coral reef that protected the tiny island's lagoon. All of the ships in the armada had dropped anchor in the deep water outside of the reef.

The men that made up his 2nd Marine Corps platoon were all young boys from different unknown towns in the United States and also from other parts of the world. They were mostly white with varying degrees of sunburn from the intense tropical sun. The sun was relentless in this part of the world. They were just ten degrees above the equator.

José was the only Chamorro in his company. He wondered if he was the only Chamorro in this fleet tasked with taking Saipan from the Japanese. To the men in his platoon José looked to be a mix of Indian and Hispanic heritage. His dark skin was ideal to repel the withering rays that beat down upon them. It was June, 1944, and the sun never took a break. The men aboard ship had shed some or most of their fatigues to deal with the intense heat and humidity. It was the white backs, shoulders and chests that were burning that day.

Chamorro? None of the men knew what this was when they were thrown together in basic training. But there were lots of Indian tribes that most had not heard of. Was this just another unheard of tribe? Hell, the Library of Congress listed 106 different tribes in North America alone. From the Achomawi's to the Yuki Indians with many, many more unheard of names in between. What was the difference? To the men of his platoon, he was an Indian.

The first people of the Northern Mariana Islands navigated to the island sometime around 4000BC. They came from Southeast Asia. The people became known as the Chamorros and spoke an Austronesian language called Chamorro. They were expert seafarers and skilled craftspeople. They settled into Guam and the Northern Mariana Islands.

José was from Guam. His island had a long history of European colonialism, beginning with Ferdinand Magellan's Spanish expedition landing on March 6, 1521. For more than two centuries Guam was an important stopover for the Spanish Galleons that crossed the Pacific annually. They sailed from Spain to Manila, taking on supplies and fresh water in Guam. The island was controlled by Spain until 1898, when it was surrendered to the United States during the Spanish American War and later formally ceded to the US as part of the Treaty of Paris.

The United States of America had control of his island of Guam until the Japanese occupation in 1941. After the attack on Pearl Harbor, the Japanese experienced an unbroken string of victories in the Pacific. Guam, Hong Kong, Singapore and the Philippine Islands were all captured and in Japanese control. The island of Saipan that the Operation Forager armada sailed to had been under Japanese control since the Marianas were taken from the Germans by the League of Nations after World War I.

José wanted to be with the American force when they liberated his homeland, but first they were to take Saipan from the Japanese.

Saipan is unknown to almost all Americans in 'the States'. It is a tiny little dot on any world map. This little dot had huge strategic significance to the warring factions of this day. Japan had created a defensive island ring of fortifications which included Saipan and one of the smaller Mariana Islands to the south, Tinian. The United States calculated that air strikes could be commenced against the Japanese homeland with regularity from these locations.

José stood and stretched, and then moved to the ship's railing. Everywhere he looked there were ships. A huge armada had been assembled to bring José and an assault force of 105,000 marines and army men to battle the Japanese. Sixty-six thousand men would attack Saipan and Tinian, while the remaining 39,000 troops would secure Guam. 700 ships were now anchored off the western shore.

Fourteen battleships and twenty six cruisers had been pounding the tiny island in the distance with over 160,000 shells. The bombardment went on for three days. The noise from these giant guns was disquieting and José felt on edge. There were also 25 carriers and escort ships in the armada, along with 144 destroyers and many, many transports.

Word had come down that the landing would begin in the morning. José s 2nd Marine Corps and the 4th Marine Corps were tasked with securing a beachhead on the western shore of Saipan, and the 27th Army Division would back up and support the Marines. There would be 8,000 marines attempting to take the beach, while 31,000 entrenched Japanese soldiers were there to spoil their attempt. That's why the men of his platoon were checking all of their equipment and making sure that their ammunition belts were full.

José was really ready to get off of the ship and walk again on terra firma. This desire was tempered with the fear he felt in facing the deadly inferno ahead. He turned to watch the men on deck. He saw some playing cards, others writing to loved ones, and several were reading bibles. One had a harmonica and was playing a soulful tune. Men had different ways to while away the time and deal with their fears about the upcoming battle. He reached into a pocket and pulled out a cigarette. As he lit up he realized that most of the men on deck were smoking—even around the ammunition boxes.

José s thoughts drifted to his family. He came from a large family. Five sisters and two brothers. He was the oldest. It felt like a long time since he partook of the family's famous barbeques. His mouth began to water as he thought of the reef fish smoking on the grill. And all of the local vegetables and dishes that his mother created. And, of course, the rice. A meal was not a meal if there wasn't rice. His time in the States had been tough because the Marine diet was potato based for the starch, and he really missed rice.

José missed all of his family, especially his mother. The Chamorro culture was strongly maternalistic. Mom ran the family and was revered by the family. He knew that he would see them all soon. The invasion force would move on to Guam after they had finished with Saipan.

The sun had begun to set on the western horizon. José grew up witnessing picture perfect sunsets, but none of the other marines had seen anything like it. The setting sun's rays turned the lazy white clouds into fiery reds and oranges. The dark blue water of the Philippine Sea had a purple glow. The ship's railing was lined with men witnessing this natural phenomenon. "Watch for the green flash as the sun touches the water," they were told. José wondered at the excitement of the men watching. He had seen thousands of sunsets just like this one.

Night didn't bring any relief to José s nerves. The cramped quarters smelled of men who hadn't showered in days. The air was still with no breeze to carry away some of the odor. The thunder from the battleships and cruisers pounded in his brain. Tomorrow this would all stop.

José squeezed his eyes tight and tried to form a mental picture of his girl on Guam. She had large deep brown eyes and long jet black hair that hung straight to her waist. She had a wilting smile that made you want to do anything she asked. And those crooked teeth. Her laughter always brightened the spirits of those around her, and thinking of her laugh made him smile now. He missed Jaime. He slept fitfully.

At 4 am the alarm was sounded.

At breakfast the men ate in hushed silence.

Just before dawn the command was given for the thirty-four LST's, or tank landing ships to move into position about 4,000 yards from Saipan's shoreline. These craft were longer than a football field. Orders were given to load the landing craft. José and the men of his platoon retrieved their gear and clambered into the awaiting LVT (tracked landing vehicle).

He didn't like the feeling of being so tightly packed into the landing craft. Once the craft was filled with the eighteen marines that it could hold, the driver revved the engine and headed the craft toward the reef. Seven hundred and nineteen landing craft headed for the western shores of Saipan. Never before had this many landing craft been used at the same time.

The LVT's, with their caterpillar-like tracks easily crossed over the reef. The light gunboats firing 4.5-inch rockets, 20mm guns and 40mm guns toward the emplacements on the shore lead the attack, but had to withdraw from the battle when they reached the reef. Eventually a path to breach the reef would be found, but that was no help for the initial wave of 8,000 Marines.

Once they crossed over the reef and entered the lagoon, the enemy fire became intense. Artillery shells were dropping all around them. Machine gun fire penetrated the air with hot lead. The Japanese were extremely accurate with their fire. LVT's were exploding and men were dying everywhere he looked. José didn't know this, but the Japanese had prepared for the invasion by placing markers into the lagoon which they used for target practice. This proved to be ingenious and deadly.

All the men in his platoon could do was crouch and wait. Off to the left a mortar round scored a direct hit and a LVT exploded. "All those poor souls." José thought and wondered if any of his friends had been aboard that craft.

Just then a Japanese machine gun began to pepper the LVT that José s platoon occupied. The thin armor was not enough to stop the deadly rounds that found their way into the bodies of the men in the front of the craft. Then a bullet found the driver and killed him instantly. The LVT began to veer off to the north. Others scrambled for the wheel and attempted to straighten the craft and keep it headed to shore. José prayed hard. They had to reach the narrow shore and land to continue the fight. They were trained to put some serious hurt on the Japs that defended the island that day.

A mortar round streaked through the air heading right for his craft. The incoming sound from the shell was unmistakable. Men tried to scramble over the sides of the LVT just as the shell exploded. A direct hit. José never heard the deafening explosion. His body was blown out of the LVT and into the lagoon. The bullets that he had so carefully packed into his utility belt the day before now lay on the sandy bottom which became José s final resting place.

That day, June 15, 1944, the Battle of Saipan began. An initial wave of 8,000 Marines attempted to reach the western shores of Saipan. By nightfall, 2,500 Marines were dead. By the end of the first day, 20,000 Americans had made it to the Saipan shore. They were badly outnumbered. These men had to hold the beachhead until morning against an overwhelming number of Japanese defenders.

The Japanese defense strategy was simple: destroy the Marine landing force on the beachhead. The Japanese commander made the first of many fatal mistakes of the battle by choosing to wait to counterattack the American positions until the second night. By then, the American Army had resupplied the meager Marine force that remained on shore and reinforced the number of men that had reached land.

PART ONE

CHAPTER 1

Saipan, Northern Mariana Islands

I was walking leisurely along the white sandy beach in front of the house that had been leased for our stay in Saipan. I looked to the sky and thought that this was a perfect morning. The sun had yet to clear Mount Tapochau to the east of us. White cumulus clouds marched slowly by overhead. Daylight, but no direct rays from the sun and their intense heat that withered anything that moved on the island between ten in the morning and four in the afternoon. Even the unmoving plants would wither except for the 21 inches of rain that fell every year. The rain insured a constant extremely high humidity that even made breathing in a deep gulp of air difficult.

Warm, but not too hot. A light breeze was blowing in from the Philippine Sea, hitting the moist droplets of sweat on my forearms and chest and it felt cooling. The prevailing wind came from the Pacific on the eastern side of the island, but the early morning allowed for onshore effect winds from the Philippine Sea. Looking west into the lagoon, I observed the turquoise water broken by occasional dark patches. I asked about the different colors flying into the island. The turquoise was created by the sun's rays reflecting off the white sand underneath the shallow waters that made up the lagoon. The darker colors represented the sea grass that absorbed the light and prevented a reflection.

I had spent the last couple of years living in Dubai. The humidity in the United Arab Emirates was noticeably less intense than Saipan. Dubai was a desert that boasted really high temperatures in the summer months, with an annual precipitation of three and a half inches. I had come to a tropical paradise from a desert climate. Everything in Dubai was man-made, while everything here grew naturally. The man-made buildings here did not look like they belonged.

I had enjoyed a large mug of great Saipan coffee on the porch in the early morning light. The man that grew the local coffee lived just above Bobbie Blizzard on Mount Tapochau. Bobbie was a legend on this tiny island, having been here since the Trust Territory days when she served as the assistant to the High Commissioner and later as the Housing Officer. Every year she hosted an all-day Christmas party that everyone on the island was invited to. The party was held on the day that Ash and I had arrived on Saipan. What an introduction to the island! That is how I met the man responsible for the coffee I was enjoying. His name was Chuck.

Chuck's coffee was much better than any flavors that I had discovered in Dubai. His company, Marianas Coffee, was started by Chuck and his wife in 2003. The coffee plantation is nestled into the hillside of Mont Tapochau. They grow Arabica beans which are known to be smoother and contain less caffeine that their counterparts, the Robusta beans. He pulled me aside at the party and told me that, by law, only 10% of the beans had to be grown locally to use a local name, but that was not the case with Marianas Coffee! Once a year they produced coffee that was 100% locally grown. Chuck handed me a bag of his dark roasted beans and told me to enjoy.

The walk was helping to clear the fog in my brain after travelling over twenty-seven hours to arrive here. There is no direct way to fly to Saipan from Dubai. The individual legs of the trip did not appear to be that long…but the airport layover times were a killer. Awful! Ash and I had flown from Dubai to Manila. The flight was just a little over nine hours…but then the layover. Eight hours in Manila? An old and dilapidated airport that offered extraordinarily little in the way of distractions and even less in the way of comfort for someone having to enjoy their 'hospitality' for an extended period. Ash and I thought of renting a car and seeing the sights of Manila. The people in the know said, "absolutely not!" If you leave the airport, it could take you hours to return. The traffic in Manila is miserable! As newly arrived guests, Ash and I chose to pass on the car and remain at the airport.

It also seemed like every scanning machine in the airport was not functioning. There were at least three times as we moved through the airport that our carryon luggage was opened and examined. And do you think the examiners put anything back in its place? No!

A relatively short flight to Guam from Manila. This leg took a little less than four hours flying time. Then another lengthy layover in Guam. The Guam to Saipan flight takes less than an hour. So, the journey took over twenty-seven hours before we finally got to Saipan. And only thirteen hours of that time was in the air. The journey sucked! How I missed flying to destinations in my own plane with no airport time unless I chose to take a break from the cockpit.

People had told me that in the boom years there were direct flights to Manila from Saipan, but that was a decade ago. The garment industry created the boom. Beginning in 1983 factories had begun to spring up all over the island producing inexpensive clothing that could still carry the label, "Made in America". All the factories had brought many Filipinos and Chinese to this tiny island seeking work. The population grew by 30,000. The workers were paid low wages by United States standards, but the wages were more than ten times higher than in their home countries.

Saipan got away with this because they were a United States Commonwealth. The islanders had voted in 1975 to change from a Trust Territory to a Commonwealth. The Commonwealth began in

1978. I have talked to people on the island that were living in Saipan through and after the conversion, and they would say to me, "Reggie, the mood was like that of the Wild West days in America." That phrase conjured up visions of gunfights in the streets and outlaws running wild through the little towns in the American west. Not very civilized!

Those factories began to close by 2005. Three lawsuits were settled in California by twenty-six retail companies and twenty-three garment factories. The signing of the North American Free Trade Agreement (NAFTA) in 1994, and the lawsuits killed a thriving industry and plunged the island into a deep depression. All the factories were closed by 2009. Many foreign workers were forced to leave the island and return to their home countries. Back to forced labor conditions at thirty-five cents an hour! Over twenty thousand foreign workers had left. Only forty-eight thousand people left on Saipan. Quite a hit…

After a decade of a very depressed economy, the tourism industry, which had thrived alongside the garment industry, became the only major industry and the island began to recover. The lure of a tropical island, beautiful turquoise water and sandy beaches on the west side of the island, and much for the World War Two history buffs to explore was a strong draw to the people of Asia. Tourists from Russia, Japan, Korea and China made up most of the visitors to Saipan.

In the States, we call them, "snowbirds," Ash intoned as we walked.

"Not exactly," I interjected, "Snowbirds come from the colder northern climes and 'winter' in the warmer southern climes of Florida and Arizona. They often spend months away from the cold. The Asian visitors here in Saipan rarely stay for more than two weeks."

"Alright…I get the point…but you do not need to be so technical!" Ash replied.

He made an 'about face' and headed back into the house. "I have to use the head," he announced, and jogged off ahead of me.

I continued to walk in silence. My thoughts were of Saipan and its history.

The islanders were placing all their eggs in one basket...tourism. What would happen if something went wrong with the tourism industry?

I was pondering how we had come to this spot and why I was in Saipan when a metallic greenish copper glint caught my eyes. I glanced down and there it was. Lying just barely into the lapping waves of seawater along the white sandy shore. A bullet. It was this object that reflected in the morning light that caught my attention. I bent down and picked the bullet up. It was crusted with a calcium-like buildup and most of the copper jacket had a green patina to it. The brass bullet head also was covered in a green patina.

As I turned the bullet over in my hand and it hit me like a locomotive. This was a bullet that was seventy years old! This bullet had found its way into the calm lagoon during the Battle of Saipan in 1944! The bullet had probably fallen out of an ammo clip belted to a dead American Marine that fell into the shallow lagoon on the island's western shore. The US soldier had died in the salty water along with 2,500 men on the morning of June 15, 1944. It had taken seventy years for the ocean tides to push the bullet that I now held in my hand to the shore.

I recognized that the pointed projectile was from a .30-06 rifle. The more popular M-1 ammunition sported a blunt, rounded bullet. This was from a Springfield! My dad had one that I used for target practice when I was growing up. Great rifle. My father used that rifle for deer and elk hunting in Colorado. I never went on those hunting trips with him. Some of the time he came home with a deer or an elk and mom would cook the venison. I never liked the taste...too gamey.

I held the bullet gently in my hand, closed my eyes, and for a few moments, forgot about why Ash Black and I had been summoned to Saipan, and imagined the battle that took place on the very beach I was walking seventy years ago.

I returned to our rented house and I carefully placed the bullet on the kitchen counter. Ash came out of his room and asked about what I had found.

"A seventy-year-old bullet," I answered, somewhat in awe.

"What?" Ash asked as he picked the bullet off of the counter.

"It's a relic from World War II. The Battle of Saipan. Fought seventy-seven years ago this year!" I replied.

"You found this right out there?" Ash pointed to our small piece of beachfront out the glass patio doors.

"Yep," I answered.

I poured Ash a cup of the Marianas coffee and refilled my cup. We took the mugs out to the patio table where I had started my day alone to talk about our agenda for the day.

"They asked us here to help them with the China smuggling issue," Ash began.

"Let's be careful with that word, 'they'," I added.

"Reggie, what the hell…this is a tiny little island. There aren't that many 'they's'", Ash exclaimed.

"We've been here less than a day and I already have a sense that there are the locals in one hand against the federal government in the other," I added.

"So, Sir Reginald, who are we working for?" Ash asked.

"Drop the 'Sir' crap, Ashonte'," I began.

"It just sounds so regal, but I'll drop it if you drop the 'Ashonte' crap," Ash replied.

"No regal here," I answered.

"So, answer the damn question," Ash intoned.

"We were called by the local Saipan government, not USCIS," I said.

"USCIS?" Ash asked.

"United States Customs and Immigration Service," I replied.

"Oh my God…not the federal government…might as well call them USELESS!" Ash retorted.

"No, Ash, not the Feds. We were asked here by the local government," I added.

"Okay, I may be the most obtuse black man on this speck of an island, but isn't this a US territory?" Ash asked.

"Absolutely right, my friend, but when the CNMI moved out of the Trust Territory days and voted to become a United States Territory, there was a huge struggle over how much of their individual autonomy the people of Saipan were willing to give up," I replied.

"CNMI…USCIS…it's too early in the morning for this alphabet soup crap," Ash retorted.

"Commonwealth of the Northern Mariana Islands," I added. "Ash, how many commonwealths are there in the United States?" I asked.

"Well, let us see…Virginia's a Commonwealth. By the way, what the hell is a Commonwealth?" Ash asked.

I cut Ash off without a response. "Who else?"

Ash thought for a moment, then replied, "What about Puerto Rico?"

"Right on!" I answered. "And they are another United States Territory."

"They're bankrupt and owe over thirty billion dollars. Not a great example of anything!" Ash retorted.

"Ash, technically, they cannot declare bankruptcy," I replied.

"You blowhole!" Ash replied.

"What?" I asked.

"They fucking owe over thirty-two BILLION dollars! Tell me that isn't bankrupt!" Ash answered.

I realized that it was pointless to continue in this line of reasoning. Besides, Ashonte' was right! How does a small island of 2.8 million people get so many billions in debt?

"And what about Greece?" Ash continued.

"We're getting way off course," I answered. "Let's get back to the Commonwealths."

"Cannot think of anything but Virginia and Puerto Rico," Ash began.

"And the CNMI," I added.

I continued, "Kentucky, Massachusetts and Pennsylvania are also Commonwealths."

"Back to my question…what is a Commonwealth?" Ash asked. "And what are those ships out there beyond the lagoon?"

"Those are Pre-Positioned ships," I answered.

"What?"

"You heard me, Pre-Positioned ships."

"And?"

"I googled the answer earlier this morning. There are thirty-two Pre-Positioned ships stationed around the world. Their primary mission is to resupply an American invasion force within seventy-two hours after the commencement of hostile action," I began. "I was told that when the Marines hit a beach, they carry with them enough provisions for three days. Those ships out there can reach anywhere in the world to support the invasion force within that time."

"You said thirty-two ships?"

"That's right, my friend."

"I count only six anchored out there beyond the reef."

"Maybe because China and North Korea are so close!"

"Oh…that's comforting," Ash exhaled. "There are two gray ships and four black and white ships…what's the difference?"

"I was told that the gray ships are Army and the black and white are Navy," I answered. "But what do I know…seems to me that the gray ships should be Navy, like all the Navy vessels."

Ash studied the ships for a while longer then turned to me and leaned into the table. "Reggie, what are we doing here? This feels like we are way out of our league. Chinese money laundering? How can we help the local government here in Saipan cut down on the number of wealthy Chinese who choose to bring their money here?"

"Ash?" I questioned.

"Listen to me, please." I asked.

"What?"

"There's another reason we are here…"

"Oh?" Ash replied, "Spill it."

"I'll explain later, once we're into our day." I hinted.

"Now, back to my question…what is a Commonwealth?"

Denver, Colorado

Lance Wood was meeting with the Denver team of five men that worked for I.N.C.I.S.O.R..

Lance had formed I.N.C.I.S.O.R. with Reggie and Ash toward the end of their first escapade thwarting the attempts of a terrorist organization to detonate a nuclear device which was buried in the Arctic National Wildlife Refuge in an area called the North Slope in Alaska. Had the Saudi terrorists been successful, all of the oil reserves that had been discovered in the area would have been rendered radioactive and useless for the next fifty years…at least. The United States would have been forced to rely on Saudi Oil for their short- and, more importantly, long-term fuel needs.

The three men, Reggie, Ash and Lance, decided to enlist their wives to help them fight terrorism, and to form two teams of five men to continue the fight against terrorism. One of the teams was stationed in Denver, Colorado, and the other team was located in Frankfurt, Germany.

Reggie had worked with the CIA to develop two unique high-tech gadgets that were proving to provide invaluable information for the fight against terrorism around the world.

The PC was a tiny device with a Nano transmitter which was implanted into the teeth of suspected terrorists in the dental clinic in Dubai. The CIA had cameras and facial recognition software installed in Reggie's clinic, and they directed the dental team to implant the PCs into certain people. The dental clinic was continuing without Reggie at the helm after his abduction by Al Qaeda. One of the Denver team had been killed during his rescue. Max Galloway was hit by a stray bullet and died during that mission.

Michael MacAteer was Max's replacement, and the reason Lance was gathered with the Denver team. Michael had broken both legs steering a speeding truck off of a ramp and into the wheelhouse of a yacht to rescue Mariola who wore the second high tech invention.

The 'mini' as it was nicknamed, was a tiny transmitter that gave extremely accurate GPS data, but was only activated when word of a kidnapping or abduction came through. The mini had allowed a rapid response and rescue of a number of terrorist and kidnap victims.

Lance and the rest of the Denver team, Lance Everett, Powers Hunt, Flex Lawson and Duncan Trevino, were evaluating Michael's recovery. His legs had not responded well during physical therapy, and it was obvious that Michael's days doing field work were over. The team would need another replacement…and what to do with Michael?

Lance had retained all of the resume's that he had acquired during weeks of interviews to put together the two teams of I.N.C.I.S.O.R.. He had placed them into priority piles with his top ten backups on top. He had already used the first of these files when he replaced Max with Michael. Who was to be next?

Dubai, UAE

Becky Nelson was just finishing with her long list of emails and stretched as she rose to move to the kitchen. She did not like their house on Palm Jumerah since Reggie was abducted by Al Qaeda. Nothing had actually happened at the house, and the CIA operatives assured her that she was safer there than Fort Knox. But Dubai now gave her a sour, even bitter taste in her mouth.

Reggie had always dreamed of owning a vineyard in Italy, and they both had a wonderful trip scoping out the available properties around Florence. Becky especially loved the rolling hills and the open feeling of the Tuscan countryside. Any worries seemed far away when she walked among the olive trees and grape vines.

Reggie and Ash had been summoned to a tiny little island named Saipan that Becky had never heard of. Reggie had also received a call from Somalia asking for I.N.C.I.S.O.R.'s help with their pirate problem. Becky was with the two men when they discussed their next venture, and she heard them talk about the instability of the government in Somalia. Maybe that was why they were off to Saipan?

As Becky waited for the water to boil, she thought about the women that she had become so close to…the wives of Lance and Ash. A tear welled up in her eye as she thought about Grace. Ashonte's wife had been killed in Israel by a terrorist bomb while visiting the wife of Israel's Prime Minister. Ashonte' never healed from that loss and became a hard, mean man who now demanded to be addressed as Ash.

Cyndi Wood was the third female that made up I.N.C.I.S.O.R.. She had returned to Denver from Dubai after Reggie's abduction, and swore that she would never return to the Middle East again. Lance was with her now in Denver, and Becky pondered whether she would ever see Cyndi or Lance again. Lance had passed on the opportunity to join Reggie and Ash in Saipan. He was not asking to get out… but he had never passed on an adventure before. Cyndi's influence? Becky wondered.

As Becky gave her tea time to steep, she thought about Michael MacAteer in Denver and had an 'aha' moment. Michael could come here to Dubai and run the command center from here…at least while she got their new digs ready south of Florence.

She picked up the phone and looked at the clock. Saipan was six hours ahead of Dubai.

Saipan, Northern Mariana Islands

"Great idea, my love!" I said into the phone. "I'll ask Lance to talk to Michael about this. He's looking for Michael's replacement right now."

"Did Lance say anything when he passed on your trip?" Becky asked.

"Nope, just wanted to stay in Denver," I replied.

"You get any vibes?" Becky asked.

"No…what's up?" I asked.

"I've got this 'gut feeling'," Becky answered.

I knew from over thirty years with this woman that when her gut spoke it was like the long-running commercial for EF Hutton. When EF Hutton speaks, everybody should listen. I sat up a little straighter. "And?" I asked.

"I don't know…I have this feeling like I will never see Lance and Cyndi again," Becky replied.

I quickly did the math…there were six of us at the end of the Saudi Oil Gambit. Grace had died. If Lance and Cyndi were done with I.N.C.I.S.O.R.…then there would only be the three of us…Ash, Becky and me. I was suddenly feeling extremely far away from Becky. Hell, we still had the two teams strategically stationed to respond to issues around the globe…but the good friends…Ash, Lance and me, and our wives, who also had become remarkably close…I did not like the way this felt.

"My love, you know your gut is the gospel in my world. I will see if I can glean anything from Lance when I talk to him about Michael. Everything okay in Dubai?" I asked.

"Okay, yes, but I don't feel good about being here anymore," Becky added.

"Well, if Michael is up for this, you can leave Dubai as soon as you have shown him the ropes," I replied.

"Good, okay…I love you," Becky said through the phone.

I missed her already. "I love you, too."

Saipan, Northern Mariana Islands

"So, my friend, what do we do with our day?" I asked.

Ash looked out at the turquoise water for a moment then turned to me. "This is a lazy, adjustment day after that wicked flight, right?"

"Yep," I replied.

"How about a jog on the beach then a trip into Garapan to find some sushi. There has to be decent sushi here." Ash exclaimed.

"Sold!" and I went to find some running shoes.

Greenville, SC

The new plane was wheeled out of the Steven's Aerospace hangar.

The paint job looked identical to pictures they had been shown of Aurora, Dr. Reginald Nelson's private aircraft.

This new plane was also a pusher prop. A new version of the Avanti, called the EVO. It was faster, rated to a higher ceiling, quieter and able to carry a larger payload.

"Beautiful! Dr. Nelson knows nothing about this," the CIA agent in charge of the project said to his associate, as they looked upon the airplane being pulled out onto the ramp.

"Our job's done here," the associate said, swatting at a mosquito. "Just in time too. These bugs have been eating me alive."

"We'll turn the plane over to the ferry crew and it will be on the way to Saipan," the first agent said.

"I wonder what Dr. Nelson will call this plane…"

CHAPTER 2

Saipan, Northern Mariana Islands

Ash and I took our rental car and headed north on Beach Road toward Garapan. Beach Road is one of two major north-south thoroughfares on the island of Saipan. Beach Road, route 33, runs along the western edge of the island, often hugging the shoreline as it winds into the major town on Saipan. It did not take us long to reach the southern end of town as we encountered our second stoplight at the Hard Rock Café.

I was navigating and my phone GPS said to turn right at this light and head east for a few blocks. Winding on the side streets for a while, we were able to spot our destination, Himawari, a Japanese restaurant and grocery store. The upstairs hotel was popular among the scuba diver crowd that flew here to Saipan to see the World War Two ship and plane wrecks. The establishment was well known for its fresh fish. We figured it would be a good restaurant to satisfy our need for sushi and sashimi.

We sat at the sushi bar and picked our lunch items from the impressive and widely varied menu. Ash and I both ordered an ice-cold Asahi super dry beer. Once the beer had been served and our order taken, I began to speak, "Ash, the money laundering gig is just a front."

"What? Like a cover?" Ash asked.

"Yes, we have another purpose for being here…" I trailed off.

Denver, CO

The team of five men had just finished a strenuous workout and had all piled into Lance's van to find a lunch place.

Lance drove north on Quebec from the Greenwood Athletic Club. At the Belleview light his van was the fourth car in line waiting for the light to turn green.

Suddenly, all four doors on the sedan in front of the van flew open and four occupants quickly exited the car. Lance Everett was riding shotgun and shouted to the other team members, "they all have automatic weapons!"

Flex, Powers and Duncan were shoulder to shoulder in the back of the van, watching the action unfold.

The four occupants ran to the back of the car in front of theirs and began to fire. Short, calculated bursts were directed at three of the people in that car. One managed to get his door open and begin to exit the vehicle. Powers saw that he was in a uniform and wore a sidearm. The man never had a chance to draw his weapon before he was cut down by the gunfire.

Powers yelled, "We have to do something!"

Lance replied, "all we have are our handguns. They are no match for that kind of firepower."

All caution to the wind, the van doors all flew open, and the team worked to extricate themselves from the automobile. The attackers in front of them did not immediately notice the activity behind them. Their focus was on killing the people in front of them.

Lance and Flex both aimed their drawn weapons on the attackers. Two of the men dropped instantly. The other two occupants wheeled and trained their weapons on the Denver team. The five men huddled behind the van doors, seeking some kind of protection from the onslaught of automatic fire aimed their way.

Flex was hit in the arm and his pistol flew away toward the rear of the van. Powers was closest to Flex and went to help Flex with his wound. The other three watched as the remaining two attackers pulled a woman from the back of the car and rushed her to their vehicle. They attempted to continue the barrage of bullets, but their weapons sprayed wildly as they were fired single-handedly. They reached their vehicle, quickly entered and sped away with bullets from the Denver team spraying their car.

"What just happened here?" Duncan yelled.

"Looks like a kidnapping," Powers replied.

"They were treating the woman with respect. Not manhandling her like a kidnap victim," Lance interjected.

"Anybody else hurt?' Powers asked. He was able to apply pressure to Flex's arm and the bleeding was contained. "Looks like a through and through."

The others indicated that they were okay and began to make their way to the severely damaged car. Two of the attackers lay on either side of the car. Duncan checked the first body. "This one has had it," he said.

"Same on this side," Lance replied.

Duncan was checking the remaining three occupants of the car. The bodies were badly shot up and all were dead. "No joy on the inside," he called out. There was blood splatter all over the broken windows, seats, dash and bodies.

Shortly after their initial examination of the scene, two Greenwood police cars sped into the area. The officers drew on the Denver team and demanded that they drop their weapons and get their hands in the air.

Lance yelled for the team to comply. The sound of an ambulance siren could be heard coming their way.

Saipan, Northern Mariana Islands

"Okay Reggie," Ash queried, "What gives?"

Just then our sushi arrived. We had both ordered the same item…the Sakura set that came with several different fish attached to a rice base. A healthy dollop of wasabi and a mound of pickled ginger rounded out the plate. The sushi plate was accompanied by a fresh green salad with Japanese dressing and a bowl of miso soup.

"Let's eat and then we can talk," I suggested as the waitress served our food.

The sushi was exquisite, although maneuvering the chopsticks was a challenge for me. Ash did not seem to struggle with them at all. I asked for a spoon to dive into the soup bowl. "No, no, no!" Ash exclaimed. "Do like the Asians do! Pick up the bowl with your hands and drink from the bowl!" I complied. This was much easier than slurping the soup from a spoon, but I knew that if my mother were to see this she would turn over in her grave.

With our stomachs comfortably full, I suggested that we retrieve the rental car and drive north. I headed the car onto the north-bound lanes of Middle Road.

"Where are we going?" Ash inquired.

"Radar Hill," I replied.

"What's that?" Ash asked.

"The Air Force installed a giant radar on top of Mount Petosukura in the late eighties, to spy on the Soviet Union. It was Cold War stuff. They built this big secret facility, named Pacbar III, which stood for Pacific Barrier Radar. The published mission was to detect and track Soviet satellites and missile launches. This was the third in a series of spy radar sites established by the United States Air Force in the western Pacific. These radar were also called Relocatable Over-The-Horizon Radar, or ROTHR."

"There was a more sinister, unpublished spy mission for this radar site, which brings me to what I have wanted to reveal to you." I paused for effect. "The CIA also added something to this site. This radar dish was not only for receiving and detection, but transmission. They could alter the transmissions coming from the Soviet Union to their satellites and rockets to interfere with the success of those missions."

"The CIA earlier had built a bunch of concrete homes on Capitol Hill to train insurgents to be used to overthrow various Communist regimes in Asia. Access by the general public to the northern part of the island of Saipan was restricted for many years. The authorities blamed the restriction on 'unexploded ordinance'."

"That's like that bullet I found along the shoreline! People find remains from the World War Two conflict every day. And it has been more than seventy years since the Battle of Saipan. I think a better excuse for the restrictions came from this radar facility," I paused again as we reached our turn to begin the climb up Radar Hill.

We turned right and Ash read the sign to our left, "As Matuis? What kind of name is that? Is this Matuis's ass?"

"No," I rebutted, "As Matuis is the name of this village."

We continued up route 320 to a large, blue million-gallon water tank, and veered right onto route 318 to continue up to the radar facility.

As we approached, Ash exclaimed," What a piece of junk!"

"You're right," I added. The site has been sitting empty since the late nineties."

"In God We Rust!" Ash added. "What does this thing have to do with anything about us?"

I parked the car and Ash and I approached the dilapidated concrete bunker and the lonely radar pointing straight to the heavens.

Ash stuck his head inside the building and shouted, "This looks like a place for teens to come to get laid! Look at all the condom wrappers!"

"Time to spill the beans," I suggested.

CHAPTER 3

Saipan, Northern Mariana Islands

"Ash, you know how the experts can tell where a batch of explosives, like C-4 were manufactured?" I asked.

"Yeah! They have placed markers in explosives manufactured after the treaty in 1991."

"What treaty?"

"Okay, it wasn't exactly a treaty. It was the International Civil Aviation Organization's Convention on the Marking of Plastic Explosives for the Purpose of Detection," I replied.

"Treaty is easier…how do you remember this crap?"

"The taggant of choice is DMNB, or 2,3-dimethyl-2,3-dinitrobutane." I continued.

"Okay, so…"

"Well, C-4 is the favorite explosive for al-Qaeda. They even publish it in their traditional curriculum of explosives training."

"How do you know this?"

"I just do! I was Googling C-4 and got hung up on the taggant. The stuff is in all C-4 and is used to detect the presence of the explosive."

"Okay, so what?"

"Well, a night after reading this article, I bolted upright from my slumber. What is the name of the taggant?" I asked.

"What did you say? DNMB?" Ash asked.

"No, DMNB, or more accurately, DMDNB. What is the name?"

"Stop teasing me! I have no idea what you said." Ash retorted.

"Very simply, dimethyl dinitro butane with some numbers stuck into the name."

"Once again, okay…"

"Pronounce the name," I ordered.

"Dimethyl dinitro buta…"

"Get it?"

"No…wait…Yes! Butane!" Ash answered.

"Good boy!" I Replied.

"Don't call me 'boy'," Ash bantered.

"Okay, sorry. I meant it like 'schoolboy',"

"So, the operative word is 'butane'," Ash surmised.

"Yes, and…"

"Butane is combustible." Ash answered.

"And..."

"I don't get it," Ash intoned.

"Butane is highly volatile," I continued.

"That is how it can be used as a taggant. I get it!" Ash answered.

"Partly," I continued, "C-4 is extremely stable as an explosive compound, but what awakened me was that butane is not stable at all."

"That's why all of the other names in the taggant. The dimethyl and dinitro part, right?" Ash asked.

"Yes and no..., let's get out of this heat and get a drink," I suggested.

Denver, CO

Flex was delivered via ambulance to Swedish Hospital. While he was being examined by the emergency team, his four compatriots arrived. They took up positions two by two on both sides of the gurney. They all began to talk at once, each recounting his experience with the shootout.

Just then the emergency room physician flung the curtain wide and entered the space.

He addressed Flex, ignoring the other men in the room, "The Xray confirms that the bullet passed completely through your arm and did no vital damage. A couple of stiches and a bandage will suffice." With his diagnosis made, he wheeled on his heels and departed, leaving the curtains wide open. A nurse entered the space and began administering to Flex's arm. "We'll get you all patched up!" The nurse was young with a hot body.

Flex looked at the others surrounding the bed and observed that none of them were looking at him. All eyes were glued on the nurse's ass.

"Hey guys, what's up?"

Now that their intent gazes were interrupted, they began to chuckle. The incident now seemed a long time ago.

The chatter around the bed resumed as the nurse finished with the bandage.

Just then an Arapahoe County Sheriff's deputy ambled into the emergency space.

"Hello boys," he intoned, "I have an update for you."

All five men focused on the deputy.

"The woman you saw kidnapped is the head of a local Mexican gang here in Denver. This was not a kidnapping, but a prison break. She was being transported from a hearing in downtown Littleton back to the Arapahoe County jail when the Sheriff's transport was hit. I thought you would want to know."

"Thanks, deputy," Lance spoke, "Who was the woman? What was her name?"

"Melania Cruz. She is head of the most notorious Mexican gang in Denver, the Gallant Knights Insane. These are bad dudes. We estimate that there are 20,000 Chicano gang members in Denver and the outlying suburbs. I think that these assholes are the worst. We have them implicated as having been responsible for crack cocaine and firearms trafficking, homicides, drive-by shootings, aggravated assaults, home invasions and robberies in the metro area."

"A one-stop crime syndicate," Duncan responded. "I always liked what Mickey Mantle said about gangs…a gang is where cowards go to hide."

"Again, bad dudes," the deputy replied. "And Melania Cruz was one of the worst. We had her dead-to-rights for a multiple homicide. She was going to be headed to Florence to live out the rest of her evil days."

"I know of that place," Flex said. "It's call ADX. It houses four hundred prisoners that the country has deemed 'the worst of the worst'. It is the highest security prison in the country! The prisoners live in long-term solitary confinement for the rest of their days on this planet."

"Not Melania, not now," the deputy said.

"We're involved now, how can we help?" Powers asked the deputy.

"I'll inform my Sheriff. See if he wants your help," the deputy replied, and turned to go.

Saipan, Northern Mariana Islands

Ash and I entered Godfathers and chose seats at the bar. We arrived shortly after they opened at 5 o'clock. The horseshoe shaped bar was manned by young Filipino girls dressed in miniskirts. One approached us as we took our seats.

"Hafa Adai, what is your pleasure?" she asked.

"Double Crown Royal on the rocks with a twist," I replied.

"Long Island Iced Tea for me," Ash added.

She put down two napkins at our places to indicate that we had ordered and went to make our concoctions. I reached for a bowl of peanuts from the place next to where I sat and moved it between the two of us. Ash seized a handful and began to shell the first peanut. I also grabbed one from the bowl.

"Hafa Adai? Like 'hello'?" Ash asked.

"Yes, that is the Chamorro's hello," I replied. "Just like aloha in Hawaii, but you pronounce it like 'Half-a-day'.

"Half-a-day," Ash practiced.

We waited quietly for our drink order to appear.

"Now to continue," I broke the silence. We had driven from Radar Hill in silence and had not spoken to each other while entering the bar. "I could not get that butane taggant out of my mind. I did a little more research. C-4 is relatively stable with an explosion temperature of 263 to 290 degrees Celsius."

"That's why those Arab idiots love it!" Ash added. "Hard to mess up."

"True, but butane has a flash point of -60 degrees Celsius," I continued. "That got me curious."

"So, I called our lab buddies at CIA in Langley and posed the question, could the taggant, butane, be excited enough to ignite automatically and set off the C-4?"

"Those lab dudes got really excited and intrigued. Soon, they were off working on a new project for I.N.C.I.S.O.R.! We have been working on this question for the last six months, conversing back and forth."

"So, what did they find? Ash interjected as the drinks arrived. "It must be something good or we wouldn't be here, right?"

"Well, yes," and I hesitated to make Ash squirm. He is not a patient man and I loved doing this to him! "It turns out that a proper radio wave frequency can excite the butane and set off the C-4 as if a detonator had been used."

"So, all of those hordes of explosives sitting in third world countries with any of the multitude of terrorist groups can be set off remotely?" "That is genius!" "That will set the terrorist trade back several decades!"

I replied, "And they won't know what hit them! At least right away."

"Here's to you," Ash said as he raised his glass. I lifted mine to meet his glass. "Thanks."

"So, our first adventure involved your invention of the PC, or Post and Core listening device placed in teeth."

"Yes," I replied.

"Next was the mini. That allowed a person to be tracked via GPS but was activated remotely so the kidnappers could not scan for the device," Ash continued.

"Right on, although the avoidance of World War Three played a major part in the second adventure," I added.

"Yep, and what was different with both of these devices? They were somewhat passive."

"I agree," I said.

"This thing is an active assault on terrorism around the world! I love it!" Ash intoned, "Another toast. What are we going to call this?"

We clanked glasses again.

"I was thinking…remember Radio Free Europe?"

"Yeah…those were broadcasts into Communist countries during the Cold War," Ash replied.

"Well, it's a little more than that…Radio Free Europe is a United States government-funded organization that broadcasts to countries in Eastern Europe, Central Asia, Caucasus and the Middle East. Anywhere the free flow of information is banned by government authorities. They have been headquartered in Prague since 1995."

"I had no idea," Ash said.

"Yeah, twenty-seven languages to twenty-three countries," I added.

"And it's still going on? I thought that stuff was during the Cold War," Ash replied.

"Still going," I took a sip from my drink.

The bartender checked in on us. "My twist is green," I commented. "It is supposed to be lemon."

"Local lemon," she replied. "Local lemons are green."

"What are limes?"

"Orange," and she left to fetch us another round.

I sat there open-mouthed, formulating a cute reply, but she was gone.

"So, Ash, I was thinking of calling this Radio Free World," I continued.

"RFW…cute…so…how's it work? I still don't get why we are here in Saipan," Ash said.

"Well, a lot of the research done over the last six months has been testing and isolating the proper radio frequency to excite the butane… that was the easy part…and then how to transmit the frequency."

"And…" Ash pried.

"It turns out that the proper radio frequency excites a wide range of objects…vibrating them to pieces," I added.

I glanced around the bar and noticed that all of the stools were occupied. Also, there were people in most of the booths against the wall. I observed two other details…almost all of the patrons were older men, and almost all of them were white.

The gent sitting next to Ash had eavesdropped on our conversation. He wondered out loud, with a strong German accent, "Where are you two from? You sound like you're from the States."

"Haven't lived there for a while," Ash replied, and the conversation grew to include men on both sides of us.

Washington, DC

"What gives with the project in Saipan?" President Marron asked.

President Steve Marron succeeded former president John James as POTUS. President James had completed his eight years as president. His two terms had been extremely busy and trying on his health. His hair was completely silver, and he looked much older than a number of his close peers.

President James had several encounters with the I.N.C.I.S.O.R. group and had not been disappointed. The new president had the same party affiliation as the former president. He was a card carrying Republican. Because of that affiliation, President James had closely counseled President Marron about I.N.C.I.S.O.R.…. President Marron understood that he could trust Reggie Nelson and all of the I.N.C.I.S.O.R. team.

"They are moving forward, Mr. President," an aide replied. "The project should wrap up in two months."

"It cannot be soon enough! I would love to strike a deadly blow to terrorism in this world, and in our lifetime!" the President spoke. "Keep me informed."

Frankfurt, Germany

The makeup of Team Frankfurt was similar to Team Denver. The I.N.C.I.S.O.R. team also comprised five men, Stirling Mason, Magnus Harper, Dick Becker, Aaron Dekker and Graham Sandler.

The team gathered at their headquarters in the hangar at the Frankfurt airport. All of the men had T-shirts and shorts on, having just finished a rigorous training for the last two hours. They were covered in sweat.

Dick spoke, "What do you think about Flex being shot?"

"Pretty interesting, those guys coming upon a 'jailbreak'," Stirling replied.

"You know, things are kinda slow here. We should see if they need our help." Aaron added.

"Yeah!" They all spoke at once.

Dubai, UAE

"Hello," Becky answered the phone.

"Hey, Becky!" Magnus answered.

"How are things in Germany?" Becky replied.

"Not much happening here…can I pick your brain?"

"Sure, what's up?"

"The team in Colorado…think we could offer them a hand?"

"Super idea. I'll get you five tickets to Denver and let Reggie and Ash know."

"Cool, Mrs. Nelson!"

"Don't call me that…I think of Ozzie and Harriet when I hear that."

"Who?" Magnus asked.

"Never mind, you young pup!" Becky said. "Can you call and check on Flex?"

"Sure, Uh, Becky."

Saipan, MP

"Hello my love," I answered.

"Hey, old man!" Becky joked. "The Germany I.N.C.I.S.O.R. team is going to head to Denver to help get things rolling on that Mexican gang situation. What is happening in Saipan?"

"Sun, sun and more sun…it is hot here! Hard to function outside between ten in the morning and four in the afternoon.

"Well how do you think it is here in Dubai?"

"I know. How much longer before you're outta there?"

"Less than a month, I hope."

"We'll be a month or so while they get the radar redone. Want to come here? We can watch each other sweat!"

"That sounds like fun. I can tell you miss me."

"I do! I didn't mean it in a bad way. You know that after this long away from you I am horny with a capital H!"

"I'll think about it. I'm missing being close to you, too."

"I love you."

"Me too, bye."

"How's Becky?" Ash inquired.

"She's good…but she's had it with Dubai…the Germany team is joining the Denver team," I replied.

"Okay…tell me more about this radar thing," Ash urged.

"Let's continue later…and get to know these guys," I responded.

Denver, CO

Lance gathered the remaining three members of I.N.C.I.S.O.R.'s Denver team at their training facility. Flex was taking some needed personal time. Michael was at his apartment, packing.

"I don't have a replacement for Michael yet. I had hoped to have one picked before he moved to Dubai, but he's going to be outta here in the morning," Lance offered.

"So, it's just us," Powers replied.

"Not for long," Lance continued. "The Germany team is on their way to join you."

"And why not Michael?" Duncan added.

"He's recovered pretty well from the two broken legs suffered in Poland, but field-ops are out of the question for him. He's still involved, but he will be our research, communication and behind the desk guy in Dubai," Lance said.

Lance Everett added, "And Becky's moving to Italy?"

"That's right…she'll show Michael the ropes in Dubai, then turn the house on Jumeriah Beach Palms over to him," Lance replied.

"So, what do we do with our run-in with the Mexican gang?" Lance continued.

"Been doing some research…bad dudes, but we have to try to get that woman back!" Powers said.

"Good lives were lost because of that Marisa Cruz," Lance Everett admonished.

"Its Melania Cruz," Lance rebutted.

"Oh, yeah…sorry…Melania, Melania," Lance Everett practiced.

"Their headquarters are on the west end of Denver. Do you think they'd be stupid enough to take her there?" Duncan questioned.

"Doubt it…but it's a place to start!" Powers added.

Langley, VA

The two CIA lab technicians were putting the finishing touches on the computers and radio transmitters that would soon be shipped to some island named Saipan in the western Pacific. Neither of them had heard of Saipan before they began work on this project, but they had both 'googled' the little dot on the globe not far from Guam. They had both heard of Guam.

They knew that Saipan was part of the United States and that the main part of the mission…their invention…would be housed on US soil.

"We are really lucky that they discovered an abandoned radar facility large enough to handle the transmission of our radio frequencies," One technician spouted.

"And not on foreign soil!" the other said. "Let's finish packing this up and set off the model once again…this is so-0 cool!"

They finished in silence and moved to the testing room. How they loved blowing things up!

Saipan, Northern Mariana Islands

"We have some time before the site at Radar Hill will be ready. We should use the time to figure this place out," I said to Ash over morning coffee on the patio. The gentle waves were lapping the shoreline in the lagoon not fifty yards from the patio where we sat.

"That shouldn't take long, Reggie," Ash replied. "The island is only twelve miles long and five miles wide. Not much real estate."

"Right, and did you know that they don't have addresses here?"

"And only two north-south roads on the island. One is close to the beach...what do you think they named it?"

"Uh...Beach Road..."

"Very good, my friend," I continued. "And the other road runs up the middle of the island."

"Let me guess...Middle Road?"

"Right, Ash!"

"So, Reggie, how do you find anything without addresses?"

"Remember, Dubai didn't have addresses either. The directions are interesting...pass the gas station on the left...go to the second building on the right...look for the orange building across Chongs refrigeration."

"Across Chongs?"

"Yep! They're lazy with their language. I went to a Pilates class this morning and the instructor even said 'ankle your knee' for the piriformis leg stretch! What a great class! They have these beds called reformers with spring resistance."

"I've heard Pilates described as expensive stretching," Ash countered.

"You know how I hate exercise just to exercise. It is fine when tied to a sport. This didn't feel like exercise. I really enjoyed the class and want to go back."

"Couldn't be the women in the class?"

"Well..."

"What time was class? The sun is just now starting to peek over the mountain." Ash asked.

"Five"

"You are nuts! Let's get some breakfast," Ash suggested.

"Not many choices…Shirley's, J's and Wild Bill's."

"Oh, definitely! Wild Bills."

"Then what?"

"We go driving…some World War Two sites to see, but we'll start at American Memorial Park. They have a theater and film about the Battle of Saipan. They broadcast the film every half hour in a different language. English, Japanese, Korean and Chinese."

"Sounds interesting."

Denver, CO

Melania Cruz looked, scowling, around the room. These were her 'homies', her gang. The GKI; the Gallant Knights Insane or also known by its previous name, Gangsters Killers Incorporated.

There were Hispanic men and women lounging on the furniture, leaning against the walls and even sitting on the floor. All had tattoos covering large parts of their bodies. All wore the GKI colors, purple and black. She had to step over several bodies to take her place in the center of the living room part of the hotel suite.

Two of her most trusted lieutenants had been killed during her successful escape from incarceration. She was furious at the loss of her compatriots.

"What do we know?" she began.

"We got the plates on the van. Checked with our contact at Denver PD. Registered to a Lance Wood. Got an address." One of the gang responded.

"Got dos homies and a car watching the place." Another added.

"Get everybody. Hand out all the weapons. Lots of ammo. Those men that interfered…they are going down!" Melania screamed.

At once, the room was buzzing with activity. Armfuls of automatic weapons were handed out. Ammo clips were checked and rammed into the guns. Slides were cocked and re-cocked. The sound of car engines being revved up could be heard from the hotel suite where they had all gathered.

"To the cars…let's go!" Melania ordered. The Mexicans in the gang clambered for the door and out into the hallway. Shouts and cursing were heard throughout the two-story hotel.

A line of at least twelve decked out and wildly painted low rider cars proceeded out of the hotel parking lot and headed east on Colfax Ave. heading to I-25. Onlookers could see guns bristling out of the car windows.

Melania was in the front car, leading the procession. Her instruction to the driver was to get there as fast as he could without causing a collision. She did not want the police aware of their presence with the chance that they could interfere with her mission. Take out this Lance Wood and his cronies.

Saipan, Northern Mariana Islands

Ash and I decided on a leisurely stroll around the grounds of American Memorial Park after viewing the film on the Battle of Saipan. Two recent typhoons, Soudelor in 2015 and Yutu in 2018, had devastated many of the grand old trees that were an important part of the park. The children's play area donated by the island's Rotarians was gone.

We made it past the clock tower and down to a sandy beach. We both shed our shoes and walked along the water's edge where the wet sand was firmer. The warm sand and cool water of the Philippine Sea felt marvelous against my feet.

"I got notice from Langley that they have finished assembling all of the components of RFW. The assembly will be on its way via military transport to Saipan. A team of technicians will join the transport at Anderson Air Force Base in Guam. I am told that they will need about three weeks to renovate the radar and install the new components. Then, three weeks of testing and we'll be ready to rock and roll!" I said, breaking the silence.

"And we just …how did you say it? Get to know the island?" Ash retorted. "How does it all work? Why the radar? It can't be aimed to hit the Middle East, can it?"

"No, Ash, you're right. When the testing began on the concept, a radio frequency had to be isolated that would excite the butane taggant…"

"I get that…"

"Then, please let me talk…they needed to test if the taggant could be excited enough to flash with enough intensity to set off the plastic explosive, which is usually extremely stable."

"Okay, I get that…"

"Then they had to comprise a mechanism to deliver the radio frequency."

"Hence, the radar on Radar Hill," Ash added.

"Yes, but not entirely…remember me saying that the frequency also causes destructive vibrations in many objects?" I asked.

"Yeah, and…"

"The first trials involved constructing a portable transmitter that could be moveable. Drive a truck-mounted gizmo wherever you want and turn it on…did not work! Truck parts were scattered all around the transmitter.

Then the thought was to have a more fixed mechanism that would be mounted on a large plane…guess what happened to the plane! Not pretty…" I added. "Then the thought was to have the device mounted onto a satellite…well, guess what…satellites are even more fragile than airplanes."

"One of the trials involved bouncing the signal off of a geosynchronous satellite 22,000 miles into the atmosphere. That would have been the easiest avenue to guide the signal. Send a satellite up with a large parabolic mirror, position it over the area where you want the signal to reach and voilà," I continued.

"And?" Ash queried.

"It worked!"

"So…"

"Then they tested the mirror theory suspended from an aircraft…and that also worked." I continued.

"I imagine that the cost involved in positioning an airplane over a target would be much less than moving a satellite into position, right Reggie?" Ash interjected.

"You're right! So, the parts now involve a large, fixed radar facility strong enough to withstand the vibrations and a mirror platform mounted on an aircraft," I said.

"God, what kind of power do you need to generate a signal from this island to a plane circling over the Middle East?" Ash asked.

"Huge…immense! But not our concern. Langley has that angle all worked out. I think it involves numerous generators hooked in tandem somehow," I added.

Cherry Hills, CO

Lance and Cyndi Wood's home is located on an acre of land in Cherry Hills Village. Access to the house is from Quincy Avenue. Their home is across from the second nicest country club in the Denver metro area, Cherry Hills Country Club. Exquisite and expensive homes surrounded the Wood's enclave of homes occupying a circular drive. The surrounding homes were older with well-established and manicured yards.

A gang member in the lead car had made contact with a source in Denver's police department and had the Wood's address up on his portable GPS with a moving map. He directed traffic by communicating to the other cars via walkie talkie. Old school, but less likely to be hacked or traced.

The line of cars turned south onto University Blvd. off of I-25 which they had taken south from Colfax, then west onto Quincy from University Blvd. The next left had them on the circular drive approaching Lance and Cyndi's home. The lot was fenced and had an iron gate to block the driveway. As circumstance would have it… the gate was open. Homes in this area had little concern for safety and security. Melania called out to the other cars on her walkie talkie, "Stealth!" The cars slowed to a crawl and the car radios were turned off.

Three cars turned up the driveway and the other cars were directed to go around the circle and line up in front of the property. The driveway curved around to display the front of the house. The three cars stopped quietly. The occupants of the three cars trained all of their firepower onto the house.

Melania was in the middle car of the three. She exited the car and gazed upon the front entrance. Then she spoke into her walkie talkie, "Fire!"

An instant later, thousands of bullets began to pepper the house from the front and back. The awful roar continued for minutes…and felt like hours.

Pieces of wood and brick flew through the air. No window had a chance. The bullets pierced through the house tearing apart furniture and artwork. Nothing was spared.

Melania shouted into her radio over the noise, "basta…enough!" The noise miraculously ceased except for pieces of the house that were falling to the ground. Sure that no living thing could have survived the onslaught, Melania ordered, "We're outta here."

The line of Mexicans re-formed on the circular drive and left the area following the same route that got them to the house.

Lance had been doing laps in their pool to relieve the stress of the day and as part of his exercise routine. When the gunfire began, he dove to the bottom and held his breath. He was sure that whoever was behind this attack would soon be scaling the wooden fence around the pool. Glass and wood fragments fell into the pool.

After a pause that seemed like minutes, he slowly moved to the water's surface, barely raising his head above the water. The fusillade was continuing so he chose to stay put rather than run for his weapon. Also, he knew that his pistol could do little against the barrage of automatic weapons fire that was travelling over his head. The falling debris cut his face in several spots. The blood mixed with the pool water to stream from his upper torso.

The attack eventually ceased. He heard cars driving away. Cars going down his driveway and exiting the front of his home that he had not heard when they arrived. Must have been the swimming he thought.

He crept from the pool and looked toward his house. It was a riddled mess! He could not believe that it was still standing. Then he remembered Cyndi. She had been in the kitchen preparing dinner.

He ran barefoot through the glass shards and wooden splinters toward the back door.

"Cyndi!" he called out. A primal cry that would curdle the blood of any who were listening.

Dubai, UAE

"Cyndi's gone!" Lance screamed into the phone when Becky answered.

"What? Woa…what did you say? What has happened?" Becky sank into a chair as tears immediately welled up in her eyes.

Lance was sitting on the floor of their demolished kitchen, cut and bleeding, but oblivious to his injuries. He held Cyndi's limp and lifeless body in his arms and cradled her for what would be the last time. He had the cell phone to his ear as he reached out to Becky Nelson.

Becky could not believe her ears. Lance was telling her about the attack, but she was struggling with his words…and then she heard the sound of sirens in the distance through her phone.

"Lance…are you okay? What can I do?" she pleaded.

Becky heard a commanding voice through the phone, "Put down the phone and move away from the body!"

She hung up and immediately dialed Reggie's number in Saipan.

"Hello, my gorgeous lover," I answered.

"Reggie…something horrible has happened in Denver," Becky broke down sobbing.

"What? What's wrong? Is Lance okay?" I pleaded.

"It's Cyndi…she's gone!" and the line went dead.

Saipan, Northern Mariana Islands

"Oh God, help me," I cried out.

Ash came running when he heard me, "What give's, Reggie?"

"Becky just called…something happened in Denver…Cyndi is dead…" My voice trailed off.

Ash asked no more questions but went into immediate action mode. He called Powers Booth. Powers had not heard yet but would get the team rolling and get to Lance Woods' aid. Powers did tell Ash that the Frankfurt I.N.C.I.S.O.R. team had arrived and was checking into their rooms at the Hyatt in Englewood. He would get them to join the Denver team and get to Lance Wood.

Ash then reached out to Becky. She did not have anything new to report. Then he reached out to his friend, Lance Wood. No answer…

CHAPTER

Cherry Hills, CO

The nine men that comprised the two I.N.C.I.S.O.R. teams converged on Lance Wood's property. The Cherry Hills, Denver and Englewood police were there already. Cars with flashing lights were everywhere. The light show was impressive. There also was an ambulance and the coroner's van parked out in front of the house. Firetrucks were dousing the structure with water to prevent any fires.

A policeman was running yellow 'DO NOT CROSS' tape across the front of the property. Duncan Trevino approached him to request passage onto the grounds to get to and comfort his employer and friend. The policeman at first denied Duncan and the others access, but his senior, a captain who knew of Lance Wood and the I.N.C.I.S.O.R. team allowed them to enter.

The men ran up the driveway and observed the front of the house. The facade was riddled with bullet holes. All of the window glass was blown out and the front door was hanging open and looked ready to fall off of its hinges.

Lance was being administered to in the ambulance. He was sitting on the back step while his cuts were disinfected and bandaged. The two paramedics stepped away when the men of I.N.C.I.S.O.R. approached.

They all had surmised what had happened. This was a typical Mexican gang hit…spray a target with thousands of rounds of ammunition…then they don't have to do the work of becoming good shots. Also, many in the gang against one or two opponents…never a fair fight. What chickenshits!

They had never seen Lance with such an absent countenance on his face. His usually proud and straight shoulders were slumped in defeat. He watched with a blank stare as the coroner rolled Cyndi's body out and into the van. The men were speechless at first.

Another senior police officer was writing and reviewing his notes in a small leather journal. Magnus Harper approached him and asked what he knew.

"Pretty damn obvious," he cursed. "It's clear to me that they were after your boss and missed. The woman was nothing but collateral damage."

"Hey, lieutenant, that 'woman' is…was Lance's wife," Magnus replied, "Show a little respect and decorum!"

"Screw it. Nobody saw a thing. None of the neighbors…nobody. What a fucking mess!" the lieutenant added.

"I think we can help. Our Denver team was caught in the middle of that prison breakout, and we took out two of the accomplices," Magnus stated.

Several of the I.N.C.I.S.O.R. team were within earshot of the conversation. They moved toward the police officer.

"You need us on this," Powers began.

"Yeah, we can help," Aaron added.

"There are nine of us…and this will be our only mission," Graham stated.

"I'll let you know," the lieutenant replied.

The men moved to surround Lance.

"We're here and ready to help," Lance Everett said.

"Yup, tell us what to do," Dick added.

"I don't have a fucking clue!" Lance Wood replied. "No fucking clue. What do I do next?"

Saipan, Northern Mariana Islands

"Awful timing," I declared. I didn't want to make the trip. It felt like we had just arrived, plus Ash and I had a new project to focus our attention on.

"Bullshit, Reggie…Awful timing? Do you not have any sense of compassion? Lance's wife is dead!"

"Sorry, you're right," I apologized. "Let's get airline tickets booked to the states."

"Through Japan or Honolulu?" Ash asked.

"Let's do Japan. The way the flights are now, we would have to overnight in Guam to make the Honolulu flight. Also, United doesn't feed you if you go via Honolulu," I stated.

"What?"

"Yeah, if we do Saipan to Guam to Honolulu to San Francisco to Denver, we technically haven't left the US. Travelling through Japan is international, ergo meals on the planes."

"I learned something new today!"

"Let's see if we can get out tomorrow. I'll call and inform Langley what happened," I said.

"We should be able to get back here before they have completed the radar," Ash added.

"Yeah, I'll find out what Becky's flight plans are."

Langley, VA

"That's just awful what happened to Cyndi," one of the lab techs said.

"But the plan won't be delayed… we're off to Guam with our package tomorrow," another tech added.

"Long flight to Anderson. On a military transport to boot! So much for comfort."

"Does Reggie know about the new plane? Or about our other surprise?"

Denver, CO

Lance and Cyndi Wood had a close-knit group of Denver friends that all came to Lance's aid when Cyndi died. They quickly put together a beautiful burial ceremony and a touching celebration of Cyndi's life.

Lance had moved into a Residence Inn off of I-25 and Arapahoe Road. He watched at the goings on and arrangements with a noticeable detachment…as if he was not there. It seemed to his friends that

Lance was in the denial phase of the grief cycle. He could not believe that she was gone. He expected to wake up each day with Cyndi under his arm. It was not to be.

Ash, Becky and I arrived in time to help with the final arrangements for Cyndi's funeral. Cyndi did not have a will in place, so Lance was asked to help with her final wishes. He and Cyndi had rarely talked about the death of either of them, but Lance truly expected to go first. He had many close calls that he went over in his mind. One of the choices Lance had to make was to bury Cyndi, rather than cremation. Friends found a cemetery plot that was passable.

I was asked to speak at Cyndi's service. I knew that I would not be able to say any words without breaking down, so I volunteered Ash to do the public speaking. Now, two of my dearest friends had lost their wives.

The three of us met with and attempted to console Lance. He looked at us with a blank stare. I was not sure he even recognized us. His grief was that profound. All he would mumble was that he had found a replacement for Michael MacAteer. Kurt Nichols was his name. The teams were now at full strength. This was the last thing that Ash, Becky and I cared about, but the only words uttered from Lance's mouth.

We left Lance in his inconsolable state and drove to meet the I.N.C.I.S.O.R. teams at a pickleball facility.

"What is pickleball?" Ash asked as we drove.

"A combination of tennis, badminton and ping pong," Becky offered.

"Yeah," I added. "I 'You Tubed' it after I heard that the guys in Denver were playing. The court is the size of a badminton court and a pickleball looks like a whiffle ball. You play with oversized ping pong paddles and score like ping pong and badminton, except those games play to 21. Pickleball plays to eleven."

"Sounds interesting," Ash added.

"Fun to watch on You Tube. They have this space close to the net that they call the 'kitchen'. You can't go in the kitchen! Is the rule," Becky said.

"No problem there!" Ash replied and let out a chuckle.

We arrived at the South Suburban Sports Complex, parked, and walked into the facility. After asking directions, we proceeded to a court that had four men playing and six men watching the game.

The play stopped as they all moved to greet us. This was our first time to meet the new guy, Kurt Nichols. As it turned out, Kurt was a Harvard grad, so I felt an instant bond with this Ivy League graduate. I had attended Dartmouth.

Once the introductions and greetings were over, play resumed on the court. I saw that the men were covered in sweat. Soon the game ended. The winning team remained on the court, and the losing team exited the court. Two more took their place and play resumed. There was a multitude of skill levels present, but all of the players got to participate and enjoy the action.

After observing a few games, it was apparent that Dick Becker was the most skilled player on the court. He motioned for Ash and me to join the action. We were still dressed in street clothes but gave it a try. I had played a lot of tennis and so had Ash. It didn't take long to get the feel of the game. It also wasn't long that I was ringed with sweat and panting heavily.

"You guys have any air up here?"

"Denver's a mile high, Reggie…no air up here! Don't you remember?"

"This is embarrassing!" I exclaimed.

"It's okay, old man."

"Who said that?" I retorted as they all had a good laugh. I noticed that Becky was laughing the hardest.

"Still trying to keep up, dear?" she said. "You've got to let it go!"

"I'll let it go!" I wanted her really badly just then.

I could see that Ash and I had our hands full with these young men, but I could also see that Ash and I would have a good time with this new sport.

"Ash, we should bring this to Saipan," I said.

"It's already there, Reggie. I saw a pickleball court in the parking lot of a dental office on Middle Road. I think the sign said, 'Paradise Dental'."

"Let's call them when we return," I concluded.

Ash and I gathered the ten men around us and got them to commit to join us in the lounge of the Hyatt Regency once they had completed their play and got cleaned up. Becky, Ash and I then left the men of the two I.N.C.I.S.O.R. teams to their game.

Ash, Becky and I returned to the Hyatt and went to our adjoining suites. Alone with Becky, I voiced my concern, "Beck…I think Lance is done."

"Nah, Reggie my love…give him time…he'll get over this funk and come around. You and Ash are his two closest friends. He needs you guys."

I left the conversation, stripped and popped into the shower for a quick cleanup. As I felt the sweat and grime from the day run off my body, I prayed, "Lord…please be with Lance and help him through this rough time."

"Hey, Beck…I'm all clean…want a quickie?" I called out from the bathroom.

"Not now, Reggie. Then you'd have to shower again." She retorted.

Cleaned up and dressed, I called Ash, "You ready?"

"Still have a couple of things to wrap up…see you in the lounge in twenty."

I turned to Becky, "Just you and me babe." I gave her a hug and kiss, grabbed her arm and we headed down the hallway to the elevator.

Downstairs in the lounge, we told the waitress that we were expecting eleven more within the half hour. Several wait staff worked to move tables into an arrangement so that we could all sit together.

Becky ordered a margarita, and I ordered my standard…. double Crown Royal on the rocks with a twist. While we waited, we spent time reviewing how our flights to arrive in Denver had gone with all of the connections, and going over the events of the day.

The drinks arrived and I raised my glass to toast Becky, "The most beautiful girl on the planet!"

"Aw, Reggie,"

"I love you,"

"I love you more," she replied, and we kissed. A passionate kiss filled with urgency. I wanted it to be later already!

Ash joined us and shortly the ten young men assigned to take on the world of crime and evil sat down. Drinks and hors d'oeuvres were ordered.

"What's up, boss?" Duncan asked.

"Mexicans!" Ash answered.

"This gang, the GKI…they went after Lance with a vengeance. Why?" I queried.

Flex began to massage his injured arm. "As near as we can figure, they read the plates off of Lance's van. That's the vehicle we were in when they hit the armored transport."

"Well, they have retaliated and shed blood," Kurt began, "We should answer. Eye for an eye stuff. Oh, by the way, I am the new guy."

Stirling added, "What about the police and sheriff's departments?"

"Good question…you are assigned to liase with them," I ordered. "But, we have better access to intel from the Feds because of I.N.C.I.S.O.R., and superior firepower to what the local cops carry."

"There is something else that we have in our arsenal," Max said. "I've been playing with a drone. Not the Amazon type in their ads, but much more capable. We can feed it GPS coordinates and it will head there. It even has object and collision avoidance software built in."

"Cool," Ash replied. "What do you propose to do with it?"

"Denver PD knows where their crypt is. We start by monitoring their internet, phones and activities. All remotely." Max opined.

"And?" I spoke.

"We look for weaknesses and strengths. How many they are at what times of the day. Look for an Achilles tendon," Magnus interjected.

"I'm getting turned on," Graham added. "When do we hit these suckers and get some of our own revenge!"

"We can't let Lance down," Powers said. "How is he?"

Becky spoke for the first time to the teams, "Lance is not good. We need to leave him outta this and give him space and time to come back to us. DO NOT reach out to him in any way!"

"Yes, Maam," they all spoke together.

"After the service tomorrow, Reggie and I will travel back to Saipan. Becky was to join us, but now she's heading to Italy. Run everything through Michael in Dubai. He'll be your planner and coordinator for this operation, understand? Your eyes, ears and brains, got it?" Ash asked.

"Yes, sir!" they all replied and began to speak among themselves about different possibilities for a strike mission.

They carried on for another hour and began to drift out of the lounge to head for their homes and apartments. Each in his own way to prepare for the upcoming service.

I paid the bill and told Ash that Becky and I had had it. We were just going to get some room service and call it a night. I looked at Becky and thought I saw a glimmer in her eyes. Maybe not call it a night so quickly…

Washington DC

President Marron called to one of the many white house aides, "When is that memorial for Cyndi Wood?"

"Tomorrow, Mr. President...10 am. Central time."

"Let us get a large floral arrangement delivered to the service. I didn't know Cyndi Wood. Never met the woman, but her husband has done much in service for this country!"

"Consider it done, Mr. President," the aide responded, turned and left the room.

Denver, CO

Lance was inconsolable. A broken man. A crumpled mass whose face was streaked with tears. He sat through the service, unhearing... staring at the coffin.

Many of the attendees attempted to offer condolences, but he didn't acknowledge their presence.

Ash, Becky and I sat in the front row with Lance. As we listened, I was saddened not only with Cyndi's death, but how my initial dream of I.N.C.I.S.O.R. and the six of us ridding the world of evil seemed to be way off in the distant past. We had lost two of us...Grace and Cyndi...and who knew about Lance. Could he and would he come back to us? Was it now just the three of us? What a horrible price we had paid for wanting to have a safer world.

Well, enough of feeling sorry for myself. It was time to get back to living. Give Lance his space. Let him reach out when he is ready. Ash and I had work to do in Saipan.

CHAPTER 5

Saipan, Northern Mariana Islands

Ash and I carried our chairs from the patio down to the beach. The ironwood trees offered us plenty of shade from the intense morning sun. Ash returned to the patio and retrieved our coffee mugs as I sat observing the prepositioned ships anchored just outside the lagoon. The sun was up high enough to illuminate the intense turquoise water in the lagoon. I thought about how tranquil the scene before me was. It was a crazy thought. Those were ships to be used in a time of war. They were packed with the machinery of war. But it was a beautiful sight, and I found a strange comfort having those ships so nearby.

Ash handed me my coffee and sat next to me. I could tell that something was bothering him.

"Reggie," he began. "What are we doing here? I'm not feeling good about what we are trying to accomplish."

"Ash, my good friend…I haven't been able to think of anything else since Cyndi's death. Why did she have to die? How does Lance's loss fit in God's plan? Why do we keep going? And, you know what? I'm not getting any answers…" my voice trailed off and we sat in silence, watching the waves lap at the sandy shoreline. An occasional crab scurried out of a sand hole and moved toward the water's edge. Iridescent white terns played in the ironwood branches over our heads.

I was thinking about how those birds stayed so white when Ash broke the silence.

"I lost Grace to a terrorist bombing in Israel. Now Lance has lost his wife to a gang attack in Denver. Your Becky wants out of Dubai where you were kidnapped, to live in Florence. She thinks that she'll be safer there. There is so much evil in the world. Can we really do anything to stop it?"

"You're right, my friend. As long as there are weak, ignorant and chickenshit beings willing to attack civilians, there will be terrorism. We cannot do much to thwart all this evil with our band of ten men plus the two of us. But, for the first time I feel that we can do something proactive. All the world has been able to do until now is react to whatever actions that evil takes. If this works, and I believe it will, we will be able to strike out against the evil before it strikes the innocent."

Ash nodded his head in agreement. I looked at my friend and remembered how it was that we became friends. I wanted to get back into Karate and Ash had a dojo in Colorado Springs. As our friendship grew, he introduced me to Lance Wood and the CIA. The Central Intelligence Agency turned out to be interested in my invention, the PC. This was a listening device that could be placed in root canal treated teeth.

Then came the dental clinic in Dubai and the three of us began battling terrorism by foiling a plot to destroy the untapped oil reserves of the United States in the Alaskan tundra, named the Arctic National Wildlife Refuge. At a breakfast meeting following that successful mission, the three of us chose to involve our wives and named our group I.N.C.I.S.O.R.. **IN**ternational **CI**tizens for a **S**afe society **OR**ganization. Lance Wood almost lost his life battling one of the terrorists. I chose to crash my plane into the helicopter carrying the terrorist with the nuclear detonator to save ANWR and stop that terrorist plot.

Our next adventures entailed saving wealthy kidnap victims around the world. I had invented the 'mini' so that we could track those who had purchased our device and services. Somewhere during these escapes, we made time to help stop Iran from attacking Israel and causing World War Three. We also had help from an act of God. A Haboob had destroyed the Iranian army as it was poised to take out Israel. It was a terrorist attack in Israel that took Grace Black from us.

I was also kidnapped by a terror cell and, even though Ash and Lance were successful with my rescue, Becky was done with living in the Middle East. She was now in transit to Florence, Italy, hoping to find a safer and more secure existence. Ash, Lance and I had realized that we needed to expand I.N.C.I.S.O.R.. We added two five-man teams stationed in Denver and Frankfurt. One of these men had lost his life rescuing me and another had crushed both legs saving a second kidnap victim.

And now my third and latest invention, RFW. I desperately wanted to see this project to its completion and Ash was with me. Lance and Cyndi had returned to Denver. It was there that Cyndi had lost her life to a Mexican gang seeking revenge. The rest of the I.N.C.I.S.O.R. team was also in Denver planning a strike on the Gallant Knights Insane with the goal of recapturing Melania Cruz, the gang's leader.

"What's the old phrase about evil?" Ash asked.

"The only thing necessary for the triumph of evil is for good men to do nothing," I quoted. "Edmund Burke stated that in the eighteenth century!"

"It's that old?"

"Yep, so, good man…do we go on?" I asked.

"'We have to see this through. Many are counting on us. A proactive strike against evil and terrorism will be a monumental step," Ash replied.

"Okay…no more feeling sorry for ourselves…let's get on with the project! What do we know about the team from Langley? They are in Guam?" I queried.

"Yes…and they will be here tomorrow. They have two surprises for you…us."

"Cool…what?" I asked.

"Hey, numb nuts. What do you think the word 'surprise' means?"

Anderson Air Force Base, Guam

It was a long flight and the two lab techs from Langley were having trouble moving their stiffened legs after the flight.

"That was awful," the first lab tech spoke.

"Can we get real seats when we return to the States?" the second tech asked.

The crew of radar and computer technicians were waiting in the hangar where the two techs were directed to enter. Handshakes and introductions went around the group and there was a palpable excitement felt among the members of this new team.

The excitement was not just about an extended trip to the tropical island of Saipan, but these men were bringing with them a chance to take the upper hand against terrorism. They were not exactly sure about what they were going to construct, but the importance of their mission had been made clear to each and every one of them.

The hangar contained the various crates with the supplies and components they would need. There was also an unusual looking aircraft being given the once over by the airframe and powerplant mechanics working for the Airforce. It was a twin-engine plane…not so unusual, but this was a pusher prop…highly unusual…and with a gorgeous paintjob that none of the men had seen before.

Two other A&P mechanics were examining a crate with four large quad propeller UAV's. These drones all would ride on platforms mounted on the roof of a black Cadillac Escalade that was parked inside the hangar.

"Let's get all of this crap loaded in that C-17 out on the ramp!" the Captain announced as she entered the hangar. Immediately, the men jumped up and ceased whatever they were doing. The drones were crated up and the car was driven onto the immense transport plane parked on the tarmac. Then, a forklift moved adroitly among the crates, lifting them onto its forks and loading them onto the plane. The hangar now stood empty except for the Avanti Evo parked to the side of the main door.

Once the loading was complete, the men milled around until one of the local airmen suggested a trip into Tumon for some sushi for dinner and then to a local strip club for some female entertainment. "Maybe some shopping for the ones back home," one of the CIA lab techs ventured. "I heard that the world's largest K Mart is right here in Guam!"

"Where we're going you can't afford the shopping. All of the DFS shops that cater to the tourists are there. Outta your league, young man," an airman replied.

"Report here at 0600. We rotate at 0630!" the Captain ordered. The airmen saluted as the others watched and off they went for a night of exploring.

Saipan, Northern Mariana Islands

Ash and I drove the rental car out to Francisco C. Ada Airport. Saipan is a small island and only has the one airport at the southern end of the island. The airport sits on an old sugarcane field that the Japanese turned into a temporary airfield in 1933.

The field was named Aslito Field after the attack by the Japanese on Pearl Harbor in 1941. Two squadrons of Mitsubishi Zeros occupied the field in 1944 until they were wiped out by the Americans in the Battle of the Philippine Sea, better known as the Marianas Turkey Shoot.

The airstrip was renamed Isley Field after Navy Commander Robert Isley once America took the island of Saipan from the Japanese in 1944. Over 100 B-29 bombers carried out massive, devasting strikes against Japan, along with bombers from Tinian and Guam.

The airfield was returned to civilian control in December of 1945 and the name was changed back to Aslito Field. In July 1976, the airfield began operation as Saipan International Airport. The airport gained its current name, Francisco C. Ada, in 2005.

We parked the car at the western end of the runway so we could observe the approach and touchdown of the C-17 Globemaster as it landed from Guam. The plane was massive, and its approach was perfect.

We drove the car around to the front of the airport and parked near the executive terminal. Very few private jets flew into Saipan, but the executive terminal also served the local airline, Star Marianas which is headquartered on the island of Tinian. They boast a fleet of single engine Piper Cherokees to provide service from the island of Tinian to Saipan, and Piper Navajo twin engines to fly to the island of Rota and on to Guam. Guam is only a little over 100 miles from Saipan, and a single engine plane could make the flight, but the FAA requires two engines on planes used for flights carrying passengers over water when land was not visible.

The C-17 was parked on the ramp and the rear of the plane was opening to disgorge its cargo. Ash and I had clearance to pass through the terminal and walk out onto the ramp and observe the efficiency of the Air Force crew tasked with emptying the aircraft.

I noticed that the first vehicle that was driven off of the plane was a black Cadillac Escalade. I had noticed several black Escalades driving around Saipan and had been told that they all belonged to Imperial Pacific, a Chinese company that ran the local casino and was building a hotel in Garapan. The Escalades all had licenses that displayed 'Best' and a number, which related to Best Sunshine. This was the previous name of the Chinese venture. My assumption was that this car was an addition to their fleet…until it was parked next to where we were standing.

Ash had a giant grin on his face.

"What is this?" I asked.

"Reggie, my old friend, this is for you," Ash began.

"What? I'm a big sedan kind of guy, Ash…"

Ash continued, "This is the new Cadillac Escalade. They call it the next generation! This car boasts a 38-inch curved OLED display with twice the pixel density of a 4K TV. And it has super cruise."

"What?"

"Hands-free driving on certain approved roads."

"Really? Any approved roads here?"

"No, and no satellite to interface with a number of functions in the car."

"Ash, what are these platforms on the roof?" I asked.

"You don't miss a thing, Reggie," Ash replied.

Just then a crewman from the C-17 brought over a large case and placed it at Ash's feet. He bent down and unlocked the case.

I peered over Ash's shoulder and viewed what looked like drones.

"These aren't just drones like civilians use for photography. They are autonomous and weaponized," Ash said. "Watch this…"

He turned a switch on each of four drones and then moved to the passenger seat of the Escalade. It looked to me like Ash was opening the glove box when I heard a whirring sound and watched a console of four TV screens unfold out of the glove box space and line up in an array in front of him.

Ash turned on the four screens and barked a voice command into an unseen microphone, "Park!"

I turned to the case on the tarmac and watched as the drones turned on, raised out of the crate and each drone moved to a designated platform on the roof of the car.

"Cool!" I exclaimed. "What do they do?"

"They are our companions and escorts," Ash continued. "The drones are capable of staying airborne for thirty-six hours. They are our 'eye in the sky' along with providing us airborne weaponry if we run into trouble."

"Why four of them?' I asked.

"They all have different functions. All are equipped with camera lenses that have infra-red lenses to see in the dark. One has a laser to be used…"

Just then I was distracted by the sound of an aircraft landing on Runway 7. The turboprop sound was familiar. I turned to watch an Avanti twin engine touch down and turn off the runway onto a taxiway heading right for us.

"Ash!" I exclaimed. "Somebody has a plane here like…"

"No, Reggie!" Ash said, cutting me off. "That is your new plane courtesy of the Central Intelligence Service. This is the Avanti Evo."

"That's why the prop wash sounded off. This bird has five-bladed Hartzell propellers."

I forgot about the car and what Ash was explaining to me and moved toward the plane as it taxied to a stop.

"The paint is just like Aurora!"

"Just like her," Ash replied as he joined me.

"Aurora two…" my voice trailed off as I watched the door open. "The Evo is faster, quieter, can fly farther and higher than the P 180 Avanti II."

The ferry pilot came out of the aircraft, "You must be Dr. Reginald Nelson." He saluted. "here's your new baby."

I thanked him but barely heard what he said. I climbed the two stairs and turned left to enter the cockpit with Ash right behind me. I moved in to sit in the left seat as Ash settled into the right seat. We were admiring the all-glass cockpit and Rockwell Collins avionics.

"Let's go!" I urged.

"Hold your horses, my boy. These flyboys have more to unload, and they need to get back to Guam. You and I need to meet the team that is here for the radar," Ash interrupted.

"Come on…they can come along!"

"No…just look for now."

One of the C-17 crew stuck his head in the door, "All done with the supplies, come meet the team."

"Après' vous," I said and gestured for Ash to go first. Reluctantly, I climbed out of the pilot's seat. One last glance back into the cockpit and I followed Ash out of my new plane.

"Aurora II," I muttered as I stepped out of the doorway and moved toward the men that were gathered by the Escalade.

Back on the tarmac, it was time to meet the other fellows. The two lab techs from Langley had travelled the farthest and been in transit the longest. It showed…on their faces and their posture. I knew them by name. Joe Cavanagh and Billy Bean came to the CIA within months of each other four years ago. We had been working on RFW for more than a year, and I felt that we understood each other and worked well together.

Now, seeing them in person, I placed a name with a face.

"Ash, this is Joe…" and touched one of their shoulders.

"No, I'm Joe," the other techie said.

"Well, I guessed wrong!"

"Should have let you talk first. You can't miss that Virginia accent, Billy."

I turned to face the men from Anderson.

"And you are…"

A snap to attention.

"Lieutenant White…Clarence White," the first announced.

"Second lieutenant Black…Brock Black," the second saluted.

"You're joking," Ash exclaimed.

"White and Black…just like us good friend," I interjected.

"We have you staying at the Hyatt. The concierge wing. Let's get you loaded up and checked in," Ash said and gestured toward the Black Escalade.

"Ash, you take the four of them in that black monster. I'm going to get Aurora put to bed, um, hangered, then I'll be along in the rental car," I added.

The radar gear had already been loaded into the Escalade. Now, Joe, Billy, Clarence and Brock gathered their things and moved toward the car. I turned to Ash.

"Good friend…we have to get this plane into the air!"

"Patience, Reggie…soon," Ash replied and walked toward the car.

I moved into the Executive terminal to secure some hangar space for the beautiful plane out on the tarmac.

Garapan, Northern Mariana Islands

Ash and the four men pulled into the Hyatt hotel circular entrance and parked to unload the men and baggage. Ash went to the check-in counter to secure the four rooms. He handed the men their key cards and pointed to the right tower where the concierge rooms were housed.

"You all get settled in and enjoy the rest of the day. There's a main pool and also a private pool for use by the concierge guests. Great burgers at the pool bar by the main pool! Reggie and I will meet you in the Regency Club lounge on the second floor at 5:00."

"Goodbye, adios, thanks." The men walked toward the elevator.

Ash climbed into the Escalade and circled around to exit the Hyatt property. He headed east to Beach road and then turned south to leave Garapan. Soon he was pulling into the rental property off of Beach Road.

"I told the guys that we'd see them for happy hour at five," Ash began as he entered the living room.

I was laying on the couch and enjoying the air conditioning and dreaming about the new plane.

"Ash, did you hear anybody talk about the air conditioning, here?" I asked as I sat up.

"What do you mean?"

"They are really lazy with their English on the island. They say, 'air con,'" I replied.

"So?"

"Just talking…" My thoughts drifted back to the airport.

"Let's spend the afternoon getting familiar with these drones," Ash suggested.

"Alright," I said and arose off of the couch.

We both headed out to the Escalade.

"Watch this!" Ash exclaimed as he pulled out his cellphone.

He punched a few times on the touch screen and all four drones began to whir. As we watched, they arose off of their platforms on the roof of the car and hovered about ten feet over us.

"Follow me," Ash ordered.

We began to walk through the back yard and out onto the beach. The four drones followed. Each one had to maneuver to clear the large Ironwood trees that lined the sandy beach. Once clear of the trees, the four drones climbed to what looked like fifty feet above us. Ash showed me his phone. The screen was divided into four sections, each with an overhead image of us standing on the beach.

"Hard to see," I complained.

"Yeah, but there are four TV screens in the passenger console. You'll be driving while I get the TV show." Ash countered.

Not seeing any activity on the beach, we walked back to the car and hopped in. I hadn't noticed, but Ash was able to remotely start the car and the cabin had cooled down very nicely.

Ash pointed to the screens in front of him.

"Here's what I see while you drive," he said.

I looked at the screens. It looked to me that the four drones had taken up positions fifty feet from the car in all four directions…front, back and both sides.

"Are they completely autonomous? Do you have any control?" I asked.

Ash chuckled, "Think of it like fly-by-wire. The computer flies the aircraft, and the pilot sends signals or inputs to the computer."

"I see, okay what about a threat?"

"The drone sees the threat first but will not react without my input… laser, missile or do nothing is up to me – or you if you are playing navigator," Ash answered.

"Why four?"

"Why not," was his smart retort. "All have surveillance capability, but that is where their similarities end. The leading drone has the laser capability. The right and left drones are armed with missiles. Air to air on the left and air to ground on the right. The rear drone emits an ear shattering sound that will stop any incoming traffic from the rear. Also, all four are armed with rapid fire machine guns that automatically reload when the drones return to their platforms."

"What kind of guns?"

"M134 GAU-17 Vulcan. It is a six-barreled machine gun with electric motors to power the barrels. The firing rate approaches 6,000 rounds per minute."

"Like they showed in 'We Were Soldiers'?"

"Newer, smaller, lighter…"

"6,000 rounds a minute? Times four? Our own little army!" I exclaimed.

"That firepower should suppress any hostile activity, if we encounter any," Ash said.

"And they just hang out while we drive?" I asked.

"Yep. We act like they're not there."

"Really? Like that will work!" I countered.

"You'll see…you'll adjust, Reggie. You're a smart kid," and he chuckled.

"It rains a lot here. What about the effect of bad weather?"

"Well, I don't imagine that we'll be out and about during a typhoon, but they'll withstand anything else that is thrown at them."

"Birds?" I asked.

"They have the best collision avoidance software on the planet."

"And endurance?"

"The drones can remain aloft for thirty-six hours. When the car is parked for the evening, you plug it in and the drones recharge on their platforms on the roof. No muss, no fuss! Enough with the questions, Reggie. Let's drive up to radar hill and test these guys out!"

And off we went in the new Escalade. We headed north on Beach Road, then jogged over to Middle Road also heading north. I had trouble concentrating on the road because I wanted to see what the drones were picking up on the four television screens. But we made it to the radar site and parked. I noticed that if I weren't paying close attention, I wouldn't hear or notice the four drones. The televisions showed images of the Pacific Ocean off to the east, the Philippine Sea to the west, Suicide Cliff off to the north and the airport and Tinian off to the south.

"What a gorgeous panorama!" I exclaimed.

"This is one tiny island," Ash said.

"Twelve miles long by five miles wide?"

"Yeah, about that. Amazing that this little dot in the Pacific Ocean played such a major role in ending the Second World War. And still plays such a strategic role in America's Asian strategies."

"These shots are really beautiful! We should record these," I offered.

"Everything that the four cameras pick up is recorded on a solid-state hard drive, Reggie," Ash replied.

"Like the 1 Terabyte SSD's that I see on Amazon for $150?"

"Not quite, Reggie…there is a 100 Terabyte storage drive behind this dashboard…and it's more like $140,000 for the drive…it automatically communicates with the cloud, so we never have to bother with downloading it,"

"Wow!" I murmured.

We sat in silence for a while and watched the displays as the drones hovered above us. Soon it was time to join the others for drinks and hors d'oeuvres at the Hyatt.

We drove in silence as Ash was playing with the displays. I pulled into the entrance of the Hyatt and noticed that there was a roof covering the entrance. I wondered about the drones just as they came in low, under the roof, and landed silently on the roof platforms.

I thought about a valet to park the vehicle. Bad idea with this sophistication. I parked in the 'handicapped' parking and locked the car. Ash had punched a button on the dash and the four displays folded into the glove compartment space. Ash then pulled out a 'handicap' placard and placed it on the dash.

We walked inside and moved to the elevator bank. I put a room card into the slot and the elevator doors opened. Ash punched the button, and the elevator took us to the second floor. A woman at the concierge desk of the Regency Club checked us in and we joined the rest of the team. They had done some rearranging of the furniture and pulled four tables together in a large square. Two chairs on each side beckoned us.

"Welcome, Reginald and Ash," Clarence beckoned. "We found two local chaps at the pool bar and asked them to join us. A chance to learn about this island."

CHAPTER 6

Denver, CO

The ten men of I.N.C.I.S.O.R. had taken up positions around the structure housing the Gallant Knights Insane gang members. The information that they had gathered from the surveillance drone told them that, at any one time, there were about twenty-five gang members in the house with a large cache of arms and munitions. The weapons and armament were varied, from shotguns and double 00 shells to a wide array of handguns…38's, 45's and 9mm. There were long guns of various types, mostly AK's and lots of ammo clips for the numerous weapons.

Unlike the ragtag Mexican group, the I.N.C.I.S.O.R. team all had identical weapons and were dressed in matching outfits. On their hips or thighs were strapped 9mm. Taurus G3ca T.O.R.O. Tenifer Luger compacts, housing twelve rounds in the clip. With one in the chamber, this weapon boasted thirteen rounds of brute stopping force. All the men had opted for the optical sight mounted on top of the barrel.

On straps slung over their shoulders each man carried an Armelite AR-10 A2 308 rifle. The sixteen-inch barrel and a muzzle velocity of over 2700 feet per second made it the team's choice for assault and sniper rifles.

The rest of the gear that each man wore was the Shellback Tactical Banshee Elite 2.0 Plate Carrier vest and the TEA Clarus communication ear buds. Under Armor supplied their lightweight black boots, black pants and T-shirts that had the I.N.C.I.S.O.R. insignia over the left breast and I.N.C.I.S.O.R. spelled out on their backs.

The men had a long discussion about headgear and, even though there were mixed feelings, they chose to forego any form of helmet.

When the men stood together dressed in similar black outfits from head-to-toe, they presented a formidable force to be reckoned with. This was a good-looking bunch of killers!

The two best sharpshooters, Powers and Magnus, took up overwatch positions on rooftops of nearby houses. The remaining eight men took up positions around the house…two per side. The German team split up and manned together with each of the Denver team. Almost like 'détente', Kurt thought as he moved to his spot.

The last video report from the drone showed that Melania was present in the house. Every man on the I.N.C.I.S.O.R. team knew that it was of paramount importance to recapture this evil 'bee-atch'. And to eliminate her if they could not apprehend her. The other gang members didn't matter. In the team's eyes they were lower than 'worthless'. They had no redeeming qualities to qualify for life on this planet.

The plan called for flash bangs shot into the house from all four sides at zero hour. The grenades would be followed by a withering barrage of bullets aimed to level the structure. If the structure was still standing, then an assault from the front and back of the house would commence. Any male standing would be shot. Everyone on the floors would be restrained. Melania was the prized target.

At 'zero hour' the attack commenced. The plan was going off just as it was planned. The flashbangs stunned the inhabitants, and the men froze. Then came the fusillade. Four clips for each man were emptied into the structure. The I.N.C.I.S.O.R. teams then moved to take the house under the watchful eyes of the overwatch. That is when chaos ensued…

As the men stormed the front and rear doors which were now just barely hanging on to their hinges, men from the gang inside raced to exit the structure. The Mexicans were firing blindly and wildly, but several projectiles found their marks with the I.N.C.I.S.O.R. team.

Lance and Duncan fell onto their sides at the front door. Aaron and Graham suffered similar fates at the back door. A melee ensued as the I.N.C.I.S.O.R. teams grappled with the Mexican gang members while Powers and Magnus took careful aim and dropped many of the gang. Then, Flex and Dick ran through the front of the house, while Kurt and Stirling entered through the back. All had their pistols drawn as they moved inside.

Once Magnus and Powers had dropped all of their targets, they moved from overwatch to assist the downed men. All four had been hit in the torso and the plate carrier vests had done their job. None of the men were badly hurt, although there were a few broken ribs among the four who had been shot.

Magnus and Powers were helping the downed men to sitting positions so that they could catch their wind. The blow to the Kevlar plates was like being hit in the chest with a baseball bat. The men were all struggling to take in a deep breath and recover.

Just then, Dick Becker came out the front door and began counting the bodies strewn around Lance and Duncan. He them moved back to the interior of the house. Kurt Nichols checked out the back door where Aaron and Graham were laboring to breath normally. With the bodies counted, he moved back inside to consult with Dick.

Aaron and Graham were helped around the side of the house to the front yard where the other I.N.C.I.S.O.R. men were gathering. Magnus counted the men. All were present and relatively unscathed.

Dick then announced the results. Thirteen dead and eleven hostages. Several of the gang needed medical attention. And now the bad news…no sign of Melania.

Saipan, Northern Mariana Islands

"Who is joining us this afternoon?" Ash queried.

"Two Haolies that happen to have lived on Saipan for a long, long time," Billie Bean responded. "We met at the pool bar and had a great time talking with them. I think that we will learn much about this place from them."

"How do you know that term? Haole?" Ash asked.

"I've been to Hawaii," Billie replied.

"Wha…"

"Jeff Beach," the first man said as he extended his hand toward me.

"Nicky Bells," the other announced as he reached for Ash's hand.

We all shook hands and moved to the drink table to make our own cocktails. I noticed that the Anderson Air Base duo grabbed cold beers from the large tub of ice. Joe and Billy poured vodka over glasses of ice and looked unsuccessfully around the table for limes. There was no bottle of Crown Royal present. I chose a bottle of Makers Mark bourbon and poured two drinks over ice for Ash and me.

The six of us then moved to the round food table and worked around the other guests to procure some 'munchie' type food to have at the table. For me that meant a plate full of sliced vegetables and a small bowl of ranch dressing for dipping.

As we settled around the table, I offered a toast, "To a great mission!"

The others held up their glasses and beer bottles and toasted. Then the two locals chimed in almost simultaneously, "What mission?"

"My bad," I began, but then Ash took over, "we're on a 'mission from God'!"

The others chuckled to the Blues Brothers reference.

"No, really," Jeff interjected. I have been here on island the longest… since the end of the Trust Territory days and the beginning of the Commonwealth. I worked with the Department of the Interior. I know a government mission when I see one." He then continued, "Guys from Langley…Guys from Anderson in Guam…and you two!" He pointed at Ash and me.

"What gives?"

Nicky took over the conversation, "My dad was with the government, too. I grew up in Japan where he was stationed, attended Harvard and worked with various Japanese working on development projects here in Saipan for the last thirty years."

"That's too bad," I interjected.

"What?" Nicky asked, perturbed at the interruption.

"I'm from Dartmouth!"

Our eyes met and I felt an instant bond with this stranger. Nicky nodded.

Ash began, "We are on a mission. All of us have been sent here to survey the decaying structure on Radar Hill. We are to make suggestions and report to the Federal Government whether or not anything can be salvaged or just remove the eyesore."

The two seemed to buy Ash's answer and it was obvious that they were more interested in talking about their island.

Denver, CO

Melania knew that she was the main target of the attack.

Once her gang had procured the house, she had them cut a hole in the floor large enough for her to drop through into the crawl space underneath. The crawl space had several air vents with access to the outside.

When the attack began she threw off the rug covering the plywood placed over the opening and dropped into the space below. The floor was dirt, and the space was filthy and full of cobwebs. A flashlight was near to where she had dropped onto the dirt. Melania grabbed it and switched it on to get her bearings. She planned her path to the closest vent and turned off the light so she would not be seen from above.

Melania crawled on all fours to the vent and then lay on her back with her feet toward the vent. She listened…there was much noise upstairs. She kicked at the vent and the surrounding cinder blocks. After a number of kicks, she stopped to listen again. Still too noisy upstairs for them to hear her. Two more kicks and the vent flew off, taking two of the cinder blocks with it. The opening was large enough.

She looked at the outside surroundings. After extricating herself from the hole in the wall she had a short sprint to the area where garbage cans were kept in the alley. Melania crouched and hid among the cans and watched the attack finish up with the removal of her trusted 'homies'. She kept still and did not move until darkness helped to cover her movements. She ran down the alley and crossed the nearby street. Two more alleys and streets and she began to feel that she had made her escape.

Melania removed a phone from her pocket and placed one call.

"I'm away and okay," she whispered into the phone. "Come get me now!"

After some brief instructions, she tossed the phone into a nearby garbage can.

"I.N.C.I.S.O.R.!" she muttered. "I will destroy them and their families!" she vowed. "Ellos estan muertos!"

Saipan, Northern Mariana Islands

"Hey Nicky…I have a Harvard-Dartmouth joke," I said.

"Yeah?"

A Harvard guy and a Dartmouth guy are in the bathroom, taking a piss. The Harvard guy finishes and says, 'At Harvard, we wash our hands after taking a pee.' The Dartmouth guy retorts, 'At Dartmouth we don't piss on our hands!'" and I chuckle.

Silence from the men around the table. I guess I did not make any points with that joke. Better luck next time.

"So, tell me about your island," I say in an attempt to recover.

The man known as Jeff Beach begins..." I've been here the longest and have seen the most change."

"We've both been here more than thirty years," Nicky counters.

"What do you want to know? Did you know that this hotel, the Hyatt, used to be the Continental? It was the Haolie hangout," Jeff continued.

Nicky added, "Yeah, the Continental and Hamilton's...that's where we went to drink."

"And the Kensington was first the Nikko when JAL came here," Jeff added.

"We passed that hotel on our way to Radar Hill," Ash said. "And that dilapidated mall across from it...what was it called? La Fiesta?"

"Yep, that's right. JAL used to fly in 747's daily and built the Nikko and La Fiesta to house and entertain the Japanese. Then the Japanese economy went south, and JAL pulled out...lock, stock and barrel. Japanese tourism has never been the same here since," Nicky continued. "They were our number one market for tourism and have slipped to third behind the Chinese and the Korean visitors. And the Japanese do not like not being number one! Most now go to Guam where they are still number one.

"Why is that?" I ask.

"No visas required for the Chinese travelers here in Saipan. Guam requires visas, so much easier for the Chinese to come here," Jeff said.

"What's here for industry besides tourism?" Ash asked the two men.

"Nothing! The garment industry days are gone...that's when the island really thrived," Jeff began...

Nicky jumped in, "We had about 70,000 people here, many garment workers from China. They weren't paid much but when the shops were closed down, they left to return to jobs paying one tenth of what they made here. The damn liberals in Washington felt that they knew what was good for the island and workers making less than minimum wage was a sin. They killed the industry and really hurt the island for twenty years…now tourism is it."

We all took a break and refreshed our drinks. Some got more munchies.

Once settled, I asked, "What can you tell me about Radar Hill and Capital Hill?"

Jeff took over the conversation. "The CIA came in here in a big way during the Cold War. They moved a giant ship-mounted radar onto one mountain and built all sorts of concrete bunker-looking homes to house the operators and trainees on another mountain. One is called Radar Hill and one is Capital Hill. They even restricted access to the north end of the island for a time.

"What do you mean? Trainees?" Ash asked.

"The CIA trained men to act as insurgent forces to counter the rise of Communism, or at least the perceived rise of Communism," Nicky added.

"Yeah, who knew then that Ronald Regan and Capitalism could out spend the Communists and bring down the USSR and the Berlin Wall!" I exclaimed.

"Anyway, that was all gone before I got here thirty years ago," Nicky continued. "So, the island was riding the tourism wave until Yutu and now the pandemic. The only economy on the island is being driven by the influx of Federal dollars. Your taxpayer dollars at work."

"I guess it's good for Saipan that the US sees some strategic value here," Ash said.

"We'd be hurting big time without the Feds," Jeff replied.

Break time again for more drinks and food. Happy Hour was coming to an end and the wait staff were ready with their rolling carts to haul off all of the goodies. We all replenished our drinks and grabbed what little food was left on the table. Most of the other guests had cleared out of the room. We gathered around the table once again.

Ash began, "So, tell me about the Northern Marianas."

Nicky jumped in first, "Guam to Farallon de Pajaros make up fourteen islands in the Northern Mariana Island Archipelago. Guam is a separate US territory and part of the northern Marianas. The CNMI, or Commonwealth of the Northern Mariana Islands includes the other thirteen islands. Magellan was the first westerner to discover the islands in 1521. He and his ships fled the islands after only three days, naming them 'Isla de Ladrones... The Island of Thieves'."

Jeff added, "So, the Spanish claimed the islands first, then the Germans until World War I. The Northern Mariana Islands were then given to the Japanese until World War II. Then the United States administered the islands during the United Nation Trust Territory days until the islands voted to join the United States. The CNMI has been part of the US since then."

"The locals blame the US for bringing them tobacco and Spam," Nicky interjected.

"Those are great cultural things to be noted for," I added. "What does Spam stand for?"

"I know that," Ash replied. "Spiced Ham. But most people know it by the UK designation…Special Processed American Meat."

"Nasty stuff," I said.

"Hold on, Reggie. It is the most popular food in Hawaii!" Clarence countered.

"That doesn't make it better," I said.

"It's huge here, also," Nicky continued. "We have Spam cookoffs and Spam Christmas trees at the local market."

"And a whole bunch of unhealthy, fat islanders," Billy added.

"Huge problem here with diabetes," Jeff said.

"I bet there wasn't much of that when they climbed trees for their coconuts and fished for their protein," I argued.

"All the government handouts sure haven't helped much. The locals can make more not working than being gainfully employed," Nicky added.

"Our US government at work," Ash concluded.

"Time to call it an evening. I have Pilates at 5 tomorrow morning," I offered.

The men around the table agreed and worked to finish their drinks. The four headed to their rooms in the Hyatt, Ash and I headed to our rental house and Jeff and Nicky headed to their homes somewhere on the island.

Denver, CO

Melania made a dozen calls to the leaders of affiliate gangs and even to some who led rival gangs. She was calling in IOU's and all of the favors that she and her gang had done to help out the Mexican gang way of life in Denver.

She had dreamed of putting together an army of angry Chicanos… an angry criminal mob to wreak her revenge. Melania had vowed to herself to destroy I.N.C.I.S.O.R.. She didn't even know that was what they were called. She just knew that these ten men had taken out her gang with precision and purpose.

Melania did not know how, but revenge served as a powerful emotion, driving her to issue a call to arms within the Hispanic community. Some came to help and some to even scores. Most gang members chose to participate because of a curiosity…and it sounded like a good time. Take out a group of meddling white dudes…even if they were ex-military. When they met to plan their attack, 100 Mexicans came to the event.

CHAPTER 7

Florence, Italy

Becky Nelson awakened and ambled to the hotel window. Her room looked out on an icon of Florence, il Duomo…the Cathedral of Santa Maria del Fiore. The beautiful red tiled dome shimmered in the morning sun. She would never get tired of this view, she thought. Becky also remembered how scared she was when she and Reggie went up the circular stairway inside the dome. The stairs were narrow and very uneven from centuries of wear from the many thousands of footsteps that had gone before. She still shuddered with relief when she pictured finally getting off of the stairway onto the solid flooring. Construction of the cathedral had begun in 1296. The structure was completed in 1436. One hundred and forty years in the making!

She was alone for this trip…call it a vacation with a purpose. Reggie had purchased a villa about forty-five minutes south of the main city on a sloping Tuscan hillside. The property was a working olive and wine vineyard which had produced oil and wine for hundreds of years. The house had fallen into disrepair, hence the main purpose of this trip…begin the remodeling.

Becky turned to the roll of architectural plans that sat on the circular table ensconced on the small balcony off of her Grand Hotel Minerva suite. She had come to appreciate the amenities of this small boutique hotel. Room service delivered a tray of fresh fruit, pastries and a flask of piping hot macchiato. Reggie loved a good cappuccino and she often deferred to him…but he was not here.

Curtis Pangelinan had designed the masterpiece that was wrapped up in the architectural plans laying on the table. As coincidence would have it, Curtis was from Saipan, but she and Reggie had contracted him to modernize and restore the villa at his Dubai office. She poured some coffee and unwound the plans. She began to study them when she took a sip…awful!

Becky was unprepared for a true macchiato! Espresso with a dollop of frothed milk. In the Dubai coffee houses they served latte macchiatos… much more steamed milk and sweeter. What a rude awakening. So much for the soft morning glow.

Time for her morning routine to become presentable and then to the rental car for the drive south.

Saipan, Northern Mariana Islands

"Let's go flying!" I announced as I joined Ash for morning coffee on the patio.

It was light out, but the sun had not cleared Mt. Tapochau. There was a light breeze, and the waves were quietly lapping the shoreline. The coffee was black and hot and inviting.

Ash looked up from his paper, "What took you so long, Reggie?"

"I'm dying to put this plane through its paces."

"Yeah, let's see how it feels."

I called ahead to the Executive terminal and had the plane topped off with Jet A. We parked the Escalade next to Aurora. With an identical paint job to the first Aurora, I felt like I was back in my original plane. We performed the walk around together, admiring the beautiful lines of the aircraft. After assuring that everything was good with the exterior, we climbed the two steps into the cabin and moved to the cockpit. I took the left set and Ash sat to my right. We both donned headsets.

After receiving ATIS on the radio, we performed the preflight check with Ash reading from the list. I then began the engine start procedure...a push of a button. I had read that this model was sixty eight percent quieter than its predecessor. As the turbines spooled up the quieter cabin was really evident. I thought about the five-bladed propellers. What a change.

After contacting ground control, we taxied to the active runway...7... and held short. We were taking off to the east into the prevailing wind.

The tower cleared us for takeoff, and I lined up the plane with the center line. I stepped on the brakes and moved the throttles forward. The turbines began to build up power and the plane shuddered as I continued to hold the brakes. I released the foot pedals. Ash and I were pressed into the seats as the aircraft lurched forward. The feeling of power was reassuring to me. As we began to speed down the runway, Ash called out the numbers. We hit 105 knots in only 3200 feet of the 8700-foot runway. I rotated the nose, and we were airborne.

Once in the air, I lowered the nose as Ash cleaned up the aircraft... wheels up and flaps to zero. He did not question what I was doing because he was used to my antics. We sped down the remaining runway building airspeed. As we crossed over the far apron, I pulled back hard on the yoke. The plane leapt into the air and climbed rapidly. It felt to me like we were heading vertically during this rapid ascent. Our steep angle of attack kept us from seeing any traffic, but there was nobody else flying around Saipan airport at our departure time.

It took less than two minutes to reach an altitude of 5000 feet. I turned the plane south toward Tinian and activated the autopilot. The characteristics of the newer plane were remarkably similar to my old standby. I wasn't missing her so much right now! We were planning on staying close to the airport, so I didn't bother programming any information into the flight director.

I said into my mike, "Your plane Ash!"

Ash immediately placed his right hand on the yoke and thumbed off the autopilot with his left. He threw the plane into a right hand sixty-degree turn. His gaze switched from outside to the instruments to make sure he was maintaining five thousand feet. No amusement park ride could feel like this! He returned the plane to level and made a similar move to the left.

I had no other thoughts in my mind except feeling the performance of this airplane and its pilot. I have noticed before that all of the world's problems that occupy one's mind evaporate in this type of flight.

"How about stalling and slow flight?" I asked.

Ash immediately pulled back on the yoke. The plane climbed and slowed but did not approach stalling until he pulled back on the throttles. After a few moments, the stall horn began to blare, and we felt the familiar buffeting as the Evo approached stall speed. The nose fell forward with no sliding off to either side. Beautiful!

"My plane," I announced and turned the Evo north to fly over Saipan. We descended to 3000 feet and flew over the top of Mt. Tapotchau, which reaches to 1555 above sea level. We continued to descend and aimed to pass directly over Okso Talofofo hill, known as Radar Hill, which reaches 918 feet into the sky.

"Circle it, Reggie," Ash ordered.

I entered a right 60-degree bank so that Ash could see the radar installation. I held the turn for a full lap around the site.

"Again," Ash commanded.

I turned the yoke further and flipped us inverted. Like the move I remembered from Top Gun.

"Asshole!" Ash muttered as his cell phone fell onto the ceiling.

I rolled the plane upright and we headed back to the airport.

"Let's shoot some touch and goes," I said.

"First let's see how the flight director will fly the ILS," Ash replied.

He dialed in the frequency and I flipped on the autopilot. The plane flew a course that connected us with the ILS, and it turned onto the final approach for runway 7. I saw that our alignment was perfect and turned off the autopilot. I flew the VASI (visual approach slope indicator) down to a nice touchdown.

Ash took the yoke and pushed the power levers forward. The Evo jumped into the air and I worked to get the flaps and gear up. We levelled off at 1300 AGL and entered the downwind leg for runway 7. I noticed that the windsock was not moving at all. He moved the flaps to 5% and reduced the throttles. The tower asked us to extend the downwind leg to allow for traffic on final…a 757 from Korea. We spotted the plane on its approach. The tower called the base turn and Ash went to 20% flaps. Shortly we turned final, and Ash dropped the gear.

"Three green," I announced.

"Full flaps," Ash said.

The plane flew a perfect approach on this windless morning. He greased the landing.

"This is too easy," Ash said and exited the runway. We parked the plane and did a final walk around.

Again, beautiful!

Dubai, UAE

Michael MacAteer was enjoying his new 'digs'. After shattering his legs during the rescue of Mariel in Poland, his days as an active operative of I.N.C.I.S.O.R. were over. He knew this and the team knew this.

The idea to move him into Becky's spot behind the scenes but also extremely important in this information age was a good fit for him. Becky had left the Nelson home in Dubai completely furnished and he was enjoying the amenities on Palm Jumerah island.

Michael had just finished his review of the world news and was looking at the 'hot spots' around the world where expected terrorists were working their evil deeds. A call announced itself on the screen in front of him. It was identified as originating from the Arapahoe County Sheriff's Department and had a 303-area code.

"You've reached I.N.C.I.S.O.R.. I'll take a bite out of crime for you," he spoke into the headset.

"Ugh, is Becky there?" a tentative female voice asked.

"Nope. She's out of the country. Can I help?"

"I hope so. There's going to be an attack."

Michael sat up a little straighter.

"Yes," he replied.

"Can you help?" the female voice asked.

"Michael MacAteer…at your service," he answered.

"The is detective Satur from the Organized Crime bureau," she announced.

"Yes, detective?"

Michael waited anxiously.

"Listen, I have a CI…a confidential informan…"

"I know what a CI is," Michael said, cutting her off.

"Oh, sorry…well this informant is a Crips member. He told me that the gangs are amassing an army to take out your I.N.C.I.S.O.R. fellows."

"I'm sure they'll be fine…they can take care of themselves!"

"No…you don't understand…they are putting together an army of one hundred Mexicans to take your I.N.C.I.S.O.R. men out!"

"Against the ten of them?" Michael pondered. "This is bad. Why are you calling me?"

"I tried the local contact number I have and no answer."

"I'll get through. When?" Michael queried.

"My CI mentioned Wednesday," detective Satur replied.

"That's pickleball day! They will be extremely vulnerable!" Michael exclaimed. "Thanks…bye," and he disconnected the phone.

He called the satellite line to Lance Wood.

"Lance…sorry to bother you…this is Michael."

"I know…what's up?" Lance sounded very distant…extremely far away…not in the present.

"I think I.N.C.I.S.O.R. is in danger!" Michael replied.

Saipan, Northern Mariana Islands

I placed the phone on the table.

"Ash, that was Michael in Dubai. It seems like there is an imminent attack against our men in Denver!" I announced.

"Tell me…what's up?" Ash replied.

I told him what I knew. Ash listened in silence while watching the Escalade parked beside the patio. When I had finished, Ash stood and walked over to the car.

"Reggie, you think the CIA has more than one of these?" he gestured toward the SUV.

"I wouldn't think that this is a one of a kind," I replied, and it hit me as I was speaking. Two of these cars armed with four drones equipped the way our SUV was equipped could attack a small army and prevail.

I picked up the phone, "Lance?"

Denver CO

"I see, Reggie, Lance replied after I laid out the plan. "I'll get on it!"

For the first time since Cyndi's murder Lance Wood became animated. First, he called Langley to see about the SUV's…yes, they had developed and armed more of the Escalades. And yes, they would airlift two of the vehicles to Buckley Air Base immediately.

Lance then called the two I.N.C.I.S.O.R. teams and had them gather at the Residence Inn, his temporary home since the destruction of his Cherry Hills home.

"Time to do battle," Lance thought.

Two hours later the eleven men gathered in a conference/TV room off the main lobby of Lance's hotel.

Lance began, "Guys…I have bad news…no pickleball this Wednesday."

The men murmured among themselves for a moment.

"Quiet! We have more important business. An attack is imminent against you all."

More discussion among the I.N.C.I.S.O.R. team members. The noise in the room was on a crescendo. Arms were flailing…the men were becoming more animated. Lance Wood liked this.

Again, "Quiet!!" This time Lance had to raise his voice.

"What's up, boss?" came from one of the men.

"I have it on good authority that one hundred Mexican gang members plan to ambush you during your pickleball session at South Suburban."

"My God!"

"It's wide open there!"

"Other people are playing…using the courts!"

"It would be a massacre!"

"Innocent lives lost."

"And, what about us?"

Lance let his information sink in and then said," I have a plan…or rather Ash and Reggie have a plan!"

Lance explained to the men of I.N.C.I.S.O.R. about the two Escalades on their way to Aurora, Colorado, and the firepower they possessed. The men quickly became involved in the discussion and planned a counterattack/ambush.

"I love it when a plan comes together," Lance thought as he listened to his men. He loved that line from the A Team's Hannibal Smith.

Dubai, UAE

Michael watched the three screens in front of him as he sat in the I.N.C.I.S.O.R. office. It was his job to coordinate the I.N.C.I.S.O.R. defense and counterattack from his perch in Dubai. He was watching aerial and street views from various cameras as the procession of twenty-five cars departed from their gathering place on east Colfax and headed for their destiny with death.

He had two thoughts as he watched…this seemed like a movie that he was watching with a sense of detachment and at the same time he was anxious for his teammates. And...this procession had to contain most of the low riders in Denver!

Denver, CO

Melania rode in the first car. She rode shotgun, allowing another Mexican gang member to drive the lead car. There were one hundred men...four to a car...following as they motored down the chosen route from east Colfax Avenue to I-25 south to the Arapahoe Street exit.

As the procession neared the South Suburban park all of the men busied themselves with getting their weapons ready. This was an armada of highly armed and motivated gang members. Their large numbers and firepower gave the men a false sense of security. Little had been done to reconnoiter the athletic facility. And now, as they approached, Melania and the men ignored the signs of impending doom.

As the cars poured into the parking lot little notice of the two black Escalade SUVs was given. There should have been concern at the lack of cars in the lot. None of the men had noticed that there were drones hovering over them, both during the ride south and now as they entered the parking lot.

There were men playing on three of the courts. They seemed to take little notice of the army that was pouring into their space. Could they be that stupid? The cars made a horribly loud racket as many of the mufflers were designed to be scary and loud. Once the cars were gathered and parked, the men exited the vehicles carrying an array of shotguns and automatic weapons. They sauntered, menacingly, toward the pickleball players.

Now, the men of I.N.C.I.S.O.R. acted their parts and all ten men hit the asphalt court surfaces. As soon as they lay in a prone position, eight overhead drones unleashed their awesome firepower. Gatling guns and missiles rained down from the flying drones onto the Mexican armada. In less than a minute twenty-five cars lay smoking and riddled with so many holes that the frames squealed as the integrity of the metal fatigued and failed. Many of the cars were smoking and on fire from the Hellfire missiles that struck them.

Almost all of the Mexican gang members were dead. Most had been killed directly from the aerial assault. A few had scrambled under their cars only to have the cars collapse down upon them, crushing them.

Melania had crawled under the lead car which had collapsed down, pinning her and making it difficult for her to breathe, but she was still alive. She lay there on the pavement trying to comprehend what had just happened. Her army was no more. She looked out from under the car to see the men of I.N.C.I.S.O.R. getting off the courts and ambling toward her. None of them had been touched! Not a single gang member had fired their weapon. "What a disaster," she thought.

Approaching sirens could be heard as cars from the Arapahoe County Sheriff's department, Greenwood Village Police force and the Littleton Police and Fire Departments began to converge on the South Suburban pickleball court facility.

Soon, uniformed men were milling around the destroyed cars and working to align and cover the bodies of the massacred gang members. Several groups of firefighters were working to extract bodies from under the collapsed cars. One group was working to free Melania. United States Marshalls were waiting to take her into custody once she was freed from the wreckage.

The men of I.N.C.I.S.O.R. had all been used as bait. They now gathered to watch in fascination as the cleanup progressed. None of them had ever seen such a display of destructive firepower. And it all had come from the small drones that were landing on their rooftop carriers atop the Escalades. I.N.C.I.S.O.R. had really taken a 'bite' out of crime today!

An array of tow trucks began to remove the riddled vehicles. None of the gang vehicles had workable tires, so tilting flatbed trucks had to be used to haul away the wreckage. Coroners' vehicles could be seen as the bodies were catalogued and placed in the vans for removal.

Not a single innocent casualty. No men in uniform were harmed during the exchange. The only weapons fired were from the eight drones. This was a good day.

Saipan, Northern Mariana Islands

Reggie and Ash watched on a similar display in their rental home, and both exhaled loudly as the mission played out before their eyes. Another successful mission. Both men also had a lot more respect for the drones sitting on the SUV outside.

"That was fucking amazing! Never seen that much firepower," I exclaimed.

"Ditto!" Ash replied. "I think we're in for a new style of warfare."

"They've been using drones, or UAVs for many years now. I've seen lots of TV footage showing drone surveillance and drone strikes," I said.

"Me too, but nothing like today and in a domestic situation," Ash added.

Washington, DC

President Marron sat in the situation room in silence after reviewing the footage from Denver. He beamed with pride inside after watching the high-tech weapons deter what should have been a devasting attack against the I.N.C.I.S.O.R. teams. Outside he maintained his famous poker face that let nobody see how he really felt about things.

The other men in the room sat in silence and waited for their Commander in Chief to react.

"Well now, what do we do about this?" President Marron asked the room.

The silence continued for a moment. Then, one of his generals spoke, "That was impressive!"

"An attack against US citizens on US soil," another commented.

"Any concern that these weren't bad guys?" the President asked, staring directly at the man who had the negative response.

Some murmuring among the top brass surrounding the table.

"No, sir, Mr. President," another exclaimed.

"So…a force of evil…a gang of thugs…has been eliminated. I do not care how this gets spun. This was a good day!" President Marron replied and rose to leave the room.

Everyone in the room stood as the President of the United States turned away from the table and departed the room.

"A good day," he repeated.

Saipan, Northern Mariana Islands

"The technicians just checked in," Ash mentioned as he hung up the phone.

"And?" I asked.

"The repairs are going well. They said that the radar site is one week away from testing," Ash replied.

"Is the plane ready with the parabolic mirror?" I questioned.

"No idea. Checking," Ash said as he picked up the phone.

Ash first called Langley for an update and then called the King Abdul Aziz air base in eastern Saudi Arabia. This base had been chosen by the CIA to serve as home base for the C-130 that was tasked with carrying the parabolic mirror to reflect the signal from Saipan.

Iraq was chosen by the CIA to be the first area for the flyover and test of the radio beam. So many IEDs had been used to injure and maim American servicemen. There must be hundreds, if not thousands, of hidden storage sites for C-4. Improvised explosive devices had been used by terrorist cells to harm the US military without actually facing the men and women of the army. So cowardly!

The CIA also knew that the bomb making activity occurred in housing projects where there were civilians. The cowardly terrorists hid among the innocent, knowing that the US military did not want loss of civilian life during the conflict. So, with the radio waves from RFW, there would be loss of innocent lives. The hope among the CIA analysts was that the civilian masses would drive the terrorists and Islamic extremists away from their hiding places among the innocents and out into the open where they could be easily dealt with.

Ash and Reggie knew that the CIA logic would only work if the RFW plan was kept secret. An errant explosion could be caused by many things…poor storage conditions, poor handling and sloppy construction. Nobody would suspect that a radio wave sent from Saipan would cause the explosive material to ignite.

"Everything is set on the Saudi side. The plane is there and ready for flight. The parabolic mirror is hidden in the belly of the aircraft," Ash said as he hung up the phone.

"Good news…we only have a little while to get ready for that dinner reservation," I replied.

The 'dinner reservation' was actually an invitation to enjoy a home cooked meal. The Pilates instructor was a really nice and generous woman who wanted to make us…the newly arrived on island… welcome. I had been told that her vegetarian dishes were legendary. Ash and I were both carnivores but could pass on meat for one evening.

We arrived at her family home just a little late. Not Saipan late, which meant twenty to thirty minutes or longer after the chosen time. I was told to bring nothing, but there was no way that Ash and I would show up for this invitation empty handed. Two bottles of white wine were a safe bet to bring for a vegetarian dinner.

There were other guests who were present and arriving as we parked. People had gathered on an outside patio where I could hear conversation and muted background music. Their daughter was in charge of the music selection. I was pleasantly surprised to hear classic rock from my college days. I did not appreciate the label, 'classic'.

CHAPTER 8

Pat, our host, had invited a local dentist and his wife to the party. I was carrying on a lively conversation with him and finding out about interesting facts of the island of Saipan. There were six private practices on the island and one government clinic at the hospital. This guy, named Charles, had claimed responsibility for bringing pickleball to the island and had the first pickleball court lines painted in the parking lot in front of his office. I told him that I had played for the first time in Colorado and loved the sport!

I looked over to Ash to involve him in our conversation, but he was being very attentive to the dentist's wife who was introduced as Carol. She was taller than Ash and was showing some nice cleavage. I wasn't sure what Ash was focused on, but I didn't interrupt him.

Shortly, Pat called us to dinner and the eight guests sat around a large rectangular table on the patio. There was a light breeze coming from the north making for a comfortable evening...not too hot or humid.

Pat blessed the food, and the dishes began to be circulated around the table. I had to keep asking Pat what the various casseroles were because I did not recognize a thing! I timidly tasted each dish of which I had purposefully placed very little on my plate and was pleasantly surprised. This was good food!

Carol, the dentist's wife, was commanding the conversation. I noticed that she was very opinionated and often cut people off in mid-sentence so that she could control the course of the conversation. I had met people like that before…conversational terrorists!

One of the other guests, named Lillian, said that she had just moved to Saipan from Colorado and was working at the hospital as an emergency room physician. She said that she had only been here for two months and was "the low man on the totem pole" at the hospital. Her statement got my attention.

"I bet you didn't know that the phrase, 'low man on the totem pole' is often misused," I began.

"What are you saying?" she replied.

"You mean to say that you have the lowest rank because you are the newest physician at the hospital," I continued.

"Yes…'low man on the totem pole'" she countered.

"You are using the phrase wrong!" I argued. "It is another one of many oxymorons."

"So now I'm a moron?" she said angrily.

"No, no, no…I'm sorry…oxymoron is what I said," I quickly replied… this was not going well.

"Oxymoron as in…" she asked.

"Contradictory terms," I said.

"Explain," Lillian ordered.

"We all know terms like this that are misused. If you know Native American folklore, they started carving on the lower part of the totem pole to tell a story. The tribal elders were carved into the pole first and then they worked their way up the pole with the newest members involved in the story on top. So, being on the lower part of the totem pole does not mean you are at the bottom of the heap," I lectured.

"But that is how the idiom is used…the low man on the totem pole is the least important," Ash countered.

I tried to wilt him with my glare. How dare he take up her side!

"I know, but it is wro.." I began.

Charles cut me off, "Like saying 'she eats like a bird' to describe eating very little."

"Exactly!" I added.

"Birds eat up to one half of their body weight every day. They are voracious eaters!" Ash added, trying to get back on my good side.

"What are other examples? Let's go around the table and everybody think of one," Dane said.

"I've got one," Mike chimed in, "Jumbo shrimp."

"Great, next," Dane pointed to Lillian who was sitting next to Ash.

"Um…pass…No!" she stuttered, "Bittersweet!"

"Yes, you've got it, Ash?" Dane said as he looked toward my friend.

Ash perked up in his chair. "Happy as a clam."

Pat was seated on Ash's other side. "My turn, how about the silence was deafening?"

"These are all great examples," Dane added.

"Okay, Reggie?"

"A joke is an extremely serious issue," I said.

"What?" Ash, again.

"Hey, that is a quote from Winston Churchill!" I replied.

"I'm not impressed," Dane said.

"Aw, come on…Winston Churchill!" I exclaimed, but nobody was buying it.

"Here's one," Pat interjected. "Walking dead."

"Good, what else?" Dane said, "Oh, it's my turn. 'Sweet sorrow'…like, parting is such sweet sorrow."

"Okay," Pat replied.

"So, that's one time around the table," I added.

Just then Pat and Dane's daughter, Heidi, brought to the table a gorgeous looking cake for dessert. It was clear to us that she had been eavesdropping. "How about passive aggressive?" she asked.

"Not bad, Heidi!" I exclaimed. Heidi was a teenager, but quite wise for her age. "What does that mean to you?"

"Like when mom tells me to clean up my room and I say, 'sure', but then I purposefully procrastinate and do not get it done," Heidi said.

"That's like a woman I know on the island," Carol added. "She is nice and says she is my friend to my face and then talks badly about me behind my back. It is so hurtful!"

"Back stabbers like that are such cowards," Lillian opined.

"I had to hear about it from other friends," Carol sobbed.

It was obvious that she was really upset. Charles moved to comfort her. "How could anybody say anything bad about you, my love?"

As Carol sobbed on Charles' shoulder, I tasted a piece of the cake and couldn't help myself, "This is fantastic!"

I felt badly as soon as I said it. I wasn't being very sensitive and concerned about Carol, but this was the best cake I had ever tasted.

After putting up with several looks of shock aimed my way, Ash began to laugh, and the others joined in.

"Reggie, your Crème Brulee turned me into a diabetic! And you love this cake?"

"This is the best thing I've ever tasted!" I said between bites. "This is how vegetarians eat?"

Pat finally got to say thank you and added that she and Heidi had worked all afternoon on the desert.

"You could sell this and turn the whole island into diabetics!" I exclaimed.

Soon it was time for Ash and me to bid our goodbyes and return to our rental home. We had a big day planned for tomorrow.

CHAPTER 9

Radar Hill, Saipan

Joe Cavanaugh and Billie Bean were waiting for us as we drove the Escalade into the compound. The radar looked just as decrepit and rusted as it did when I first saw it. If anything had been accomplished to update the facility, nobody would be able to tell.

"Come see!" Joe yelled to us.

We got out of the SUV and walked to the building closest to the radar. As we entered, I noticed that all of the beer cans, Soju bottles and condoms had been cleared out and tables full of equipment had been placed around the room. It looked like miles of black and colored cables ran around the room and most exited into what I assumed was a hidden tunnel that led to the radar.

"This is a lot of stuff!" I exclaimed.

Ash shook his head in acknowledgement as he looked around the room. He and I had no idea that all this equipment was going to be necessary for Radio Free World.

"It is 8 am here in Saipan, what time is it in Baghdad?" Ash asked.

"Baghdad is seven hours behind us, so 1 am there," Billie said.

"The transport took off and is circling over the southern part of the city…ready to go to work!" Joe informed us.

"And we're ready?" I asked.

"Yep,"

"Let's do this!" Ash added.

Baghdad, Iraq

The policeman looked at his watch. One o'clock in the morning he thought. The only people up now are up to no good. He glanced down the block, swiveled, and checked behind him. No cars or pedestrians were to be seen. He pulled out a pack of smokes and his lighter.

As he fumbled to remove a cigarette from the crumpled pack, he looked into the night sky. It was a moonless night, but he saw that many stars dotted the black sky. His world seemed so peaceful right now.

Just as he struck his lighter a loud explosion could be heard.

"Did I do this?" he thought as the flame ignited from his lighter. He quickly put out the flame and looked toward the explosion. He could see a building on fire less than two blocks away. He began to run toward the flaming building as a second building exploded and erupted into flames.

"Whaaa?' he began to cry out as a third building exploded.

He now made the choice to run in the opposite direction and escape the carnage. He thought he could hear wailing and cries for help as he ran for safety.

"Not from me!" he muttered under his breath as he ran for his life.

Soon, sirens could be heard as fire trucks approached.

Saipan, Northern Mariana Islands

Video feeds were streaming in from the belly of the C-130 flying over Iraq. Three buildings all in one square block in the southern part of Baghdad had smoke pouring out of them and into the night sky. When the camera lenses were switched to infrared mode, it was clear that the buildings were all ablaze.

"At first glance it looks to me like the test was a success," Billie Bean concluded.

"Yes! A success!" Joe Cavanaugh added.

Ash and I knew that much more information had to come to the island of Saipan and also to Langley before the true results of the testing of Radio Free World could be analyzed, but we also were all smiles along with the young technicians who had travelled so far and worked so hard to make the Radar Hill site a functioning entity. Their enthusiasm was infectious.

I walked outside and looked upon the rusting radar. I was not sure if I expected the radar to do something, but I stood there expectantly. I looked into the forest and saw that the flame trees were beginning to bloom. The Japanese had brought these beautiful trees to the island during their occupation of the island between World War One and World War Two. The trees' blossoms were a fiery red color which stood out against the dark green leaves. Nature is utterly amazing on this small tropical island in the western Pacific.

Langley, Virginia

"Sir, all of the information that has been transmitted from Baghdad is telling a positive story. The initial test broadcast of the Radio Free World site in Saipan was scheduled to last for one minute. The site in Saipan performed well, with no immediate problems noted. The C-130 intercepted the beam from Saipan and directed it into a one block area in the southern area of Baghdad where we had intel that bomb-making activity was present.

Three stashes of suspected C-4 explosives all were ignited when the radio beam passed over them. The amount of C-4 present at the three sites was unknown, but there was enough explosive to bring down three buildings. We are calling this test a success!" the supervisor told his CIA chief.

"And casualties?" the chief questioned.

"Too soon to tell, sir...the three buildings are now piles of burning rubble. Lives were definitely lost, but no telling how many were civilian casualties," the supervisor replied.

"And the reports from the Iraqis?" the chief asked.

"Initial reports of possible missile attacks, Seal team incursions, infighting among various terrorist cells...nobody has a clue," was the response.

"Great! Good news...talk to me once the sun comes up over there and the ground assessment units have a chance to react," the chief commanded as he turned to leave the room.

Washington, DC

"POTUS is in a meeting," the White House Chief of Staff announced. "Tell me what you've got."

"The preliminary reports from the first night all point to success. Three suspected caches of arms and explosives were destroyed and nobody knows why," the aide assigned to Dr. Nelson's new venture said.

"This is great news! Just what the President needs…a positive blow against terrorism. When will you know more?" the Chief of Staff asked.

"Full report in two days," the aide replied.

"Let's meet again in two days. I'll make sure that POTUS is here for the news," the Chief said as he wheeled to attend another briefing.

Baghdad, Iraq

Members of Iraq's military were milling around concrete rubble piles. The piles were the remains of three buildings in the block that had been brought down by sudden and severe explosions. The men were kicking and prodding at the piles looking for survivors and corpses. The corpses outweighed the survivors by twenty to one.

The military commanders had gathered in a tent erected at the end of the street. After a brief period of silence and uncomfortable shuffling of feet, a colonel spoke, "What do we know?"

"Three explosions…all unrelated…all from unknown causes," an officer announced.

"No claims of responsibility," another officer added.

"How many dead?" the colonel asked.

"One hundred and fifty and counting," an officer looked up from his notes. "Less than ten survivors have been transported to hospital and several are not supposed to live."

"Missing?" the colonel asked.

"Still looking for about fifty more bodies," another officer added.

"And we know nothing about the explosions? Were they internal or external? Anybody?"

More shuffling and silence.

"Get me answers! I want answers!" the colonel ordered.

The officers seemed like they were tripping over each other to get out of the tent the fastest. They would head back to their respective troops to yell and order the men around. The Iraqi army was at a complete loss as to the cause of the destruction and loss of life.

Denver, Colorado

"Chalk up another in the 'win' column for Reggie and Ash!" Lance shouted to the other I.N.C.I.S.O.R. team members as several heated pickleball matches were going on.

Several of the team had some experience playing tennis and had a marked advantage over the other team members. Several others had played ping pong at a fairly high level and also picked up the game of pickleball quickly.

All of the players were in great shape and had athletic physiques that made them the envy of the players that came out to watch them.

The men had brushed off the attack from the multiple Mexican gangs and had come to the South Suburban facility to lose themselves in the new game. Some of the I.N.C.I.S.O.R. team were so aggressive that observers were wondering if the game would become a contact sport!

Melania Cruz, gravely wounded, had been captured and was under armed guard at the infirmary of the Arapahoe County Jail. Some had argued that she needed a hospital and more involved treatment, but the public's safety had won out. She would have to make her recovery at the county jail facility.

Her Mexican gang, the GKI, was no longer in existence, as most of the gang members had lost their lives during the awesome attack of the eight drones that had been tasked with protecting the I.N.C.I.S.O.R. men. Melania still commanded a strong presence south of the border and was therefore a valid threat. If she ever saw the light of day again!

"Que pasa?" Duncan Trevino called out from a far court.

"RFW was tested and looks like it was a success," Lance yelled back at him.

The I.N.C.I.S.O.R. men stopped their play and moved to gather around Lance on the first court.

"So, the damn thing worked!" Stirling Mason exclaimed.

"What happened…how did the test go?" Graham Sandler asked.

Lance donned a professorial air and began, "As you know, Saipan is seventeen hours ahead of us here in Colorado. At 8 am today, which was our yesterday at 3 pm, they fired up the apparatus on Radar Hill and beamed a radio frequency to a C-130 flying above Baghdad. Baghdad is seven hours behind Saipan, so at 1 am their time three buildings in a one block area blew up and were reduced to rubble.

The local military and police have no idea what happened to cause the carnage. The test looks initially that it was a complete success!"

"That calls for a toast!" Magnus Harper announced and headed to the cooler to retrieve the chilled beer bottles.

Bottles were handed out to all of the I.N.C.I.S.O.R. team.

Powers Hunt stepped in to announce, "A toast to our leaders! Lance, Ash and Reggie! Hurrah!"

The bottles were clanked together, and the men pulled deeply on the ice-cold beer.

Saipan, Northern Mariana Islands

"Reggie, you did it!" Ash said as he gave me a hug.

"We did it, my good friend," I replied and hugged him back.

"Let's get to Godfathers…I could use a drink!" Ash exclaimed as he headed for the Escalade.

"Me too, I'm thirsty," I agreed and went to let Joe and Billie know what we were doing and to ask them to join us.

As we drove down the hill and headed for the town of Garapan I felt a queasy sense in my stomach. I had felt like this before…an impending sense of doom.

PART TWO

CHAPTER 10

Baghdad, Iraq

Achmed surveyed the dusty pile of broken concrete. He kicked absent-mindedly at a piece of rubble that lay near his feet. He glanced at the remains of what used to be a five-story building. There were shards of wood and glass mixed in with the pile of concrete and twisted rebar. He guessed that they were probably somebody's furniture just a little while ago.

"How did this happen?" he questioned.

An Arab man standing nearby, clad in a checkered cloth wrapped loosely around his head and partially covering his face, replied, "We had weapons in an apartment on the second floor."

"Well…where are the weapons?" Achmed asked, his voice getting louder.

The man reached into the pile that once was a building and pulled out a metallic gun barrel. "Right here," he retorted, looking down at the broken weapon in his hands.

"All gone…all destroyed…how? Is it like this with the other two buildings?" Achmed continued to question.

"It is the same with all of the buildings. All three had different amounts of munitions that were stored in them. All of the weapons suddenly exploded. All of the explosions happened at the same time. We do not know why," the man said.

"We must find out why this happened. We must!" Achmed stated and turned to leave. "Get me some answers!"

Langley, Virginia

In a large, cavernous room a group of analysts had gotten up from their cubicles and myriad computer screens to gather around the supervisor's desk.

"All reports from Iraq are scattered and meaningless. They have no idea what has happened to them."

"Great work on the first test of Radio Free World! You are all to be congratulated. I'd break out the bubbly, but the word from the hill is to prepare for a second test…a larger test. This test will involve four square blocks, also in downtown Baghdad."

"Back to your terminals…let's get ready for this next test. Washington wants the test in two days. This has been a good day!"

Saipan, Northern Mariana Islands

Ash finished his call and placed his phone on the round patio table next to his cup of coffee.

I had been absently staring at the turquoise water and lost in thought. When he placed his phone down my attention returned to the present.

"So, Reggie…Washington wants another test of RFW in two days. Is that enough time to prepare?" Ash asked as we sat on the outside patio watching the lazy waves of the Philippine Sea lap against the sandy shoreline.

"Should be, my friend. The target is still Baghdad…just a larger area. We will move the coordinates to another hotspot in the city and have the aircraft fly at a higher altitude so that the one emission from the radar site here will encompass four square blocks," I replied.

"Does the beam we send out need to be stronger? Can the plane handle a stronger emission from us here in Saipan?" Ash continued with good questions.

"Don't know until we try…probably start at the same settings and be ready to crank up the volume when we get reports from the plane," I answered.

"Let's meet the guys at Spicy Thai for lunch. We can catch them up on the next test," Ash suggested.

"Great idea! I've wanted to try their buffet. I like Thai food," I said.

Washington, DC

The President of the United States was sitting in the oval office with the Director of the CIA. Both were enjoying tumblers of a single malt scotch over ice.

They waited to begin their conversation until the steward had finished using tongs to drop ice cubes into their glasses. Both men swirled the amber liquid in their glasses to allow the ice to chill the scotch. As the door closed behind the steward, they smelled the aroma rising from the glasses.

"From what we can tell, nobody…including our allies and Russia… has a clue as to why there are three buildings in downtown Baghdad lying in ruins. There are reports of earthquake, drone strikes, gas leaks, etc.," the Director opened.

"No idea?" President Marron asked.

"None! The next hours, days and weeks will allow them time to sift through the crazy theories to see if any of them work," the Director replied as he sipped his scotch.

"This tastes really good."

"It tastes better when you have a win…congratulations!" President Marron added.

The Director gloated for a moment. Wins these days came so infrequently.

"What's next?" the President asked.

"Next test is in two days…" the Director replied as his voice trailed off. How would this go? How long could the secret be kept? He had many concerns about going forward.

Denver, CO

The Frankfurt team faced off against the Denver team in a makeshift pickleball tournament. Stirling Mason took on Lance Everett in a best 2 out of 3 games of singles. Magnus Harper and Dick Becker went against Powers Hunt and Flex Lawson in a best 2 out of 3 games of doubles. Aaron Dekker and Graham Sandler teamed up against Duncan Trevino and Kurt Nichols for the second doubles match.

The Frankfurt and Denver I.N.C.I.S.O.R. teams were playing each other for the 'BIG DILL' trophy and pickleball bragging rights until the next tournament was announced. The large trophy looked like a large dill pickle holding a pickleball paddle in one hand and a trophy in the other hand.

"Zero…zero…" Stirling called out as he served the first serve of his match to Lance. Play continued in a close match with Lance winning the best two out of three games…it took all three games for him to beat Stirling. First win to Denver.

The first doubles match was also extremely close and the other I.N.C.I.S.O.R. team members cheered on their teammates. The Frankfurt team prevailed in this contest.

The winning team would be decided in the third and final match. As the four men took the court to begin their duel, the cell phones of the two team leaders began to ring simultaneously. Play was halted as Lance and Stirling moved to the side bench to retrieve their phones.

The two calls were placed from the United States Marshalls office. The news was really bad! Melania Cruz had escaped during her transport to Florence, CO. Had the transfer to the maximum-security prison there been successful, Melania would never be heard from again. Now she was out and who knew what she was planning next. All any of the I.N.C.I.S.O.R. team members knew was that reprisal and revenge were her two favorite words…Repesalia…Venganza.

The pickleball match was stopped as the men returned to the Denver training facility to shower and clean up and prepare for their next mission…track down Melania…stop her before she hurts them.

Saipan, Northern Mariana Islands

Ash and I joined Joe Cavanaugh and Billy Bean at Spicy Thai. I had just learned about Thai food during our stay in Saipan. The food was known to be quite spicy with unusual seasonings. I had become particularly enamored with the papaya salad, which I was endeavoring to eat with my awkward use of chopsticks.

Ash was enjoying a ginger beef salad with more adept use of chopsticks than me.

Joe and Billy availed themselves of the lunch buffet and had returned to the table with full plates of food. "Oh, to be young again," I thought as I watched them dig into their overflowing plates.

"You know you can go back…its all-you-can-eat," Ash remarked to the two CIA technicians.

"We're fine," they replied in unison as if rehearsed.

"Okay," I said to get their attention.

"The next test is to be in two days. Still in Baghdad, but a four-square-block area," Ash added.

"Easy peasy!" Billy replied.

"We'll be set by tonight," Joe said. "Can we take tomorrow to sightsee? I want to see Suicide Cliff and the Grotto."

"Banzai Cliff and some beach time at Pau Pau Beach for me," Billy intoned.

"If you guys are ready, then take the day," I said. "We'll meet for the test at the same time as the first test…8 am…in a day and a half."

"Great!" Billy said

"A day of exploration," Joe added.

We continued to eat in silence. Then Ash asked, "When is Becky due?"

"She is on the 4:50 am United flight from Guam tomorrow morning. Gets in at 5:30. Luckily, she won't have to quarantine like most of the visitors and returning residents are required to do. I have Pilates at 5. Be done by 6, and I'm planning on picking her up at the airport at 6:30 to give her time to clear customs and immigration," I answered.

"I hate all this Covid stuff and people running so scared. How did she get out of the quarantine?" Ash replied.

"A call from the President to the Governor of Saipan," I said.

"Wow! Just for us?"

"Yep!"

"She bringing the kitchen sink?" Ash joked.

"As always…Becky cannot be without her stuff! She has one suitcase just for her bathroom stuff…I have never understood this, but I am glad we have an Escalade to get all of her stuff!"

Baghdad, Iraq

Mustafa was working extremely carefully to put the finishing touches on the bomb packed with C4 in the open backpack sitting on the bench in front of him. This was the fifth device that he had assembled and the final bomb on his list of requests from the local terrorist cell that he worked for. They provided him, his wife, two boys and daughter with a substantial apartment on another floor of the building and plenty of money for food and supplies.

He also received an ample supply of C4, detonators, wiring and cell phones to remotely trigger his bombs.

A courier had come by within the hour to pick up the four completed devices. They were carried carefully to an awaiting car and Mustafa watched as two men gently placed the bombs into the trunk of the car. The car slowly pulled away from the curb and out into the street.

Mustafa watched the car pull away from the building where he worked and lived. He returned his focus to the bomb. As he worked, the C4 suddenly became too hot to touch. He pulled away from the table and began to cry out…no words were uttered. He and his lab were incinerated in a white flash of a C4 ignition, followed by an incredibly loud explosion.

The building crumbled. Many other buildings within the four-square block also imploded upon themselves. The car that had just left also evaporated amid a loud explosion. Adjacent buildings to the ones housing various caches of explosives and weaponry were also irreparably damaged and lay in various states of destruction and disrepair.

The immediate area around the explosions looked like a dreary scene from a futuristic apocalyptic science fiction movie.

CHAPTER 11

Saipan, Northern Mariana Islands

"Alright! Shut down the transmitter!" I ordered.

Joe Cavanaugh took the lead and began to shut down the equipment that had produced the emission that had been directed to the aircraft circling over Baghdad at a higher altitude than it had been circling in the previous test.

Billy helped to silence the electronic gear arrayed in front of us. "Equipment off. Second test is complete."

Ash turned to me, "What now, Reggie?"

"We wait for the analysis from Langley," I replied. "Good job, guys! Ash and I will contact you at the Hyatt with the results."

I walked out of the building and looked up to the decaying radar dish in front of me. "In God we rust," I muttered while thinking how decrepit the radar looked. Nobody would suspect that the facility was now the latest weapon in the war against terrorism.

Ash and I walked to the SUV and drove to our rental home on the beach. Becky was in the kitchen when we entered.

"Iced tea…anyone?" Becky asked.

"The hostess with the mostest!" I replied. "I'd love some."

"Me too!" Ash added.

"I'll bring a pitcher and glasses out to the patio," Becky said.

Shortly, Becky joined Ash and me at the patio table. She placed a large tray with a glass pitcher filled with amber liquid, glasses filled with ice and a bowl full of tangerines picked from a tree in the side yard. She placed two glasses in front of us and poured from the pitcher. She poured a glass for herself and placed the bowl of fruit onto the table.

"How did the test go?" she asked.

"Flawless on our end," Ash replied.

"The equipment was on for ten minutes before the transmission, warming up, and the actual transmission lasted less than a minute. Then five minutes to power down the transmitters. We were only at the radar site for a half hour. Two cars…four men…if anybody was watching. We were just exploring the rusting site of one of the remnants left from the Cold War," I added.

"We are waiting to hear from the States about the results from test number two," Ash said.

"I would expect that initial reports are already pouring into Langley from Baghdad," Becky opined.

"You're right…should hear something very soo…" Just then Ash's phone began to vibrate. He rose from the table and answered the call. Quickly he returned to the table and turned on the speaker function of the cell phone. "You're on speaker with Reggie and Becky and me."

"Test two is beginning to look like a success. Satellite imagery shows much destruction within the test area. Many buildings levelled. No damage outside of the test radius. Reports from the ground are beginning to trickle in. Much devastation and loss of life…and no initial idea why," the voice on the phone said.

"And our response?" Ash asked.

"Washington has reached out to the Iraqi government to offer whatever aid they need. Right now, except for immediate humanitarian aid, Baghdad doesn't know what to ask for. They are in the dark! Congratulations! To I.N.C.I.S.O.R.!" and the line went dead.

"So, can I assume that it will take days for a complete assessment?" Becky asked.

"Yeah, we have some time to kill, no pun intended," Ash replied.

I looked toward Becky with my best bedroom eyes, "let's get away from stuff around here for a couple of days," I suggested.

"Sounds good, where do you want to go?" Becky replied.

"I've heard that the Kensington is really nice and the highest rated hotel on the island," I said.

"Great, when?" she asked.

"How about we pack right now. I'll call for an early check-in and we can stay for a couple of nights," I replied.

My call to the Kensington went quite well, they were putting Becky and me in a junior suite on an upper floor with a beautiful view of the Philippine Sea. I was able to make reservations for the East Moon restaurant for tonight and Loria for tomorrow night. They were to have a nice fruit bowl in the room and some chilled champagne delivered once we were settled. I hoped for a romantic couple of nights with Becky. I was already getting aroused!

"We're all set and can leave when you're ready," I informed Becky. "How long do you need?"

"Give me an hour," she replied.

"I'll let Ash know what we're doing," I added and left her to pack and went to track down Ash.

"Old friend, I'm getting away with Becky for a couple of nights. We need some alone time," I said to Ash.

"Bullshit! You are just a horny bastard!" Ash retorted. "Where are you going? Guam?"

"Nope, staying right here. I heard the Kensington is nice," I replied.

"What's it matter…you'll be horizontal the whole time!"

"I wish," I said. "Do you want to drop us off so you can have the car?"

"You'd leave me without transportation? For two days?" Ash complained.

"No, we can get a taxi, you baby!"

"I can take you…when do we go?" Ash asked.

"Half an hour," I answered and went off to pack.

An hour later, Ash, Becky and I left the beach house and drove north to the Kensington hotel. Ash could not believe that Becky had packed three full size bags for our two-day stay.

"What the hell! I didn't pack that much stuff for my undetermined stay here in Saipan!" Ash exclaimed.

"You don't own that much stuff," Becky retorted.

"Why is this one so heavy?" Ash grunted as he hefted the bag into the Escalade.

"That is my bathroom stuff," Becky replied.

"Did you take the fucking sink?"

Becky did not reply, and Ash could see that she was pissed off.

"Reggie…help me…what's up with this?" he pleaded.

"Can't help you man…I've put up with this for thirty years. She's actually proud when the airline puts a 'heavy' sticker on her bags!" I answered.

More silence and an evil glare from Becky. My romantic dream for the two days was beginning to fade.

We pulled into the grounds of the Kensington hotel. I could tell that the property had slipped somewhat from its heyday as the Nikko in 1998 when it was owned by Japan Air Lines. When JAL went under, ownership transferred to the United Micronesia Development Association, Inc., and the property was renamed the Palms Resort in 2008 for a brief period, and then the E-land group took over ownership in 2012 and named the hotel the Kensington.

Ash helped me unload all of the baggage and we said our goodbyes.

We went through the check-in process and were taken to an all-glass elevator with views of the extensive hotel grounds hidden from the road. We could also gaze out onto the sandy shore and waters of the lagoon.

A short walk delivered us to our room and the bellman opened the door and began to place the luggage. The suite was nicely appointed with a couch and chairs around a coffee table that had a large bowl of fruit. The bed had a 'welcoming' look to it. I tipped the bellman and investigated the bathroom. It was a huge bathroom with a shower, separate tub and separated room for the toilet.

"Very nice!" I thought. "This is a good start."

Becky and I were in the process of unpacking our bags which had been placed on the king-sized bed when the suite's doorbell rang. I had taken off my shoes and padded barefoot to the door. A young female was waiting to push a cart with a bottle of champagne on ice into the room.

She parked the cart in front of the coffee table and transferred the bucket onto the table. She then looked up at the two of us and asked if we wished the bottle to be opened. I looked at Becky and decided that we would wait for a more appropriate time. I tipped her and she left with the cart.

Becky was at the bathroom vanity unpacking some of her bathroom things. I moved up behind her and reached around her to clasp her stomach just under her breasts. As I pressed against her I could feel a stirring in my loins. I loved it when I became alive down there! As I squeezed her, I could feel her become tense. I immediately stopped my advance and backed away. I looked down. "Sorry little guy," I thought.

"I'm sorry," she said looking into the mirror.

"No, I am," I replied, and caught her gaze in the mirror. She turned and touched my check with her lips.

I moved to the couch and turned on the television. Disappointment and frustration were welling up inside me. What had happened to us? Did Becky no longer find me sexually attractive? I absently fumbled through the cable channels. I stopped on Law and Order/Special Victims Unit. I could find that show on almost any hour in any hotel room in the world!

Becky reached a stopping point with her organizing and sat with me on the couch.

"Now what? Want to walk the grounds and get our bearing?" she asked.

I thought for a moment. I felt like we needed to talk, but maybe not now. "Sounds good," I replied and moved to get my shoes.

We walked around the property and watched the children enjoying the pool and water park. The foliage was bright and colorful. We moved past the pool and walked on the sand at the water's edge. The sounds from the pool were muffled and it looked like we were the only ones on the beach.

We sat on two chaise lounges under a beach umbrella that offered shade from the afternoon sun. I let my mind drift to the project that had brought us here; to the loss of Grace and Ash's slow recovery; and to the loss of Cyndi which had so devastated Lance.

The waves were lapping against the shoreline in a rhythmic pattern that made me fall asleep. Becky awakened me after what seemed like a minute.

"You have been snoring for the last half hour!" she exclaimed. "Even the lifeguards have checked to see that you are okay!"

I arose quickly. "Sorry." It seemed to me I was saying that a lot today.

We walked back to the hotel, taking a circuitous route past the wedding chapel. I thought of our wedding and love at a younger time. Was I feeling sorry for myself?

We checked on the dinner reservations and I thought that the restaurant looked inviting. We would be back in a few hours to find out.

Back to the room and Becky wanted to lay down for a bit. I didn't feel tired after my brief nap on the beach, so I propped up the pillows and lay down on the couch. I had brought along a new Harlen Coben novel and was soon lost in the book. About twenty chapters into the book, I closed my eyes.

Becky awakened me again, but this time it was to get ready for dinner. She had taken a bath and suggested that I shower before we went downstairs. The shower had the right effect and I felt awake and rejuvenated.

We prepared for dinner, sometimes finding each other side by side in the bathroom vanity doing what we needed to do to prepare for an evening out. For me that meant some Bleu by Chanel as the finishing touch.

The dinner proved to be genuinely nice, but I was disappointed in our conversation. I was trying to talk about intimate things to lead us into a romantic evening, but Becky wasn't buying it. She would fog me and steer the conversation away from anything personal. I could feel my frustration continuing to grow.

We returned to the suite, and I noticed that a thoughtful attendant had replaced the melted ice in the champagne bucket. I asked Becky if she cared for some, and she agreed. I removed the cork and poured the bubbling liquid into two flutes. We clinked glasses and tasted the champagne. It tasted really good, and I had another sip.

Becky also took a second sip and said she was going to get ready for bed. That got my attention and my mind moved to sexy lingerie…maybe a revealing robe…fabulous perfume?

I earnestly worked to find the music channels on the cable television. I wanted a channel that had classic rock with Karen Carpenter, or Fleetwood Mac or anybody else that played romantic love songs. I could not find a thing! Frustrated, I used my phone as a fallback and looked up Pandora. I found a channel that sounded good and turned the phone's volume up. I filled up both glasses.

Then the doubt started in. Do I take off my pants and shirt and sit here in my underwear? What would she want that would turn her on? When we had talked about it in the past, she made me believe that what I was wearing didn't matter. I loved her in sexy underthings, but she always complained that they didn't stay on for long! Yep! So, I hung up my shirt and pants and took a seat on the end of the bed waiting for Becky to come out of the bathroom. I held a glass of champagne in each hand. I looked down at my paunch and was not pleased that I had gained weight. I made a mental promise to work on that! My mind did not see my body looking like this. I thought of a seminar with Denis Waitley. He suggested getting completely naked and standing in front of a full-length mirror with a bag over your head with two eye holes cut in it. You will see your body as it really is and not in your mind's eye. I've never had the guts to do it.

Becky came out of the bathroom wearing a nightgown like she was ready for sleep. Nothing revealing…no cleavage…no deep slits up the thigh…not even see through.

My thoughts for romance were immediately dashed. I handed Becky her glass and moved to the chair next to the couch to drink my drink. While I finished, Becky had placed her glass on the nightstand and gotten under the covers. I went to the other side of the bed and slid under the covers.

Becky was on her back, and I moved beside her and reach across to her shoulder with my hand. She grabbed my hand and pulled it down to her vagina.

"Is my pussy wet?"

I moved my finger inside and she felt moist.

"Yes," I whispered.

She moved to get me on top of her. I obliged, but noticed that I wasn't even hard, yet. In my youth I wouldn't have needed any foreplay, but tonight I did.

"You can't do it?" Becky asked.

"Not like this," I replied, and she rolled on her side away from me.

"That's It?" I pleaded. "No cuddling…no foreplay…no oral sex?"

"You can't get it up, we can't have sex," she answered.

"We need to talk!" I blurted out in frustration.

"Not now, goodnight," she replied.

I rolled on my side away from Becky. Between the naps and sexual frustration, I did not sleep well that night.

Early the next morning I had arisen and finished all of the coffee, regular and decaffeinated that was provided with the Keurig in the room. The television was on, and the volume was muted. I was watching at the TV, but not really seeing. My thoughts were on the previous night and what was happening to our sex life. What a cliché our life was becoming. I was not ready to let go of our sex life. I was not willing to 'act my age'.

Becky began to stir about the time that Ohas was to open. I was hoping for a better cup of coffee, and they had an espresso machine! I went downstairs to retrieve two chocolate croissants, a white chocolate mocha for Becky and a large cappuccino for me. She was up and sitting in one of the chairs in the sitting area when I returned to the room.

I spread out my purchases on the coffee table. Becky took a croissant and her warm paper cup. I sat in the opposite chair and picked up my drink. The barista had done an excellent job with my coffee, and the croissant was warm, fresh and tear-apart tender. The room smelled of fresh coffee and warm bread. A pleasant way to start the day.

"Becky, can we talk about last night?"" I asked.

"I don't like sex anymore. What if we stop? We can still have the friendship and companionship with our marriage…that's important, right?" she replied.

"No…that's not okay with me…what has happened…what is going on?"

"I don't feel sexy anymore," she blurted.

"What? Why? All of the years with the bioidentical hormones and all of the Suzanne Somers books about supplements. What was the one called? 'The Sexy Years'?" I asked.

"I don't know…I have gained weight and all the diet books don't seem to help. I look in the mirror and don't like what I see. I'd rather not deal with the sex than worry if you are going to find a wet pussy or if I am going to be too dry for intercourse. When you have to reach for the KY jelly, it is just awful for me. A real buzzkill…A complete turnoff."

"When I look at you, I get turned on. When I touch you, I start to get aroused. When I hug you, I begin to get hard."

"Why?"

"What you need to hear is that I still want to have sex with you. I want a sex life with you. I am not ready to become Archie Bunker!"

"But I need to feel attractive to feel sexy…"

"No, that's bullshit! You still care enough about your appearance to want the latest hair style and color. You care enough to have a whole beauty routine that you go through in the morning…even though you know that it drives me nuts waiting for you. I tell you that you're beautiful. Does it change your routine? No! You care about your outfits and how they make you look. You know that you are attractive and that is important to you. You get your nails done…you get a facial once a week…you get your eyebrows and eyelashes done."

"Enough! I get it. But I am here to tell you that you that seeing me as a sexual object and wanting to have sex with me is not enough."

"Then what is?"

"I don't know. I do know that I cannot look in the mirror and like what I see."

"This is like that thing Ash told me about. White girls look for flaws when they look at themselves in the mirror, while black girls look at all of the same flaws and say, 'I'm all that!' They think a large 'bootie' is sexy. They pull the stretch pants up over rolls of fat and think that looks good. They go out with junk hanging out all over and walk like they were at the Oscars."

"It's not that…I don't know…I'm just not happy with me anymore."

"With us?"

"No."

"Well, you might as well be…this is about us," I stated and got up to go to the bathroom.

When I returned, Becky was sobbing. I sat in silence and let her cry. My coffee now tasted bitter, and the croissant had lost its appeal. "How could this be happening?" I thought, "What did I miss?"

Minutes later Becky stopped crying and looked at me. "I want to leave. I want to go be with Robin. She needs me."

"Your sister does not need you and running away doesn't solve a thing. If anything, it is a nail in the coffin of our relationship."

"But I still love you."

"Not like this."

"Listen, you have said many times lately that we are in our final act of this life play. I don't like the finality of that, but I understand what you are saying. You also say that you want this act to be spectacular… better than the first two acts, right?" I asked.

"What do you mean, 'the first two acts'?"

"Well, I figured that a play usually has three acts, right?"

"Yes."

"And each of our first acts were not with each other. We had other lives that didn't work out. And then we found each other."

"Yes."

"And our first years together were really our second act in this life play."

"Yes, okay."

"And now this is the third act. I like the sound of that more than your 'final act'. That gives us room for more acts and even an encore or two! Hey, I only get two acts of this life play with you in it. I want them to be special. I love you."

"Why did you bring this up? This 'third act' stuff."

"Spectacular…for me…is going to include sex."

"But I can't participate if I don't feel sexy."

"So, how do you feel sexy?"

"I don't know…I just know that I don't."

The discussion ended and I felt really disappointed. I wanted and desired to have sex be a part of our love life…and it seemed to me that Becky could 'take it or leave it'. I wanted her to say that she would work on her bio-identical hormone replacement therapy… Becky had loved the book, 'The Sexy Years' when it came out…or that maybe plastic surgery would help to make her feel sexier. But nothing encouraging? So much for a romantic couple of days!

CHAPTER 12

Baghdad, Iraq

"Am I right that Mustafa…our best bomb maker…was killed in the blast?" Achmed, the leader of the local militia for this sector of Baghdad asked.

"Praise Allah…that is true," was the response.

"And the destroyed buildings and cars?"

"Just like before. All had storage facilities with explosives, ammunition and weapons,"

"All destroyed? Everything gone?"

"Yes, sir,"

"And the casualties?"

"So far one hundred deaths and two hundred injured. Many of them were our fighters and their families, like Mustafa."

"Did he do something wrong?"

"No way to know…he was working on a bomb…but it wouldn't explain all of the destruction in this four-block area."

"Continue looking…we must find out why this has happened…twice!" Achmed pleaded for answers. "Why is that group forming…must be one hundred of them!"

The gang approached Achmed and his rag tag handful of militia men. Several of the militia raised their AK 47's and leveled them at the mob.

"Why are you here…go to your homes…it will not be good if you stay here," Achmed shouted.

One man stepped forward. His hands were clasped behind his back. It was clear that he did not carry any weapons. He moved to stand in front of Achmed and looked him in the eye. This was disconcerting to Achmed who had grown accustomed to the civilian population being pliant and cowardly.

"You have hidden among us for years. You use us to shield you from military action against you. We have allowed this to happen. But now you hide weapons and ammunition that are unsafe. Many of us have died because of you. You cannot blame 'The Great Satan' for our suffering as you have in the past. You must not live among us anymore. We want you out…we want you gone."

Shouts of support came from the angry mob that had gathered around the militia men. Shouts of 'get out' and 'be gone' were growing in intensity and Achmed felt afraid for the first time among his countrymen.

He pulled out his pistol, immediately aimed and shot the spokesman in the head. The man fell backward from the force of the gunshot, as his blood seeped into the concrete rubble. The militia men opened fire with their weapons into the mob. Men and women scattered and ran from the gunfire. Several lay dead among the ruins.

Achmed turned to his men and gestured for them to get in their vehicles. "Let's be off before they return!"

Achmed knew that the mob would return and would grow in numbers. He knew that they would not be unarmed next time. This was the beginning of the end of hiding behind the skirts of women and children that had been so effective for the last twenty years. They would be exposed and become easy targets for the Western Allies. But that was the least of his problems. Why were his weapons blowing up? Why were so many of his men dead…or dying? "A council of the Elders…that was the ticket!" he thought out loud. Collectively the various cells would find the answer that eluded him! The two Toyota pickups sped away from the devastation.

Washington, DC

President Marron opened the folder that his secretary had handed him and began to read. He reached for his phone, "Get me the Director of the CIA!"

While he waited, he continued to read the pages of intel contained in the folder. A grin was beginning to widen on his face. By the time the Director arrived, the President was grinning from ear to ear.

"This is great news! The second test accomplished everything we could have asked for and more," POTUS exclaimed.

"Yes, Mr. President. It looks promising," the Director of the CIA replied.

"We can use this anywhere. For the first time in our fight against terrorism we can be Proactive rather than just reacting to their actions and movements,"

"Yes, sir!"

"America can take the fight to them...and WE CAN WIN!"

"Yes, Mr. President."

"So...what is our next move?"

"Not sure, sir...we are still sifting through reports. Maybe we do a flyover and clear out Baghdad. Maybe other cities. Maybe other countries..."

The President cut off the Director, "We must not dally...this is our moment! Get me a plan within the next forty-eight hours! No moss will gather on these rocks!"

"Yes, Mr. President. On it," the Director replied and pivoted to leave the Oval Office. As he reached the door, he heard President Marron call to his secretary...

"Get me Dr. Nelson!"

Denver, CO

Magnus Harper looked around the large room filled with all of the I.N.C.I.S.O.R. electronic gear. There were five cubicles down one side of the room for each of the Denver team members. Each cubicle had a desk with three monitors displayed on the desk. There were name placards on each desk with the five Denver team members' names, even though the desks looked identical and interchangeable. He noticed that none of the cubicles contained any personal or family information…no pictures or other identifying features that would indicate that the Denver team members had a life outside of I.N.C.I.S.O.R.

At the back of the room a space had been arranged like a classroom, with a dozen chairs, arranged in a semi-circle, facing a large television monitor surrounded by six smaller monitors. The six monitors displayed real-time information from six principal areas of the world…Asia, Europe, Africa, North America, South America and the Middle East. The live feeds were supplied by the CIA from their posts around the globe.

The rest of the room housed the training weights and equipment to keep the men in superior shape. A door across the room from the cubicles lead to their locker room, bathroom and shower facilities. Magnus remarked to himself, "Just like home." The Frankfurt facility was identical to the Denver facility.

He was the last to enter and joined the nine other team members, taking a seat facing the large monitor. Lance Wood was standing beside the flat screen television and looked impatient. "Can we start now?" he remarked, glaring at Magnus.

"Sure…let's go…" came from among the chairs.

"Melania Cruz," Lance began. "We need a plan to find her."

He clicked a remote and a satellite image occupied the big screen.

"This is her escape," Lance continued and clicked the remote again.

The men watched intently as the overhead images showed the armored transport vehicle heading southbound on I-25 somewhere between Colorado Springs and Pueblo. A number of motorcycles could be seen coming up on the transport vehicle from behind, and then several moving past the transport to take up positions in front.

All of the motorcycles had two men riding them. Soon the rear passengers all opened fire upon the transport. The firefight was intense. The bullet-proof glass windows all shattered, and the armor plating was riddled with holes.

"Depleted uranium, armor piercing rounds," Lance announced. Ten heads were nodding as the men observed the carnage.

The vehicle swerved off the interstate and came to rest on the gentle slope of the shoulder just off the pavement. Several motorcycles pulled off of the road and men approached the rear of the vehicle. An explosion could be seen as the rear doors flew open. The guards inside had already died in the hail of hot lead.

Melania was curled in a fetal position on the floor of the transport. Two men could be seen helping her out of the vehicle and freeing her from the chains that bound her. She hugged one of the men.

"That is Juan Cuellar. The leader of Mexico's fiercest drug cartel, Los Zetas. Really bad dudes," Lance added.

As the footage continued, the men and Melania mounted their rides and proceeded south on I-25. Soon they were out of the satellite camera's range. Lance clicked the remote again and the images disappeared from the screen.

"What do we know?" Lance asked the team.

"No witnesses," Lance Everett began.

"Precision strike...well planned," Magnus added.

"Armor piercing ammunition...hard to come by," Graham Sandler continued.

"Melania knew to get down, so someone got to her. We know that she was not allowed any outside contact once she was captured. They had inside help!" Powers Hunt exclaimed.

"They knew the schedule, the route and the vehicle. Again, leading to an inside job," Aaron Dekker opined.

"Well planned…with the right amount of manpower," Dick Becker added.

The men sat in silence, deep in thought.

"Anything else?" Lance Wood asked.

"How did you know who that man Melania hugged was?" Flex Lawson questioned.

"The FBI is involved. They have also reviewed this footage and used their facial recognition software to identify Juan Cuellar," Lance replied.

"How? He had a helmet on," Duncan Trevino asked.

Lance rewound the footage to immediately after the rear doors were blown open.

"Right here!" he exclaimed.

The men all watched intently. There was an instant immediately after the explosion that one of the men glanced up. All ten I.N.C.I.S.O.R. men had been distracted by the blast and had not noticed, but the FBI analysts hadn't missed that mistake.

"Are we to assume that this Mexican gang rode their motorcycles all the way across the US border and into Mexico?" Kurt Nichols spoke.

"No and stop with the conjecture!" Lance Wood cautioned. "You men are to study this footage. Piece together their escape route. How and where they entered Mexico. How they smuggled Melania Cruz into that country without papers. And where they are holed up now. You have twenty-four hours. We meet here tomorrow, same time to devise an attack strategy to get that woman back. She will pay for murdering my wife!"

Lance placed the remote on the monitor and walked out of the room, leaving the men staring blankly at each other.

"Let's move!" Magnus announced and they moved in teams of two to the five cubicles to begin the work of finding Melania Cruz somewhere in Mexico.

Baghdad, Iraq

The top leadership from twenty of Iraq's thirty-seven known militia groups gathered in a northern suburb of Baghdad to discuss the recent destruction. Representatives from al Qaeda in Iraq were also in attendance. The building was surrounded by armed men, but the men inside did not carry weapons…at least that one could see.

The rhetoric was loud and bordered on yelling as the men jockeyed for power and recognition among their allies and rivals in the room. Twenty-five men were present, which made for much shouting.

Finally, Achmed attempted to take control and yelled out for silence. Most of the men complied, but there was much grumbling among them.

"It is my district of Baghdad that has seen most of the devastation!" he yelled. "Let me speak!"

The grumbling died down as the men turned their attention to Achmed. He stood on an overturned wooden crate so that he could be seen by the other men.

"I have lost men and armaments from the recent explosions and collapse of many buildings in my sector. Each of the buildings contained one or more caches of arms and explosives. The cars that were destroyed all were transporting bombs to be used on Western targets. I have lost much, and I do not know why. My men also are being forced out of their apartments and no longer allowed to live among the civilian population. They assume that it is our fault that these buildings have been destroyed. I need your help! I praise Allah that you will be able to help me."

A militia leader from a nearby city spoke next.

"Were these drone strikes by the United States?"

"The buildings all collapsed at the same time. I do not believe that the United States could have coordinated simultaneous missile strikes against us."

"What about bombs that were remotely detonated?"

"How could anyone but me know where all of our arms were kept? It was only the buildings that we kept munitions that were destroyed, and same with the cars…they had our bombs in them!" Achmed replied.

"What else could it be?"

"Not an attack from the outside? Not an attack from the inside?"

"What about Russia?"

"Same as the US. They could not have coordinated a simultaneous attack on our munitions supplies…and they do not know where they are…or were," Achmed answered.

"No, no, no. I did not mean that Russia was behind this! I meant that we need to reach out to them for help. They may know something that we do not know. I can reach out to them in Syria and ask for their help."

The grumbling among the men increased in volume. The men in this room knew that Russia would not help them without asking much in return. These men were fiercely independent, and it would not be easy to involve Russia in their situation.

"Any other ideas?" Achmed asked.

More grumbling, bordering on yelling as the noise in the room increased.

"If we cannot answer what is happening to us then we must involve Russia," Achmed announced, and the meeting slowly broke up and the men began to leave.

Moscow, Russia

"Look at these satellite pictures!" an analyst announced.

Several men gathered around him.

"What are we seeing?"

"Look at this plane…looks like a C-130."

"Where is this?"

"Oh, I apologize. These are images of Baghdad when the last blast occurred. Now, look at this plane!"

"So, the United States has many military transports into and out of Baghdad every day."

"No! This plane is in some type of holding pattern directly over where the blast happened. See…look at these pictures!"

The others looked on and came to the same conclusion. The plane was circling over the area that had been decimated by multiple, simultaneous blasts. But…what did it mean?

Washington, DC

President Marron had just finished consulting with the Russian ambassador to the United States. He summoned the CIA director to the Oval Office.

"The Russians know that something is up with Baghdad," the President began.

"How so?" the director asked.

"They say that one of our planes was captured on film hovering over the blast sight just before and during the event. They think that the plane somehow caused the devastation and want us to explain its presence there."

"So, the Russians think they caught us in the act. I will come up with a plausible denial and explanation for the plane being there. Is that all they have?"

"I did not hear any more from the ambassador, but this says we better move forward carefully. Don't we know when their satellites fly over Baghdad…or anywhere else for that matter?" President Marron added.

"Yes, we do. It must have been an oversight for the second test."

"Like I said, we need to be more careful. Fix this!"

President Marron dismissed the director with a wave of his hand. "Bad luck," he muttered to himself.

Nuevo Laredo, Tamaulipas

Melania Cruz lounged on the chaise drinking an iced tea.

"Nice digs, Senor Cuellar! Thank you for my freedom," she said.

"My honor, senorita," Juan replied and took a sip of tequila. "What are your plans for the future?"

"Do you know this group, I.N.C.I.S.O.R.?"

"No, senorita, I have not heard of them."

"They were responsible for my capture and wiping out most of the Mexican gang members in Denver. My beloved Gallant Knights Insane is no more," Melania hissed. "I want them dead!"

"Ah, what do they say? Revenge is best served cold?"

"Actually Juan, the phrase is 'revenge is a dish best served cold'." Melania corrected.

"It means that the recipient knows it is coming and can worry and fret about it. Does this group know you are coming?"

"No, they do not. As far as they know I am rotting away in Federal prison. I will take my time plotting my revenge. Can you spare some of your men?" Melania asked.

"Mi army es su army!" Juan replied.

Melania thanked him and drank from her cold glass. Her thoughts turned to the future, her return to Colorado and the demise of I.N.C.I.S.O.R.

Saipan, Northern Mariana Islands

Hey, Reggie!" Ash called out to the patio from the living room.

"What?" I replied.

"The guys in Denver are really getting into the pickleball scene. We should play more while we're here! Who was that dentist we met that started it up on the island?"

"Charles….and his wife was Carol," I remembered.

"Did you get a last name or number?" Ash asked.

"What am I…your secretary? No, I didn't, but I do remember something about Paradise Dental. I think that was the name of his clinic. They had a court out in front of the office if I remember correctly."

"They were friends of Pat and Dane from that dinner party," Ash remembered. "Call Pat."

"I'll just call information and get the number for the dental office," I replied, and dialed 411.

With the number in hand, I called the office.

"Thank you for choosing Paradise Dental," was the response over the phone. I asked to speak to Dr. Charles…I didn't remember his last name.

"Please hold," was the reply.

"Dr. Cram is with a patient. This is Carol. How can I help you?"

"Carol…his wife?" I asked.

"Yes, who is this?" she answered.

"This is Reggie from the dinner party!" I replied.

"Reggie…Oh! Reggie and Ash? From Colorado via Dubai?" Carol responded.

"Yes, Ash and I were wanting to play pickleball."

"Tomorrow morning, 6:30, know where we are?"

"Nope…and new to the island," I answered.

"Middle Road, Gualo Rai, orange building, across Chongs," she said.

I chuckled quietly at her lazy English…across Chongs?

"We'll find it,"

"Good, see you tomorrow!" and Carol hung up the phone.

I had many more questions…what about paddles and balls, etc. but let the phone go.

"Ash, we have a game in the morning!" I called into the living room.

"Who's playing?" was his reply.

"No idea, we'll just have to 'wing it'," I answered.

Langley, VA

The Director of the CIA was meeting with the top supervisors reviewing the state of the world and the bad characters wishing to bring harm to the United States of America. It seemed to him that the world's hot spots and bad actors were increasing. Whenever he heard the growing list of known terrorists, he always had an unanswered but nagging question…where did the money come from to support all the bad stuff?

The Director had just finished reading a report that the United States spent sixteen percent of its annual discretionary budget fighting terrorism. This staggering percentage amounted to 186 billion dollars per year over the last seventeen years. Amazing, but also so saddening. This money could be used for good. Instead, it had to be earmarked to combat terror around the world.

The conversation found its way to I.N.C.I.S.O.R. and the final report on the second test in Baghdad. Very simply, mission accomplished! The terrorists did not have a clue what had happened, Iraqi intelligence had no idea what had caused the buildings to collapse in downtown Baghdad, and the world, including Russia seemed to be clueless also.

The Director assigned the task of designing and implementing the third test to two of his trusted supervisors in the room. This test would be larger and encompass more of the country of Iraq. What about more Middle Eastern countries? Were the properly stored munitions in the US and NATO allies' lead-lined bunkers safe from the emissions? What about home-grown terrorists? What if the world found out what America was doing?

The meeting adjourned and the two supervisors began immediately to design the scope of the third test.

Saipan, Northern Mariana Islands

"Eleven, twelve, one," Ash announced as he placed his underhand serve deep into the opponent's cross court. The forehand return landed long.

We switched places and Ash readied his serve to the add court. "Twelve, twelve, one," he said. The serve was placed well, and the return was short and down the middle. I hit a backhand down the middle, splitting the two opponents, for a winner.

We switched again and Ash was serving for game point. "Thirteen, twelve, one he called out. Another deep and well-placed serve. This time the return came cross-court to Ash who hit the third shot down the line. Both opponents had moved to the kitchen line and a quick-fire volley ensued. We won the point and the well-fought game.

I was dripping wet. My shirt felt like it weighed an extra five pounds! We all came to the net and touched paddles. What a fun sport. The players all had so much fun.

Ash and I helped take the portable net apart and retrieve the balls scattered around the parking lot. A group was going out to breakfast at Wild Bills, but we chose not to join them. I wanted to get home to Becky and get a shower.

Denver, CO

Lance Wood placed the phone in its cradle.

"That was Becky Nelson," he announced to the ten men of I.N.C.I.S.O.R. "She wants an update on our plans to recapture Melania Cruz."

"Were almost there, Lance," Powers responded. "Just working on the timing."

"How's your Spanish?" Flex joked. "We will be ready to leave for Nuevo Laredo tomorrow."

"Here's our plan," Kurt began.

Over the next hour the Denver and Frankfurt teams brought Lance up to speed. They had done their homework and prepared for all contingencies…except one.

"I'm going also," Lance announced at the end of the presentation.

Most of the men could see the faulty thinking on the part of Lance Wood. The ten of them were younger and moved more quickly than Lance. They were also more agile and had endurance that Lance did not exhibit. And most of all…the death of Cyndi was still a raw wound affecting his heart and mind. At best, Lance would be a liability. At worst, he could blow the mission and place the men in more peril than they had bargained for.

"Meet here at 0400. We will take four cars to Laredo, Texas. Two of the vehicles will be the new Escalades, Lance added. "Gear up and get some rest."

Lance departed the conditioning room.

"What do we do now?" Stirling asked.

"I'm calling Reggie and Ash right now," Aaron answered.

Saipan, Northern Mariana Islands

Ash, Becky and I sat at the patio table looking at each other after the call was ended.

"I don't like it," I began. "Lance is too important to us…to I.N.C.I.S.O.R."

"I disagree," Ash countered. "If we were there one or both of us would go."

Becky listened to us, smiled, and began, "You must know that you two are no longer spring chickens. I love you both, but you must learn to trust the young men that have joined you in our fight against worldwide terrorism. Have faith in them. Tell Lance not to go."

Ash and I nodded our agreement to Becky's words, even though they were bitter and difficult words to hear.

"I'll call Lance," Ash added and moved inside the house to place the call.

After a while, he reappeared on the patio. "No answer…goes straight to voicemail…Lance has turned his phone off. I'll call the team. Is Michael up to date and in the loop?"

CHAPTER 13

Laredo, TX

Six rooms had been booked at La Posada hotel. The hotel was situated near the Puente Internacional Solidaridad-Columbia bridge which the team would cross to gain access into Mexico. The men would use their American passports to pass through US and Mexican immigration.

The four vehicles that had made the trip from Denver to the southern coast of Texas stood out like sore thumbs in this small city of 250,000 residents. They would stand out even worse once the crossing into Mexico occurred. They were new...and clean, not like the majority of cars in this town which looked like they had 'been rode hard and put away wet'.

The decision was made to cross over under the cover of darkness, raid the Los Zetas compound, re-apprehend Melania Cruz and escape to the American side of the Rio Grande before morning.

Powers and Magnus were sitting in the front passenger seats of the two Escalades. Each Escalade carried a drone tasked with surveillance, and these two drones were now flying over the Rio Grande, heading for the Los Zetas compound. The drones possessed stealth technology so that spotting them would be extremely difficult. Lance Wood sat in the back seat of one of the Escalades and watched as the two men sent electronic inputs to the drones streaking over the Nuevo Laredo sky.

The video was crystal clear, and the compound was coming into view. A high wall surrounded the compound. Most likely made of reinforced concrete to repel most attacks. A large double gate with four trucks outside and four trucks inside the gate came into view. At least four men were manning the gates armed with automatic weapons. Teams of two were walking along the front wall of the compound. Was all this security normal, or were they expecting an attack?

One drone circled the complex, following the perimeter wall, while the second drone flew over the structures inside the wall.

It was clear that the wall was substantial and that the well-guarded front entrance was the only access to the property. Inside the wall were six structures. A barn and dormitory were the easiest buildings to identify. The main house was a Hacienda-style home with four sections built around a central courtyard. Three other smaller buildings were present inside the wall and their function could not be determined from this flyover.

Many people, both men and women, were moving around the compound inside of the perimeter wall. Many carried weapons. Others carried goods into the main house. Smoke was observed rising from the house and Powers clicked a pin on the display in front of him which labelled the area of the smoke as the kitchen. There were no architectural or building plans for the house that the I.N.C.I.S.O.R. team had been able to find during the research and planning phase of the mission. Therefore, they could only guess about the layout of the mansion.

The cameras also captured the faces of the men and women who did not wear hats or scarves covering their heads. Facial recognition software in the vehicles was working to identify those they could identify. At one point, Juan walked out the front door and glanced upwards. He was easy to spot with his balding head and goatee. Melania was not spotted during the flyover.

Back in Lance Wood's suite, the men gathered to watch the footage. It looked like the eleven of them would be up against a private army of around fifty men, armed with automatic weapons. Mounted M-60's and grenade launchers could be seen in the truck beds and atop the perimeter wall. Cameras were spotted at various points along the perimeter wall and no blind spots were identified.

The I.N.C.I.S.O.R. men were outnumbered by over five to one, and the compound looked impenetrable. Daunting? Not for these men. They had the element of surprise, superior training, including night operations, mostly thanks to Uncle Sam, and technology on their side. The men had seen what the drones were capable of and felt secure that they would have the advantage.

They would go tonight!

As the sun began to set in the West, the men returned to their rooms to check and double-check their equipment. They donned their tactical gear and gathered back in Lance's suite. Lance did not have much of a motivational speech prepared, and said only, "I want Melania alive. That bitch must spend the rest of her days on earth suffering for taking Cyndi from me."

The men moved to the four vehicles and headed to the bridge entrance. All of their senses were on alert. The SUVs would cross into foreign country at 7 pm. They all knew that the bridge closed at midnight. They must finish their business and cross back into the United States before 12 am, or spend the night exposed on Mexican soil.

The vehicles were parked in an abandoned building within a half mile of the Los Zetas compound. Eight of the men would 'hoof' it from the building and seek shelter outside of the wall. Powers and Magnus would stay with the Escalades to monitor all of the drone activity. Lance Wood had agreed not to leave the vehicles.

The men donned their night vision goggles and began their trek toward the compound. Powers and Magnus got all eight drones up in the air. The two surveillance drones led the way while the other six hovered just over the men as they walked. The journey was completed, and the eight men took up positions. The attack on the compound would begin at 9 o'clock sharp!

At 8:55, a pickup truck approached the main gate to the compound. Several of the I.N.C.I.S.O.R. team were caught in the glare of the truck's headlights. The driver called out an alarm.

"Go...Go...Go!"

The command to begin the attack went out. Graham opened up on the pickup and the driver's body jumped about as he was riddled with bullets. The drones had each targeted the vehicles at the gate, and they too were obliterated.

A drone missile took out the front gate, and six of the team moved inside the perimeter wall. Another drone moved to the front door of the mansion and a missile made the reinforced door disappear.

Four of the team entered the main house while the other four mopped up in the yard with the help of the drones. Any movement was dealt with swiftly. Soon, the majority of Cuellar's security force had been neutralized. Outside, there was only sporadic gunfire.

The four 'men in the manor' spread out once they entered. One team of two headed right, and the other team of two headed left. The house was well lit, so night vision goggles were not necessary. The goggles were perched on the foreheads of the four men. As they moved through the mansion, any movement was met with silenced bursts from their weapons. Each and every door was opened, and the rooms cleared of live men or women.

Two master bedroom suites lay at the back of the house. One room was empty, but the other housed Juan Cuellar, who immediately threw his hands up in the air and surrendered.

"We are not here for you. Where is Melania?"

The question was met with silence.

"Donde es Melania Cruz?"

More silence.

"Kneecap him!" Kurt whispered.

Stirling placed the muzzle of his assault rifle against Juan's kneecap.

"Melania Cruz!" he demanded and waited for an answer.

"Nothing?" as he fired his weapon.

Cuellar screamed in agony and fell to the ground holding his wounded and bleeding knee.

Stirling placed his rifle against the other knee.

"Where is she?" he demanded.

Cuellar was sobbing as he pointed to an armoire across from the bed.

Kurt moved to the armoire and opened the doors. All that he could see were clothes hanging from an inside rod. "Nothing here," he announced as he pushed the clothes aside. An opening was evident at the back of the hutch. "Hey, Stirling! There is a secret passage in here!"

"When did she leave? How much of a head start does she have? Where does this go?" Stirling questioned Juan.

"Nothing?" as he fired a bullet into the other knee.

Juan screamed again and rolled on his side in a fetal position.

"No help, here," Stirling announced as he placed a bullet in Juan Cuellar's forehead.

"Let's go!" Kurt shouted as he disappeared into the passageway. Stirling followed and radioed the team that they had found a tunnel.

When Powers heard Stirling, he switched one of the drones to infrared cameras. These cameras had the ability to penetrate concrete and look inside structures. If the tunnel weren't too deep and the concrete too thick, maybe he could pick up a signal.

There it was! A glowing red mass moving beyond the back of the mansion and two other red images moving fifty feet behind the first image.

"Fifty feet ahead of you!" Powers exclaimed. "Keep moving!"

Melania knew that she had to move quickly through the dark tunnel. She felt her way and tripped several times, almost falling once. At the end of the passage there would be a door and an underground garage housing her escape vehicle. A four-wheel ATV to handle the desert landscape.

She could see the door ahead as she heard footsteps running toward her. Melania threw the door open as bullets ricocheted off of the concrete walls.

"Halt right there!" she heard them yell. She did not heed the warning and jumped on the ATV. She pressed the ignition switch and the engine belched to life. Melania gunned the throttle and engaged the clutch. The ATV jumped forward as the hidden doors opened to reveal her escape route. Almost instantly she was speeding into the night in the desert. The dim headlamp on the ATV provided very little illumination and several times she almost dumped the vehicle as she hit depressions and plant life in the landscape.

Stirling and Kurt entered the garage. There was one more ATV parked and ready to go. Kurt mounted the vehicle as Stirling radioed for help. Magnus immediately directed a drone to pursue, and it had quickly overtaken Melania. A bright halogen lamp shone upon her.

Melania opened fire at the light, and the drone withdrew. It then returned and laid down a line of gunfire ahead of her, causing Melania to turn sharply and dump the ATV. As she lay on the ground, gathering her thoughts, she heard another ATV approaching. Melania began to run but was limping badly. The drone lay down another burst of gunfire ahead of her escape route. She froze in place.

The drone reactivated its spotlight and illuminated Melania with her hands on her head and hopping on one leg.

Kurt pulled up alongside and quickly forced her face down into the desert sand. He roughly pulled her arms behind her back and secured them with a plastic zip tie. Kurt pulled her up into a kneeling stance and guarded her with his weapon while he waited for the team to respond.

Two of the men had run back to where the four SUVs were parked. They joined Magnus and Powers, and each drove a vehicle into the compound. Magnus steered his Escalade behind the compound and located Kurt with his prey.

Stirling and the other team members were retrieved, and the SUVs headed back toward the bridge and the safety of the United States. Melania was drugged and was sound asleep when papers were produced at US Immigration. All four vehicles re-entered the United States without incident.

They chose to spend one last night in Laredo before the long drive back to Denver. Melania was placed in Lance's suite with a team member to watch over her in the living room. The team members rotated watch throughout the night, mainly to ensure Melania's captivity, but also to make sure that Lance Wood left her alone.

While the team unwound and slept from their successful mission, a tornado was brewing. Not the cyclone-type of storm that most people think of when they hear tornado, but the angry Mexican cartel-type of storm about to be unleashed against I.N.C.I.S.O.R. Juan Cuellar was related to the leader of the Sinaloa Cartel by marriage. All of the Los Zetas gang members at the compound were dead, including Cuellar, their leader. The carnage and devastation at the compound drove the Sinaloa Cartel leader to the verge of madness. He swore revenge and, in his rage, dispatched a large number of his gang to hunt down and destroy whoever had done this to his brother-in-law.

Saipan, Northern Mariana Islands

Ash walked into the living room after being absent for a little over three hours. I looked up at him from the couch. He looked like he had been sleeping somewhere.

"Hey, good friend. You look beat," I began.

"Man, I am!" Ash replied.

"Where have you been?" Becky asked. She was sitting next to me on the couch. We were watching a movie on Netflix.

"Getting a massage," was Ash's answer.

My interest in my friend's actions was now heightened.

"Chinese or Thai?" I queried.

I had been told by Jeff Beach that the Thai massage parlors were legitimate and that they gave great massages…especially if you liked a hard, deep massage. The Chinese massage parlors had been described as 'fronts' for prostitution.

"Chinese," Ash answered.

"And?"

I wanted all the details, but Ash probably felt awkward giving me much in the way of information with Becky sitting right next to me.

"It was great!"

"Happy ending?"

That question got Becky's attention and she looked up from the computer screen after quickly pausing the movie.

Sheepishly, Ash looked at Becky, "Yes…and more."

Becky let out a smirk and then said, "I don't get this 'Asian Flu' crap that I hear so much about! What is it that guys from the States find so attractive about Asian women?"

We both stared at her, not wanting to reply.

"I'm serious…what is it? They are tiny and have no tits."

"It could be that they take better care of their men than American women do," Ash began.

"Bullshit!" Becky answered.

"No, I mean it!" Ash countered; I have watched the way Reggie treats you…you are up on some kind of pedestal and that he worships you.

He takes great care of you. And…what do you do? It seems to me that a lot of his gestures go unrequited!"

"What do you know, dammit!" Becky retorted.

"I know what I see…and I don't see much from you. I think you expect to be pampered, like you earned it. Like it is your right or you deserve it."

I was becoming extremely uncomfortable with their argument, but I couldn't fault Ash and his thought process. I did not ask for much from Becky…but would have liked more.

Becky stood up in a huff. "You men are all alike! All you think about is sex."

Becky stormed out of the room and slammed the bedroom door.

"And?" Ash called after her.

Ash and I looked at each other is silence and I shook my head.

"Now tell me," I asked once Becky had left the room.

"Sorry, Reggie. I was probably too harsh in my criticism. I shouldn't have picked on Becky."

"Forget that, tell me about your 'massage'!"

"Well, it began as a typical massage. She told me to get undressed and left the room. I was to lay face down on the table. So, I got naked and lay on my stomach. I pulled a towel over my back and covered my ass."

"When I get a massage, I leave my underwear on…but I've never had a happy ending, either," I replied.

"Okay...and?"

"After a bit I heard her return, and she pulled the towel down to uncover my back. She oiled up her hands and began the massage. Honestly, I have had better massages, but she was doing okay. She moved from my back to my legs, pulling off the towel. After some time, she started caressing my ass cheeks. This was unexpected but felt great."

I was salivating in anticipation, "And..."

"When she was done with my backside, she signaled me to turn over. Now remember, I had lost the towel! The lights in the room were dim...almost dark...but as I rolled over and got comfortable, I saw that she was naked. Cute, tight body, long black hair, and no body hair below her eyebrows! Reminded me of a little girl."

"Okay..."

"Hey, let me talk. She massaged my chest and stomach. Then moved to my lower legs and worked her way up to my thighs. I was becoming aroused, and it must have shown. She placed a well-oiled hand on my dick and began to rub it. Her touch was exciting, and I knew that this was not her first rodeo, so to speak."

"And..." I was becoming impatient with the story. Ash seemed to be dragging the story out for effect.

"While she was stroking me, I reached up and rubbed her tiny, brown nipples. They both were hard and erect. I could feel that I was getting close to coming. At that moment she placed a condom in her mouth and expertly placed her mouth over my dick... The condom slipped on easily because I was well-oiled at that point. She then threw a leg over me and quickly mounted me. She had a small, tight pussy, but I slipped inside her easily. She began to rock rhythmically on top of me and it wasn't long before I moaned and exploded inside her. She continued to ride me until my orgasm had passed. She then grabbed a warm, moist towel, slipped off the condom and cleaned me off. She kissed me once and left the room. I lay there composing myself for a few moments, then got up from the table and dressed. Now, I need a nap!"

Ash left the room, and I heard a bedroom door close. Now, I had to go and deal with Becky.

Laredo, TX

The chamber maid was putting the finishing touches on the last of the six rooms that had just be vacated by the I.N.C.I.S.O.R. men. Three dark, swarthy men rushed into the room, brandishing machetes. She was able to scream once before the three subdued her. They dragged her out of the room and down an outside staircase. She was pulled in front of about thirty men, she guessed. The three captors manhandled her into a kneeling position in front of their leader.

"What is your name?" he asked.

Silence was the only answer.

"Como te llamas?" he seethed.

Now she understood him. She had learned truly little English as a Mexican maid in Laredo.

"Maria," she replied.

"Where are the men who were staying here?" and then he remembered... "Donde es los hombres?" as he pointed to the now empty rooms.

Maria shrugged her shoulders. The men were gone when she started her shift. She had no idea where they had driven off to. She did know that they were American…and good tippers.

"Last time," the leader announced.

Nothing but a blank stare from Maria.

One of the three captors that had dragged Maria out into the hotel parking lot, raised his machete and brought it down swiftly on her neck from behind, severing her head from her body. The body crumpled to the pavement as the head bounced away. Blood spurted from the open neck wound.

When the Laredo police arrived at the hotel, they found a gruesome site. Several of the hotel staff had been beheaded and their corpses left to the buzzing flies that were in the first stages of consuming the dead human flesh.

The police questioned neighboring businesses, but there were no witnesses. Nobody had seen or heard a thing. The Mexican gang members were nowhere to be seen…just the carnage left in their wake.

"Los Zetas," one of the detectives stated, remembering the gang's penchant for cruel beheadings.

"We'd better get in touch with the Mexican police in Nuevo Laredo and see what they know. This could be a drug hit, or the beginning of a drug war between rival gangs," the Lieutenant assigned to the investigation announced.

The Sinaloa Cartel gang members chose, on a hunch from their leader, to head north on I-35 into San Antonio. The plan was to head west on I-10 from San Antonio to Albuquerque. He had heard about the Mexican gangs being attacked in Denver. Maybe there's a connection there. Maybe that's where these guys are heading. The gang would travel north on I-25 from Albuquerque to Denver. Somebody will have seen something between Laredo and Denver!

Saipan, Northern Mariana Islands

I sheepishly opened the door to our bedroom. Becky was sitting on the end of the bed, shaking her head. She looked up at me with an accusing look in her eyes.

"Want to get a massage?" I asked, somewhat jokingly.

Becky stared at me for what seemed an eternity.

"Yeah, okay. I'd like that," she replied, choosing not to engage with me about her spat with Ash.

"Great! I'll call Traditional Thai," I said and headed back to the living room.

Becky joined me on the couch. They could see us right now, I told her, and we packed to leave. The drive to the massage parlor was made in silence.

A darkened room had been prepared with two Thai massage beds positioned next to each other. Soft instrumental music was playing through hidden speakers.

Becky and I stripped down to our underwear and lay down on the beds. I had learned that I prefer Thai massage beds because they are wider than the traditional massage bed so that the masseuse can climb onto the bed so that she can exert more pressure during the massage. Elbows, knees and even walking on my back!

We had scheduled a two-and-a-half-hour massage. The two masseuses joined us and covered us with towels and began our massage odyssey.

They began by kneading our backs through the towels, and then the towels would be peeled away, and they would ply us with oil to continue the massage.

Somewhere during the first half of the massage I fell asleep and had to be awakened when it was time to turn over so that she could complete the massage. Not once was there any hint of impropriety or suggestive touching. In fact, the deep tissue massage that I prefer leaves little room for relaxation. I thought about how different our experience was compared to Ash's description of his massage.

San Antonio, TX

"So, that is the Alamo," the Mexican gang leader thought as he looked upon the small chapel and mission that had been so instrumental in delaying Santa Anna's march north to reclaim Texas as Mexican territory. A rag-tag group of just over one hundred North American frontiersmen and Texians held off his Mexican army of fifteen hundred soldiers for thirteen days in 1836.

The men had stopped in San Antonio to refuel and refresh. During their stop some information had been uncovered. Four SUVs had gassed up just six hours before. Several of the men in the vehicles had escorted a female to an outside bathroom, and then back to one of SUVs. That had to be them! And Melania was still alive!

The gang posse continued west with an earnest that came from the news that they were on the right track. Twelve-hour head start. They could make that up…probably not on the next leg to Albuquerque, but they should be able to overtake the four vehicles somewhere between Albuquerque and Denver!

The Mexicans were speeding, averaging close to 100 miles an hour. They were able to close the distance on the Americans significantly during the normal eleven-hour drive between San Antonio and Albuquerque.

They would make the trip in seven hours. In Albuquerque, they would have closed the gap to under two hours!

Langley, VA

The Director of the CIA sat at his desk and debated in his mind about the third test. The technology seemed flawless after the first two tests. Now, it was time to test how far RFW could be pushed. Could the signal be alive for longer periods, allowing the aircraft to cover greater distances. What about the wear and tear on the equipment on Radar Hill in Saipan and the plane that was reflecting the signal to earth? Could the signal and its origin be detected? Were the US stores of C-4 safe in the hardened storage bunkers? What if Russia developed a similar weapon? Would they use it against terrorism? Or to topple regimes that the United States supported?

His mind was spinning with all of the possibilities when one of the floor supervisors knocked on this door.

"Sir, the parameters for the third test are ready for your review,"

"How does it look?"

"Broader in scope and a longer test is what we have planned. The aircraft will take off from its Saudi base, climb to altitude, signal Saipan that it is ready, and the beam will be launched. The plane will fly a circuit over Saudi Arabia, north into Iraq, west into Syria, south into Jordan and then returning to base in Saudi. The circuit will take approximately three hours to complete."

"And the RFW transmission?"

"Active for the whole flight…except for take-off and landing."

"Any issues with the equipment?"

"We do not know, sir. That is the main purpose of the test…endurance."

"And the US storage bunkers?

"Also unknown, sir. Our expectation is that any unprotected C-4 will be detonated, but that our lead-lined bunkers will be safe."

"What about detection?"

"Well, sir, the transmission will last for hours…if everything goes well. That gives anybody who is paying attention a good chance to detect the emissions."

"What about the report we intercepted from the Russians? Something about a plane being located over where the destruction took place in Baghdad during the second test?"

"Right, sir. The plane may be spotted by their satellites. Actually, we do not know where the terrorists store their munitions in Saudi, Iraq, Syria or Jordan."

"So, we just hope for some detonations?"

"Director, sir…that's why they call this a test!"

CHAPTER 14

Washington, DC

President Marron was pacing in the Oval Office after reviewing the parameters for the third test of RFW. What was America's ultimate goal with this new weapon against terrorism? Yes, we wanted to drive the terrorists out into the open and not allow them to hide behind innocent civilians. We wanted public sentiment in the Middle East to turn against all of the Jihadi groups that existed with their sole purpose to destroy America. What about our allies like Saudi Arabia? What if there was destruction within their borders? We knew that they have housed and trained terrorist cells for years. Hell, bin Ladin was a Saudi!

"Get me Dr. Nelson!" POTUS said into the intercom.

Saipan, Northern Mariana Islands

I realized that I was standing at attention on the outside patio while I was talking with the President of the United States!

"Relax!" I muttered to myself and glanced at Ash. He had a huge smile on his face, watching me perform.

"Yes, sir, Mr. President," I said into the phone. "We will be ready for the third test within twenty-four hours. I understand the parameters for the third test are quite a jump from the first two tests, but it is time to see what RFW can do. We will be in close contact with the aircraft when it departs the Saudi base, and Langley will receive real-time data as the test is commenced. I understand that a satellite over the Middle East has been tasked with following the plane's flight path and will be ready to record all ground incidents when and if they happen."

"Sounds like you're ready," President Marron replied. "I wish you all the best for this next test. Your technology may turn the tide against global terrorism. We need this to work!"

And the line went dead.

Just then Becky appeared on the patio with a tray of glasses and iced Thai tea. My glass had the orange tint of the plain tea. Becky and Ash preferred their tea combined with milk.

"Who was that?" Becky asked as she place the tray on the table. She looked at me with a quizzical look. My demeanor must be different, having taken a call from the President.

"That was the President!" I answered. "I should have a real drink!"

"And?"

"He was wishing us luck on the third test. Ash, we had better get with Joe and Billy to review our protocol for the test and make sure we have covered all the bases."

"I'll get the FBO. Let's meet with the boys and then head out to the airport. Time to go flying!" Ash replied.

Ash drove the Escalade while I maneuvered the drones. As we approached the turnoff from Middle Road onto As Matuis and the road up to Radar Hill, one of the drones caught the rental car belonging to Joe Cavanaugh parked outside of the building housing the new electronic gear.

"They are already inside," I commented as we proceeded up the hill.

"Good…I want to get to the airport!" Ash said.

The meeting was brief, and we were reassured that Joe and Billy were both ready for the test tomorrow. They walked us through the changes and how the radar transmission would track with the airplane as it flew its circuitous route over four countries in the Middle East. Ash and I departed shortly and drove to the airport.

We chose to fly north from Saipan to check out the northern islands that made up the rest of the CNMI. There are a total of fourteen islands, including Rota, Goat Island, Tinian and Saipan. Ten smaller islands stretch out to the north and west in a gentle curve.

As we flew over Pagan, we could see a plume of smoke exiting the volcano. Pagan was located two hundred miles north of Saipan. The recent volcanic activity had caused the evacuation of the eight families that inhabited the island. The volcano on Pagan had erupted in 1981, spewing lava across most of the arable land and the island's runway. The eruption continued until 1985, with ten smaller eruptions over the years, including the current eruption. Pagan is the fourth largest island in the Northern Mariana archipelago.

"Look how that lava cut the runway right in half!" I exclaimed as we circled the volcano. We could both see how the lava flow from the volcano eruption in '81 had flowed over what was (once) a nice landing strip and (had) cut it literally in half.

"What's left is just that grass strip," Ash pointed out. "What do you think, Reggie? Fifteen hundred feet?"

"Yes, and grass," I added. I was thinking in my head. The Avanti Evo needed thirty-two hundred feet for comfortable takeoff and landing distances. And that was on a nice, well-maintained asphalt or concrete runway. We weren't going to be landing here any time soon!

The island is deemed by many to be uninhabitable, even though a handful of hearty souls choose to call it home. The United States military has plans to use the island for live-fire training, and this has been met with strong online dissention, including one group wishing to have a particular snail on the island declared an endangered species! It's a pretty safe bet that the US military will get their way if they wish to pursue the use of the island for live fire training purposes.

We circled over the island twice and then continued our journey northward to see the other islands. We flew over the northernmost island, Farallon de Pajaros, just shy of four hundred miles from Saipan. Ash was flying the plane at this point and headed back to Saipan.

As we headed across the tarmac to park Aurora II, my phone rang. I answered with my favorite line from a Harlan Coben character, "Articulate!"

There was silence on the line…and then a sheepish response, "Dr. um, Nelson?"

"At your service," I replied.

"This is Charles…er…Dr. Cram,"

"Yes, I remember! You and Carol brought pickleball to Saipan!" I spoke.

"Yes, that is us…we want to invite you to our house for dinner. We have some nice steaks that need barbequing."

"I love to burn animal flesh!" Man, I was in some mood. I bet that this Charles character was beginning to regret his invitation. "Becky, Ash and I would love to come."

"Great, we have the northernmost house on the island," Charles said.

"How do you know that?" I asked.

The 2020 census people told us when they did our interview at the house," he replied.

"Can we bring anything?"

"Nope, Carol and I have it covered…oh, we don't drink…so, if you care for a libation other than water or tea, please bring it."

"Ice, too?"

"No, Reginald, we have ice," he said, offended.

"How do we find you?" I asked.

"Do you have Google Maps on your phone?"

"Yes,"

"Punch in Matansa Drive, one mile north of the blue million-gallon water tank," he suggested.

"I go by that almost every day heading to Radar Hill," I stated.

"Yes, that is route 318. You want route 320," Charles replied.

"It turns into a dirt road just past the water tank," I remembered.

"Yes and bear left at the quarry. Ours is the only house between the water tank and Suicide Cliff Road. Five-thirty? You have to be here in time for the sunset. We have a spectacular view looking west toward the Philippine Sea."

"Ash, Becky and I will be there at 5:30 on the dot," I announced.

Ash had parked Aurora II and was opening the cabin door to exit the aircraft.

"We have a date, good friend!" I yelled from the right seat of the cockpit.

"Let me check my calendar…oh, I'm free," Ash joked.

I called Becky to give her time to prepare. We were going out!

just outside Florence, CO

The two I.N.C.I.S.O.R. teams were travelling in caravan fashion on Colorado route 50 heading northwest out of Pueblo toward Florence. The most notorious federal prison for the worst of the worst had been constructed outside the town of Florence. It had been affectionately nicknamed the Alcatraz of the Rockies.

The two Escalades had been in first and fourth position in the caravan. They had all of their drones airborne. Melania was riding in the third vehicle along with three of her captors, including Lance Wood, whose wife had been murdered by Melania's Denver gang, the Gallant Knights Insane. Lance rode shotgun so that he did not have to glare at Melania.

The trip had proceeded quietly and without incident since departing Laredo, TX. An overnight stop at the Holiday Inn in Albuquerque, once they made their way onto I-25 northbound had given the men much needed rest. They had partaken of the free breakfast before the men continued their journey north into Colorado.

One of the drones that was following the convoy sent an alert to the trailing Escalade. A large number of cars were gaining on their position. The men discussed the meaning of this intrusion and voted that they should prepare for an attack.

The lead Escalade pulled out into the oncoming traffic lane and let the two middle SUVs pass and assume the lead while it took up a position ahead of the fourth vehicle. Traffic was extremely light, allowing the cars to maneuver.

All eight drones were directed to take up positions in front of and alongside the intruders' cars. The drivers and passengers in the pursuing cars had not noticed the presence of the drones overhead. Mexican license plates were captured on the Escalades' video screens and the license plate numbers were sent off to be identified.

Information was beamed to the SUVs that the plates belonged to members of the Sinaloa Cartel. It was decided by the I.N.C.I.S.O.R. men that the Mexicans in those cars that were quickly approaching the convoy were after revenge for their compatriots in the Los Zetas gang whose bodies were left scattered around the compound in Nuevo Laredo, and that they probably wanted Melania back…preferably alive.

As the team members watched the surveillance video, several men noticed that many of the cars were carrying many men. Several of the older beater cars had not fared well during the high-speed chase north and had to be abandoned along the roadside, causing the overcrowding in some of the cars.

There were at least forty cars counted as the Mexicans closed the distance on the I.N.C.I.S.O.R. teams. That would mean eighty to one-hundred men were involved in the assault. The eleven men in the four SUVs checked out the surrounding land and found it to be desolate and without much to offer in the way of cover. Strong feelings of being outnumbered were present and concern was evident in the lines of their faces.

The decision was made to let the drones handle as much of the attack as they could as the cars kept moving toward Florence, and then they would park in a semi-circle across the road and use the cars for protective cover while the eleven managed their defense against the onslaught.

Flex pulled a needle out of a medical bag and stuck it in Melania's neck. "Bye, bye for now, adios," he murmured as she slumped onto the floor.

When the attackers had closed to within one hundred feet, the two drones equipped with sonic disrupters, activated their amplifiers and a number of the first attack cars swerved off the road as their drivers reached to cover their shattered eardrums from the piercing sound. Several other cars crashed into the rear of the first cars, and the attack was halted…temporarily.

The Mexicans quickly adapted and placed cotton, cigarette butts or whatever they could find into their ears to offer some protection. The damaged cars were pushed off of the highway. The pursuit then continued with the vehicles that were left.

Next up was the air to ground missiles which took out the next batch of attacking cars. Men were seen running from the exploding cars while others screeched to a halt. The Mexican gang members ran for the ditches on either side of the road. They aimed their gunfire at the flying objects that were creating such havoc.

The drones now took up phalanx positions, four on each side of the road. The gatling guns opened fire and rained down a hell storm of bullets that decimated the Mexican ranks.

Several cars in the rear now attempted to turn around and escape the carnage. Each of these cars were pummeled by the guns and left as burning hulks.

"Wow!" Magnus breathed.

The firefight was over, and the eleven men had not fired a shot, although there were very sweaty palms being wiped on their pant legs.

The drone controllers recalled the drones to their positions on the roofs of the Escalades. The drones would refuel and rearm automatically while they rested in their cradles. By recalling the drones, their surveillance capabilities were gone.

The drones had failed to pick up a trailing car that was not part of the attack force. The leader of the Sinaloa Cartel force sent to enact revenge on the Americans had watched the carnage through his binoculars. He figured out where they were heading and why. He would make his play for Melania just outside the prison entrance… they would not expect an attack now!

CHAPTER 15

Langley, VA

Reports were flooding in from the third test. There were reports of explosions in Saudi Arabia, Syria, Iraq and Jordan. Reports of decimated buildings, and much carnage were piling up on the analysts' desks.

Saipan, Northern Mariana Islands

We had no trouble following Charles' directions and were ensconced on their back patio as the sun began its journey into the Philippine Sea.

"What a phenomenal view!" I exclaimed as I looked out on Managaha Island. The property was perched above a cliff with unobstructed views of downtown Garapan, the reef line and the prepositioned ships.

There were occasional cumulus clouds dotting the horizon, but none would interfere with the sun's march into the sea.

"We always watch for the green flash," Carol spoke.

Ash and I had heard about the green flash, but this was new to Becky.

"What is a green flash?" she asked.

"Just when the sun touches the water sometimes you can see a green flash just above the upper rim of the sun. It only lasts for a couple of seconds," Carol replied.

I took a sip of Crown Royal and asked, "Becky…wasn't that restaurant on the beach in San Diego where we went for breakfast called The Green Flash?"

"Yes, Reggie…good memory!" Becky said.

We sat and looked out over the large, sloping back yard. The pack of dogs that had greeted our arrival so loudly were now playfully bounding up and down the slope of the grassy yard. Two of the dogs had short white hair, one had long white hair, two were brown in color and two were mostly white with brown and black spots.

"How many dogs do you have?" I asked.

"We have six and our neighbor has one. There are seven dogs on the property," Charles answered.

"What are they?" Ash queried. He was nursing a local beer from the Saipan Brewing Company.

"They're called Boonie Dogs," Charles added.

"What is a Boonie Dog?" I asked, having never heard of the breed.

"Boonies are descendants of the war dogs that the US soldiers brought to the island to sniff out the Japanese. The Battle for Saipan was the marines' first experience with the Japanese hiding out in mountainous caves. The dogs, with their superior sense of smell would 'alert' if a Japanese soldier was lurking ahead. The dogs saved many American lives during that battle. They were also used in the battle to retake Guam from the Japanese. There is actually a Boonie Dog Memorial in Guam," Charles continued.

"I've seen the movie, War Dogs of the Pacific," Ash offered. "Those dogs were German Shephard Dogs and Doberman Pinschers. They were used as attack dogs."

"Not so much, here," Carol added. "The dogs that the GIs brought over were bloodhounds, Rottweilers, Labradors and German Shepards. The dogs were used mainly to sniff out the Japanese where they hid, not to attack them. The tough part was that many of the dogs were left here when the GIs moved on and they have spent over seventy years breeding among themselves. Most of our Boonies came from the local shelter, but three just appeared out of the jungle!"

"Wow! Great story. They always bark like that?" I asked, remembering our arrival.

"They are extremely protective and a wonderful deterrent. They are better than any house alarm!" Charles replied. "Let's walk out back and I'll show you where I'd like to build a pickleball court."

We walked down the back lawn and Charles pointed out where he wanted to build a pool and pickleball court. The dogs bounded down the back lawn and played among themselves. They were so fast!

"Something else you should know about our Boonies," Charles began. "Our dogs' names all begin with 'S'. Spencer is the oldest. He is almost eight and the leader of the pack. Sully is the long-haired one. He came out of the jungle. He watched us for about a year before he came to join us. Scooter also came out of the jungle. When he came to our patio, he looked so emaciated that I guessed he had less than twenty-four hours to live. Stella and Sophie are the white ones. They are sisters and came from Saipan Cares for Animals. SCA is our local shelter. Stormy is the new puppy. She also came from SCA.

"What is with the 'S' names?" Becky asked.

"It's a Carol thing," Charles replied.

"You have so much room here, you could do two courts!" Ash opined.

We turned to go back up the slope to the house.

"Tara!" Becky exclaimed. She was from the South and loved the movie, Gone with the Wind. "The pillars! This looks like Tara!"

We all glanced up at the rear façade of the house as we hiked up the slope. Sure enough, it looked like Tara did in the movie.

Charles grilled up some fabulous looking New York strip steaks and Carol placed a dollop of garlic infused butter on each one. He had prepared earlier mashed potatoes with the skin on and chunky with only butter and whipping cream…and a little salt. My favorite way to eat mashed potatoes. Carol worked to create before us a Caesar salad that complemented the steak and potatoes well.

Carol and Charles did not drink, so Ash, Becky and I enjoyed two bottles of a Jordan cabernet with the meal. An unforgettable meal.

Amman, Jordan

The Russians had flown in three of their experts in satellite imagery. The terrorist leadership from four Arab countries was convening to discuss what in the world was happening to their stores of munitions. The discussion was loud and full of conjecture. All of it was wrong.

The Russian imagery was being displayed on a large white sheet by a projector twenty feet away. The men gathered around the sheet so that they could see better. Sometimes one forgot and stood in front of the projector. These mistakes were immediately met with loud disapproval.

The Russians followed a plane as it took off from a Saudi airfield, circled to reach an altitude of 10,000 feet AGL and then headed in a north-northwest path. The images were changed frequently as the plane was being tracked. Ground explosions could be seen on the imagery and the Russian experts pointed out the explosions to the Arabs gathered there. The flight was followed over Iraq, Syria, down into Jordan and back into Saudi Arabia. All along the flight path were explosions and destruction.

The lights came on when the presentation was completed. The Russians had completed their presentation and packed up to leave.

"Whoa! What…nothing else?" one of the terrorist leaders exclaimed.

"Yes! What did this plane do? Did it drop some kind of bomb?" Another piped in.

"We have nothing more than what you saw! We do not know how this plane accomplished the destruction of your supplies. But, we have shown you proof that the plane is the cause of your losses."

There was much grumbling and shouting in the room. The Arab terrorists were no closer to an explanation than they had been before the Russian presentation.

"Do svidaniya!" the Russian trio called out as they left the Arabs to yell among themselves.

Dubai, UAE

The image capturing and identifying software at the American Dental Clinic had a hit on a gentleman who had just entered the clinic. The CIA analysts in Virginia had been alerted by the software and they quickly placed a call to the office. A young associate who had been groomed to replace Dr. Nelson came on the line.

"You have in your chair the suspected leader of a Hezbollah faction in Iraq. What does he need?"

"I'll go see why he is here," the associate said into the phone. "Please hold."

In less than five minutes he was back on the line. "He has a toothache and wants to save it."

"Please insert a P&C into his tooth." And the line went dead.

The associate did as he was directed and two hours later the CIA was listening to the Arab leader talking to the front desk as he paid his bill.

Florence, CO

The I.N.C.I.S.O.R. team huddled together in an impromptu debrief after the attack. Assuming that the danger was now over, they gathered together and left Melania asleep in one of the vehicles.

Nobody saw the car approach their parked vehicles. A dark-skinned Mexican quietly exited the passenger door of the car and sneaked up on the four SUVs. He spotted Melania lying prone in the back seat of one of the vehicles. He moved to the driver's seat and worked the wires to hotwire the car…something he had done hundreds of times.

As he touched the wires together the car engine came to life and startled the gathered men. He put the car in gear and gunned the engine. The SUV sped away in a cloud of dust.

Lance Wood was the first to react. He ran wildly toward the car, screaming, "They have Melania! She killed Cyndi! Stop!"

As he ran toward the escaping car, a man in the Mexican car raised his weapon and fired a burst…

CHAPTER 16

Saipan, Northern Mariana Islands

I placed the phone on the table. I still was not believing what I had just heard. I placed my head in my hands and began to sob. Breathing became difficult as I struggled with the news.

Ash could see that I was visibly moved by the phone call. He waited patiently for me to gain some bit of composure…

"Lance was just gunned down in Florence. Lance is dead…" I cried as my voice trailed off.

"Oh, God…No," Ash whispered, and he placed his arm around my shoulders.

Half of the original six I.N.C.I.S.O.R. team members were gone. I got up but felt unsteady on my feet. I moved shakily to find Becky in the kitchen. My heart felt so heavy with grief that I thought it would stop beating. She looked at me and saw that I was crying.

"Reggie? What has happened?"

"Lance…" was all that I could say.

She led me to the bedroom, and we sat on the end of the bed. She attempted to comfort me but knew inside that something desperately wrong had happened to Lance.

"Ash," Becky called out.

He came into the room looking distraught and dejected.

"Lance was killed," Ash said as he sat on my other side.

Florence, CO

All ten men of I.N.C.I.S.O.R. opened fire on the remaining occupants of the Mexican vehicle as it attempted to speed away. The car exploded in a large fireball as fumes from the ruptured gas tank caught fire and engulfed the car and the bodies within.

Magnus raced back to one of the Escalades and signaled the drones to take flight and pursue the escaping SUV. The car had not gone far when it was overtaken, and a Maverick missile was launched into the body of the car. The explosion and ensuing fire cooked the driver and Melania as she slept in the back seat.

Dubai, UAE

Michael MacAteer fielded the call from Saipan. The news was devastating to him. He couldn't imagine the pain that Reggie, Ash and Becky were experiencing. Two of their closest companions gone? Lance and Cyndi Wood were no longer with them. One of the original three couples that had formed to fight terrorism around the world was gone. What would that mean for I.N.C.I.S.O.R.? Would the three remaining founders be able to recover and provide the superior leadership and guidance to the other ten team members and to himself?

He calmed his mind and put the questions out of his thought process. He alone would be responsible for the three in Saipan to return to Colorado for another funeral and service to say their final 'goodbye' to their friend.

Michael busied himself with all of the arrangements. He almost forgot to book his own tickets to attend with the other team members.

Englewood, CO

Lance Wood was a retired Marine. He was afforded a full military funeral with a trumpeter and honor guard at Ft. Logan National Cemetery. The fort opened in October 1887, on two hundred and fourteen acres, and operated until 1946. Later, the fort expanded and over three hundred more acres were added. The fort was closed shortly after World War Two and was turned into a mental health hospital, and seventy-five acres were set aside for the cemetery. The cemetery began in 1950. It is located just south of Hampden Avenue between Federal and Sheridan boulevards. Over 148,000 veterans and their families are buried there.

The I.N.C.I.S.O.R. group of eleven young men, Ash, Becky and myself stood quietly as a Pastor read through the funeral rites. The honor guard fired off a twenty-one-gun salute, which meant that seven men fired their rifles into the air three times. The American flag that draped the casket was folded with much pomp and circumstance into a triangle, while taps was played by the bugler.

Becky was the only woman in the group and received the folded flag from the commander of the honor guard. I heard her catch her breath once as she was handed the flag. We three had done much crying over the past few days and that well was tapped out.

The team members slowly moved past the casket and each one reached out and touched it. This was our final goodbye. I was the last to go and immediately choked up with a knot in my throat and tearful eyes.

"Hasta, good friend, see you soon," I whispered as I touched the cold wooden lid of the casket.

The team waited for me at the limos that had been rented for the day.

"Let's meet up at the Perfect Landing restaurant out by Centennial Airport," I announced.

The drivers punched in the coordinates to their moving maps and off we went. I had called ahead, and the restaurant prepared a large table for fourteen for our arrival.

We gathered around the table and a round of dark rum shots was ordered. Lance's favorite drink was a Cuba Libre.

"To Lance!" Flex toasted.

"To Lance," we all replied and downed our glasses.

Another round of Jack Daniels was ordered. Again, the glasses were raised.

"To Cyndi!" was the toast. Her favorite drink had been a shot of Jack with a coke chaser.

We sat and ordered. Oysters came out and soon the restaurant had finished their allotment for the day. The waitress apologized and pointed to the menu…they would shuck the oysters as long as they had them. They were out!

Dinner came next. I noticed that most of the young men at our table ordered steak. They served a good rib-eye here! Becky and I were having the Walleye Pike. It was flown in daily from Minnesota. Ash ordered the Cioppino. The stories began around the table of experiences with Lance and Cyndi. Lance had been responsible for hiring all of the men that were involved in I.N.C.I.S.O.R. I remembered times from Project Loudmouth and the minis, and places we had been around the world. I chose to keep the memories to myself.

When there was a break in the conversation I asked, "Any of you young pups know what Centennial Airport was called before?"

They looked around the table and nobody knew.

"It was named Arapahoe County Airport. When I got my pilot's license I was sixteen years old. That was in, um…1969. I used my lawn mowing money that summer to pay for my flying lessons. I trained with Star Aviation at Stapleton Airport. My instructors were all United pilots who moonlighted as flight instructors."

I took a drink and continued, "At that time, Arapahoe County Airport was an uncontrolled airport."

"That means no tower," Stirling interrupted.

"Yes, only Unicom. We flew out here one day to shoot some touch and gos. As my instructor and I approached the airport, we saw two planes landing at each other. Coming at each other from opposite ends of the runway!"

"Oh, damn!" Flex exclaimed.

"My instructor had seen enough, and we flew out to Jefferson County Airport to practice my landings," I continued.

"When did it get renamed…the airport, I mean?" Magnus asked.

Arapahoe county expanded their north south runway to accommodate larger aircraft. When they lengthened the runway, they ran onto Douglas County land. Well, Douglas County was fine with the expansion but told the airport that it couldn't be called Arapahoe County airport any longer! Hence, the name, Centennial Airport. The name change happened in 1984.

"You used to keep a plane here, didn't you?" Lance Everett asked.

"A long time ago…" I answered and drifted off in thought.

"You've been flying since you were sixteen? That is a really long time!" Kurt remarked.

"You trying to make brownie points, young pup!" I countered. "This is not the way!"

Ash interceded at this point. "Reggie has not been flying for all that time. He's just had his license for that long."

"What do you mean?" Powers asked.

"I could not afford to fly in college and dental school. Once I had my dental practice in Littleton, I could get back into flying. Five of us bought a Cessna 172, and I logged a lot of hours in that plane. Then I stepped up to a twin-engine Cessna 310 and got my instrument and multi-engine ratings in that airplane. I kept both of those planes at Centennial," I continued.

"Where are they now?" Michael asked.

"No idea. Meg, my ex-wife took the plane in my divorce. She hated flying but knew that I loved it…so…she took the plane, all my stuff and my children. What an evil witch," I said.

"Well, let's change that subject!" Becky suggested. She had heard those stories for thirty plus years and did not want them to continue now. "What is the plan for the future? Where do we go now? Keep the teams or disband. Do Denver and Frankfurt still make sense?"

I had a long history, growing up and living in Denver and Littleton. The thought of leaving Denver for good was a tough nut to crack. But Becky and I had not lived there in a decade. The other questions I was not prepared to answer.

Ash must have sensed my discomfort with Becky's line of questioning. "Let's wait for awhile and let Lance rest in peace."

The others gathered around the table were in agreement and the evening continued with stories about Lance and Cyndi and shared experiences with them. Grace's name was mentioned in several of the tales that were told around the table. I really missed these three.

CHAPTER 17

Washington, DC

"Radio Free World is an astounding success!" Director of the CIA assured President Marron.

"And that business with Lance Wood?" POTUS asked.

"A bad loss, Mr. President…"

"And I.N.C.I.S.O.R.?" the President interrupted.

"I don't know, sir," the Director replied.

"You are not much help!" POTUS exclaimed and waved for him to leave.

Moscow, Russia

"The FSB has some information for us, comrade," Ivan announced.

"FSB? I don't trust those guys! They're just the KGB with new letters. They are all nationalists that want the Soviet Union back in power!" Dmitriy countered.

"Watch your tongue!" Ivan ordered. "You do not know who could hear you and what they might do!"

"I do not care," Dmitriy replied. "I am for a strong Russia, but I do not want to return to the days of the USSR. Those were dangerous times!"

"Well, back to the news," Ivan said, redirecting his friend's angry remarks. "The FSB analysts have a theory about the recent explosions in the Middle East. And we may be able to use this information to damage the United States' influence in that region."

Russia had been doing all they could to counter and disrupt America's presence in the Middle East. They were especially effective in Iran and Syria. It had been Russian technology and equipment that had led to the development of the nuclear reactor at Bushehr in Iran. And, the Russians had flown in troops and military equipment to bolster President Assad's reign over Syria since the civil war began in 2011. Russian planes had been used to combat insurgent forces that fought against the Assad regime. The Russians were not afraid to target hospitals and medical centers with their missile attacks. Many believed that Assad would have fallen before now if the Russians had not come to his rescue.

"And what is that so-called theory?" Dmitriy asked.

Ivan continued, "A radio beam was launched from the airplane to disrupt the stores of ammunition hidden in those places."

"What places?"

"Where all the explosions have been occurring!" Ivan yelled, frustrated at Dmitriy's ignorance.

"So, like the James Bond movie…Diamonds are Forever. A laser beam with enough power to destroy anything in its path…"

"No comrade!" Ivan interrupted. "Not everything is being destroyed. Only weapons! And not just weapons. Guns and bullets are not the targets. Explosives are what are being ignited."

"And this laser beam selectively finds these explosives…"

Ivan interrupted Dmitriy again. "C-4 is the target!"

"Okay, C-4. Plastique…this laser can selectively target plastique?" Dmitriy asked.

"Stop saying laser. Laser is light transmission. This is radio transmission."

"So?"

"Get it right!" Ivan ordered.

"A beam of light or a beam of radio wave…what's the big deal?" Dmitriy countered.

"It is a big deal!" Ivan instructed. "Laser is the **L**ight **A**mplification by **S**timulated **E**mission of **R**adiation. It burns holes in anything it touches at this intensity. Radio wave emissions penetrate structures and can seek out targets within the structures. That's how radios can receive signals from stations miles away. The waves pass through things."

"So, this plane sends out a signal strong enough to cause this kind of damage?" Dmitriy asked. "That would be a very large transmitter!"

Ivan faltered with his answer, "Well, Dmitriy, you have a point. I do not know if there is a plane large enough to house a transmitter of this size…Even the Antonov may not be large enough!"

"And we know that this plane was smaller?" Dmitriy said.

"Yes, the satellite made it out to be a C-130," Ivan replied.

"A C-130? That is not a very big transport! I do not think our FSB comrades know what they are talking about!" Dmitriy added.

"We need to get a look at that plane," Ivan suggested.

"Yes, comrade…and we know where! King Abdullah Air Base," Dmitriy said.

"Let us approach the FSB about a covert mission to examine that aircraft!"

Dhahran, Saudi Arabia

The King Abdulaziz Air Base in this eastern province of Saudi Arabia was under attack this night. The Royal Saudi Air Force was not aware of the attack on the air base, or of the Spetsnaz force that attacked it.

Ten men assaulted the base under the cover of darkness. Security at the base was very light. The Saudis had not been at war with any of their neighbors in quite a while. The men snuck up to the perimeter fence behind the hangar where the C-130 aircraft was stored. Eight men scaled the fence and climbed down inside the complex. Two were left to guard the entry/exit point and prepare for extraction when the mission was complete.

A roving patrol was noted and observed until the two guards moved away from the hangar to cover the rest of the base. The eight men moved toward the hangar and left two outside as six men picked the lock on a rear door and entered the hangar.

Several planes were inside the structure, but only one sported markings of the American Air Force. Four men were left outside the plane and two entered the aircraft. The four men outside the plane took copious photos of the exterior of the plane. Special doors…almost like bomb bay doors…were noted on the underbelly of the transport.

The two men inside also took many photographs. They observed the lack of any special radio equipment but did see a large parabolic mirror stored inside the fuselage…just inside of a pair of doors.

The elite Russian team of commandos completed their mission and escaped from the air base without detection.

The special plane that had been used for the three RFW tests was no longer a mystery. The digital photos were transmitted to Moscow for review and further investigation. The absence of radio equipment and the presence of a giant mirror would create much consternation and debate within the FSB ranks.

Langley, VA

The CIA director sat in his office reviewing the final reports following the third test of Radio Free World.

All of the indicators were positive.

Stores of C-4 had been eliminated in massive explosions. Properly stored munitions were immune from the emissions.. Many terrorists had been killed, but there was also a large number of civilians that had been killed.

The effect was more than the Director had hoped for. The civilians were driving the terrorists out of their neighborhoods. The bad men of the Jihad movements were gathered in quickly constructed, ramshackle structures that could be easily marked and targeted for future elimination. And they were not close to civilian homes, schools or hospitals which the terrorists had loved to hide behind.

The war on terror had taken a turn for the best. The world, including the Russians who so often blamed the Americans for anything that went wrong in the Middle East, was not aiming its vitriol at the United States. The various terror cells were being blamed for improper storage of their arms and the loss of innocent lives.

"This is great!" the Director spoke to his empty office.

Baghdad, Iraq

Russian advisors had flown from Moscow to Syria and then traveled by Land Cruiser into Iraq and the city of Baghdad. They were meeting with and advising the local militia and terror organizations about the discovery in Saudi Arabia.

One of the attendees to this meeting had recently had some dental work done in Dubai. And a technician in Langley, Virginia was listening to and recording every word spoken in the meeting.

"Comrades! Attention!" the first advisor began.

The room became quiet as the Arabs listened with eager anticipation. They needed answers about why their munitions were exploding.

"We know how your depots are being sabotaged!" the second advisor announced.

"It is the United States that has caused these attacks," the first advisor took over. "We have concrete proof that it is…what do you say…The Great Satan."

Murmurs around the room began and grew in intensity. Now there was yelling. The Arab terrorist leaders began to chant, "Death To America…Death To America…Death To America!"

The two Russian advisors let the Arabs continue. One said to the other, "These are stupid people."

Eventually the chanting died down and the advisors continued.

"It is your stores of Plastique explosives that are the target. They are being ignited remotely."

"But that is not possible!" shouted one of the Arab leaders. "Plastique is safe until a detonating pin is placed in the material. Then it can be exploded directly or remotely!"

"And many different storage places ignite at the same time!" another leader shouted out. "You do not have the answer!"

"Da! We do have the answer. Please listen to us!" the first advisor shouted.

The yelling among the Arab terrorists grew louder.

"We do not believe you…You lie…It was you that destroyed our weapons!"

"No…No…No!" the second advisor pleaded.

The Arab leaders had become an angry mob and rushed upon the two advisors with all of their knives drawn. Screams from the two men could be heard over the angry voices of the mob. The two Russian bodies soon looked more like Swiss cheese than human form.

The Arab terrorists had not let the Russians explain. If these two did know how the C-4 was being ignited, the answer would stay with them. They would never speak again.

Langley, VA

"What just happened?" the CIA techie said as she listened to the digital recording that had just been produced from a secret meeting inside Baghdad, Iraq. The PC that had been implanted in the terrorist leader's molar worked perfectly and the CIA had a complete transcript of the interaction and conflagration that had taken place on the other side of the world.

She rushed to her supervisor and demanded that he listen. He did as she requested, then immediately phoned the Director for an audience. Soon the Director was listening to the recording.

"They really did this? They didn't even listen to what these men had to say! Well, the cat is out of the bag…now. I wonder if Russia really knows about RFW? Or are they just guessing. I need to see the President!" The Director shooed away the supervisor and picked up his phone and spoke, "The White House…now!"

Washington, DC

President Marron sat on one of the couches in the Oval Office and listened to the recording for the third time.

"They don't say a thing. The Russians accuse us but that is all. What do they know?"

"A video camera, you know, like one of those 'cop cams' was hidden inside our plane in Dhahran. It picked up two Russian special forces commandos inside that C-130 in Saudi. We have video of them taking pictures of the parabolic mirror." The Director added.

"So, am I to assume that Russia knows about the mirror?" President Marron asked.

"Yes sir, Mr. President. We at the CIA believe that Russia knows about the mirror and will piece together that the mirror was used to reflect a signal of some sort."

"Will they be able to figure out where the signal came from, or what the signal is?" the President inquired.

"Unknown, Mr. President."

"How would they find out?"

"They would need a receiver aimed in the direction of the beam at the precise moment that the beam was active to pick it up," the Director answered. "And then the Russians would know where the beam came from, also."

"What is the focus of the RFW beam from Saipan?"

"It is very narrow. Only a receiving disk aimed in the direction of the beam would pick it up."

"Well, then…I choose to believe that the Russians know Jack Shit about what we are doing. They are grasping at straws. Let's warn Reggie and Ash about this, though. Better be safe than sorry. Are they back in Saipan yet?"

"No, Mr. President. The I.N.C.I.S.O.R. team is all still in Colorado. Ash and Reggie should be back in Saipan within seventy-two hours," the Director replied. He stood to depart.

"That was ugly stuff in Colorado," President Marron added. "Make sure they have everything they need from us."

"Yes, sir!" the Director said, and he left the Oval Office.

Denver, CO

"I vote that we go on," Ash began, as the third round of drinks was served.

Ash, Becky and I were sitting in the bar at Flemings. We had heard about their fabulous bar food during happy hour and, if I didn't know better, Becky was acting like she was in love with the bartender who was serving Ash and Becky wonderful, chilled vodka Martinis. I was enjoying my signature drink, the double Crown Royal on the rocks with a twist. The Martinis were half-off for happy hour, but not my choice.

We had been discussing our future during the first two rounds. Becky had been ready to throw in the towel after my kidnapping in Dubai. Ash went through a really dark period after the loss of his wife, Grace. Now, fate saw to it that Cyndi and Lance were taken from us.

I wasn't ready to call it quits. I didn't know if I had any more inventions in me, but I hoped that I did. I also knew that we were getting older and fighting the terrorists around the world was a young man's game.

The PCs were working well. The minis had gone far in putting a damper on kidnappings around the world. Now, RFW was working well and giving America an offensive weapon to combat terrorism.

No, it wasn't time to quit.

"You are right, my friend," I answered and held up my glass. "To I.N.C.I.S.O.R.!"

Becky and Ash joined me in the toast.

"We need to include the eleven others," Becky added. "They need to know our plans and if they have a future with us."

"Right on!" Ash added. It was obvious he was feeling the effects of the three Martinis.

"So, what do we want to tell them?" I asked my wife and friend. "Do we keep a team in Denver and Frankfurt? Is our focus going to be on the Middle East? Do we need to expand?"

"One thing at a time, Dr. Nelson," Ash interjected.

"Okay, let's talk about Denver. Ash, you and I have history here. A lot of history. Hell, I grew up here. But we don't live here anymore. The only thing that has brought us to Denver is funerals! Not a good draw for me," I said.

Becky added, "But what about the team of five that we stationed here?"

"Lance was the one who did the recruiting and made sure they kept up with their training," Ash replied. "Without him, why keep them here?"

"One of the reasons we had a team in Denver was to deal with home-grown terror issues. And, they have proven very valuable going up against the gangs that have caused problems in the past. What am I saying? Not just the past…but the present! Lance and Cyndi are no longer with us because of Mexican gangs from both sides of the border," I said.

"And Frankfurt?" Becky asked.

"Well, same thing," Ash took over. "The Frankfurt team could respond quickly to anything that came up in Europe. And, they have been useful."

"I think that we are answering our own questions," I remarked. "What I am hearing is keep both teams in their current domiciles."

"Okay, and leave Michael in Dubai?" Becky queried.

"I say leave everything just like it is," Ash reacted.

"And what about growing I.N.C.I.S.O.R.?" Becky added.

"I, personally, don't see the need to become bigger. I like our size just the way we are," I replied.

"Also, with this new unmanned drone technology, it is like we have more men," Ash added.

"Right! I forgot about that," Becky said. "Watching the drones in action has been amazing!"

"So, all our questions are resolved?" I asked.

"Yep."

"Yes, sir!"

"Let's get with the others and let them know what their future holds," I said. "Another round?"

Englewood, CO

The eleven young men of I.N.C.I.S.O.R. answered their summons and were all present at the Denver training facility. They all pulled up chairs around the wide screen monitor and sat at attention, military style. They had talked among themselves and anticipated bad news.

Ash was the first to speak. "Men, we are keeping the teams together and in their present locations. Frankfurt and Dubai…you depart in the morning. Time to get back to work!"

I added, "Men of I.N.C.I.S.O.R., you have performed beyond our wildest expectations. Our hats, if we had them, would be off to you. I am proud of each and every one of you!"

The men rose up and let out a cheer. Then, Lance Everett spoke up, "we would like to have the two facilities named after Lance and Cyndi."

"Yes!" Becky said. "Denver is now Lance and Frankfurt is Cyndi. I like it."

The men gathered in a tight group and talked among themselves. I turned to Ash and Becky.

"Time to get back to fighting the good fight."

"I'll head back to Florence to continue the renovations," Becky added. "Reggie, you and Ash have more to do in Saipan?"

"Yes, there were four tests planned for Radio Free World. We are more than halfway through, but still a ways to go before we are done," Ash said and joined the others in lively conversation.

"One more night of hotel sex?" I whispered in Becky's ear.

"Um!" she replied with a smirk on her face.

CHAPTER 18

Langley, VA

"Reggie and Ash are back in Saipan and awaiting our input for the fourth test," the CIA Director announced.

A group of technicians and analysts had gathered in one of the conference rooms. They were all sitting around a large, rectangular table with their laptops humming in front of them. Several were reading email messages. The rest were listening to the Director.

"We know that Radio Free World can reach from Saipan into anywhere in the Middle East. We now need to see if it can reach into the United States to help with the nationalist militia groups and other home-grown terror cells. Also, to reach other bad apples that have been smuggled into the States," an analyst opined.

"How far is it from Saipan to California and the west coast?" another asked.

The Director interjected, "So, the fourth test is about distance? Is that right?"

"Yes...accuracy and endurance have already been tested. Now we need to know how far it can reach," one of the techies replied.

"Back to my question. How far is it from Saipan to the west coast?"

"An analyst looked up from her computer, "Almost six thousand miles."

"Hold it!" a technician interrupted. "Iraq is over six thousand miles from Saipan. Where is the distance test?"

"We start with a flight up the west coast, making sure to overfly all of the known militia compounds from California to Washington. Then we move east, and see how far we can go," an analyst said.

"So, we are recalling the plane from Saudi Arabia?" the Director asked.

"Yes, sir, so we think a series of three flights. One up the west coast, one up the western side of the Rockies to include Idaho and Montana. Lots of survivalist camps there. Then a flight up the Midwest from Texas to Michigan, and a final flight up the east coast from Florida to Maine," the first analyst answered.

"And this is on US soil. Possibly targeting US citizens. You all okay with this? This is way beyond our purview!" the Director exclaimed. "We will be in direct violation of the Attorney General Rules. I know those rules are old news and the rules are about collecting data on United States citizens."

An analyst stood up, "We are not collecting data, sir. The FBI has already done that for us. Many of these groups are in their crosshairs. We are simply flying a plane overhead with a mirror suspended underneath the aircraft. If something bad happens, so what!"

"Do we know if the transmission will disrupt any existing radio traffic or microwave emissions?" the Director asked.

"The frequency of the transmission should not interfere with any known broadcasts," a technician replied.

"Good! Let's get that plane to Miramar," the Director ordered.

Lake Como, Italy

Five members of the 'Ndrangheta syndicate followed Marta Fascina southwest as she was driven from Arcore into Milan. The two men and three women followed Marta's car in two cars of their own. Their plan was to take Marta by force when her chauffeur dropped her off for a hair appointment.

Marta was the domestic partner of Silvio Berlusconi, one of the most famous of the Italian politicians. He was a member of the Forza Italia party, known as The People of Freedom. Silvio's net worth was over eight billion dollars. He was listed by Forbes magazine as the 190th richest man in the world. He had held the office of Italian Prime Minister for the longest period since World War Two.

The syndicate wanted a good chunk of his money and they planned to kidnap Marta and hold her for ransom.

The car pulled up to the curb in front of Gli Scarano Srl salon. Marta had an appointment for color and style and told the driver that she would be two hours. She stood on the sidewalk out front to enjoy a cigarette, a habit that she knew she should change. The driver pulled away, leaving her thinking about what he would do in Milan for two hours.

As she contemplated about her chauffeur, two cars screeched to a halt in front of her. Three women jumped out of the two vehicles and grabbed her. Her cigarette fell to the ground as she was forced into the trailing car. Two women jumped into the rear seat, one on each side of Marta. The third woman entered the lead car. Both cars had heavily tinted windows so that the occupants could not be seen by passing motorists.

A double zip tie was applied around her wrists. The tie was pulled taut, and a piece of duct tape was placed over her mouth. The women were very rough with her. She attempted to protest, but her mouth was covered. Marta noticed that a man was behind the wheel of both cars. The cars pulled away from the curb and entered traffic.

They drove east to Viale dei Mille and headed north. The road circled to the west, and they joined route E62 northwest until they entered route A9 which they drove into the town of Como. Traffic was light at this time in the afternoon. The trip took less than an hour.

The crime syndicate had rented Villa Sardagna outside of the town of Como. The villa was on the eastern side of Lake Como and offered beautiful sunset vistas. The complete villa had been rented for a month, with an option for a second month if negotiations dragged on.

The two cars entered the gate and continued up the drive to the main house. The driveway curved and ended on the north side of the villa. Marta observed that the villa had a three-story façade facing Lake Como. The property backed up to a mountain on the eastern side, with only the third floor being above ground.

She was pulled out of the car and pushed into the house. Her captors took her to a second-floor suite. Her zip ties that had bound her wrists were cut off. She was ordered to remain quiet, and the door was slammed. An old tumbler lock was activated. Marta heard the key as it rattled in the lock. She imagined that there was at least one guard stationed outside her room.

Marta remembered the mini that her husband had inserted in the heel of her shoe. She reached down and removed the shoe. Silvio had shown her how to twist the heel to activate device. It made no sound.

She didn't know if the thing even worked! But, she had nothing else to try. They had taken her purse, her phone and her jewelry. Even her watch was yanked off her wrist. One of the women had even frisked her to make sure that nothing was missed.

Dubai, UAE

Michael Mac Ateer was sitting in the I.N.C.I.S.O.R. office on Palm Jumerah island watching You Tube. He was learning more about pickleball so that he could play better when the teams would meet again. Even though his legs had been broken during the rescue in Poland, he felt good when he played pickleball.

An alarm sounded and the computer monitor immediately switched to a world map. As he watched, the map began to zoom in, first over Europe, then over Italy, then northern Italy, then Lake Como, and came to rest on the Villa Sardagna.

A mini had been activated!

Michael thought about what to do and then remembered his training. He placed the cursor over the indicator on the monitor and right clicked the mouse. A display window opened with the name of the owner of the mini. "Marta Fascina," he read out loud.

He moved to another monitor and punched in the name. All of the relevant information filled the screen in front of him.

Michael read through the information and then placed two calls. The first was to the Frankfurt team to apprise them of the activated mini. They would now set a rescue plan in motion. The second call was to Becky Nelson in Florence. Becky still felt the need to act as the main go-to person for these rescues. She wasn't quite ready to let Michael fend for himself and be the lead during the pending rescue.

Frankfurt, Germany

Stirling Mason was on duty, receiving calls when Michael phoned and informed him that a mini had gone live. Stirling immediately punched a series of buttons and several large screens in front of him came to life. He was seeing the same information as Michael saw in Dubai.

"Thanks, Michael…We're on it!" Stirling said and hung up. With a few more keystrokes, the other four men's beepers had been activated, informing them to get in. They had a mission!

Stirling watched the screen displaying the location of the mini while he waited for the others to arrive. "Lake Como?" he thought out loud. "Isn't that where Reggie, Lance and Ash rescued the first kidnapping victim that possessed a mini?"

CHAPTER 19

Saipan, Northern Mariana Islands

It was 6:00 am. I had just finished a Pilates workout which I had come to love and had made it a regular part of my routine three days a week. The workout room housed five reformers, but this morning only Pat, the instructor, and I went through the paces of the workout.

Pat had asked me about pickleball for her daughter, Heidi. I explained to her how much I enjoyed the game and that I believed that it was a sport for all ages and all degrees of skill. I told her that I would be seeing Charles Cram in a few moments. We were playing pickleball at 6:30! Pat said that she knew Charles and his efforts to bring pickleball to the island of Saipan. She would call him.

I proceeded to the Mormon church. There were three courts striped in their parking lot. The surface was asphalt and a little rough, but it worked just fine for our needs. Charles told me that the USAPA just appointed him Ambassador for the sport in Saipan and Guam. I was happy for him. He was receiving some of the recognition for his work in introducing the sport to Saipan.

"How did he learn about it," I asked him while we were trading volleys at the kitchen line.

Two years ago, he needed a hip replacement. The hip had become so painful that he needed a cane to maneuver, and he had to give up tennis. The surgery was successful, and he found himself pain free for the first time in years.

He told his wife, Carol, that he was ready to get back into tennis. Her sister, Diane practically jumped through the phone saying that he had to try pickleball.

Charles got on You Tube and watched many videos from beginning instruction to professional match play. Soon, he ordered a net, some paddles and a dozen pickleballs.

He and Carol striped the first court in their dental office parking lot, using red duct tape. Later he hired a painter to permanently stripe the court. People began to play and drivers on Middle Road wondered about the sport. Many stopped in to give it a try.

"Pickleball is just a little over a year old in Saipan," Charles said. "And we have a core group of about twenty regulars! Hence the need for the three courts we are on."

"What does the future hold?" I asked.

"I want to see a six to eight lighted and dedicated court facility at the Oleai Beach Sports Complex, and another similar facility at Memorial Park next to the tennis courts. I would be a happy camper if those courts get built!"

"Great story," I said and moved back to hit some ground strokes.

The matches that morning lasted until 9:00. My clothes were soaked with sweat, but I had learned from another player to bring along a dry shirt. I changed and we drove to Wild Bills for breakfast. The talk was lively! These were good people playing this sport.

I realized that I had turned off my phone and reactivated it. I had six missed calls from Ash.

"What's up?" I asked when he picked up.

"A mini in Italy has gone active. The location is Lake Como! You believe that?" he answered.

"No, really? Lake Como?" I thought about our flight to northern Italy during our first rescue mission.

"Finish your breakfast, Reggie. Everything is in motion just like we set up. Not much for us to do but observe," Ash replied.

"I'll be there shortly," I announced and ordered a refill on my coffee.

Frankfurt, Germany

The team members were gathered in a circle. As they faced one direction, each man checked the gear that was strapped on his teammate's back. When the checks were complete, the men lined up to head out to the waiting aircraft that would fly them into Como, Italy.

Michael had requisitioned a private aircraft for the short hop from Germany to upper Italy. Frankfurt to Como would take a little over an hour in the medium-sized jet resting on the tarmac.

They stored all of their equipment in the baggage compartment behind the cabin and climbed on board. An attendant poured them all soft drinks and Pellegrino in crystal glassware. The cabin of the jet had typical seating with four of the chairs facing one another. Magnus sat on the forward side-facing couch. Stirling and Dick faced one another, and Aaron and Graham took their seats on the opposite side of the center aisle.

They had worked through the plan so many times that each man felt they could perform the mission in their sleep, but they still used this last hour for one more run through from top to bottom. What was the old saying by Abraham Lincoln? "If I only had an hour to cut down a tree, I'd spend the first forty-five minutes sharpening my axe."

Como, Italy

Michael MacAteer had booked the team into the Albergo Milano Inn, a short distance from Villa Sardagna. This was the first time that he was left to his own devices to coordinate all of the planning, preparation and provisioning. Becky Nelson had always handled the background work in the past. She was in Italy and purposefully left Michael alone to accomplish all that was necessary for the mission to have a chance of success.

It was Michael's work that procured the jet and the two vans that were waiting to whisk the team to Albergo Milano. So far, everything in the plan was going well. The team gathered their gear from the vans and entered the Inn. They looked down the hill from the Inn and could make out the roofline of Villa Sardagna.

The plan was to hit the house in the pre-dawn hours. The men knew from experience that vigilance on the part of the captors would be more lax at the end of the night. The team would attack from the boathouse, moving up the gentle slope to the house with the aid of night vision goggles. Outside guards would be overcome with knives. Surveillance of the villa had indicated there would be two assigned to watch the exterior, while three would guard the hostage.

Florence, Italy

Becky Nelson was glued to the computer monitor as the rescue attempt began to unfold. The Frankfurt I.N.C.I.S.O.R. team wore body cams that were activated when they moved. One of her computer screens was divided into six parts and five of the six had movement as the men gathered in the boathouse of Villa Sardagna. Their approach to the boathouse had gone off without detection. Not even a dog was barking this night.

As she watched, Becky remembered the missions that she had provided all of the behind-the-scenes support in the past. She looked with a keen eye at each step in the process, looking for mistakes that Michael might have made.

"So far, so good!" Becky announced to an empty room.

As she watched, the two roving outside guards were quietly dispatched from the planet by Aaron and Graham who both used the Ba-1008 12-inch knife. The two guards no longer had patent airways or intact carotid arteries. In fact, it did not look like there was much left of either man's neck, Becky observed.

Dubai, UAE

Michael was watching the same show on his large monitor in the office. He was watching with an intensity even stronger than Becky Nelson's. He, too, was looking for mistakes and places where he could have done more, and also with the strong desire or wanting to be there with the men as they continued with the mission.

Lake Como, Italy

The I.N.C.I.S.O.R. team approached the house and spied into the villa through first floor windows. Surveillance footage over the last twenty-four hours had shown that the original five kidnappers had been joined by seven others. The math said that there were now ten bad people in the house along with the victim, Marta Fascina.

The team observed that four men were lounging in a great room watching an Italian football game which was turned up loud enough for the men to hear the play-by-play from outside the house. Two women and a man were in the kitchen carrying on an animated discussion over a large pot, which the team assumed was spaghetti sauce simmering. Two were stationed outside Marta's room on the second floor…a man and a woman. One was missing…bathroom maybe?

Two of the team scaled the brick façade to the second story and quietly entered Marta's room. She was lying on the bed when Dick snuck up to her and covered her mouth with his hand. Magnus worked to restrain her arms for the brief period that she writhed on the bed. The two signaled to Marta that they were the good guys and she stopped struggling.

Once Marta had calmed down, Magnus let loose of her arms and Dick removed his hand from over her mouth. Magnus held a finger in front of his lips, indicating that she was to remain silent. Marta did as she was told and sat up on the bed. Dick whispered into her ear that she should call out to the two guards on the other side of the bedroom door.

Marta complied and called out for help. The I.N.C.I.S.O.R. men took up positions on either side of the bedroom door. They could see the doorknob slowly turning and heard the latch free itself from the strike plate. The door opened about a foot wide and one of the guards stuck her head in. The glint of Dick's knife was the last thing she saw as the blade was thrust deep into her neck. She could not cry out through her severed vocal cords. Dick withdrew his knife as Magnus pulled the limp body roughly into the bedroom and threw it on the floor. As soon as the guard's feet cleared the doorjamb, Dick lunged for the second guard.

The remaining male guard was alerted to the sound of his partner's demise and began to raise his automatic rifle which was slung around his neck. Dick's lightning fast knife action severed the man's throat before any sound of alarm was issued. His trigger finger convulsed and would have alerted the house if even one round had been fired, but, as luck would have it, the finger was not inside the trigger housing and convulsed in dead air.

Dick checked the hallway and saw and heard nothing. "Five down... seven to go," Dick thought as he did the math in his head. Magnus was checking on Marta as Dick re-entered the bedroom.

"Everything good? Can she move?" Dick asked.

"Good as can be...just a little shaky," Magnus replied.

"Let's go!" Dick whispered and began down the hallway to the top of the stairs. Magnus helped Marta as they followed Dick. At one point a floorboard creaked, and they all froze.

The sound on the television was quite loud, but one of the captors was alerted by the sound.

"Calmatevi...quiet! Shut that thing off!" he shouted.

The man clambered to his feet just as Stirling dashed into the room and sprayed the four kidnappers with hot lead from his silenced weapon. All four died and dropped to the ground, although not as quietly as they had been dispatched. Stirling turned his attention to the swinging door into the kitchen. He put his ear to the door...

Just then the door was flung open by the full force of a man on the other side. He slammed into the door, and it caught Stirling completely off guard and threw him onto one of the dead kidnappers. He lost his footing and fell backward as his knees buckled and his arms flailed up in the air.

The man who threw his body into the door regained his balance and fired his weapon at Stirling. His aim was effective as Stirling's body received at least six direct hits from the automatic weapon. Stirling's death was immediate as he bled onto the body under him.

Dubai, UAE

Michael MacAteer watched the shooting from Stirling's body camera. He reacted as if he, himself, was being shot. After the reaction passed, he jumped up from his chair and yelled, "Oh God!"

Florence, Italy

Becky Nelson had an identical reaction! Another I.N.C.I.S.O.R. team member was gone…

Lake Como, Italy

The remaining female kidnapper retrieved her cell phone, kneeled down in the kitchen to hide and placed a call to alert the gang members that weren't at the villa that they were under attack. The two men entered the great room from the kitchen and viewed the carnage on the floor. Four of their comrades were lying there, lifeless. Stirling was dead on top of one of them. Another creak from a board on the old stairway alerted the two to the movement. They took up positions on either side of the stairs with their weapons trained on the landing. The kidnappers failed to look out the windows.

Just then, Aaron and Graham fired through the windows into the entryway, taking out the two remaining men.

Aaron was the first to react. "Two down at the stairs!"

"We're on the stairs!" Dick announced urgently.

"Weapons secure," Graham said.

The two team members continued to escort Marta down the stairway.

The five gathered in the entryway.

"One's missing," Aaron announced.

"Yeah, the female in the kitchen," Dick added.

Magnus stayed with Marta as the other three team members headed into the kitchen. A back door was flung open and there was a strong, pungent smell of gas lingering in the air. Aaron saw it first…the gas line to the stove had been severed.

"Clear out!" he yelled to his friends.

Dick headed out the back door while the other two headed for the front of the house. Just then a shot was fired into the kitchen from the back yard. The bullet struck a cast iron pot, and the ricochet caused a spark that ignited the gas building up in the room. A massive explosion rocked the villa and blew out all of the windows.

The force also ejected the I.N.C.I.S.O.R. team and Marta outside. The concussion left them writhing on the grass and all of the communication equipment ceased to work immediately. Becky and Michael's monitors turned to snow, and the audio was gone.

Becky picked up her phone and called Michael in Dubai.

"I saw the same thing that you did," Michael replied.

"Can you tell if any of them made it out?" Becky asked.

"Their comms and body cameras are all down. I have no idea!" Michael announced.

"So…now what?"

"All we can do is wait…"

PART
THREE

CHAPTER 20

Saipan, Northern Mariana Islands

Reggie and Ash sat together at the patio table each inwardly contemplating the news about Italy. Stirling Mason had been killed in the exchange with the kidnappers. His death was witnessed by the I.N.C.I.S.O.R. team before visual and audio communications stopped. All that Reggie, Ash, Michael, Becky, and the Denver team could do was wait…and hope…and pray.

Langley, VA

The CIA had tasked one of their spy satellites to be positioned over Italy and the technicians at headquarters were scouring over images sent to them from the satellite. The techies witnessed the approach to the Villa by the German I.N.C.I.S.O.R. team, and the elimination of the two outside guards.

Infrared imaging gave them a distorted view of the entry by the rescue team into the house, and the location of the kidnappers and their victim. The supervisor joined the technicians, and all watched with interest as the red figures moved on the big screen projecting the show up on one of the walls in the room. As the kidnappers were eliminated the bright red image that had portrayed them began to fade to black as the heat signature waned. They all watched in rapt fascination as the red images danced on the screen.

At one point the screen turned white and a snowy screen followed.

One of the technicians shouted, "An explosion!"

Another shouted, "It came from the kitchen area…may have been a gas explosion!"

The supervisor added, "Calm down, people. We need analysis…not reaction!"

Soon the snowy screen cleared, and they had a still shot showing five red images laying in a grassy area outside the kitchen door. None of the five were moving. A sixth red image was seen moving quickly off of the image before them.

"That's the female kidnapper!" a technician announced.

The people in the room seemed glued on the five motionless red images. This was what remained of the I.N.C.I.S.O.R. team and their rescued hostage.

"Hey! The red images are not fading like the others did! They are alive!" a technician announced.

"How long is the satellite here?" the supervisor asked to the room.

"We're losing the image…now! And the monitor went blank.

There was a brief moment of silence and then bedlam hit the room as every technician scrambled back to their cubicle to re-establish some contact with the Villa on Lake Como, Italy.

Washington, DC

An aide to President Marron burst into the Oval Office and announced, "Something went wrong with the rescue in Italy. There was an explosion! We think the hostage is alive, but we do not know her condition."

President Marron looked up from the papers he was studying. He dismissed the overt intrusion without even a knock and asked the aide to keep him informed as they got more information.

The aide apologized and quietly left the room.

President Marron sat quietly and absorbed the news. An explosion. Something went wrong. Alive, but how were they?

He clasped his hands on top of the desk. "God, please help them," he prayed.

Denver, CO

The turmoil that was happening at the Denver facility was intense as the five team members watched the event unfold in Italy. The atmosphere in the room was slowly turning to a quiet sadness as each of the men dealt with his own feelings of loss. Stirling had died right before their eyes. His body camera recorded the kitchen door smacking him hard and driving him backward. The camera moved to an image of the ceiling as he fell backward over the inert body of a man he had just killed. The camera then focused on the kidnapper who came through the kitchen door and fired his automatic weapon at Stirling. The body cam jumped with each bullet's impact into his body as Stirling's torso recoiled from the bullet's force. It was as if each one of the Denver I.N.C.I.S.O.R. team had personally taken the blows from the bullets.

The five members all knew that Stirling was gone.

They did not know the status of the remaining four Frankfurt team members or their hostage.

A quiet pall enveloped the room.

Vladivostok, Russia

"Our two comrades in Iraq have been murdered by that angry mob of terrorist leaders," Ivan commented as the two men walked down a corridor. The military boots made a distinct 'clicking' noise on the polished tile as they walked.

"What is wrong with those people? Do they not know that we are on their side?" Vladimir replied.

"We must contact our troop commander in Syria and get him to send more envoys to these idiots!"

"Da! We must get the terror cells back on our side and show them that we wish to pomoshch'…to, how do you say? Help. We must succeed in turning them against America."

"Do svidaniya comrade!"

Lake Como, Italy

Dick was the first to have some of his senses begin to return. He heard groans from the others around him. He ventured first to sit up and get his bearings. Then he kneeled as his head continued to clear. He attempted to stand but moved too quickly and fell back to his knees.

Dick crawled to Marta who was on his right. He felt her stomach and placed his ear over her mouth. She was breathing! He looked over her body and his own and did not notice any overt signs of injury. He looked to his left.

Magnus was beginning to stir and made it to his feet. He was wobbly and his head was woozy. He swayed in place as he waited for his head to clear. He also had no outward signs of injury. Magnus moved to Marta and Dick to see how he could help.

Aaron and Graham were also sitting up, but these two were both sporting injuries.

Aaron had blood oozing from a wound on his left side. He had removed his tactical belt and was applying pressure with a gauze bandage. Although most of his attention was focused on treating his wound, he glanced up to see that Magnus and Dick were kneeling over Marta and that Graham was close by and tending to his injury.

"Is she alive?" he questioned. Nobody responded quite yet.

Graham looked to be the worst for wear of the four remaining I.N.C.I.S.O.R. members at the site. His left arm was hanging limp at his side with blood dripping off of his wrist and the arm hung like a useless appendage. He was attempting to minister to the wound with his right hand, but his actions did not seem to slow the flow of blood.

Marta began to come to life as Dick and Magnus checked her for injuries. She screamed as she tried to sit up. A severe pain came from her right hip. Dick helped her lay back down and she lay prone while a wave of nausea passed over her. Magnus moved to help his two friends and teammates with their injuries.

The sound of sirens approaching was heard by the five survivors as they gathered on the Villa's lawn outside of the remains of the burning kitchen. Help was on the way.

Dubai, UAE

"Becky, the polizia and ambulanza are arriving at the Villa as we speak. I called them as soon as my screen went blank. All of their communication equipment is still down, probably taken out by that kitchen explosion. We should get a report from the Como police soon," Michael said to his boss on the other end of the call.

"Good work, Michael…let me know when you hear something," Becky answered.

"You and Reggie will be the first to know!" Michael replied.

Langley, VA

"What do we hear from Italy?" the Director of the CIA asked as one of the supervisors entered his office.

"The latest from the Italian paramedics is that one of the I.N.C.I.S.O.R. team has a shrapnel wound in his abdomen, one has a broken arm and severed artery, and the hostage has a shattered hip that will require replacement. All have cuts and bruises. One of the team was killed just before the explosion. Don't know which one, yet" the supervisor announced.

"And the kidnappers?" the Director asked.

"All dead…oh…except one. We think a woman escaped and the explosion thwarted any possibility of the team giving chase. We'll get her," the supervisor added.

"Anything else?"

"No, sir. That is all the news that we have for now."

"Get back to me in two hours with an update! I want to know that everyone is okay…except that one poor soul."

The supervisor gave a short nod toward the Director and left the office.

Saipan, Northern Mariana Islands

"That explosion was too well timed! Do you think they knew we were coming?" Ash asked.

"Ash, my good friend…you know it's too early to know. It could be serendipity that that gas line exploded. What if it was old, or rubbing against something sharp the wrong way? What if it was cut in haste to mask a getaway? Or, like you suggest…It was planned to take out our team! You know, also that, I trust your instincts more than I do my own, so…if you think it was a setup…I'll believe you," I replied.

"You are right, Reggie. We need to wait for the analysts in Langley to do their thing. Once we have that information, and their best guess as to what happened at Lake Como, then we can decide what to do and what action to take. What about Stirling?" Ash asked.

"Becky is reaching out to his parents. I think they are in Iowa… or somewhere in the Midwest. Michael is collaborating with the authorities in Italy to see what they can recover. I talked with Becky, and she is fine taking care of helping Stirling's parents with the funeral arrangements they want. I hope there is something left of him to send home. That was a horrific explosion!" I added. "You and I need to focus on this next test in California. The plane is already there. Did you say it is in Sacramento?"

"Nope…that's where your friend moved to. You know…that friend from Arizona!"

"Right," I said. "Well, where is the damn plane?"

"Edwards," Ash replied.

"Oh, all right. What is the plan for the test?" I asked.

Ash took the next hour explaining how the CIA technicians would align the radar so that the signal generated by RFW would be directed to and follow the aircraft with the large parabolic mirror as it flew along a route plotted south to north through California, Oregon, and Washington.

California alone had seventy-three anti-government groups operating within its borders. Oregon had another nineteen groups and Washington boasted twenty-five such groups. The authorities knew that not all of the over one-hundred groups were militias that were busy arming themselves against some type of future doomsday event. The estimate was that less than twenty-five percent of the known anti-government groups were active militias with arms caches.

The scheduled test would go a long way in helping to determine how accurate the government estimates were. We would also show the level of munitions that were hidden away in rural and mountainous depots. Did these groups have guns or more serious weaponry?

The equipment that was my brainchild and brought to life by the CIA technicians, Joe Cavanaugh and Billy Bean had performed well in the previous three tests. Each test was harder on the equipment than the previous test. The second test was harder on the equipment than the first, but RFW had performed well. The apparatus had performed well through the third test. This fourth test was going to be even harder. A test on the west coast of the United States, one just east of the Rocky Mountains and the third and hardest test along the Eastern Seaboard. So, actually, three separate tests over the next week. Why was Langley calling this all one test?

Florence, Italy

Becky Nelson walked quickly and purposefully toward the main hospital entrance. She had been working behind the scenes to secure the best trauma surgeons in Italy and have them all flown to this hospital in Florence. The Careggi University hospital was known in many circles to be the best facility in northern Italy.

The trauma teams were already working to save Graham's left arm. He had suffered a shrapnel wound that had severed the brachial artery and damaged the nerve plexus that innervated the arm. Even with the tourniquet that had been applied to his arm in Como, there was concern about blood loss and function for his arm.

Aaron's wound to his abdomen was examined by a second trauma team and there were no major organs involved. He was in the process of having the final sutures placed in his side.

Marta's right hip turned out to be irreparable and a third trauma team was prepping her for surgery. An orthopedic surgeon was standing by to perform a lateral posterior hip replacement surgery. The implant would give her twenty good years…but no running, jogging, or jumping…ever again.

When Marta heard the restrictions, she actually thanked the surgeon!

The other team members had their minor cuts and scrapes attended to and were waiting in an ante room when Becky walked in.

"Buona Sera," she said as she walked up to Dick and Magnus and gave them each a hug. Becky gave them both a careful look from head to toe and decided that they would be okay.

"How are the other three? She asked.

Magnus replied first, "Aaron's almost done. No organ damage. He'll be sore for a while, but he will be okay. They want to keep him overnight for observation."

"Not such good news with Graham," Dick added. "They have his arm under a microscope attempting to re-attach some severed nerves and an artery. He lost a lot of blood and only time will tell if he will have use of his arm. Nerves are the slowest tissues in the body to heal. They take longer than even bone to recover. Graham's going to be on a long, slow road back to decent function…if ever. At least he gets to keep the arm. That tourniquet was on for a long time."

"What is the time limit for that?" Becky asked.

"Two hours…after that there is permanent damage," Magnus chimed in.

"And Graham?" she asked.

"Close to that," Dick said.

"And Marta…where is her husband? He should be here for her, already!" Becky blurted out.

"At some political fundraiser-type function," Graham answered.

"He doesn't seem that interested that she is alive…or that she is in surgery getting a new hip," Dick added.

"You know," Becky brought up, "Ash thinks that the kidnappers knew that your team was coming."

"You think her husband may have had something to do with this?" Dick asked. "Kinda makes sense with his lack of interest that she escaped…with our help…"

"And the loss of Stirling!" Magnus added.

"I don't like this one bit," Dick seethed through gritted teeth.

"Hey, calm down!" Becky interjected. "This is all conjecture. We have no proof."

"Yeah, but…it is still weird that he is not here for her now," Magnus added.

"We may need Ash to talk with him…he'll get our answers!" Becky offered and took a seat to wait on news of Marta's surgery.

Dubai, UAE

Michael finished his call with Becky Nelson and was happy to have an update, although the news could have been better. He focused his attention on the computer screen in front of him. What could he find out about Marta's husband? What was his name… Silvio Berlusconi? What kind of politician was he? Was he in any kind of trouble? Why did the kidnappers choose his wife to kidnap? The assumption made by the I.N.C.I.S.O.R. people was that it was about his money, being the 190th richest man in the world. Was there more to the story?

Time for Michael to do some digging! He started, as he always did with research, with the Google machine to get as much general background about this man and his wife as he could. Then the real work began…he would dig deeper, peeling away one layer at a time. Becky had mentioned involving Ash. What could he do? Michael had heard rumors about Ash Black and his tactics. He had heard that Ash could break any man or woman. Michael heard that sometimes the truth cost lives. One of their own was dead. Michael shuddered to think what would happen if foul play were discovered!

Edwards Air Force Base, CA

The aircraft took off to the north and began a lazy turn to the west and continued in that direction until it was over the Pacific Ocean. It then turned southeast and flew until San Diego could be seen off to the left of the plane. By this time, the ordered flight altitude had been reached. Even though the cabin was pressurized, the pilot and co-pilot had donned oxygen masks, as was protocol for a test flight of this nature.

The pilot banked the plane to the left and began a wide U-turn that placed the plane on a northwestern path which began over Mexicali, Mexico. The aircraft was aimed toward Sacramento and would fly over the mountainous terrain beginning with the Sequoia National Forest then traversing the Sierra National Forest, Yosemite, Stanislaus National Forest, then over to Sacramento and following I-5 north into Oregon. The route continued into Washington as the plane flew east of I-5 toward Seattle.

Once the flight reached Seattle, Washington the plane would turn east and fly to Spokane and then turn southwest to fly over Bend, Oregon, then head southeast to fly over Lake Tahoe and head directly back to Edwards, continuing the southeast direction. This path would take the plane over extremely remote areas of California, Oregon, and Washington states.

The flight path was overlaid over a map of known anti-government establishments with known depots of munitions.

At various points during the flight, lights on an instrument panel in the fuselage would indicate that an emission from Radio Free World had been received and bounced toward the ground by the parabolic mirror.

The onboard instruments indicated that over one-hundred emissions had been received. The technician on the flight wondered why the signal from Saipan was not continuous, but he also knew that it was not his place to question the test process.

The pilot and co-pilot only noticed one flash from the ground that they assumed was an explosion at an ammunition depot in the wasteland of eastern California. They had no idea how many stores of C-4 had been ignited as they flew overhead.

The flight landed back at Edwards Air Force Base without incident and the longest test of RFW had been concluded. The test had consumed almost ten hours of flying time and it showed on the crew as they disembarked from the aircraft.

After a mission debriefing, the pilot offered to buy the first round and the crew headed off to Riley's to throw down some cold beers.

Unbeknownst to this Edwards crew, while they were busy imbibing in the ice-cold beers and throwing down their favorite chasers, the C-130 was refueled and a skeleton Edwards crew boarded the aircraft to ferry it to Albuquerque for its next test. That test was to happen the next day.

CHAPTER 21

Saipan, Northern Mariana Islands

Ash, Joe Billy, and I were enjoying our favorite cocktails while sitting in the Chambre lounge in the newly renovated and renamed Crown Plaza Hotel in Garapan. We were discussing the recent test and how well the equipment had performed. One hundred and twenty signals had been sent from Radar Hill in Saipan to an airborne plane over California, Oregon, and Washington states. The test had shown that the equipment had endurance and could be counted on to perform over extended periods of time.

The next test, tomorrow, would involve a continuous signal from Saipan to the plane flying a route from Albuquerque, New Mexico to Cheyenne, Wyoming. The plane would fly north over the Rocky Mountains, staying west of I-25, then fly south, returning to Albuquerque on a path east of I-25…out over the Great Plains.

While we were discussing the mission, Jeff Beach and Nicky Bells came through the front door of the lounge. Ash and Billy pulled over two more chairs so the two of them could join us.

Nicky sat down next to me, and I noticed that his shirt was soaked with sweat.

"Pickleball?" I asked.

"Tough match! Singles…" Nicky replied.

"You are seventy years old!" I exclaimed.

"I still got it, Dartmouth Dude," he answered.

"Good for you," I said and turned to Ash.

"What do you think about Italy? You thinking of making a trip?"

"I am…but I hate flying commercial. Want to make it the first mission for the new Aurora?" Ash asked.

"Can you wait til we get past the next couple of days? We have the final two parts of the fourth test of Radio Free World. I know that these two…" I pointed at Joe and Billy, "…can manage it but I'll feel better being here, just in case."

"Well, the cat in Italy can wait…I guess, but I want to know if we were set up. If that is why Stirling is dead…things will get ugly," Ash threatened.

"Ash, my friend, you put together a flight plan for Aurora II and I'll babysit RFW," I said.

"Babysit? You don't do a thing!" Joe added.

"Well, Joe, it is his baby. I'm all right if he hangs around," Billy countered and then looked at me with a menacing look, "but keep your hands out of the cookie jar, Reginald Nelson!"

Albuquerque, NM

The C-130 was fully fueled and parked on the ramp in front of the New Mexico Air National Guard hangar, where it was housed for the previous night. The Air National Guard is located on the northeast end of the Albuquerque International Sunport. A pre-flight check found no problems with the aircraft. A Denver crew had been flown down the day before and was now boarding the plane. The crew had been briefed about the previous tests. They had also been informed that this test would be the first involving a continuous emission from Saipan, and that they were to monitor the aircraft's systems and the new instrumentation installed in the belly of the craft. The crew had been warned about the emissions literally shaking the test satellites apart! That was why this workhorse of an airplane was being monitored for its effectiveness and durability.

This was the next to the last test of the plane flying over United States soil. There were probably numerous groups that would have objected to the mission…hence its 'top secret' classification. Any C-4 that was held by one of the anti-government militia groups that was ignited today would surely violate somebody's civil right to bear arms. The ACLU and other quasi government protection groups would have a heyday if the purpose of this flight were uncovered.

The flight path would take them on a northern track following I-25. They would fly to the west of I-25 and continue north to Buffalo, Wyoming and then head east across Wyoming following I-90 to Murdo, South Dakota and then turn south. The plane would follow route 83 and fly over North Platte, Nebraska and then cross over I-70 at Oakley, Nebraska, continuing south to Amarillo, Texas and turning west, following I-40 back to Albuquerque, New Mexico, and the conclusion of the flight. This would only be a six-hour flight. The California test was the longest, by far, but this flight was the most strenuous test of the plane and equipment so far.

The number of anti-government groups operating in all of the states to be overflown was over 140. The government analysts guessed that around twenty five percent of the groups had a militia contingent to them. The unknown was how many of the groups stored the 'nasty' weapons. The flight test of Radio Free World would go a long way to either alleviate government concerns or to reinforce concerns.

The pilot and crew spent the majority of the flight glued to their instruments, looking for any small variations or fluctuations that may indicate that the plane was adversely affected during the test. Surprisingly, the avionics, especially the GPS systems did not seem to be affected by the aircraft receiving emissions from Saipan and reflecting them onto the ground below. The plane and the instruments performed well and no ill effects from the test were observed.

After returning to their base at the Albuquerque International Sunport and parking the aircraft outside the hangar at the New Mexico Air National Guard, the crew proceeded to the debriefing area. The interviews did not take long because there was extraordinarily little to report about their flight. The crew drove to the other end of the Sunport and entered the Rio Grande Brew Pub and Grille inside the main passenger terminal. The crew shared pitchers of Rio Grande Desert Pils and wolfed down several orders of Brisket Street Tacos and hot wings.

Just like the previous night, a ferry crew was assembled, the aircraft refueled, and flown to Dover Air Force Base in Delaware.

Langley, VA

Information was cascading into various computer terminals within the surveillance room.

The sources varied from witnesses, both amateur and professional, on the ground near to where the explosions occurred, flights, both private and commercial where explosions were observed from the air, and military and national guard maneuvers near to the explosions.

There were also reports filed by FBI operatives who were specifically positioned to observe certain anti-government group compounds for any unusual activity. The FBI agents had been warned about the test and for what to watch.

Reports from the west coast and the Midwest indicated that there had been just a little over twenty explosions, all occurring in remote and rural locations. The analysts at Langley were beginning to do the math based on the numbers of known anti-government groups and the percentage (less than 25%) of those groups that sported a militia wing. They knew about 120 groups on the West Coast and about 140 in the Midwest. The expectation was that one-quarter stored arms and that these groups were well-stocked with weaponry. The math said to expect over sixty explosions.

Only twenty explosions had been reported or recorded. This meant several different things to the analysts…and raised many questions.

Were the militia groups not as well organized and stocked as the government entities believed? All puff and pageantry and no power?

Was it possible that the militia groups stored their munitions in hardened bunkers like the military did?

Did the fly over not cover enough territory?

Did Radio Free World not work as well as they expected?

The data was still pouring in from the western half of the country while the test was ready to commence along the eastern seaboard.

Dover, DE

The third and final flight as part of the fourth test would leave Dover Air Base, fly west over Delaware, Virginia, and West Virginia, turn south to fly over Kentucky and Tennessee, into Mississippi, turn eastward to fly over Alabama, Georgia, and South Carolina, then northeast over North Carolina, out over the Atlantic and land back at Dover.

The test would be the shortest distance but covering states that hosted 145 anti-government groups.

The choice was made to focus the third American test on the Southern states and leave the New England states alone. Yes, there were anti-government groups in New England. Heck, the state motto in New Hampshire was "Live Free or Die"! But the third leg test was more about how far away from Saipan the signals could travel and how effective the emissions could be in exciting stores of C-4 at this distance.

It turned out that the fewest number of explosions were recorded on this test. But there were explosions! RFW worked…even at this distance! The technicians at Langley and in Saipan would be thrilled with this news.

Saipan, Northern Mariana Islands

Ash disconnected from the call he had just received, "Shut her down, boys! That completes the fourth phase of the testing of Radio Free World!"

"What are they saying?" I asked.

Billy and Joe busied themselves with making sure all of the equipment was turned off and stowed away properly.

"Word from Langley is that all four tests were successful. The two tests in Baghdad, the test involving four Arab countries, and the three legs in the States showed the CIA that RFW is effective in activating stores of C-4 that are not stored in protected bunkers. Properly stored C-4 was safe from the emissions. Exposed plastique can be ignited anywhere in the world from this one location," Ash announced.

"Time off definitely for you two!" I announced as I watch Joe and Billy finish putting away the equipment.

"Fantastic!" Billy said.

"Great! What is next?" Joe asked.

"No idea, Joe," I replied. "As far as I know, Langley has several weeks of analysis of all the data collected from the four tests. They will also be paying close attention to the reactions from around the world. Washington will then need to decide what to do with RFW."

"In the meantime, you two should get yourselves to Guam. For residents on Saipan, it is like going to the big city," Ash suggested.

"How do you mean?" Billy asked.

"Guam is three times the size of Saipan. There are about fifty thousand people living here, and one hundred and fifty thousand on Guam," Ash clarified.

"Also, Guam has a Macy's, two Rosses with a third opening soon, and Home Depot, and…the largest K-Mart in the world!" I added.

"And the big military presence…Anderson Air Force Base and the Naval Base…and they are building a Marine base there also," Ash said.

"Okay, we're sold," Joe replied.

"Not too big on shopping, but there has to be more choices for fast food and restaurants," Billy added.

"Yeah, Lone Star, Outback, and more," Ash replied. "Man, Reggie, I want to go now!"

"Maybe we'll join them," I answered.

"Let's pack it up here. You think those cases are secure? You know, this place is called the 'Island of Thieves'!" Ash intoned.

"What?" Joe and Billy asked together.

"Magellan gave Guam and Saipan that moniker when he sailed here in 1521, the 'Isla de Ladrones'. It was a cultural misunderstanding, as the locals describe it. The Chamorros sailed their tiny Proas out to the big Spanish galleons and took things from the Spanish ships, including the iron nails that held the planking to the sides of the ships! The locals thought they deserved the items for bringing the Spanish sailors food and water," Ash added.

"Really?" Joe asked, incredulous.

"That's the story I heard," I replied.

"Well, yes…the cases are all secure. Nothing can be moved without a crane, so I feel good that we can be away from this place for a while and not have to worry if somebody becomes curious," Billy answered.

"I'm ready for a drink," I offered.

"Hey, maybe we can catch the sunset on the beach at PIC!" Ash added. "They have those great potato skins!"

"Those are really good…and they are free with your drinks," I added. "Let's move!"

The four of us moved to the Escalade and headed to the southern part of the island for some food and drink.

Dubai, UAE

Michael had been busy with the research he was doing on the Italian that was suspected of setting up the Frankfurt team during their rescue effort.

Marta's husband, or as they called it in their home, 'domestic partner,' had not acted thrilled to have his wife returned to him so quickly. Although her hip had been shattered, the hip replacement surgery had been successful, and she was well on her way to walking without the help of a cane.

She had been a fabulous patient and responded to the extremely painful physical therapy like a real trooper. From the shock of being made to get out of her hospital bed in blinding pain that same afternoon following the surgery to doing laps around the recovery ward with a walker, the staff was amazed how she responded in recovery. Marta left the hospital after only three days to finish her recovery at home.

Michael was digging deep into Silvio Berlusconi. When he got stuck he reached out to Becky who also helped with the research. Why was this man not pleased to have Marta back? Did he want her gone? He had almost eight billion dollars…did he not want to share if they split domestically?

His three terms in the Italian parliament had proven to be extremely turbulent times. Numerous political challenges occurred during his tenure. He was blamed partly for Italy's weak economy and criticized for his backing of the United States invasion of Iraq.

Added to this was a sex scandal during his third term in office which involved a minor. His second wife divorced him over his alleged improprieties.

Even during his time out of office, his media empire proved to cause him much controversy. He was convicted of tax fraud. Berlusconi was also convicted of publishing police surveillance tapes of one of his political rivals.

"Not a nice guy!" Michael thought as he was putting the finishing touches on a report about Silvio to Reginald and Ash. Michael was focusing his report on three facets that stood out to him…Silvio was extremely wealthy…Silvio was in his mid-eighties…Silvio had immense influence through his media empire.

In Michael's eyes, Berlusconi had Marta around as nothing more than eye candy. She had just come into his life in 2020. This would not be a woman he would share confidences with, have financial alliances with, or have sexual intimacy to strengthen their relationship.

Michael and Becky could find nothing overtly tying Berlusconi to Marta's abduction. No funny payments or contact of any sort with the kidnappers and the Italian gang they belonged to. He was just an unsavory character!

Saipan, Northern Mariana Islands

Ash and I finished reading the report at the same time.

"I want to go!" Ash began enthusiastically.

"And…why is that? There is nothing here," I retorted and pointed at the laptop screen that I had been reading.

"One…we need to fly somewhere…get off this island for a while. Two…I want to have some fun with this nasty man. Three…you can be with Becky, and we can check out the improvements to the Villa in Florence. Four…" Ash continued.

"That's enough!" I interrupted. "You had me at let's go flying. The rest of it will work itself out. Do me a favor, though…don't kill the guy!"

"Hey, he's an old dude. Already had heart surgery and stomach surgery. No guarantees!" Ash argued.

"Okay, okay…how about we do some flight planning," I said.

"I was wishing you'd say that!" Ash gleamed a big smile. "I have been doing some work on just that. Here is what I propose…"

"You've already done your homework?" I asked. "Let me get us a couple of drinks."

I ambled into the kitchen and poured myself a double Crown Royal over ice with a twist and poured one for Ash. I knew it wasn't his favorite, but so what.

"We fly Aurora II from here to Manilla. That's 1652 miles, and 3.6 hours flying time right? Aurora's speed is 460 MPH?"

I nodded, thinking of the route over the water of the Philippine Sea.

"We refuel and take a stretch break, then head to Hanoi. That's 1102 miles and 2.4 hours of flying time," Ash instructed, and took a sip from his drink. "Really, Reggie…your signature drink? I am not a fan!"

"You need a more sophisticated palate, my friend," I interjected. "So that is day one? Saipan to Hanoi?"

"Yep…and we take a day or two there to explore. Viet Nam was our generation's war, and it may be uncomfortable to be there, but I have heard that it is beautiful," Ash replied.

"Okay, I'm with you…and?" I spoke.

"Don't you have family in Hanoi?" Ash questioned.

"Yes, a nephew. He and his wife live in Hanoi. I think he is a teacher working for the United Nations, or something. I don't think he's been doing much teaching with this Covid stuff," I answered.

"United Nations is in New York, Reggie…I'm beginning to worry about you!" Ash countered.

"No! They have some kind of school in Vietnam…in Hanoi!" I said.

"Maybe they could show us around the city," Ash suggested.

"I'll ask, so continue with the trip," I urged.

"Next leg is Hanoi to Myanmar, which is 634 miles or 1.4 hours, quick potty break, get a little gas, then Myanmar to Mumbai which is 1507 miles, or 3.3 hours, another break to stretch and get fuel, then Mumbai to Dubai, or 1206 miles and 2.6 hours. Long day, a little over seven hours in the air, plus the time on the ground, but then we spend some time with Michael and make sure everything is okay at the home office. I figure we need a day or two there," Ash continued.

"Then?" I asked.

"Dubai to Ankara is 1645 miles, or 3.6 hours in the air, take a break, get some Jet A, and then the final leg from Ankara to Florence is 1502 miles and 3.5 hours. Three days in the air and three or four days exploring new sights," Ash finished.

"So…a week to get there," I deduced.

"Fun and flying…what more could you ask for?" Ash questioned.

"I would like a week with just you and me to decompress from all that has been going on," I added. "When do we leave?"

"We're done here for a while, right?" Ash asked.

"As far as I know we are done with the testing from Radar Hill in Saipan," I replied. "I guess we are not finished until Langley and the President say so, so we have to be ready to see what more they want from us."

"Then I say we start our week tomorrow morning! The two CIA techies will be off to Guam tomorrow, so no more babysitting duties. Langley is busy reviewing all the data. POTUS has been quiet. Let us be off!" Ash declared.

"And we have no issues to deal with on the plane," I added. "What about the weather enroute?"

"Severe calm and clear…a few of those afternoon thunder boomies to avoid," Ash said.

"I'll call Becky and you call Michael…let them know we're coming," I finished.

We sipped on our drinks in silent contemplation of the upcoming adventure.

"Another?" I asked

"Sure"

Denver, CO

The team had voted unanimously to take a road trip to visit Stirling's parents in Des Moines, Iowa. The five would drive straight through on I-80. The team would take the new Escalade that had been provided by the CIA. Even the drones would come along for the nine-and-a-half-hour drive to the capital of Iowa.

Each man would spend two hours behind the wheel, spreading the driving load out equally. Eastern Colorado and Nebraska provide extremely flat geography with nothing but farmland to look at. Nothing much of interest to break up the monotony. The three in the back seats did have the two video monitors in the backs of the front seats to watch Netflix and make the time move more quickly.

The team members were also all ex-military and had become expert at passing the hours during long transport to remote deployments.

The men also used the driving time to create various scenarios for the drones and they practiced simulated attacks on unsuspecting cows and oncoming traffic. They also enjoyed and became skilled to a man with landing the drones on the trailers of semi-tractor trailers that they passed and that approached them travelling westbound on I-80. The drivers of these big rigs that were used as moving landing pads were oblivious to their involvement in the team's games.

This trip was also the first time that any of the men had experienced Super Cruise. Their Escalade allowed for hands-free driving along all of I-76 flowing northeast to I-80 from Denver to Ogallala, Nebraska, and then all along I-80 into Des Moines. The car even made automatic lane changes when the car determined that it would be optimal! Some of the men struggled with hands-free and paid even more attention than they would have when they controlled the steering wheel.

The team would spend almost a whole week on this road trip. Two of the days were used up getting to and from Des Moines. The rest of the time was used by the I.N.C.I.S.O.R. team members to visit with Stirling Mason's parents, bid Stirling their final farewells at his gravesite, and to evaluate the pickleball ability of the residents of Des Moines.

CHAPTER 22

Hanoi, Vietnam

The first two legs of our trip to Italy in Aurora II had proceeded flawlessly. There was lots of down time on the radio, which gave us much needed time to talk and reconnect on a more personal level.

Ash was in a much better place now than he was when Grace was murdered by a terrorist bomb in Israel. He had made his way completely to the dark side and had gone on quite a killing rampage. He was skillful enough with his craft not to leave any clues that would come back to haunt him, but I knew that all of the murders were at his hand.

Ash still had no need for an alive terrorist. In his mind…and mine… they were the scum of the earth. Any person that chooses to infringe on the rights of innocent civilians by killing and maiming them in the name of some god does not deserve any of the oxygen that we breathe. At least now enough time had passed since Grace was taken from him that he would at least use the terrorist for valuable information before their time on this planet was ended.

What to do with this mega-wealthy Italian blow hard? Ash would let him say his piece, but if there was any inkling that he had any part in Stirling's death…even just by remote association…the man's life would be worth extremely little. There was no amount of money that could assuage Ash or make him amend his ways, either.

I had already decided that I would be conveniently busy with Becky and her new project. Like an ostrich sticking its head in the sand, I was choosing not to be aware of Ash's motus operandi or his tactics used to question the man who had purchased the mini. I knew enough that I would not like Ash's tactics, but he was always effective. My error would be one of omission, not as an accomplice.

But here we were in Hanoi. Fifty years since I lost ten of my dormmates from Lord Hall at Dartmouth to that war. The military draft was a mandatory thing when my age group turned eighteen. We were required to register and be counted in the draft. My roommate and I both received high draft numbers and therefore would not be called into action. We would not have to enlist in a safer branch, like the Air Force, or run to Canada to avoid being drafted into the Army to do infantry work, slogging through the wet jungles of Asia.

My nephew, Noah, and his wife, Stevie, were waiting at their five-bedroom house on the lake called, West Lake, in Tayho. A taxi dropped us at the house, and we were greeted warmly, and shown to our bedrooms. Noah and Stevie lived alone in this large home with their two dogs. They used one of the bedrooms for themselves and a second for Noah's studio. He produced interesting audio and visual media from that room. I did not expect separate bedrooms for Ash and me, so this was a welcome treat.

They were leasing the home but were lucky enough to be the first occupants once the dwelling was completed. They also did not have a car. They maneuvered around the bustling city of Hanoi on scooters! Taxis were used only when they had to get more home than their daily food, and much of that was delivered…also by people on scooters.

One of the more popular experiences that is talked about by visitors to Hanoi is the street food. From Pho (pronounced Pha) to Bun cha and goi cuon, the special experience was watching the food prepared in front of you at tiny street booths. My favorite treat that I discovered this trip was Vietnamese egg coffee at the Café Pho Co coffee in Old Town. When milk was in short supply during the war, beaten egg yolks served as a substitute, which became over time egg cream with egg yolks, condensed milk, and sugar. The cream mixture was floated on top of a robust coffee. Fascinating experience sitting in the café, sipping Vietnamese egg coffee, and watching the people walk by!

While we were watching the milling crowds, Ash asked me about John Vann.

"I used to do a lot of flying with John before I knew you," I replied.

"No, No, No...his father?

"Oh, John Paul Vann," I answered.

"Yeah, he was some kind of big wig here during the war," Ash continued.

"Yes, the only civilian awarded the Presidential Medal of Freedom and the Distinguished Service Cross since World War II," I added.

"He died here, right?" Ash asked.

"Yep, 1972...his helicopter crashed. It was argued that the South Vietnamese caused the crash because they hated him. He was really harsh with them and was not known to mince words. He would demean an officer in front of his men and formed many lifelong enemies among the South Vietnamese," I said.

"His son ever talk about him?" Ash queried.

"Never! I found out about him from friends…and the movie with Greg Kinnear. What was it? A Bright Shining Lie: John Vann and America in Viet Nam," I answered. "John Vann had one of the best quotes about that war…our war. 'We don't have twelve years' experience in Vietnam. We have one year's experience twelve times over'."

"And that means?"

"We didn't learn a damn thing! It was a stupid war. Did you know that we never lost a battle and yet we lost the war? Another example of politicians messing up everything they touch!" I exclaimed.

"Oh, Reggie…tell me how you really feel!" Ash said with a big smile on his face.

The second day was spent wandering around Old Town where over thirty streets display vendors of the same craft or guild. If you wish to buy something for the kitchen, you go to kitchen street.. You want linens…linen street.

"Where is Walmart when you need it?" Stevie exclaimed. She had been looking for a large paper clip and could not figure out which street she needed to find her item!

"Or a Bed, Bath and Beyond!" I added. Wandering these streets was fun as a tourist but seemed very inefficient as a way of shopping.

Ash and I bid our farewells and made it to the airport before the throngs of people hit the streets. Aurora II was fueled and ready to begin the second leg of our journey.

It was during the third part of this leg that Ash and I experienced our first hiccup. We were halfway between Mumbai and Dubai when Ash asked me about the temperature reading in the right engine.

"Reggie! Isn't that a little high?" Ash asked.

I tapped at the indicator as if it was a real instrument. Bad habit from the old days and stuck dials.

"Yep…and climbing," I noticed.

"Pulling back on number one," I announced, and gently pulled back on the power lever. Now I had to compensate by adding more left rudder. I quickly trimmed the rudder to manage the decreased thrust from the right engine.

"Ash, can you grab the owner's manual? What does it say about single-engine operation?" I asked.

"Reggie, we are only about thirty minutes from beginning our normal descent into Dubai…Let's just begin a slow descent now," Ash said.

"Good thinking, my friend," I replied and pulled back on the left engine to match the right power/thrust lever. "How's the temperature look?"

"Still high but not climbing," Ash added.

"Watch it," I said stupidly. Our eyes were going to be watching that gauge from now until the engine was shut off and the turbine was spooling down.

I contacted Dubai approach and informed them of our deviation from the published…and allowed…approach plan. We were approaching Dubai from the east. Only the country of Oman would be a problem if we deviated from the published approach vectors. Dubai approach acknowledged and agreed to contact Oman to inform them of our change.

We continued our approach and then suddenly there were two F-16 fighters on each side of us. When I got over my shock, I turned to Ash, "What the hell?"

"Must be a slow day in Oman's armed forces," Ash retorted. "I'll call approach and see what's up."

The F-16 on my left had corrected his course to fly alongside of us and, as I watched, saluted me. He then pointed his finger down to indicate that we descend. I told Ash, who was busy on the radio.

"Dubai approach…Avanti 121 India Romeo…the Royal Oman Air Force is wanting us to land…now!" Ash said into the microphone.

"Avanti 121 India Romeo…Dubai approach…we're talking to Oman now…hold steady."

"You mean to continue our descent?"

"Negative…hold altitude!"

"Dubai approach…we have a hot engine…"

"Hold altitude!"

I inched both throttles forward. The right engine temperature gauge began to immediately climb. Ash saw the same thing that I observed.

"Dubai ap…"

"Hold!"

"What is up with these idiots?" I announced, feeling like I was preaching to the choir.

"Don't know, Reggie…but that…" Ash pointed to the middle glass panel. "…Is almost in the red!"

"I know, dammit! I'm pulling back," I said as I pulled the throttles toward me. We returned to our descent.

"Dubai approach…"

Just then the two F-16's pulled up and out to assume firing positions behind us.

"Dubai approach…the two fighters are getting ready to fire on us!" Ash yelled into the microphone. "What are you guys doing?"

"Avanti 121 India Romeo…Dubai approach…do you have an emergency?"

"Wha…" Oh, Reggie, I get it! "Dubai approach…Avanti 121 India Romeo declaring an emergency!"

"Avanti 121 IR…Dubai approach…descend and maintain flight level 10…expect to intersect the ILS runway 12 left at frequency 110.10. Clear to land…contact tower on 118.75."

I began to object.

"Reggie, I read about this!" Ash began. "These Middle East countries will shoot your ass out of the sky it you deviate from your published flight plan unless you 'declare' an emergency!"

"So, what about those two assholes that were about to give us new assholes?"

"They're gone…all gone…they have gone home," Ash replied and breathed a sigh of relief.

"Man-O-man!" I exclaimed. "That sucked!"

We crossed the localizer beacon and the autopilot turned us onto final and followed the ILS approach into Dubai International Airport. At five hundred feet above ground I clicked off the autopilot and landed

Aurora. My hands were noticeably shaking. After a short runout, I taxied to the I.N.C.I.S.O.R. hangar which still housed Aurora I.

Just as we were finishing with the A&P mechanic, Michael pulled onto the apron in my 750IL.

"Hey Michael! You look good in that car," I yelled.

"You kidding? Too old for me," he retorted.

"Trouble getting laid in that?" Ash added.

"No…no trouble at all! Michael replied and we had a group hug.

Damascus, Syria

The Russian FSB agreed to meet with the Iraqi terror cells one more time. The terrorists had a quasi-religious reason to attempt to bring down the United States of America which the FSB wished to play into and capitalize on. The problem was that these religious zealots were like rabid dogs…easily provoked into attacking anything that they felt was in their way.

These rabid terrorists had already killed two of the Russian FSB, hence the meeting in Syria. Russia had a military presence here that gave the FSB a sense of safety from being attacked as they were before.

Ivan began the presentation.

"America is behind the recent explosions! We have proof," and he signaled Vlad to turn on the projector.

Ivan pointed toward the image on the screen.

"This is a Russian satellite image of an American plane…a transport…flying directly over the area of destruction," he continued.

"An American plane flying over Baghdad!" Ivan went slowly to let his words and the image sink in to the terrorists crowding the room. He also knew that if he was not careful; he and Vlad might end up the same way as their two comrades who tried before.

There was grumbling from the floor, but the reaction was opposite from what Vlad and Ivan expected.

"So, what!"

"How does an American transport cause damage like that?"

"No bombs were dropped!"

"No missiles launched!"

The mood was turning foul as the tension mounted and the shouting began.

"Please, please!" Ivan pleaded and he signaled with his arms to calm down…to no avail.

"There are American transports flying in and out of our airport all the time!" another shouted.

"Yeah…so what!"

Vlad put up a second slide on the screen.

"This is the same American plane overhead when the four-square block area was damaged," Ivan continued.

"How do you know it is the same plane?"

"The Americans have lots of transports here!"

"Yes! I know this plane…a C-130! A lot of those here in Baghdad!"

The shouting continued and the tension rose.

"You have no proof!"

"You treat us like fools!"

Ivan was perspiring profusely. Vlad threw up the next image.

"Here is your proof!" Ivan yelled above the crowd noise.

The two images had been merged into one showing the same aircraft identifying markings.

"It is the same plane!"

Ivan paused and let the news sink in. The mob became quieter.

"How did they do this?"

"It was only buildings where ammunition was stored!"

"How is this possible?"

"I can tell you with authority that the aircraft beamed a signal…an emission down to the surface that caused the stores of munitions to ignite," Ivan offered.

"The signal came from the plane?" one of the terrorists asked.

"No!" Ivan countered. "The signal came from somewhere else. The plane just reflected it…like a magnifying glass reflects and intensifies the sun." Ivan's mind wandered to all of the ants that he had fried and small fires he had started as a child with his magnifying glass.

Vlad then ran through a series of photographs that had been taken inside the hangar in Saudi Arabia.

"This is the inside of the plane," Ivan continued. "And this is a parabolic mirror!"

For the first time in what seemed like hours to the two Russians there was silence in the room. The men pushed forward from their chairs to try to get a better view of the screen and the photographs that were displayed.

"Where is this plane now?" one of the terrorists asked. "Is it still in Saudi? We can take it out! We will destroy it!" The grumbling began again.

Ivan thought to himself, "That's all you idiots are good for…destroying things."

"We have tracked the aircraft to the United States. It currently is hangered at Dover Air Base in Delaware, Maryland," Ivan announced and began to relax. They were buying the story! He and Vlad just might live…

Dubai, UAE

Michael drove Ash and me to the I.N.C.I.S.O.R. house on Palm Jumeirah. We took some time to settle into bedrooms and then joined Michael on the patio. I let Michael prepare cocktails and I took the time to call Becky in Florence. An unsettled calm had come over the I.N.C.I.S.O.R. world. All was quiet in Italy. I told Becky that I missed her and would see her in two days.

Michael brought the drinks and mine was prepared exactly right. The hint of lemon on the rim of the glass made my tongue tingle. As we sipped our drinks and looked out onto the water from the back porch, Michael filled Ash and me in on his research into our Italian politician. Ash was extremely attentive, and I could see the wheels in his mind turning as he planned a strategy to deal with this man, his lack of concern about his significant other and our loss of Stirling.

I chose to wait until we were on the final leg of our flight to query Ash and try to understand what his thoughts were about this guy.

As Michael was telling us about his exploration into Silvio Berlusconi's life, the phone rang. The A & P mechanic was checking in from the Dubai International Airport.

I listened on the phone as the mechanic described a bleed air leak that caused insufficient airflow through the compressor to the right turbine. The was the cause of the temperature gauge to indicate a dangerous temperature level in the right engine.

He explained that the turbine had not experienced any damaging detonation and that he was able to correct the bleed air leak with a simple tweak. Aurora II was good to go! I told him that was great news, thanked him and hung up the phone.

"Aurora is all fixed!" I announced to Ash.

"What was it that almost cost us our lives?" he asked.

"Bleed air problem," I glanced at Michael's quizzical look. "I'll explain in the air."

"Got it, so no delay to our itinerary?" Ash asked.

"Nope! We're good to go either tomorrow or the next day," I answered.

"So, Michael…you lonely here?" I asked.

"No, I love it here," Michael replied.

"What about companionship?" Ash interjected.

"Have you seen the Russian women here? Whew!" Michael retorted.

"Don't you have to pay for those women?" I asked.

"Not all of them," Michael said.

"And what about the clinic?" Ash questioned.

"Running like clockwork. They are expecting you tomorrow for a visit."

"Thanks for setting that up," I replied.

"I'm still thirsty!" Ash exclaimed as he rose to gather our glasses for a second round. "And, what about dinner?"

Washington, DC

President Marron was studying a brief that had given him to prepare for an upcoming international summit. The intercom buzzed and his secretary announced that the Director of the CIA wished a moment of his time.

POTUS looked up from the pages in front of him as the door to the Oval Office opened.

"You know, Director, that your news is almost always bad?" President Marron began the conversation.

"Yes, sir…I apologize. Today the news is mixed," the Director replied.

"Bad news first," the President said.

"It looks like the Russians have photographs of the plane."

"Well, we couldn't keep it secret forever. What, did one of their satellites pick it up?"

"Well, yes sir…but they also have pictures of the plane…in the hangar…in Saudi Arabia…and shots of the inside!"

"What the hell? How'd they do that? The Saudis have some piss poor security!"

"You got it, Mr. President."

"And the good news?" the President asked.

"The three tests are complete over the US. Radio Free World has performed well, and we are done with the testing. Still have many reports to sift through and analyze, but it is my opinion that we have added a new and tried weapon to combat terrorism at its source."

"Well, what about the United States?"

"Fewer detonations than we expected. It is our belief that the home-grown anti-government groups that we were targeting are not as well armed as we were prepared for."

"So, Mr. Director, what is our next move?" President Marron asked.

"We finish analysis and prepare a plan to implement this device into our armamentarium. This definitely goes into the 'win' column!"

"Good and thank you, Director," the President said as he donned his readers to continue delving into the pages in front of him.

The Director took his cue and departed the Oval Office.

Langley, VA

"This group has been formed to create a plan to implement RFW. The test phase is complete. We are to suggest a platform to use this weapon. Now that Research and Development of Radio Free World is complete, we are to discover other means to make the system useful. In other words, can RFW do anything else besides excite and explode C-4 explosives? What happens when the beam is directed at…for instance…a satellite? We know that the testing satellites became unstable in the initial tests and were not good reflecting platforms. That is how they chose an aircraft as the reflecting platform of choice. Can we permanently disable them? Do we want to? What happens when the world figures out what we have? And on and on and on. Get it?"

Florence, Italy

Ash was in the pilot's seat for the final leg from Ankara, Turkey to Florence. The pilot in command sits in the left seat, while the first officer, or co-pilot, sits in the right seat. When I researched why airplane pilots fly in the left seat and helicopter pilots fly in the right seat, which flies in the face of conventional wisdom, the main thing I could find was that the torque from airplane engines spinning to the right made the aircraft want to veer left. Therefore, most landing patterns have left-hand turns to accommodate pilots compensating for their engines. The opposite is true for helicopter pilots whose engines mounted over their heads provide torque in the opposite direction.

I was working the radios and had been handed off from Florence approach to Florence tower on 125.10. We were cleared to enter a right-hand base leg for runway 05. Ash flew a beautiful approach and turned to final splitting the VASI lights. Touchdown was uneventful, except that the right engine temperature was starting to read hot, again, and power had been reduced during the letdown and approach into Amerigo Vespucci Airport, Florence. The reduced power should have allowed both engines to begin lowering their internal temperatures…there must be more wrong with the right engine than just the bleed air system.

"Hey, Ash," I suggested. "Aurora was manufactured in this country. Let's fly to the Piaggio facilities and get her checked out!"

"Where are they?" Ash asked.

"Not exactly sure, but somewhere around Genoa," I replied.

"And that is…?" Ash continued.

"A hundred and fifty miles west, northwest of here," I said.

"That's a quick up and down," Ash concluded.

"Yes, but the Piaggio facility is fifty miles further southwest of Genoa at the Villanova d'Albenga Airport," I added.

"Why didn't you say that before?" Ash scolded. "Still an up and down for us. Especially flying across the Mediterranean sea. Haven't they renamed that airport? I read something about that. Yeah, it is now called the Riviera Airport!"

"When did that happen?" I asked.

"No idea, but it's a sexier name!" Ash countered.

"You got me there! Let's put her away," I finished, and I climbed out of my seat to get the cabin door open. As I opened the door, I saw Becky waiting for us on the tarmac.

Once we had finished with Paramount Business Jets, the FBO operator at the Amerigo Vespucci Airport we grabbed our bags and headed to her car. Becky had purchased the car without consulting me and had gotten just what I would have wanted for our estate in Tuscany. When you think about Italian cars, Ferrari and Lamborghini come to mind as sexy and fast. Then you think of Fiat and Alfa Romeo as cars that are too small for our needs. That leaves the Maserati as my Italian car of choice and exactly what Becky was driving!

Ash and I loaded our luggage into the back end of her Maserati Levante Trofeo. I claimed 'shotgun' and climbed into the front passenger seat. Ash squeezed into the back seat. Luckily, he was smaller than me because the Italians do not believe in lots of legroom for the back seat passengers.

"Hello, beautiful!" I exclaimed and reached over to kiss Becky. I rested my hand on her thigh for support and it felt good to touch her again.

The drive to the estate took about an hour with the traffic. We were in no hurry and the countryside was beautiful. Ash and I talked about our journey and Becky brought us up to speed on the progress at the estate. There had not been any major developments with I.N.C.I.S.O.R. during our adventure from Saipan to Florence.

As we pulled up to the ancient farmhouse, it looked to me like there were construction crews everywhere with scaffolding, piles of new material, piles of used brick and rubbish, concrete trucks and pumper trucks, and pickup trucks of all sizes and models spread around the front of the house.

"What the hell!" I exclaimed.

"You did know we were coming?" Ash asked Becky.

Becky ignored our comments and said, "Let me show you around!"

She acted like all of the workers were not even there. Becky walked us around to the side of the house so that we could see the building that housed the olive press and bottling facility.

We watched as huge bins of olives were weighed and dumped onto a shaker to begin the process of removing twigs and debris. A conveyor moved the olives up a story and then it entered the building.

Becky showed the way as Ash, and I followed her inside. The smells were earthy and intense. We saw where the conveyor belt entered and watched the olives fall into a water bath. The whole water bath vibrated and there were large agitators to keep the water and olives circulating as the dirt and debris was removed.

The olives moved into the cold press where three large stone wheels mashed the olives and remaining leaves into a paste that was transported into the separating room by giant augurs. Water was separated from the oil and then the cloudy oil passed through filters to become the oil that appears in kitchens all over the world.

The canning room, I could see, was a term left over from previous efforts. Now, the filtered oil was dripped into plastic bottles of assorted sizes. The storage room next door contained pallets full of boxes.

"Do we sell this stuff, Becky?" I asked.

"No, Reggie, we contract with a broker who sells about ninety percent of the olive oil production. I am told that our oil is some of the best in the region," Becky smiled as she answered.

"And the other ten percent?" Ash asked.

"In here!"

Becky led us into a small, dark room and turned on a wall light. The room had shelf after shelf of earthen jugs lining the walls. A small table was in the center of the room with two rickety-looking chairs on either side.

"We keep the best from each press in here," she said and showed off the room with both arms raised.

"That's a lot of oil!" I exclaimed.

I moved to the table. There was a plate with Italian bread slices and a small carafe of oil and another of balsamic vinegar. I sat down, grabbed a plate, and picked up a piece of the bread. I poured some olive oil onto the plate and then poured a small amount of balsamic vinegar into the oil. I dipped the bread into the oil and vinegar mixture and tasted it. The taste was superb! I had never tasted olive oil like this!

"Wow!" I shouted.

Ash moved in to try a piece of bread for himself.

"Ditto! This is out of this world!" Ash announced.

Becky then moved next to us.

"This is Italian butter…the best Italian butter," she said.

"No argument here!" I said and moved to get another piece of bread.

"No, Reggie, bad boy! You'll ruin your dinner," Becky scolded.

"This isn't dinner?" Ash countered.

"No, Sir Black, now get up…there's more to see," Becky ordered.

Vladivostok, Russia

"The emissions came from the Western Pacific, comrade," an analyst schooled Ivan.

"Thanks for narrowing that down for us," Ivan replied sarcastically.

"Let's see," Vlad added. "I just Googled it. You have limited our search to, let me read from here…Australia, Brunei, Cambodia, China, Cook Islands, Fiji, Japan, Kiribati, Laos, Malaysia, Marshall Islands, Micronesia, Mongolia, Nauru, New Zealand, Niue, Palau, Papua New Guinea, Philippines, Republic of Korea, Samoa, Singapore, Solomon Islands, Tonga, Tuvalu, Vanuatu, and Vietnam!"

"Comrade please," the analyst begged. "Let me finish!"

"We have kind of triangulated the signal by recreating the time of the explosions and placing the aircraft over those sites at the identical time…that the signal came from the Mariana Islands!"

CHAPTER 23

Langley, VA

"Mr. Director, sir…ah…thank you for seeing me," a CIA analyst stuttered.

"Come on, man…get on with it! I don't have all day," the Director replied, perturbed.

"We have some intel from Russia," the analyst attempted to continue.

"I would hope so!" was the Director's response.

"I am sorry, sir…this is about Radio Free World," the analyst added.

The Director of the CIA now sat at attention at his desk as the analyst fidgeted in front of him.

"The Russians believe that they have isolated the emissions that caused all of the destruction in the Middle East…mainly Baghdad…"

"I know…I know!" the Director chided.

"The signal is from the Mariana Islands!" the analyst blurted.

"What!" the Director stood up fast, causing his chair to hit the credenza behind the desk.

"I'm sorry sir," the analyst apologized. As if the news was his fault.

"How do they know that?"

"A simple re-creation of the events and times."

"Okay, get out!" the Director rudely ordered.

He sat back at his desk and pondered the news for a few moments.

"Get me Reggie Nelson or Ash Black," he ordered into the intercom on his desk.

Florence, Italy

As Becky led us to the winery behind the main house, a man sauntered up to our group.

"Gene Ramos," he announced and shoved out his hand.

"This is our head vintner," Becky introduced Juan to Ash and me.

"Oh, so you grow the grapes?" Ash asked.

"No, I work on all of the areas of wine making…" Gene began.

"The grape growers are called Vignerons!" I interrupted.

"You are right, Reggie…can I finish?" Gene was not happy that I interrupted him.

"Go right ahead," I waved my arm and bowed. Inside I was thinking that I owned this damn place…and I did not like him very much.

What do they say about first impressions? How long does it take? Seven seconds? I probably wasn't making his list of favorite people, either.

"I oversee every aspect of the wine making from the harvest to the bottle," Gene continued.

"You look Mexican," I observed.

"Si, senor," he replied.

"I grew up in the Napa Valley. My parents were migrant farm workers. My family picked the grapes at harvest. I then got my degree in viticulture from UC Davis and returned to the Napa Valley to work," Gene added.

"What brought you to Italy?" Ash asked.

"I retired and my wife always wanted to see Italy…so we moved here," Gene said.

"And you're working?" I asked.

"Retirement sucks! I was just eating and drinking and getting fat. This keeps me busy, and I feel alive, again," Gene replied.

Becky asked him to show us the operation.

Gene started with the end of the operation…the finished product… the vast underground cellar where the oak barrels were stored. He picked up what looked like a giant pipette and plunged it into one of the barrels. Gene then poured two small glasses for Ash and me to taste.

"This wine has been aging for ten years. I think it is ready," he announced.

I looked at the translucent reddish liquid and swirled the glass. I then smelled the glass, wishing that I had some sense of smell left after too many years of smelling nasty mouths. Then I tasted the liquid, letting it sit on my tongue for a moment before swallowing.

"Chianti?" I asked, noting the smooth and complex taste as I took another sip. I was liking this guy more with every sip.

Ash was performing his own introduction of the wine to his nose and mouth.

"Very good! Very smooth," he commented.

"Yes, Reginald, this is one of our better Chiantis and we will bottle this under our own label," Gene replied.

We have our own label…how cool, I thought.

The rest of the tour involved many stainless-steel vats and tubs where the grapes were processed into wine and any additions to the wine were added under Gene's guidance.

"Good crop this year. Should be a good vintage," Gene announced at the end of the tour.

The three of us left Gene and moved to the rear entrance to the villa. The inside still looked like it was part of a house that was hundreds of years old, but I knew that the house had the latest in technology of all kinds. Even the wiring within the walls had been changed out to fiber optic cable that ran outside to the mini-satellite farm by the winery.

Becky showed us the kitchen first which had been outfitted with a stainless-steel kitchen array, including a gas Viking stove, Sub Zero refrigerator and freezer and a commercial cappuccino coffee maker. I could envision some culinary creations from this room.

There was a new door off the kitchen that led to an underground level that had been excavated under the house. The engineers supported the existing house and then dug out underneath it to create the lower level.

This space housed the new nerve center for I.N.C.I.S.O.R. When the room was equipped, we would shut down operations in Dubai. This was Becky's wish. She hated that Emirate after my kidnapping ordeal.

"I'm impressed!" Ash commented.

"Yes, this is nice…excellent work, Becky," I added.

"Thank you, thank you," and she took a bow.

"Let's get some wine out on the back patio," Becky suggested, and she led the way to a cozy area behind the house.

Three bottles from different years spanning the last two decades were already sitting on the table, along with some bread, olive oil, balsamic vinegar, fruit bowl and an antipasto tray. A veritable feast!

Gene was there to serve and explain the wine to us.

"You must begin to understand the subtleties produced by the different years. Changes in the amount of sunlight, changes in the amount of rainfall, etc. affect the same plant and their grapes each year. The good years are represented here. I will explain them to you," Gene began.

"I would also like to taste an off year," I said. Especially if my palate is going into training!"

Ash smirked but got his glass ready for a taste.

After an evening of catching up and storytelling, I wanted to retire with Becky. Ash suggested that he was going to visit an Italian politician tomorrow, and could he borrow a car. The way he phrased his upcoming visit did not pique any interest from Becky. I knew what he was headed to do…

Denver, CO

Powers Hunt had assumed a leadership role with the Denver I.N.C.I.S.O.R. team. The other members seemed to be okay with his willingness to take on more responsibility…a role that they had left to Lance Wood who was one of the founders…the original three team members…and their boss!

A vacuum always wants and needs to be filled, and now it was.

"I have been looking over Lance Wood's records of the interviews that he had to find us five here, and the four in Frankfurt plus Michael in Dubai. I didn't know that there was such a large pool to pick from. Lance had done an excellent job picking us…" there were chuckles around the room, "and I don't have the skill or experience at interviewing and screening that he had," Powers began.

"What if we had a committee?" Lance Everett asked.

"I was almost thinking that…but…a committee of, let's say three, when there are only five of us seems crazy to me," Powers continued.

"Then we're all in to help!" Flex added.

"One for all…" Duncan Trevino began.

"And all for one!" Kurt Nichols finished.

"It looks like Lance Wood had a short list of ten names to pick from. Can we assume that this is a good list to work from?" Powers asked.

"Let's do that," Duncan said.

"Two a day for five days…we'll have this done in a week!" Lance added.

"Give us the list…we'll get to calling," Kurt suggested.

Baghdad, Iraq

The leaders of the various terror organizations that chose Baghdad as their home came together for a meeting about the information they had been given in Syria.

"So, you believe the Russians?" Achmed asked the room.

After much grumbling among the players, "Yes! Yes, we do."

"Russia is on our side with these incidents," another terror leader spoke.

"Do not be fooled friend," Achmed added. "Russia does not care about us! Russia cares only about Russia, and their foreign policy is based on lies, misdirection and denial. They look at us as their lackeys in this fight against America."

"But it is our fight against the Infidel!" another shouted.

"Yes! But remember that Russia will help us to bring down the United States only as long as our war fits with their plans for world domination," Achmed countered. "We cannot trust them…but we can use them!"

"How do we verify that the information they gave us in Syria is accurate?" another terrorist leader asked.

"We cannot…our cells do not have the ability to check on the validity of Russian claims…we must take the intel on face value…how would it serve the Russians to lie to us?" Achmed added.

"So, we believe them at this point…but do not trust them!" a leader shouted.

"For now, yes. That must be our position. There has been no other explanation offered as to why our ammunition stores blew up! I mean nothing!" Achmed said.

"Our only information…however implausible…is still our only information," another added.

"This news does not make me feel comfortable. I would rather hear from an ally of the United States than a foe," a leader added.

"So…what are we to do?"

"I have a contact in the French embassy in Dubai. We all know how the French hate the Americans, right?" Achmed announced.

The grumbling in the crowded room grew in volume.

"The only use the French have for America is to save them from their wars!"

Shouting and laughter filled the room. The world seemed to know that the only need France had for the United States was to sacrifice their young men to right their wrongs. Between wars and conflicts France had no use for America.

"I will go to Dubai and see this man. I will find out what France knows about our destroyed buildings and dead Iraqi citizens. If France knows about this…I will get them to leak the information to me," Achmed said and concluded the meeting.

There was nothing more for these men to do until more information was available. They were forced to hide in anticipation of another strike against them. No further attacks against the West were being implemented, or for that matter, even planned. The terrorists had their first sense of being impotent. They had no idea how to respond…and who to respond against.

More information was vital!

Lake Como, Italy

There were flashing police lights and cars parked everywhere at the boat dock. Most of the vehicles belonged to the police, but there were two ambulances and the coroner's van parked, waiting to carry off what the police boat carried as it neared the dock.

Once the ropes were tied off and the boat was secured to the dock, several uniformed men jumped on board. As a group they lifted the body that had been found tangled in fishing line and detritus from the lake up, and off the boat and onto the awaiting gurney. The color of the face alone was enough to show the ambulance teams that they would not be needed on this day at this scene.

The medical examiner moved in to do a visual examination of the corpse and obtain a liver temperature to begin to establish the time of death. Cameras were clicking as official police photographers and some free lance photographers shot picture after picture of the scene and the body. Press vehicles were pulling up and reporters were pushing their way into the crowd like unwanted pests at a picnic.

A plastic body bag was produced, and the body was placed inside the coroner's van. An autopsy would be performed to attempt to determine the cause of death, but many at the scene recognized the disfigured face as that of the famous man that had served for so long in Italian politics and had so many stories of troubled times while he served.

Florence, Italy

I was enjoying a cappuccino in the kitchen and Becky was enjoying a cup of herbal tea when Ash came into the room to join us.

"We have one less 'mini' account," he announced.

Becky and I looked at each other and then at Ash. Becky nodded that she understood, but I wanted to speak, "The papers have the death of Silvio Berlusconi plastered all over the front pages. Is that the account you speak of Ash?"

"Yep! He won't be making any more yearly payments to I.N.C.I.S.O.R." Ash added.

"And…you were able to discover what you were after?" I asked.

"Yep, Stirling's death has been avenged. Ain't retribution a bitch!" Ash said.

"I guess…I just hope his hands were dirty," I replied.

Ash bit into an apple he picked up off of the kitchen counter. "Filthy!" was all he said and took another bite.

"Onto another subject, you two," Becky began. "Langley called. The Russians know that the Radio Free World emissions came from somewhere in the Northern Mariana Islands. I'm sure their first impression will be that the signal came from Guam…but it won't take them long to discover the radar on Saipan. You two need to get back to Saipan and wrap things up!"

"How did they…?" Ash began.

I was thinking the same thoughts as my best friend. I always assume that Russian technology is way behind the United States, but then they do things like place a man in space before us and work on the development of hypersonic aircraft and missiles.

Becky cut Ash off mid-sentence. "Ash! They know! That's all that really matters. You are done in Saipan. Get back there and finish up! Put this project to bed."

Ash stared at Becky for a long moment. There were few people on this planet that talked to him that way. At least living people. But he loved Becky and understood that she was protecting him. She had Ash and my best interests in her heart.

"Do we leave Aurora here?" I asked in Becky's direction.

"And not have a plane at our disposal while we finish up in Saipan?" Ash countered.

"Listen guys," Becky continued. "The CIA is pulling Billy Bean and Joe Cavanaugh out now. They have been ordered to pack up the gear and prepare for a transport from Guam to arrive tomorrow."

"Then I want the plane with us," I said.

"Sold!" Ash added.

"We'll leave in the morning and fly the same route back to Saipan. We'll just leave off the sight-seeing and connection time. We should be able to make it in a day," I surmised.

"And…what kind of shape is Aurora II in? Did you fly to Piaggio while I was visiting the dead Italian politician?" Ash asked.

"Yes, Ash," Becky spoke. "I flew in the right seat! And then we drove to Monaco and had a wonderful night at the casino."

"How was that drive?" Ash wondered.

"Easy! About sixty miles. We took a leisurely drive, and it was an hour and a half. Did you know that thirty percent of Monaco's population are millionaires?" I questioned.

"I did not," Ash replied. "But I did know that it is the second smallest municipality in the world. Only the Vatican is smaller…And I have heard that real estate there is ridiculously expensive!"

"And no taxes! Explains why the wealthy are there," Becky said.

"Back to Aurora II…Piaggio Aero gave her a really thorough going ever, from head to toe. The right engine problem has been addressed and corrections were made. She did fine getting back to Florence but it's a pretty short flight. We'll just have to watch it going to Saipan and make sure that the problem, whatever is was, is resolved," I opined.

"So…we're out of here in the morning, Reggie?"

"I guess so,"

"What time do we leave?"

"How about takeoff at 0600."

"So, I have to stop drinking this wonderful wine at ten tonight?"

"That's what the regs say…how about no more alcohol after six tonight?"

"Okay, Reggie, okay. Where is that Chianti?"

"It is all Chia…" Becky began to correct Ash, but then paused. "Wine for breakfast? Yuk!"

Ash chuckled that he had been able to pull Becky's leg.

"Can we just spend time together here today? I don't feel like any more sight-seeing," Ash announced.

"Fine with me!" I agreed.

Washington, DC

"So, the Russians are on to us," President Marron stated.

"Well…" the National Security Advisor began.

"And we have intel that the terror cells in Baghdad know," the CIA Director interrupted.

"I was going to say…" the Security Advisor tried to continue.

"Our two CIA technicians in Saipan have already been pulled out of Saipan. Dr. Nelson and Ash Black are on their way back to Saipan to finish with their business there and close up shop," the CIA Director continued.

"And…" the Advisor attempted.

"What is your suggestion for what to do next?" President Marron asked.

"The…" the Advisor tried.

"There were three ROTHR facilities established in the late eighties during the peak of the Cold War. These were radars that were built in the sixties. The radar in Saipan was originally mounted on a World

War II ship that was decommissioned. The radar was hauled up to the mountain now referred to as Radar Hill. The facility was completed in 1989 and only used until the early nineties when the Cold War ended with the Soviet Union," the CIA Director instructed.

"Who was President then? Reagan? Bush?" POTUS asked.

"Both!" the National Security Advisor blurted out.

President Marron looked at the Advisor and waited for him to continue.

"Reagan was '81 to '89, then H.W. Bush from '89 to '93."

"So, the project began under Reagan and ended with Bush," the CIA Director continued. "ROTHR has been continued and used for drug interdiction in the Caribbean. In fact, we just negotiated a new contract with Raytheon to continue and maintain the ROTHR facilities in Puerto Rico, Virginia and Texas."

"I remember reading about that contract!" the President added. "There are six facilities…six of them each covering two and a half million square miles. That's a lot of space!"

"Yes, sir, and our plan is to relocate Radio Free World to an existing ROTHR facility and continue the project," the CIA Director answered.

"So, no more Saipan?" POTUS queried.

"Nope…" the Security Advisor tried to begin.

"We are done with our testing program there, Mr. President," the CIA Director interrupted.

"Well then we should get those two off of that island!" President Marron stated.

"Yes sir, Mr. President, I'm on it," the Director said and rose to leave.

"Hold on a minute," the President ordered.

The CIA Director resumed his seat.

"How do we know that the Russians know about RFW?"

"A 'PC' placed in a terrorist leader identified in Dubai who had a bad toothache," the Director began.

"So, another I.N.C.I.S.O.R. device?"

The Director cringed. "It is a CIA device. There have been several improvements to the listening devices over the years, but Dr. Nelson did come up with the idea. That's why the United States government is still working with his group."

"And they are all civilians?"

"They now have a number of ex-military types working for them now, but, yes, they are all civilians," the National Security Advisor finally got a full sentence in.

President Marron smiled at the Advisor. "Way to go, T.J.! You completed a sentence!"

"Anything else?"

"Not at this time, sir," the Director answered and rose again, expectantly.

"You can go," POTUS ordered.

CHAPTER 24

Langley, VA

"How are we doing with other uses for Radio Free World?" the CIA Director queried.

"We are studying what other materials are excitable by this same frequency," one of the analysts offered.

"We know that satellites in space are not sturdy enough to handle much in the way of transmission. That is an avenue...knock down satellites," another suggested.

"Good, but most of the stuff in space is Russia's and ours...and Russia knows that we have RFW," the Director countered. "I want uses that can remain unknown initially...keep this secret as long as we can."

"What about disrupting electronics?" an analyst asked.

"What do you mean?" the Director queried.

"Like aviation electronics...remember the movie, Die Hard 2? The terrorists were able to 'fool' a plane's avionics and made it crash while the captain and first officer thought they were right on the ILS approach," the first analyst said.

"Yeah! And in the late 80's I read that electromagnetic interference caused five crashes of Blackhawk helicopters by affecting their electronic flight controls. Very strong radar and radio transmitters were found to be the culprits. Isn't that exactly what we have? The best of both of these?" an analyst exclaimed.

"What are we hearing from Baghdad?" the Director asked, switching the subject.

"The Russians have told the Iraqi terror groups that the emissions that caused all the destruction in Baghdad and took out much of their ammunition stores came from somewhere in the Northern Mariana Islands," an analyst replied.

"How do the Rus…" the Director began and then stopped himself. "It does not matter! So, the Russians know and have told the terror cells that were affected. What do we do about this?"

"Keep listening and see what Russia will do to pinpoint the emissions… and inform Dr. Nelson and Ash Black to watch their backs!" the first analyst answered.

"Great stuff…keep at it!" the Director urged and concluded the meeting.

Saipan, Northern Mariana Islands

"Did you see all those prepositioned ships just outside the lagoon?" I wondered.

"How could you miss them! I counted eight prepositioned ships and the one war ship," Ash said.

"I read that there was a submarine spotted here with the tender ship while we were gone. I wonder if the sub is still here, also," I added.

"Do you know why they are all here?" Ash replied and reached for his phone to take some pictures.

"I bet some people are buying up extra stores of food and water…probably thinking that we're going to war or something," I continued as I lined up Aurora II for the approach for runway 07 into Francisco Ada Airport. "I heard from that local dentist…what's his name? Oh yeah, Dr. Cram, that between four and five prepositioned ships are here on Saipan pretty much all of the time," I paused my monologue to complete the pre-landing checklist with Ash. Once finished, I continued, "he told me that the only time he has felt nervous is when they all sail away…to deep water…to ride out bad storms and typhoons. The island residents get really nervous when the prepositioned ships sail away. He told me that he feels safer when the ships are here, although he knows they play no role in defense of the island. Gear down…three green."

We completed the flight and were now back in Saipan to conclude our stay in this tropical paradise. We drove north from the airport toward our rental home on the beach. As we drove along Beach Road Ash commented, "Reggie, look how different those ships look from here."

"No depth perception…they look like they are right on top of each other!" I exclaimed and continued, "Could you imagine the feeling that these locals and the Japanese for that sake, had when an armada of seven hundred ships showed up in 1944? Holy shit, batman!"

"Same idea, but what about the feeling those GI's had when they awakened one morning, and all the American ships were gone?" Ash said.

"That's right! The whole armada sailed off to meet the Japanese Navy steaming to rescue Saipan from our invasion. What did they call it? The Great Marianas Turkey Shoot!" I added.

"It was the Battle of the Philippine Sea, Reggie…no turkey shoot!"

"Okay, Okay, what's with all the correcting…you sound like Becky!"

"How about getting it right…occasionally!"

"Okay, Ash…The Battle of the Philippine Sea," I corrected.

"Pretty much did in Japanese naval aviation," Ash said.

"Yeah, could you imagine losing over six hundred planes in one single engagement?" I wondered.

"And we lost, what…eighty?" Ash asked.

"I looked it up while we were in Florence, that battle was the largest carrier battle in history. There were twenty-four carriers in the battle and over thirteen hundred aircraft!"

"That was the last carrier battle of that war in the Pacific. I can't imagine all those planes in the air at once. Had to be just…crazy!" Ash finished.

"And all that hardware at the bottom of the sea…" I wondered.

We finished the drive to the house in silence.

Denver, CO

The I.N.C.I.S.O.R. team gathered to complete the process of replacing Stirling Mason on the Frankfurt team. The short list of ten men had been whittled down to three outstanding candidates.

"How do we decide between these three?" Flex asked.

"I want all three!" Duncan exclaimed.

Powers listened and then suggested, "I have a clever way to break the impasse we seem to be facing. Let's send all three of them to Frankfurt and see if the team that they will be working with has a favorite!"

"Great idea," the others echoed, glad not to have to make the decision. "See what those four think."

Lance Everett made the call to Frankfurt, Germany and let the Frankfurt team know that the three finalists were being sent into their midst to see which one fit the best with the German team.

Frankfurt, Germany

Magnus Harper gathered the four remaining team members together after he hung up the phone after finishing the call from Denver.

"Three guys joining us tomorrow. The Denver team had narrowed the list of replacements for Stirling to three men. They matched up evenly and the Denver team couldn't make a choice," Magnus announced to the other three.

"If they couldn't decide, how are we?" Dick questioned.

"Aw, I bet we'll just know. Spend a little time with three different men and one will feel right," Aaron suggested.

Graham chimed in, "I hope you are right…richtig," practicing his German.

"Let's prepare for our guests," Magnus said.

Manilla, Philippines

"We're getting close! I can feel it," Romel shouted over the clanging of the jackhammer.

Manny was operating the tool and it was shaking him silly as he chipped away at the layer of concrete ahead of him. He and Romel had been working secretly in this hidden cave north of Manilla for several months now.

Romel had stumbled across the cave while he was hiking in the jungle. The cave was well hidden, and the average passerby would never have noticed the change in the jungle landscape that indicated the entrance to the cave. He returned to Manilla to get his good friend, Manny and show him his discovery.

"Do you think it could be Yamashita's treasure?" Manny asked when Romel showed him the cave opening.

"Wouldn't that be awesome?" Romel replied as his brain wandered into a world of make-believe thinking about wealth and fortune.

Tomoyuki Yamashita was a Japanese general known as The Tiger of Malaya. During World War II, war loot that was stolen by the Japanese from Southeast Asia was rumored to have been hidden in caves, tunnels, and underground complexes throughout the Philippines. Yamashita was the general who conquered Malaya in seventy days and wrested control of that land from the British.

Treasure hunters have been lured to the Philippines for over fifty years hunting for Yamashita's gold. In the late eighties a Filippino treasure hunter actually sued Ferdinand Marcos, claiming that Marcos' soldiers had stolen the gold and artifacts that he had found. The Hawaiian court found that the treasure did exist, and that Marcos had taken it.

The two men were careful to preserve the hidden entrance to the cave as they began their spelunking. Neither could afford a helmet equipped with a light so they got by with weak flashlights that cast weird shadows along the cave walls. Once Romel and Manny made it past the overgrown jungle at the entrance, the cave was well preserved with only an occasional spider web to contend with and brush away from the cave walls.

They had to crouch only slightly. The cave height allowed them to almost stand upright, and they could walk side by side as they descended deeper into the cave. About fifty feet from the cave entrance their excitement level shot through the roof! Man-made concrete! An area on the floor of the cave almost as wide as the cave opening was filled with a concrete slab! The slab was smooth compared to the rough and rocky floor of the cave. Somebody had sealed the floor of the cave for some reason! What would they find if they removed the concrete!

Manny and Romel had made plans to bring up a generator and tools to chip away at the concrete slab. They had decided not to use explosives because the noise would have given away their location. They also chose not to invite others to join them in their mission so that they could keep their motives as secret as possible.

The two men had no idea how thick the slab was as they chipped away at the concrete. There were no maps that they knew of describing the cave and whatever was hidden by the concrete. It had been three months since their discovery, and they had chipped away about two feet of concrete. They had to work slowly so that the people close to them in Manilla did not get suspicious.

Suddenly the jackhammer began to 'thud' against a piece of wood! Manny stopped immediately and called out to Romel who was checking on the generator. Romel turned the generator off and the two men checked the opening in silence. They both grabbed hammers and stone chisels and began to chip away the remaining concrete chunks off of the wooden support.

Once the concrete was cleared away, they began to explore around the edges of the wood. It looked like it was jammed into the sides off the cave floor. Romel and Manny could not tell what was hidden behind the wooden shield.

Romel started up the generator and Manny grabbed a hammer drill and a one-inch auger bit. He chose to drill into the wood in a triangle pattern out from the center. He began to drill, and the wood did not give way easily! That told him that the wood was very old…then he broke through with the first bore. Manny determined that the wood was about an inch thick by dropping his tape measure into the hole. He continued with the two other holes and finished just as Romel returned to the excavation site with three hooks attached to nylon rope.

Manny took the apparatus and affixed the hooks into the three holes. Romel then fetched a tripod with a pully system that he lined up over the opening. Manny attached the three ropes to a single rope dropping down from the pully. Romel pulled the rope taught and looked at Manny. They were both filled with anticipation! Was this the treasure from World War II?

Manny grinned at Romel, "ready?"

Romel tugged on the rope…nothing! He braced himself against the walls of the cave and pulled harder…nothing!

"Manny…come help!" Romel called out.

Manny joined him and they both put all of their strength and effort into pulling on the rope. As they pulled, at first there was no sound or movement. And then…as if sprung on them by surprise, the wooden plug came flying out of the opening and the slackness in the rope caused them both to tumble onto the cave floor.

Once they gathered themselves together and stood up, they headed to the opening with their hearts pounding both from the exertion and the anticipation. Both men had their flashlights on and trained toward the opening. Initially all they could see was dust caused by disturbing the wooden cover that had been in place for decades. As the dust cleared, Manny and Romel viewed a cavern that appeared to be about twenty feet by forty feet.

"It's an underground pickleball court!" Manny thought. He had just started playing the game in the Philippines. A pickleball court is twenty feet wide by forty-four feet long.

"Look at all those wooden crates!" Romel exclaimed.. Some of the wooden boxes were strewn about while other boxes of the same size were stacked in the corners of the cavern.

"Looks to me to be about two stories from here down to the floor," Manny judged.

"Okay," Romel suggested, "enough excitement for today. We need two rope ladders to descend down into the space and some better lighting. How are we going to get that stuff out of there?"

Manny thought and then said, "A better tripod and pully system and an electric winch."

Manny and Romel placed the wooden cover over the opening, policed the area where they had been working, and headed out of the cave. They decided who would pick up the different supplies and a time to meet back at the cave tomorrow. Both looked like smiling fools! Neither would sleep tonight as they anticipated their discovery.

Frankfurt, Germany

"Team Frankfurt! Meet the new guys," Magnus announced as he escorted the three men into the I.N.C.I.S.O.R. facility.

"Who do we have here?" Dick said as the seven men sized each other up.

"This is Dale Denby," Magnus said as he grabbed Dale's shoulder, "and this is Gary Grayneck," as he grabbed Gary's shoulder. Magnus moved to the third candidate and patted him on the head. "This is Dick Giles."

"And you hail from…actually, just take a minute and tell us about yourselves," Duncan suggested.

"Well, I'm Dale…you can call me Double D…" Dale began.

"We'll call you Dolly before we call you Double D!" Aaron interrupted.

"I grew up in Breckenridge, Colorado. Raced for Breckenridge through high school and then went East to Dartmouth to race for them. Couldn't handle the ice in New England so my racing days were over. I enlisted after my freshman year. College wasn't for me, but I loved the Army Rangers," Dale continued.

"So, jumping out of perfectly good planes was your idea of a fun time?" Graham asked, chuckling.

"Any combat?" Dick asked.

"Two tours in Iraq and one in Afghanistan," Dale replied.

"And you?" Dick turned to Gary.

"Spring Valley, New York was home," Gary began.

"Just outside New York City?" Aaron asked, "drove through there once."

"Yep, then off to Middlebury for college, and…"

"Vermont?" Magnus interrupted.

"Yes, sir," Gary tried to continue.

"Don't call me sir!" Magnus retorted, "I work for a living."

"I am also a Ranger. Enlisted in the Army after my sophomore year. I'm a pretty good shot. Had a lot of sniper training and experience in Afghanistan," Gary finished.

"And what is your story…Dick?"

"I'm from Tempe, Arizona. Went to ASU and then also joined the Rangers. Wanted to fight ISIS in Iraq."

"Well, welcome to Germany! What do you know about us?" Dick asked.

"Lance Wood interviewed all of us and told us that we get to continue fighting the good fight against terrorism in the world, but now we get paid better," Dale began.

"And we know that I.N.C.I.S.O.R. is made up of two five-man teams headquartered in Denver and Frankfurt. There were six founding members of the group, but only three remain. We have not met them," Gary added.

"And there's one more team member in Dubai…we can't forget about Michael!" Aaron opined.

"And we are here for a final test? You four are to pick between us. Is that right?" Dale asked.

"That's right, Dolly, and boy do we have a doozy of a test for you three!" Graham said.

Vladivostok, Russia

"We have a surveillance van that looks just like the ambulances on Saipan," Ivan began.

"But it does more?" Vlad asked.

"Yes, comrade, the roof of the van elevates and a dome similar to those used by the United States Air Force in their AWAKS planes…" Ivan attempted to continue.

"Those big domes housing radar?" Vlad interrupted.

"Yes, comrade," Ivan continued, "except this dome houses the most powerful receiver in the world! We will be able to check for the emission source and cover the whole island in less than a day."

"And we are just going to fly an Antonov into Saipan without raising any eyebrows?" Vlad questioned.

"No, comrade, the Antonov will have a whole belly full of similar transports to be given to the people of Saipan. Our country did this after the typhoon, Soudelor. The Antonov flew to Denver, Colorado…"

"In the United States?" Vlad interrupted again. His interruptions were beginning to annoy Ivan.

"Yes, comrade, the United States. Russia picked up many electrical trucks and crewmen in Colorado to work on all of the downed power lines after the typhoon and flew them to Saipan. The residents there are used to our big plane!"

"And we're giving them stuff, too?" Vlad asked.

"The stuff is a rouse, comrade, to hide the fact that we wish to discover where on the island those emissions came from," Ivan finished.

Langley, Virginia

"So, you assume that Russia has narrowed its search for Radio Free World to Saipan?" the Director asked.

"You know what assume is? Right?" the Director continued.

"An ASS of U and ME," he concluded.

"Well, yes sir. Their intel has focused on Saipan, and we know that they are flying an Antonov into Saipan, supposedly for humanitarian reasons which they say are tied to Covid," an analyst began.

"Covid!" the Director almost shouted. "Hell, Saipan is the safest place in America from that virus! Only twenty-nine deaths and two of those were the Filipino missionaries that brought the virus to that island! And that is out of a total of nine hundred and forty seven thousand total Covid deaths worldwide! Do Reggie and Ash know?"

"We're reaching out to them as we speak," another analyst said.

"They are the only ones there still, correct?" the Director asked.

"Yes, sir. Our two technicians are back at headquarters, nursing some nasty sunburns, and the gear is in Guam waiting for us to decide what to do next. The C-130 is still at Dover," the first analyst added.

"Good! Let's get those two out of there! I don't want them to run into the Russians," the Director finished.

Baghdad, Iraq

Achmed gathered the various terrorist leaders for a conference. There had been no calamities in Baghdad for over a week and the terror groups were beginning to relax.

"The Infidel…The Evil Satan…is behind the destruction! If we choose to believe the Russians, which I am choosing to believe," Achmed began.

"What do we do?"

"How do we strike back?"

Grumbling and shouting happened among the gathered men.

"The Russians are still pursuing leads and pinpointing the origin of the attack. Once we have these details, then we can formulate a plan to strike at the Infidel!" Achmed shouted over the grumbling.

"And here?" a terrorist leader asked.

"Russia says that we are safe now to resume our activities," Achmed announced.

The leaders were noticeably relieved and began to think of ways to move back into the civilian communities and hide among the innocent. Like roaches after a bug bomb had been set off. They will crawl back into their dark places to plot more evil.

Saipan, Northern Mariana Islands

"The CIA wants us out of here, pronto!" I said to Ash as I placed the phone on the table.

"You worried?" Ash asked.

"Not a bit! Well, 'The Russians are coming, the Russians are coming, everybody to get from street!' What movie was that from?" I put on my best Russian accent.

"It was from 'The Russians are Coming, The Russians are Coming,' Reggie. The actual line that the Russians practiced was, 'Emergency, everybody to get from Street,'" Ash corrected.

"You remember that? From the sixties, right?" I asked.

"Yep, so what do we do?" Ash questioned.

"I'm not quite ready to go yet. I want to get with those two guys who have been here forever…what were their names…Nicky Bells and Jeff Beach!"

"Oh, and what about those two?" Ash asked.

"I think there's a lot more to this place than a quaint little third world island that America thinks is important enough to pour millions of federal tax dollars into every year," I answered.

"What about the strategic value? I think that there is something to that," Ash opined.

"I just want to hear more from those two. Thirty years here must account for something!" I replied.

"Yeah, okay. What's the hurry anyway? To hell with what Langley says. I'd like to get in some more pickleball, also," Ash said.

"You know what? I just read that Saipan has been accepted into the International Pickleball Federation as its sixty-seventh country. Did you know that a sport needs to be played competitively in seventy-five countries to be considered for the Olympics?" I added.

"I did not know that Sir Reginald! So, pickleball should be there in another four years," Ash said.

CHAPTER 25

Manilla, Philippines

Manny and Romel descended down the two rope ladders into the cavern below. They looked around at the wooden boxes and wondered which one to open first. Manny shone his flashlight on a nearby box. Romel moved to the illuminated box and worked a chisel under the lid. He pulled out a hammer and drove the chisel to loosen the lid. He pried up the lid and peered inside.

Manny aimed the flashlight to light up the inside of the box…a glorious, golden tint lit up the box. Romel reached for one of the bars. It was quite heavy as he pulled it free from the other bars inhabiting the box. He held it toward Manny, "Gold!" he whispered.

Manny and Romel's teeth reflected the golden light as both men had huge smiles on their faces. Upon close examination, both men had teeth missing which showed with big smiles. Manny took the gold bar from Romel and Romel pried a lid off of another box. The second box was also filled with gold bars. Romel moved to a smaller box that was shaped differently than the first two. The opened box displayed golden jewelry…rings, necklaces, tooth crowns, and even tiaras.

Romel ran his fingers through the jewelry and pulled out his palms with necklaces and chains hanging from his fingers. Manny looked at Romel's hands and exclaimed, "we're rich!"

The two men examined a few more boxes and then reality began to sink in. How do they get the booty out of the cavern and out of the cave stealthily? Do they attempt to cash in their huge find in the Philippines? That's what happened with that treasure hunter in the eighties. Do they attempt to get the loot off island to a safer country? So many questions! Romel suggested to Manny that he call his friend in Saipan. He had several businesses in Saipan and had helped Romel find his way back to the Philippines.

Manny wasn't sure if this was a good idea, but every thought they had was wrought with flaws. Romel's friend was a stranger to Manny. It could be the two of them against him. He knew that this thought process was paranoid, but what choice did he have? This land boasted bandits, terrorists, crooked policemen and corrupt politicians. All of them would kill the two to get to the gold.

At least they had each other…for now.

The two did agree to take some of the jewelry to fence in Manilla for extra cash to purchase more equipment so they could begin the removal process. Extracting the gold from this cavern would be a slow and tedious process.

Saipan, Northern Mariana Islands

Igor answered the phone after a few rings. He looked at the screen on the cell phone and saw that it was Romel calling. The last that Igor knew, Romel was running an import business at the Manilla airport. Igor had invested in this business because he trusted Romel, but nothing had come of the investment because of the Covid scare and the business had virtually no clientele wishing to offset taxes and tariffs on goods coming into the Philippines. Igor had spent thousands keeping this business of Romel's afloat.

"Kumusta," Igor said into the mouthpiece. A Filipino 'hello' with a Russian accent was extremely difficult to understand, but Romel knew what Igor was attempting.

"Hello, my friend," Romel answered.

"Magandang araw," Igor replied as he thought that his command of Tagalog was quickly coming to an end.

"Yes, Igor, Good day to you also…er…dobryy den," Romel answered.

"Very good, my friend…you remember some Russian!" Igor exclaimed.

"Da, comrade," Romel added.

"What can I do for you?" Igor asked, expecting another request for money to fund what was beginning to feel like a lost cause.

"Do you still have a boat?" Romel asked.

"Yes, in fact I sold that little boat and bought a bigger boat. More space and a more powerful motor. Why?" Igor wondered.

Romel had argued with himself about how much to tell Igor once he decided that he would ask for his help. He and Manny had made the choice to use Igor's boat to get as much of the loot out of the Philippines. Now he needed to lead Igor on with as little information as possible. Enough to entice Igor and get him to commit the boat, but not enough to have their secret exposed.

"We need to get some supplies out of the Philippines without involving Customs," Romel offered.

"You want to use my boat to smuggle goods?" Igor deduced.

"Yes, my friend, and it may take as many as five round trips from Saipan to Manilla. And we have to load the boat here under the cover of darkness. How fast is your craft?" Romel asked.

"I can do ten to forty miles per hour…empty. How heavy is the cargo? It better not be people! I will not get involved with human trafficking!" Igor replied.

"No people, but the stuff is heavy…we will load the boat with every ounce it can carry, but there will be space on board. The craft will not be top-heavy," Romel said, and he thought about the weight of the boxes. Each gold bar weighed in at almost twenty-eight pounds, and there were ten bars in each box. The boxes weighed almost three-hundred pounds each! It was going to take a lot more trips than the five he had told Igor!

Romel and Manny had written an inventory of their discovery in the cavern of the hidden cave. There were two hundred boxes. The two had not taken the time to open and explore each box, but one hundred and eighty boxes were the same size as the one they had opened with the ten gold bars…and therefore were packed with the same prize, the two assumed. Twenty of the boxes were different and were filled with loose items and jewelry like the second box they had opened. The two made this assumption also without checking all of the twenty boxes.

They had also had some fun with a few calculations to get a handle on the amount the gold booty was worth. A four-hundred-ounce gold bar came with a current price tag of over $750,000 dollars! There were ten bars in each box and one hundred and eighty boxes, or so they assumed.

So, each box was worth over seven and a half million dollars today. All one hundred and eighty tallied in at over one billion dollars! And that did not count the jewelry boxes and their contents.

The two men would become wealthy beyond their wildest dreams. They would never have to work again. They also worked out a plan to share the wealth with the people they trusted to help them realize their dreams. The two men would keep seventy percent of the loot and allow thirty percent to be parceled out to those who helped them.

Each ten percent would have a value of one hundred thirty-five million dollars. Even that small percent would be life changing to almost everybody on the planet!

The first man that Manny and Romel approached was Igor.

"How much weight can your boat carry in one load?" Romel asked.

"About two thousand pounds," Igor answered, "Including the crew."

Romel was doing calculations in his head as Igor spoke. Ten boxes weighed in at three thousand pounds. At ten boxes, eighteen trips would be involved. Crazy! And if Igor was not willing to overtax his boat, then the number of trips increased to twenty-six trips. And that did not include the jewelry. So many variables with each trip. So many things to go wrong...

The conversation continued, "how many days to travel across the Philippine Sea to Manilla?" Romel asked.

"I bet I can make it in four days with mild weather and calm seas," Igor answered.

"My God!" Romel thought. Eight days for a round trip! And twenty-six trips total! More than a half year to remove the prize from these islands. Impossible! Romel expanded his thinking. He needed an armada of small craft to make the trip from the western shores of Saipan to the eastern shores of the Philippines. It was time to come clean with Igor. No more beating around the bush. Igor needed to know and enlist help from other boat owners and sailors from Saipan.

"Igor, I have not been completely honest with you," Romel said into his cell phone.

"I had a feeling that you were dancing around the truth," Igor replied. "You remember that I am in Rotary here in Saipan, and our number one rule is, 'is it the truth'!"

"Yes, I remember, and I apologize…" Romel hesitated. "Okay, here's the deal. A friend and I…did you ever meet Manny? We have discovered gold."

Romel paused to let this bombshell sink in.

Igor also was silent for a moment as he wracked his brain for a hidden memory.

"Yamashita!" Igor announced. "The Japanese general that supposedly hid gold and treasures from his Malaya campaign in the Philippines!"

"Yes, that is what we think we have found," Romel almost whispered into the phone. "We cannot have it verified here in the Philippines because we fear that our discovery will be taken from us…or worse, but there are Japanese markings on the gold bars."

"Now, was that so hard to come clean with me?" Igor asked.

"Yes, how much can I trust you?" Romel answered with a question. "Money can do awful things to a person!"

"Okay, tell me about your plan," Igor requested.

"We have lined up trucks to ferry the recovered boxes from the cave where we discovered the loot north of Manilla across to the east side of the island travelling on route 601. The trucks will arrive at the Infanta, Quezon Municipal Fish Port and the load will be offloaded at the Dinahican Boat Terminal there. We thought about one of the resorts, but the port is a better place with facilities to deal with the heavy loads we will have. Also, the port is going to be accustomed to boat traffic and hopefully not so many eyebrows will be raised. There is also a concrete pier that hopefully can sustain the weight of the loaded trucks. There is even a ferry that docks at this port."

Igor punched buttons on the laptop in front of him at his kitchen table. He was able to find the longitude and latitude of Romel's proposed location to punch into his GPS. That way he would have very little 'sailoring' to do as the boat would steer itself from Smiling Cove in Saipan to this place, Infanta, in the Philippines that he had never heard of. He then pulled up his calculator on the laptop.

"How many boxes?" Igor asked, already knowing the answer.

"Two hundred," was the reply.

"And each box weighs?" Igor continued his questioning.

"Just shy of three hundred pounds."

Igor did the math quickly in his head…ten boxes would put him overweight by half a ton! He also did the number calculation and murmured to himself, "this is too many trips to make."

"Romel…this is too much for me to accomplish alone!" Igor exclaimed.

"I was afraid that you would say that," Romel replied.

"Can I recruit some more boats?" Igor asked.

This is what Romel feared the most…having a whole bunch of people involved. It only took one person with a big mouth to have their whole scheme blow up. "Loose lips sink ships" took on a too real scenario for him.

"Do you have people you can trust?" Romel questioned.

"Let me see what I can round up," Igor said.

"Please keep this as quiet as you can…please!" Romel replied.

"Give me a week," Igor asked and hung up the phone.

Manilla, Philippines

Manny and Romel continued the task of bringing each of the boxes in the cavern to the improvised pully system. It took both men to heft one box and move it to the opening. The box was then secured to the pully and one of them climbed up the ladder to begin straining on the pully ropes. The other manned a rope to keep the box being lifted from shifting, as any movement affected their system.

They had been careful, so far, not to involve any others except a local jewelry dealer in Manilla who was known to fence jewelry that might have come from illicit sources. If the dealer's curiosity had been piqued when he compensated the two for their jewelry, he did not let on.

Romel told Manny about the conversation with his friend in Saipan. He told Manny about his fear that many others would have to become involved for them to have any chance of getting the bounty off of this island and to a country where they could live. It was important to both of them that they live through this ordeal. Dead millionaires was not the goal. And they both knew that they could not stay here in the Philippines with all of the corruption and dirty politicians.

They were averaging an hour to lift each box out of the cavern and onto the cave floor above. They worked late into the night to achieve their goal of ten boxes a day. Romel's friend was calling back in a week. Manny and Romel decided to push themselves and get all two hundred boxes moved before they got the call.

A week later they had worked themselves ragged. Their bodies were near exhaustion. The two men were filthy dirty and smelled of stale sweat. They had both asked for a week off from their regular jobs so that they could meet their goal to complete the extrication of each and every box from the cavern. They were down to the last two boxes when Romel's phone rang. Both men stopped stacking the boxes along the wall of the cave and collapsed against them.

"Hello, Igor!" Romel said after looking at the name on the screen.

"Hello, friend," Igor replied.

"Do you have news for me?" Romel asked.

"Do I have news! If you wish, I will leave Saipan tomorrow morning with twenty-four other boats," Igor suggested.

"Twenty-five boats?" Romel asked in awe. "How?"

"As I know you remember, Saipan has a rich fishing history. In fact, before America brought processed meat to the island, the villagers fished for their protein. I just went to one of their gatherings and asked for help. I also offered each of the boat owner/operators one million dollars to make the round trip with me and no questions asked," Igor continued.

"Do they know what they are hauling?" Romel asked.

"No...a million bucks is a fortune to these fellows."

"And they will wait to be paid until we have located a buyer?" Romel questioned.

"Yes, Romel, they are fishermen. They are used to waiting for their money. And they will not have to fish for money anymore!"

"How did you decide on one million each?" Romel asked.

"Easy…you offered me ten percent and I see that it is possible to have the ten percent worth one hundred and twenty-five…"

"One hundred and thirty-five million," Romel corrected.

"So, giving up twenty-four million leaves me over one hundred million dollars! I think I can get by with that amount…just barely though!" Igor laughed.

"When do you depart?" Romel wondered.

"I looked at the weather forecast and there is nothing brewing southeast of Saipan for the next ten days, so we will leave tomorrow. Also, better to leave sooner than later because, you know, 'loose lips sink ships.' See you in five days," Igor finished and disconnected the call.

Romel did some quick math in his head. As he understood it, Igor was going to stay within his ten percent and was not asking for a bigger cut. That would amount to one hundred and thirty-five million. Romel had promised the truck drivers one million Philippine pesos, which amounted to twenty thousand dollars per truck, and he had requested five trucks. One million pesos was a huge windfall to the men driving the trucks. He had planned on paying the truck drivers from some of the jewelry he could cash in. That left twenty percent, of two hundred and seventy million dollars to spend on a fence of crime syndicate to give him cash for the loot. Manny had told him that a seven percent fee is standard for dealing in stolen goods. Romel began to argue with Manny when he classified their find as stolen, but then he stopped. As soon as the gold were to depart the Philippines, then it would be stolen loot!

Manny and Romel had a nice cushion built into their plan for any contingencies that may arise that they had not prepared for. They would have at least one hundred million dollars to buy their way out of any problems that could pop up.

The trucks were to arrive at the cave in two days. Manny had taken care of recruiting the drivers. He focused on younger drivers with the hope that they had not been around when the tales of the lost World War II cargo that had supposedly been hidden in the Philippines by the Japanese. If the chosen drivers had not heard about the lost treasure, they would not question the origin of the boxes that they loaded onto their trucks from the cave entrance.

Of course, curiosity gets the best of most of us, and the drivers were included in the curious bunch. What were the heavy wooden crates that they were asked to carry out of Manilla and off to the eastern shore? Manny's story to the drivers was that the boxes contained iron ore to be shipped to a refinery off shore. Luckily for Manny and Romel the two hundred boxes had no Japanese writing or characters stamped onto the wood.

The drivers helped each other load the boxes…forty boxes per truck. The trucks then lined up and proceeded through Manilla and onto route 601 in caravan formation, with Manny and Romel bringing up the rear. The two men had chosen not to arm themselves because neither had any experience with guns. They had agreed that if there was an armed conflict, they would be the most dangerous if they carried weapons. Their purpose in joining the convoy was to help if any of the trucks ran into mechanical trouble or if there was an accident of any sort.

Manny and Romel had at least two conversations about the Islamic terrorism that had plagued the Philippines for the last two decades. Kidnappings and attacks of foreigners was quite frequent, but only in the southern islands of the Philippines. Mindanao and the Sulu archipelago were the sites of most of the activity. ISIS, or the Islamic State, had re-energized the militant activity in the south, but the terrorists were not venturing north to areas around Manilla. At least, not yet…and now the Taliban's takeover of Afghanistan sent a psychological boost to these Islamic extremists, and their activities were on the rise. Why did all of the problems seem to be tied to Islam Manny asked. Romel had no answer to this question.

Their other concern was highway robbery. On occasion, various crime syndicates and para-military groups set up roadblocks along the more rural routes around Manilla and relieved drivers and passengers of money, jewelry, and any valuable belongings that they had unfortunately chose to travel with. Sometimes there were beatings and rarely death because a driver or passenger chose to resist. The plan was to stay on route 601 and not stray off of this road. The road was well travelled and there was a military presence that should made the journey safe.

All five box trucks had the capacity to carry up to fourteen thousand pounds. Each truck was loaded with approximately twelve thousand pounds of gold cargo. The trucks were newer with good tires, sound suspension, and well-tuned engines. Romel thought that they had covered everything that could go wrong in their preparation. He liked to be meticulous! The drive was less than one hundred and fifty miles. The duration of the excursion would be under four hours.

Each of the drivers was handed a walkie talkie. There were six handsets all tuned to a unique frequency. Cell phones were taken from the drivers. They were told not to stop and only communicate with the radios they had been handed. The drivers mounted their cabs and Manny approached each driver with a route change as they started up their vehicles. Romel had suggested this last-minute route variation. They would travel out of Manilla on the Marcos Highway, rather the route 601. Only Manny and Romel knew of this change until the last minute, so that any prying ears could not be planning an ambush!

If there had been a sphygmomanometer available to check Manny and Romel's blood pressure, it would have registered sky-high! The two men were not expecting to be as anxious as they were, but this was the beginning of a journey that would create for them magnificent new lives…or cost them their lives…

CHAPTER 26

Saipan, Northern Mariana Islands

Igor was enjoying breakfast at Shirley's with his good friend, Charles Cram. Dr. Cram was sipping on a mug of Marianas coffee as he listened to Igor.

"Charles! This is huge! I need your help. I have two boxes of stuff that I need to get here to Saipan from the Philippines. I am leaving for there in my boat, but I want you to get these two boxes over here as soon as possible. You know a guy who knows a guy…Does that dentist you met have a plane? You doing anything today?"

"Whoa, partner! Slow down. Which question do you want me to answer first?" Dr. Cram exclaimed.

"Okay, sorry, sorry…Didn't you meet that guy that is visiting here? Dr. Nelson?" Igor asked.

"Yep, we've played pickleball together," Charles said.

"Did I get the name right?" Igor continued.

"Yes, Dr. Reginal Nelson DDS," Charles replied.

"Oh, he's a dentist?" Igor queried.

"That's how we met. He wanted to see my practice. I have the pickleball court in my parking lot," Charles added.

"Yes, I've seen you guys playing. Looks fun," Igor said.

"You should try it," Charles offered.

"Back to our topic…doesn't Dr. Nelson have a plane here?" Igor asked.

"Yes, a really sexy plane! It's a pusher prop and it has a fabulous paint job. It looks like the Aurora Borealis," Dr. Cram replied.

"Pusher prop…Is that fast?" Igor questioned.

"The fastest turboprop in the world!" Charles exclaimed.

"Would he fly to the Philippines?" Igor asked.

"All I can do is ask…in fact…I'll call him and see if he can join us. Then you can ask him yourself!" Charles said and pulled out his cellphone.

Langley, Virginia

"What's the scoop from Saipan?" the Director asked.

"Dr. Nelson and Mr. Black are still on the island," was the answer.

"What!! I want them out of there! Things could get ugly when the Russians arrive," the Director exclaimed.

"I do not know why they are still there," the analyst said.

"Well, get on it! They need to leave…the sooner the better!" the Director announced.

Frankfurt, Germany

"The three are all great," Magnus began. "Can we keep them all?"

The three candidates for the German I.N.C.I.S.O.R. team had all performed flawlessly through the battery of tests, both physical and psychological that the three had been faced with. The team of four had gathered to discuss their findings and make a decision.

"I think it is worth asking the top brass," Flex added. "They are all going to be wonderful additions to our team."

"Yeah, I would hate to choose," Dick offered.

"I'll make the call," Magnus said.

Washington, DC

At the daily national security briefing, the Director of the NSA began to speak, "Russia is requesting clearance for an Antonov 225 to enter US airspace and land in Saipan with a load of ambulances they are donating to the island."

"Ambulances for Saipan? Does the island need ambulances? I thought that we just allocated Federal dollars to replace police and emergency vehicles," President Marron interjected.

"Yes, Mr. President, if I may finish…the NSA analysts believe it is a rouse. You remember that we intercepted transmissions from Vladivostok about Radio Free World? They are attempting to narrow their search and the Russians are beginning with Saipan. We believe that there will be a surveillance vehicle that they will offload among the ambulances that they are donating to Saipan."

"And…what are they going to find?" the President asked.

"Nothing! The technicians have already cleared out and are back at Langley. The RFW equipment is safely ensconced in a hangar at Anderson Air Force base on Guam. Dr. Nelson and Mr. Black have been ordered to get out of Saipan immediately," the Director continued.

"So, I say we let them in, and they can have their fun looking all over that island. Then what? Are the Russians going to look on Tinian? What about Rota? Do they then try to enter Guam?" POTUS was having fun with his knowledge of the Mariana Islands. "Hey! Maybe they'll look on Pagan!"

Saipan, Northern Mariana Islands

Ash and I joined Igor and Charles just as they were finishing their meal. We ordered coffee and watched as the waitress cleared away the breakfast plates.

"So, Charles…here we are…what will you do with us?" I asked. "You ready to lose at pickleball…again?"

"Yeah, I'm ready to kick some butt!" Ash exclaimed. "Do you play?" Ash was looking at Igor.

"No, I do not," Igor replied and looked around the coffee shop before he continued. Covid restrictions had reduced the number of tables that could be occupied in the restaurant. Shirley's was utilizing every other table during this time. There was no one within earshot of the conversation.

Igor continued once he was satisfied, "I have some secret news and I need your help."

Ash, Charles, and I leaned forward, intent on hearing the news.

"I have a friend in the Philippines. He has discovered what he feels is Yamashita's treasure," Igor began.

"Who? What treasure?" Ash asked.

"A Japanese general who was rumored to have hidden gold in the Philippines in World War II. Google it!" Igor replied.

"So, your friend has found a stash of gold," I said.

"And he wants to smuggle it out of the Philippines," Igor continued.

"How will he do that?" Ash asked.

"I am taking a fleet of twenty-five fishing boats from Saipan to transport the gold here," Igor announced.

"Why are we here?" I wondered. "We don't have a boat here."

"No," Igor began. "We need your airplane. We want to transport one box of jewelry and one box of gold bars to Saipan immediately and I have a Russian contact that will help us to move the gold."

"Two boxes…Aurora can handle that. Do we fly into Manilla?" I asked.

"No. We want you to fly in to Alabat Airport. The boxes are being delivered to Infanta by truck…" Igor began.

"Truck?" I interrupted. "How many boxes are there?

"Two hundred!" Igor whispered.

Charles let out a slow whistle. Ash looked at me with wondering eyes. I knew what he was thinking…how much gold?

Igor read the looks on our faces. "It's over a billion dollars."

"Jesus Christ!" I exclaimed, which got some heads to turn. I apologized to the others in the restaurant and continued, "Do you have a map?"

Igor produced a map that showed the location of the cave, the route that the trucks would take and the destination in Infanta.

"How do you get the boxes from Infanta to Alabat?" Ash wondered as he studied the map.

"My friend in the Philippines has lined up a speedboat to make the short run to your airport with the two boxes," Igor replied.

"And the other one hundred and eighty boxes? Your armada?" I asked.

"Yes, Dr. Nelson. We only need your help with two boxes," Igor said.

"And once we are back in Saipan?" Ash questioned.

"I have a Russian friend who will pick up the shipment at Francisco Ada airport. Your job will be done. So, one round trip? A few hours there and a few hours back? You in?" Igor asked.

"Well, let me think about it…" I began.

"No!" Igor cut me off. "No time to think but right here, da! I leave with my ships in the morning. We need to know now."

I looked at Ash.

"All we have to do here is pack," Ash said. "We can take a day or two for adventure."

"This airport, Alabat. Does it have Jet-A fuel? It looks like a general aviation airport that hasn't seen many turbines." I questioned.

"Already covered," Igor continued. "The fuel will be delivered in fifty-five-gallon drums with an electric transfer pump."

"And the field…the landing strip?" Ash asked.

"How are your short field takeoff and landing characteristics?" Igor stated. "The strip is short."

"Aurora can do short fields, but it's built for speed, not utility flying," I replied. "How long is short?"

"A third of a mile. Seventeen hundred feet," Igor answered.

"I've seen an Avanti land in fifteen hundred feet, Reggie. Anyway, what's the fun without a little 'pucker factor'!" Ash said.

I looked at Ash and wondered if he was out of his mind. I knew that the landing gear was robust and could take a hard landing, but I didn't want to break the plane! We would both have to stand on the brakes and immediately reverse thrust upon touchdown. He just smiled back at me with a crooked, devious smile.

"So, we fly from here to the Philippines, pick up two boxes, refuel and return to Saipan and some Russian dude takes the boxes off our hands…is that it?" I asked.

"Da…da," Igor replied.

"And we are paid?" Ash continued.

"Five million dollars for one day's work!" Igor announced.

Charles let out another low whistle.

I looked again at Ash, hesitated…and then said, "We're in. We'll leave at daybreak!"

Igor stood and shook our hands. He left to phone Romel about the good news.

Romel thought about the airplane and the different airport and the speedboat to get the loot to Alabat and having to get the fuel for the airplane to the airport. This scheme was getting more complicated with every step...

Vladivostok, Russia

"The plane is completely loaded, comrade and the technicians are on board. The markings for the surveillance van match exactly the markings of the ambulances. We are ready," Vlad explained to Ivan.

"Let us begin our mission," Ivan ordered, and the pilots began to start the six giant engines on this monster plane.

As the pilots proceeded through the engine runup, Ivan reviewed the flight plan. The journey was approximately 2096 miles and the Antonov 225 cruised at 474 miles per hour. They would fly directly over Japan and continue to Saipan with a planned touchdown in a little over four and a half hours. Not a bad start to this mission of spying on the Americans, he thought. He wondered what he would discover in Saipan.

Saipan, Northern Mariana Islands

Ash and I headed out to the airport, arriving at four in the morning. The early flight ensured that there would be relatively smooth air for the flight over to the Philippines. As we lifted off, Igor's group of small fishing boats were leaving the lagoon to begin their journey. The boats looked like toys on the water as we gained altitude and they became tiny dots on the water as we headed west across the Philippine Sea.

The flight was uneventful and as we began our descent into Alabat, Ash and I went over the short field characteristics of the Avanti Evo. The important part was to get the airplane on the ground as fast as we could once we crossed the end of the runway and not to worry about greasing the landing.

At one thousand feet above ground level, we circled the airport. There was no tower, and the only radio was a Unicom frequency. We listened to the radio as we circled. The Filipinos were speaking Tagalog and it sounded like gibberish to us. So much for English being the language of the skies! The windsock was still, indicating no wind, so we entered a downwind leg for the runway, and announced our arrival in English. The radio went silent. We saw no other planes in the pattern.

We turned to base and lowered to full flaps and got the wheels down. As we turned onto final, I focused on touching the plane down right on the runway numbers. We approached and the land proximity warning sounded. Just then Ash yelled at me to go around! I pulled back on the yoke and applied power. Ash worked to clean up the landing gear and flaps.

"What's up?" I asked, startled.

"Look!" Ash exclaimed.

There was a cow with a young calf standing at the end of the runway. As we gained altitude, we flew directly over them which must have scared them because they ran off into the jungle which looked like it was creeping toward the runway asphalt.

We re-entered the downwind leg and flew the landing pattern. This time the approach was uninterrupted, and I put the plane down hard on the numbers and we both pressed our feet on the brake pedals as I pulled the engine levers into reverse thrust. The far end of the runway seemed to be coming really fast, but the plane slowed and then we turned around at the far numbers.

"That was fun," I said facetiously.

"Still…wonderful job, my friend," Ash congratulated.

We stopped and saw two flat bed trucks come toward us.

We hopped out onto the runway and stretched while we watched two men carry boxes to the cargo hold and two others begin to pump gas into the plane. I check the fifty-five-gallon barrels that they were filling Aurora II from, and they all were labelled Jet A.

The men finished loading the crates quickly and left. It took longer to fuel the plane, but soon they were done and the truck with the fuel pulled off the runway.

Ash and I looked at each other.

"Wonderful visit!" Ash exclaimed.

"Absolutely!" I replied and we re-entered the plane and settled in for our return trip.

Ash moved into the left seat for this leg of the journey. We ran through the pre-flight checklist and then proceeded to the starting sequence for both turbines. Soon the gauges indicated that the two engines were humming along within normal limits. I looked to the right and Ash checked to the left.

He moved the throttles forward and Aurora II began to move down to the far end of the runway. I operated the radio and informed Unicom that we were taking off on the active runway. Ash moved the throttles forward to takeoff speed and kept his feet on the brakes. The aircraft wiggled and bucked as the power increased. She wanted so badly to dart down the asphalt. Once the turbines reached full power, Ash released the pedals and Aurora II sped down the runway. We had almost reached rotation speed when I pointed and yelled, "Holy fuck!"

A small high-wing plane, probably a Cessna 152, was landing directly at us! I had grabbed the yoke and pulled hard. Ash looked at me and pulled back to help me. We both willed the plane into the air. Aurora jumped into the air, and I turned the yoke to the right. The stall warning blared in the cockpit. Ash reached to clean up the landing gear and flaps.

We were close enough to the approaching plane to see the pilot with his mouth hanging open. The left landing gear glanced off the other plane's left-wing tip. Once we cleared the oncoming obstacle, I levelled the wings and let the airspeed build before we continued our climb.

"Jesus Christ!" Ash exclaimed. "That was too close…no more uncontrolled airports, Reggie. Oh no…the gear didn't come up clean. We have no red light on the panel."

"Your plane," I said and cycled the landing gear switch. The gear came down, but the indicator didn't give us 'three green' as we had hoped.

"We have green lights on the nose gear and the right main gear," I announced. Can't tell about the left main gear. Don't know if its up or down, but it is not locked." I raised the landing gear lever.

"We better fly to Manilla's main airport and do a fly over to let the tower observe Aurora's underbelly," Ash suggested.

"How is she handling?" I asked.

"Feels fine. A little more right trim than normal. Must be the drag from the left main," Ash announced.

"Let's just proceed to Saipan and get out of this damned country. Remember that we have what the authorities will call 'stolen booty' if they search us," I said.

"Alright, Reggie, we'll continue east, and, I hope, make the journey to Saipan." Ash replied, and then added with a laugh, "I guess it's better to crash on US soil!"

CHAPTER 27

Saipan, Northern Mariana Islands

Ash flew over the tower as we arrived at Francisco Ada Airport. I was on the radio communicating with the air traffic controller.

Typhoon Yutu destroyed the airport's tower and a temporary tower had been transported to Saipan and mounted on an empty shipping container. I had talked with one of the air traffic controllers who told me about how little they could see with the tower at ground level. The controllers also had to sit to see anything. They were not able to stand and move around when they were on duty, which made their shifts very difficult.

I informed the tower that we had a damaged left main landing gear and could not get a green light for that gear in the cockpit. TJ, the controller on duty, grabbed a pair of strong binoculars and moved onto the container so that he could see up and observe our plane as we flew over the tower.

TJ informed us that the gear looked like it was down, but he could not guarantee that it was locked, or that it would not collapse when we touched down and put the weight of the aircraft on the gear. I thanked him for the help, and he asked if we were declaring an emergency. I responded that we were not.

Ash entered the pattern of the downwind leg and flew a normal approach. We had discussed our options on the flight over. We talked about everything from ditching the plane in the lagoon to a belly landing on the grass next to the runway to attempting a normal landing but keeping the weight off of the left main as long as we possibly could.

That option was the one that Ash prepared for…he flared over the runway and let the ground effect buoy the aircraft. Ash then allowed the right main to make contact and kept the yoke back as long as he could. The left main and nose wheel made contact with the ground almost simultaneously. Ash and I both cringed, expecting the gear to collapse…

It held!

"Aurora II, you are amazing!" Ash exhaled as he patted the dashboard.

"Good job, Ash!" I exclaimed. "Good girl, Aurora II."

The runout was uneventful, and we received permission to taxi to our hangar.

"Welcome home and nice landing," TJ said over the radio.

I thanked him and we both exited the aircraft as soon as the engine off checklist was completed. The door to the cabin is on the left side, so we both paused at the left main gear to take a look at the damage.

The plane whose wingtip had hit Aurora II had struck the gear assembly just above the tire. We could see white paint where the contact had been made. The metal gear assembly was bent ever so slightly, but it was enough that the landing door would not seat properly when the gear was raised, and the damage was enough not to give a 'down and locked' indication when the gear was lowered. Ash and I both realized that we were lucky. The gear was robust enough to hold even with this damage.

I called to an A & P mechanic who was working on a Piper Seneca which was parked on the tarmac adjacent to our hangar. He took his sweet time but ambled over to take a look.

"I've seen more landing gear damage from hard landings than you boys have!" he exclaimed.

"Really?" I asked the mechanic.

"What's this paint here on the gear?" The mechanic pointed to the gear housing.

"We hit another plane on takeoff. They were landing. It was an uncontrolled airport in the Philippines," I offered.

"My God!" The mechanic exclaimed. "You almost had a head-on crash? Wow!"

"Yes, we were very lucky," Ash said.

"Yep, sure enough. You two must have someone upstairs watching over you," he stated and then spit a brown streak of saliva onto the asphalt.

"Beetle Nut," I whispered to Ash.

"Nasty!" he added.

"I can hammer this out in nothing flat," the mechanic began. "But I'm tied up for now on this other bird. Have to get that into the air by sunset."

"No hurry," I said and added, "tomorrow's fine. Then we need to fly it around the pattern and cycle the gear? Make sure everything is good?"

"About noon should be good for you all to take it for a spin," the mechanic confirmed. "Nice bird, by the way."

"Thanks!" Ash offered and moved to get away from the mechanic before he spit again.

"Now you understand the signs we see all over the island. 'No chewing or spitting'. It makes an awful mess," I said to Ash as we moved away toward the Escalade.

As we waited for the air conditioning in the car to make the inside bearable after it was baking in the sun for the day, Ash asked, "What's up with chewing Beetle Nut?"

"I asked Dr. Cram about that when I saw the sign outside his office. I got quite the lesson! He told me that about one fourth of the world's population chews. And the nut is not a beetle nut. It comes from the Areca palm," I began.

"So why call it beetle nut?" Ash questioned.

"No idea. But Dr. Cram said that the locals take this nut and wrap it in a leaf with lime and tobacco. It's called a 'quid'. Then they chew on this," I continued.

"And that is pleasurable?" Ash asked.

"I guess…Dr. Cram said that there is a 'high' associated with chewing the nut, but it is highly carcinogenic. Plus, they add tobacco and lime, also both carcinogens. A triple whammy!" I spoke. "Dr. Cram said he has seen more oral cancer on this island in eight years than he did in the states in thirty-five years."

"Geesus!" Ash exclaimed.

"The locals also wear their molars down to the point where the nerve tissue is exposed and they lose the elasticity in the muscles around their mouths, so they cannot open!" I continued.

"This is just crazy," Ash commented.

"Dr. Cram told me that in the old days chewing beetle nut was reserved for the tribal elders. It was a perk of being the leader of the tribe! Now, everybody chews. He has even seen parents giving it to children in strollers!" I added.

"Now we're getting ridiculous!" Ash said.

"He said that they just passed a law a couple of years ago that you have to be eighteen to buy beetle nut in the stores," I finished.

"One quarter of the earth's humans does this? Again, nasty!" Ash opined as we drove out of the airport and headed for home.

"Hey, what about the loot?" Ash asked.

"I almost forgot…we were just supposed to fly the boxes here and not touch them. A Russian friend of Igor's will come to the airport to retrieve the boxes once I call him to let him know that we have arrived, which I will do right now," I said.

I pressed the voice recognition button on the steering wheel. "Call Igor," I told the car.

"Calling Igor," the car replied in a nice female voice.

"This hands-free stuff is kinda cool!" Ash said.

CHAPTER 28

Frankfurt, Germany

"Just heard from Michael in Dubai. Reggie and Ash have approved keeping all three of you. We will each have six men," Magnus said.

"That is great news," the three recruits said in unison. "What do we do now?"

"Fly back to Denver and pack up your stuff. Finalize your affairs and end whatever leases and contracts you have going there. You have two weeks! Report back here and begin your German lives on Monday, two weeks from now," Aaron ordered.

"Here are your tickets to Denver. Flight leaves from the other side of the airport in two hours. You'd better move it!" Dick urged.

Denver, CO

"Did you hear? We are to add to our roster here." Flex said.

"Now we'll have even teams for pickleball," Kurt joked.

"Who was next on that short list?" Lance asked.

"This will be good…when we break into teams, somebody will always have your back…kinda like a wingman," Duncan said.

"Yes…two-man teams will be a plus," Powers added.

Saipan, Northern Mariana Islands

The approaching Antonov 225 had drawn quite a crowd of dignitaries and curiosity buffs to the Saipan International Airport. Many watched from windows in the air-conditioned terminal building. The dignitaries waited in the sun for the event to begin. Many held umbrellas, not to ward off the rain, but to keep the tropical sun from frying their foreheads.

The behemoth plane touched down and cruised to the last exit from the runway. It ambled toward the crowd that had gathered. The pilots proceeded through the engine shut down routine. Once complete, the nose of the aircraft lifted up and a metallic ramp extended from inside the belly of the plane.

The crowd stood in awe as the plane opened up and then they heard the blaring of sirens as twelve new ambulances were driven out of the plane's cargo hold. The ambulances parked in a semi-circle facing the temporary podium that had been erected on the tarmac. The sirens fell silent, and the ambulances were shut off.

The governor and several other dignitaries from the government and the hospital took their turns to speak to the crowd. Thankfulness for the international cooperation and how fine the new vehicles looked and how important these would be to the island were the recurring topics of the bevy of speeches.

There were two men in the cab of each of the vehicles. They stayed in their seats during the speeches and then turned into welcoming hosts as the crowd moved to check out the new emergency ambulances. Not one of the crowd noticed that one of the vehicles had an articulated roof that could raise up to expose a powerful transceiver that would spin three hundred and sixty degrees inside a protective dome.

The backs of the ambulances were not opened for the crowd to observe. If they had, it would have been easy to recognize that the one vehicle was filled with electronic equipment and not a gurney and medical supplies. When the show was completed, the vans moved in single file off of the tarmac and through a gate that led to an outer airport road and the exit.

Only eleven vehicles were delivered to the hospital. One van had turned off Middle Road and pulled into a cargo container. The container's doors were closed as soon as the two men exited the cab of the surveillance van. The men were driven to their comrades at the hospital. All of the drivers and passengers were placed on a bus at the hospital and driven back to the airport. They boarded the Antonov, and the nose was lowered. The pilot requested clearance for a flight plan back to Vladivostok and started the six turbines.

Soon the plane rumbled to the runway and roared into the sky, turning north for the return trip to Russia. The first phase of the mission was complete and news of this was radioed to Vlad and Ivan sitting in their FSB headquarters.

Langley, Virginia

"Dr. Nelson and Mr. Black are still there?" the CIA Director asked incredulously.

"Yes, Director, they have not departed the island and the Russians have arrived," an analyst allowed.

"Damnit!" the Director cursed. "Why don't these guys listen to me! I want them out of there now! Pronto! I don't want them mixing it up with the Russians! Get on it!"

"Yes, sir," the analyst replied and rushed out of the office.

At his terminal the analyst placed a call to both Reginald Nelson and Ash Black. Both men answered their phones.

"I want to be completely clear here! The Director is pissed! You two should have been out of there by now," the analyst began.

"Hey…what's up with the Russians and the Antonov?" Ash asked.

"You weren't supposed to be there for that!"

"Well…what is it?" I asked.

"The Russians have tracked RFW to the island of Saipan. Or at least they think they have. They have smuggled in a surveillance van in hopes of pinpointing the origin of the signal from Saipan," the analyst said.

"Well, this is fun!" Ash answered and he looked at me with a glimmer in his eyes.

I had seen that mischievous look so many times. He was up to something.

"You men need to leave!" the analyst urged. His voice had raised an octave when he spoke.

"We'll get right on it," I replied and hung up my phone.

Ash put his phone on the table and said, "Well, well, well."

"We're ready to go but I want to have some fun first," I agreed.

"Yes, Reggie…let's have some fun…" Ash urged.

I moved to the kitchen and retrieved the Crown Royal bottle. I filled two glasses with ice and took out a lemon and carved two twists from the peel. I rubbed each glass around the rim with the lemon peel and dropped it into the glass. I poured a double shot each of the Canadian whiskey into the two glasses and carried them to the patio. Ash thanked me and we toasted to our new adventure.

CHAPTER 29

Florence, Italy

"Reggie, you're slurring your words. What is going on?" Becky asked into the phone.

"I miss you, my love," I answered.

"Put Ash on," Becky demanded.

"Hello, my dear," Ash said when I handed him the phone.

"You are worse than Reggie! What have you two been doing?" Becky questioned.

"We're drinking!" Ash replied.

"Oh? Thanks for letting me know. What is the occasion?" Becky asked.

"Do we need one?" Ash countered.

"Let me talk to Reggie!" Becky demanded.

"We love you," Ash said as he handed the phone back.

"Reggie, I need you to focus! I just got off the phone with Michael. You two were supposed to be out of Saipan days ago. You have the CIA Director upset and you've even pissed off the President. What are you doing?" Becky queried.

"Oh, my love…"

"Stop with the amorous crap!" Becky cut me off. "This is serious. You need to get out of there before the Russians find you."

"Only a couple more days…we have a plan for the Russians!" I replied. "I love you."

"You and Ash could drive a woman to drink!" Becky exclaimed. "Take care of each other and try to stay out of trouble…bye for now."

Saipan, Northern Mariana Islands

"That sounds like a great plan!" Ash said when we had finished plotting against the Russians.

"So next step is to get with Jeff Beach and Nicky Bells and see what they know about abandoned properties around here," I said and phoned the two Saipan men that had more than thirty years each living in Saipan.

"Where are we meeting?" Ash asked when I finished with the two conversations.

"They didn't want to go back to the Hyatt, or Godfathers. They both want to sit on the beach at PIC, drink, eat potato skins, talk, and watch the sunset. Nicky feels that the atmospheric conditions are good for a green flash. Jeff said that there shouldn't be many people around because the resort was used for Covid quarantine and is just getting back to normal operations," I announced.

"But the tourists aren't back yet," Ash countered.

"That's why it shouldn't be too crowded. Let's finish these drinks, get cleaned up and head to the Seaside Grill at Pacific Islands Club! We want to get there before sunset, according to our two pros," I said, and we both downed our cocktails.

PIC was located almost at the southern end of Saipan. There was another resort truly at the southern end, called Coral Ocean Point. Both resorts are owned by E-Land corporation, and both were badly damaged in typhoon Yutu. Coral Ocean had not reopened yet, but Pacific Islands Club had been fully restored. We parked the Escalade by the tennis courts and walked through the pools and water park to get out to the Seaside Grill and the beach.

Nicky and Jeff had already procured a table on the beach and their drinks, and the first round of potato skins had already been served.

"This is a beautiful setting!" I exclaimed as I looked over the beach scene displayed in front of me.

"Ditto!" Ash said, but he was already eyeing a table of cute young things in bikinis.

We took our seats and the waiter promptly appeared.

"Double Crown on the rocks with a twist," I ordered.

"A be…no, not a beer tonight. Bring me a Cuba Libre in honor of Lance," Ash said.

"Mixing rum and Canadian whiskey?" I asked. "That smart?"

"Who are you, my mother?" Ash countered.

We said our 'hellos' to Nicky and Jeff and had a few minutes of small talk while we waited for our drinks. Nicky, I had remembered, was heavily involved with helping several Japanese ventures begin on Saipan, and Jeff had been with the Department of the Interior. Both men were a wealth of information about the inner workings of this island. Ash and my drinks arrived with another boat of potato skins.

"How can we help you two gentlemen?" Nicky asked after we tested our drinks and the potato skins.

"Tell us about all these abandoned properties we see when we drive around the island," I began.

"One of the bigger problems on the island. In fact, I heard a man say years ago that this island was 'Paradise with Warts', and I think that fits pretty well. Often times the buildings are damaged in a typhoon…like all the abandoned buildings you saw when you drove down here to PIC. And the property owner is often different than the building owner or the business owner. So, the buildings just decay away and look awful," Jeff said.

"Yes, and they get mold and all sorts of other nasty stuff," Nicky added.

"Why doesn't the local government do something…like bulldoze them!" Ash questioned.

"The local government has been asked that same thing for years," Nicky began.

"And all they do is blame it on zoning," Jeff added.

"And then you have the buildings where complete industries folded and left the island. Did you see all the abandoned warehouses and barracks along Beach Road?" Jeff asked.

"Yeah, it really looks sad," I said.

"Another example is La Fiesta, up north. When Japan Air Lines folded, they pulled out of here in a big way and the Japanese market has never recovered. La Fiesta was a thriving mall when the Nikko resort was going strong. Now the buildings just sit and decay as the jungle overgrows the concrete structures," Nicky added.

"Now to the point…we want access to one of these abandoned properties," I began.

"Where very few people will take notice if there is some activity there," Ash added.

"How big a property?" Nicky asked.

"Are you looking for a house? Or a larger structure?" Jeff added.

"What do you know about the Plumeria Resort just north of the Aqua Resort?" Ash asked.

"It has been closed since 2008," Nicky offered.

"I think it had one hundred and ninety-eight rooms when it was a functioning hotel," Jeff said.

"And it has been sitting empty and rotting since 2008?" I asked.

"There was talk once that Bridge Capital was going to restore the resort in 2015, but you've driven by it…nothing!" Nicky added.

"So…we could use it as a base to cause some mischief and nobody would be the wiser?" Ash asked.

"Mischief?" they both said in unison.

"There are some Russians that just arrived, and they will be snooping around the island for a while. I'd like to cause them some grief and make sure they have a miserable time," I continued.

"What are they snooping for?" Jeff wondered.

"The reason why we're here. We were testing a device, which I am calling Radio Free World. The device sends out a signal that excites the explosive, C-4, and makes it unstable. Did you read about all those explosions in Baghdad recently?" I asked.

"Sure," Nicky said. "That you?"

"It was, it was!" Ash interjected.

"So that was what you were doing on Radar Hill," Jeff deduced. "You sent the signals from Saipan!"

"You got it, and it worked. It was a huge blow to the terrorists in the Middle East. They're afraid of their stockpiles of plastique explosives now. It's harder for them to hide among the civilian community now. Good stuff!" I spoke.

"Those other two guys we met at the Hyatt?" Nicky asked.

"Joe and Billy," Ash said.

"Yeah, they have a role?" Jeff wondered.

"Yep, they are technicians with the CIA. They set up the equipment and ran the tests. Joe and Billy are back in the States now," I answered.

"So, what are the Russians going to find?" Nicky asked.

"A whole lot of hooey!" Ash said. "Time for another round!"

"Watch the sky," Jeff announced.

"Yes, look at the horizon…no clouds tonight. Perfect for a green flash!" Nicky added.

We all gazed west over the Philippine Sea to watch the sun set. It was a beautiful sunset. The waiter arrived with another round and asked if we saw it.

"Nope…no green flash tonight," Jeff replied.

We sat for a few minutes enjoying the scenery as night crept upon us. The outside lighting came on and candles were lit at every table. Tonight, it was hard to imagine that there were bad people and bad things happening in the world.

"Tell us about your plan and how we can help," Jeff began.

"Yeah, I'd love to put a world of hurt on the Russians!" Nicky added.

PART FOUR

CHAPTER 30

Saipan, Northern Mariana Islands

Igor had met with his Russian contact whose responsibility was to find a buyer or buyers for the gold bars and jewelry. This was a mountain of gold. More than all of the men would ever see. One buyer would be easy, but it may take several buyers to accomplish this task. Igor knew that the more people that were involved, the more chances there were for a leak. He did not want the ignominy for being the one that allowed the Philippine government or, for that matter, the American government to seize the gold and end so many prospects for the future.

He had taken one gold bar and a bag full of the jewelry to the meeting. They met at the Russian's home on the top of Navy Hill. The house had full-length windows on the western façade with a spectacular view of Garapan and the turquoise water of the lagoon beyond. Beyond the reef the Philippine Sea was dotted with six prepositioned ship and one US warship. The tiny island of Managaha was just to the north of the ships beyond the lagoon. Igor guessed that the warship was a guided missile frigate. The view captured his imagination and he forgot for a moment why he was at this house.

The meeting was held in private so that there were no prying eyes and ears. Showing off the gold bar and jewelry would not have been possible in a public place. Russians on Saipan had no restaurants lately where they could enjoy dishes from their homeland. Igor remembered the Siberia restaurant in Garapan with fondness, although his homemade version of borscht was much tastier than the restaurant served. He had become the best Russian cook on Saipan.

His contact had a digital scale on the table in front of them. He first weighed the bar and wrote down the weight. He turned to Igor and asked him how many bars there were. Igor told him that there were eighteen hundred bars on their way to Saipan. The contact let out a low whistle. He wrote down that number next to the weight of the one bar. There was a calculator next to the scale. He punched some buttons and then wrote down another number on the paper.

The Russian contact then grabbed a jewelry loupe, placed the eyepiece against his face and examined a few of the gold jewelry pieces that Igor had brought. A widening smile was growing on his face. Russians rarely smiled.

"This is excellent quality! These are vintage pieces, and they are eighteen carat or better," the contact said.

The contact asked Igor how many pieces there were. Igor told him that there were twenty boxes of jewelry of the same quality and vintage also on their way to Saipan. The contact's grin grew wider.

The Russian then dropped his pen and exclaimed, "I know what this is! This is Yamashita's treasure! That wily Japanese general that stole all the gold during his campaign in Malaya and hid it in the Philippines. That is what this is! They found it!"

Igor was silent while his contact raged on about the discovery. He looked up on Google about Yamashita and read what was known about the mystery of the gold. His lips curved up in a thin, smug smile.

"And you got it out of the Philippines? How!" the contact wondered.

"It is on its way to Saipan by boat as we speak," Igor announced without directly answering the question about how.

"I have to make some calls…wait here…I'll be back in a minute," the contact offered and moved into a bedroom off of the main living room.

Igor waited and looked at his watch. It was about twenty minutes when the contact returned. He stood while Igor sat. His gaze alternated from the gold on the table to the panorama outside.

"I'll be able to own an island like Managaha!" Igor whispered to himself.

The Russian contact returned to the living room with his arms in a gesture of magnanimity.

"I will get for you one and a half billion dollars, sight unseen!" the contact offered.

Igor was glad that he was sitting because his legs felt weak. He was willing to take a finder's fee of five percent, down from his normal seven percent, because Romel was a friend. He did the math in his head…he had just made seventy-five million dollars! Never before or probably ever again would he receive a commission this enormous! He may not ever have to work again! It was hard for him to fathom.

"And how much for your cut?" Igor asked his contact.

"The buyers will pay for my share. I will keep some of the gold. It is not part of this transaction. Do we have a deal?"

Igor thought for a moment that maybe he should hold out….a first offer is usually low…but no, this was an amazing amount of dollars! "Yes, comrade, we have a deal." Igor rose and shook his contact's hand. A servant appeared with a tray of expensive Russian vodka, and both men toasted to their success and enjoyed some caviar and toast points.

With their business complete, Igor packed up the gold bar and jewelry. As he walked to his car, he thought about calling Romel, but chose to stay calm, drive down Navy Hill back to his home, and gain his composure before he picked up a phone.

Infanta, Philippines

Romel gently placed his phone on the table. Manny watched his friend with an eagerness he had not experienced before. He felt like his bladder was ready to let loose!

"Well?" Manny could not wait for Romel any longer.

A wry smile appeared on Romel's face.

"Ah Manny, my friend, do you remember what we agreed we would have as our piece for finding the treasure and getting it out of the Philippines?" Romel began.

"Yes, yes…we each get a little over four hundred and seventy-two million," Manny answered.

"Well, can you spend a little more?" Romel added.

Manny's grin grew into a full-fledged smile, "What? Tell me," Manny urged.

"They buyers are offering one-point-five billion dollars sight unseen!" Romel exclaimed.

"Wow!" Manny said. His mind could not grasp what that vast amount would mean to him or how his life would be altered.

"That's $525 million for each of us!" Romel calculated.

"And our work is done," Manny hinted.

"Yeah, we just sit and wait for the payday," Romel finished.

The two men headed to the Infant-resto bar they had found up the road from the municipal fish port where the fleet of boats had been loaded. Manny and Romel both ordered a Las Islas. A Las Islas was similar to a mojito, made with light rum, triple sec, peach schnapps, mint, and muddled mangoes. The drink had a tangier taste than the sweet mojito.

They toasted to their success.

All that had to happen for their wildest dreams to come true was that the fleet of fishing boats from Saipan make the return trip to their home port. Four days...

Vladivostok, Russia

Ivan and Vlad listened to the radio report from the technicians cruising around the island of Saipan. They were on their second day of investigating a possible signal. Day one had provided no signal. Not one clue! The island was tiny. They only had twelve miles from north to south and five miles from east to west to check. But there were vast areas of uncharted jungle and mountainous terrain that did not have roads.

The Russian technicians were used to travelling hundreds of miles to perform their task of pinpointing where signal sources came from. This small island was baffling to them. Where could the signal be hidden?

The van had begun at the northernmost end of the island known as Banzai Cliff. The Americans had driven the Japanese to the north end of Saipan in the battle of 1944. As the American soldiers closed in upon the Japanese position, the Japanese soldiers chose to jump into the Pacific Ocean off of the northern cliffs rather than surrender. The area where they jumped to their deaths was named Banzai Cliff and there were many memorials and shrines erected to the Japanese that died there.

It was the Japanese suicide rather than surrender that convinced the American President, in 1945, to use the newly developed nuclear bomb against Japan. The theory was that if the Japanese had been so brainwashed into believing that suicide was better than surrender, then huge numbers of American soldiers would be lost if Japan was invaded. The bomb brought Japan to the bargaining table which led to their surrender without invading that country.

The van drove slowly south on Middle Road, scanning from the Philippine sea side of the road to the mountainous terrain to the east, and then turned down Micro Beach Road to transition to Beach Road. The Russians moved through the main town of Garapan and continued south on Beach Road past the major resort hotels to the antennae farm at the southern end of Saipan. The road turned east at this point.

Ivan and Vlad had suggested that the likely culprits were the major resorts and the antennae farm. There was nothing to be picked up from any of these places on the west side of the island.

The investigation continued around the southern tip of Saipan until the road turned north and joined Isla Drive. Their sensitive receiver was strong enough to pick up any transmission from the northern end of the island of Tinian, just a few miles south of them. There was no contact. The road meandered to the eastern side of Saipan. There was one major resort to check out on the eastern side at Lao Lao Bay in Kagman. Nothing coming from this area either.

Mount Tapotchau in the center of the island required the Russian van to drive along both sides of the island. Their equipment was sensitive enough to pick up signals within a ten-mile radius, but the mountain would have interfered with any transmission, making their search more difficult.

At the end of day one, the van had travelled most of the paved roads on the island of Saipan with no positive results. All of the major resorts had been checked. The antennae farm on the southern tip of Saipan had been investigated. The sensitive receiver had even been trained on the antennae on North Field on the neighboring island of Tinian with no results.

The investigators ended their first day empty-handed. The two Russian technicians transmitted their negative findings to Vladivostok. Vlad and Ivan returned to their large map of Saipan and their white board to think of other options to check out on the island of Saipan.

Or was it possible that their triangulation efforts were off by enough to mean that the signal was from another island in the Mariana archipelago…maybe even Guam with all of its military complexes. The Russians knew of the large Air Force base and the growing American naval presence in Guam. Ivan and Vlad would have one more day to check other places on Saipan before expanding their search south toward Guam. Vlad was certain that the signal had come from Saipan!

Saipan, Northern Mariana Islands

Ash and I discussed the plan…this was going to be fun!

A stop at the computer electronics store provided us with ample material to pull off the plan. Back at the rental home we unpacked the new electronic toys and got out our tools. Soon we had fabricated a transmitter and an electronic multi-frequency generator.

I contacted CIA headquarters in Langley and obtained the frequencies that had been most effective at exciting the C-4 plastique explosives. Our multi-frequency generator that we had built from various computer store electronic parts was adjusted so that the frequency transmitted by our device covered the frequencies that had been used in Baghdad, Iraq. The same frequencies that the Russians had deduced as the cause of the conflagration that had occurred at two separate times in the Iraqi city.

We then retrieved the quadcopters from the roof of the Escalade parked next to the house. Each of the drones was equipped with different armament, but for this mission they would all be the same. Smaller versions of the parabolic mirror that had been carried below the C130 aircraft that flew the missions over Iraq and the United States were mounted below each of the drones.

Ash hopped into the Escalade front passenger seat and fired up the electronic display for the four drones. He issued the command for the quadcopters to take flight and hover twenty feet into the air, each taking up a position over the back yard. I moved around the back yard and placed small receivers on the ground. The receivers would emit a high-pitched squeal if they received a signal.

As each drone flew silently in place above us, I directed the small transmitter at each of them and activated the signal very briefly. One-by-one the receivers were activated, and we heard the squeal. We knew from each of the squeals that the signal transmission from our little device worked. Four for four! The equipment was all functioning properly.

Ash directed the drones back to their perches on the Escalade and joined me at the patio table. He had a large grin on his face. I knew exactly what he was thinking! We were ready! Time to spoof the Russians!

Philippine Sea

The first half of the return trip had proceeded smoothly…but now there was trouble. Three of the fishing boats that made up the twenty-five-boat armada had experienced mechanical troubles. For several different and varied reasons, the engines on these three had quit functioning. This was an expected occurrence when so many boats sailed together. Ropes were extended to the three disabled boats and three of the larger boats hooked up to them and began to tow them back to Saipan. The other boats in the armada slowed down to accommodate the towing boats. This would slow their return to Saipan. Two days of this and they would be back in the warm turquoise water of their home lagoon.

The sailors awakened on the morning of the third day to a beautiful sunrise with orange-red wispy cirrus clouds to the eastern horizon. Igor thought to himself the old seaman's adage…'Red Sky at Morning, Sailor's Warning, Red Sky at Night, Sailor's Delight.' He wondered if the sky was a harbinger of dangerous weather to come.

Halfway through the third day of the return, the weather began to take a turn for the worst. This was not typhoon season, but tropical cyclonic storms could materialize extremely fast. The Marianas trench lay just to the east of Saipan. This was the deepest place in the ocean. The colder water spawned many a storm that grew in strength as the winds pushed them over Saipan and into the warmer waters of the Philippine Sea.

The meteorologists and forecasters were routinely wrong with their predictions, which in Igor's case had foretold balmy conditions and calm seas.

As the storm brewed up to the east of the armada, the clouds became heavier and much angrier looking. The cumulous clouds reached up thousands of feet as they sucked the warm water of the Philippine Sea up into their centers. The bottoms of the clouds became darkening shades of gray until a solid bank of black clouds approached.

The swells grew to between ten and twenty feet. The majority of the fleet of fishing craft were less than forty feet in length. For them, the wave-height danger zone begins at twelve feet high. These waves were exceeding that height.

Also, many of the boats had taken on more weight than the craft were designed and built to absorb. Greed had won out over safety. Most of the vessels were riding low in the water. Now the waves began to crash over the sides of the boats and wash over the decks of the craft. The three disabled boats had their tow ropes dropped. The towing craft could not risk being pulled under by the disabled craft. They were left to flounder as the storm passed overhead. They had lost the ability to turn into the oncoming waves and were pummeled from the sides as the boats were tossed from wave crest to wave trough.

The waves were so high at their crest that the sailors could no longer see the horizon. When they looked over the top of the waves, they saw only the sky which was black and covered with boiling clouds. The younger men were afraid. The older seamen knew not to be afraid, but to bail with all of their might.

Many other craft were taking on more water than their bilge pumps could keep up with or handle. Several of the boats looked like they would just sink below the surface of the Philippine Sea.

The wind had grown in intensity and the visibility had disappeared. Igor extended the anchor on his craft, knowing that the water was too deep for the anchor to grab the ocean bottom, but the anchor would have a stabilizing effect on his boat. It would function much like a keel on a sailboat. He went to his GPS locator and marked their location. Igor thought about a saying he had just read about that was attributed to Joseph Campbell which said, "We must be willing to let go of the life we planned so as to have the life that is waiting for us." Right now, life was out of his hands. And then he prayed…

On the morning of the fourth day Igor grabbed his binoculars and scanned the horizon. All around him were stranded boats that looked on the verge of succumbing to the Philippine Sea. The sailors were on deck and working laboriously to save their vessels. His first count made for five ships that were in big trouble. The total count was twenty-one visible craft. There were four missing. He expected that the three disabled boats would have drifted in the storm. But there was another boat missing.

Igor got on his radio in the wheelhouse of his boat and began to reach out to the other seamen. Most were able to answer him that they were okay, and they talked about the various levels of distress the boats were in. The majority of the craft remained somewhat seaworthy… as long as another cyclone didn't pass. Right now the seas were calm and the sky was clear.

Four of the twenty-five boats that began the journey were missing. Once Igor finished checking out his boat from bow to stern, he fired up his engine and set the autopilot for the GPS spot he had recorded yesterday. He figured that was a good place to start the search. Igor enlisted the help of three other boats who followed him to the GPS starting point. Once there, he scanned the horizon again and worked the radio to raise the other boats.

There was nothing but static on the radio…no response from the missing boats. Igor was not concerned yet because the three boats that had lost their engines may have run out of battery power during the night. The batteries had no way to recharge without a working engine. He studied the movement of the waves and decided to begin his search by travelling five miles to the west…back toward the Philippines.

Each of the other boat captains took a line from their compasses and travelled five miles along that path. The four boats kept in constant radio contact as they moved out to begin their search. Igor scanned the horizon ahead of him. After about a mile he saw a small dot bobbing in the gentle waves. He turned the wheel and aimed his boat at the speck. He communicated his discovery to the others.

As he approached, Igor could make out the shape of one of the disabled boats. He could begin to make out the shapes of two men who were working hard on the manual bilge pump to rid the boat of water. The electric pump had stopped during the night when the battery ran down. When he could, Igor hailed the men on the other craft. He steered his boat alongside the floundering boat and the men lashed the two boats together.

One of the men continued working the manual bilge pump while the other regaled Igor about their night of being tossed about like a feather in a tornado. Igor heard about the battery dying and the frightened men huddled in pitch black night. They could not even see the stars! The two were freezing cold and could not eat or drink. Both had wretched bile over the side during the ordeal and were beyond exhaustion. Dry blankets were immediately provided, and the men hunkered down and began to warm up.

Igor radioed to the other boats and told them of his position. All three craft headed directly for the new coordinates. The first boat to make it to Igor's location tossed a tow rope to the disabled boat. Igor untethered the boat from his own and watched as the larger boat began to head toward Saipan. He waited for the two others to arrive, and the three boats began once again to search for the three remaining boats that were missing. Igor assumed that the other boats would probably have drifted in a similar fashion to the discovered boat. The three captains agreed to motor in concentric circles with Igor in the middle position.

Almost as soon as they began their search pattern, the inner boat radioed that they had a sighting! As they closed the distance, they radioed that they had found the second of the disabled boats. The captain and mate were waiving frantically as they approached. It was determined that for now the boat was seaworthy enough to continue being towed and the tow rope was attached. The two craft began their journey to Saipan.

Igor moved his boat to the inner circle of the search pattern and the outer boat closed the diameter of their circular pattern also. Igor was now in the southwest tangent of the pattern when he heard from the other boat that they had also made a sighting. This time the news was not good. The boat's transom had flown loose in the high winds and had hit the captain in the head. He had died immediately. The mate had spent the night in darkness with the body of his captain and no communication equipment.

The boat was also listing heavily to the starboard side and was no longer seaworthy. The decision was made to move the wooden cases onto the larger boat. The captain's body was also hefted onto the craft and the mate jumped on last. The damaged boat was abandoned, and the tow boat captain turned the bow of his boat eastward toward Saipan.

One boat to go and all three other boats had been found in close proximity to Igor's position. He now continued the search pattern alone. The other boats were soon out of sight. He completed the circular pattern and then made the decision to stop the search and aim his boat on a path to Saipan. The last GPS location plus the two other locations were recorded…maybe he could ask Reggie to fly over these locations to continue the search. For now, Igor tallied up one dead and two missing sailors from their armada…and one boat unaccounted for…

Igor picked up his phone to place a call to Reggie.

Saipan, Northern Mariana Islands

Reggie and Ash looked around at the seventh-floor room whose window faced to the north. They had hauled the electronic gear up seven flights of stairs that were dark and dingy and had to step over lots of debris that had accumulated on the stairs and around the abandoned property once called the Plumeria Resort.

Reggie and Ash had stopped on each level as they climbed the concrete stairway. The lower floors limited their view of structures and landmarks to the north. Finally, on the seventh floor they had visual access to the areas they wanted to project a signal. Unlike the ROTHR radar site that they used for the four tests of Radio Free World, which beamed signals over the horizon, their small transmitter would only work by 'line of sight'.

It took the two men four trips to get all of the equipment up to the higher floor. Reggie was feeling his muscles in both legs and knew that he would be sore in the morning. Ash commented that this was great exercise! He loved running stairs.

They were looking out the window and planning how they would mess with the Russians when Reggie's phone rang.

"Dr. Nelson," I said into the mouthpiece.

"Reginald, this is Igor...do you remember me?" Igor questioned.

"Da, of course I do...we brought the two boxes to Saipan for you that your Russian friend picked up just like he was supposed to. How are you doing?" I answered.

"I need your help, again," Igor began. "We had a fleet of twenty-five fishing vessels that went to the Philippines to pick up the other boxes. There was a bad storm."

"I saw that on the news!" I interrupted. "It came up out of nowhere… dumped a lot of rain here on the island."

"Da, that's it. Well, a number of boats were damaged last night. One sailor has died. The damaged boats are being towed into Saipan," Igor replied.

"How can we help?" I asked, not sure what he was going to ask and knowing that seamanship was definitely not my forte.

"I fear that one of the boats has gone down with two on board. We have not been able to locate them. I am asking if you can use your plane to search an area around coordinates that I will give you. We get no response to radio calls and no distress signal has been intercepted. You can search more quickly and cover more distance in your plane than I can in my boat," Igor advised.

I looked at Ash and covered up the mouthpiece of the phone, "We need to go help some people, Ash!" I whispered.

Ash gave a nod.

"We're in, Igor. We'll leave now. I am handing the phone to Ash. Give him the coordinates," I ordered, and the two of us headed for the stairs and the long trek to the ground level. The Russians would just have to wait…I hoped that they would continue their search for at least another day.

We stopped by the house on the way to the airport for another pair of binoculars and a new toy that I had been working on with the technicians at Langley. It was a hand-held radar/sonar device for underwater mapping above the water surface and also able to look below the surface up to one hundred feet down. Sonar systems were available for mapping the bottom of the ocean, but the units were bulky and had to be mounted on a ship. This was a portable unit.

As we drove to the airport and readied Aurora II for the mission, Ash and I talked over and designed a search grid and pattern that we would fly beginning with the coordinates that Igor had given to Ash and expanding out to fifty miles in all directions from the beginning point. We would fly low and slow so that our powers of observation would be better. I would use the autopilot as much as we could so that we could both scan out the sides of the plane. I would use binoculars and pay attention to Aurora II and Ash would alternate between using binoculars and the handheld combination detecting device.

As we flew toward our rally point, we flew over a number of small craft making their way to Saipan. A couple of the boats looked like they were being towed in to port. The last boat we flew over was Igor's, and he called to let us know that we were close. The distance measuring equipment on the plane agreed that we were close to beginning our search pattern.

CHAPTER 31

Florence, Italy

Becky Nelson was seething mad.

"Mad as a hatter!" Becky thought, and then wondered, "What does that mean…mad as a hatter?"

She sat at her desk and called up the Google machine. In the search bar she typed, 'mad as a hatter'. Becky quickly discovered that her phrase did not describe how she was feeling. 'Mad as a hatter' referred to being insane or crazy…not angry. In olden times, men in the hat making business used mercury nitrate to moisten the fibers and make them mat together more efficiently. The process was called carroting and produced better felt and higher-quality hats. The problem was that many of the hat makers were driven insane from mercury poisoning.

Becky decided to use 'angry' to describe her state. Reggie had done it again. He and Ash were supposed to get the hell out of Saipan before the Russians arrived. Now, the Russians were there and searching for them. Then he told her that he was off on some crazy rescue mission with Ash. Then they wanted to play tricks on the Russians before they departed Saipan. The CIA and even POTUS had ordered them off the island, but the two of them were going to do whatever they damn well pleased.

She was pissed off…and afraid. Reggie and Ash should know better than to get in hairy or dangerous situations with the Russians. What would happen to I.N.C.I.S.O.R. if their involvement in Radio Free World were discovered. Becky wished that Reggie would consider the bigger picture for once when he acted.

That was it! Becky called Michael in Dubai and told him that she was booking a flight to Guam. Michael was ordered to call the Denver team and the Frankfurt team and get the twelve I.N.C.I.S.O.R. men to Guam. Michael was to arrange rooms at the Westin for her and the two teams for the next two weeks.

Michael chose not to argue with Mrs. Nelson. He followed her orders and contacted the twelve men, made travel arrangements, and booked the hotel for twelve rooms and a suite.

Denver, Colorado

Lance Everett downloaded his team's ticket information and travel itinerary. He sent the digital ticket for each of the six men to their cell phones.

"No paper anymore," Lance thought as he looked at his phone. All a traveler had to do these days was to call the airline ticket up on their phone display and scan it at the gate.

Lance checked the itinerary. The commercial flight took them from Denver to Narita, Japan. The team would have a short layover in Japan and then catch a flight to Guam. He hoped the layover in Japan would be long enough for him to show the other team members a fabulous sushi restaurant at the airport. The duration of the flight from Denver to Tokyo lasted just over twelve hours. It always amazed him that those giant planes could stay aloft for that long without refueling. The flight was so long that two flight crews were required to pilot the plane. Lance rechecked the information that Michael had provided and then made sure the team knew when to report to Denver International Airport.

Frankfurt, Germany

The six team members had gathered to hear about their next mission. It seemed like Becky Nelson was the force behind this mission. They were going to Guam to help out their bosses, Reginald Nelson and Ash Black. The crazy part of this trip was that Reggie and Ash did not know they were coming, and probably would have disapproved of their mission.

The men looked over their travel arrangements that had them departing the Frankfurt Airport in the morning and arriving in Guam almost eighteen hours later. The German team was also transiting through Narita, Japan. Magnus thought about the ANA lounge on the southern end of the Narita airport and its automatic Asahi beer machine that produced a perfect head of beer for every glass.

Becky Nelson was hopping a short flight from Florence to Frankfurt and then joining the team for the long trek to Guam. The only difference was that Becky was flying first class, which meant a nice bed for the longest leg of her flight.

The men from both teams had a myriad of questions. Becky deferred all of the queries, telling the young men that she would brief them about the mission once they were all settled into the Westin in Guam.

Saipan, Northern Mariana Islands

The two Russian investigators were halfway through their second day of searching. They had decided that the search mission would take three days and they were now halfway through their search with no results. Their fancy receiver had not found a thing! Not even a hint of a signal emanating from Saipan.

The two comrades were becoming frustrated in their lack of results. They would continue to follow the search pattern that had been mapped out for them, but they were tiring of watching the equipment and listening for something to wake up their senses.

While the Russians searched for Reggie and Ash, the two I.N.C.I.S.O.R. men were flying their own search pattern over the Philippine Sea west of Saipan. Unlike the Russians, they had just had a positive indication that the missing boat had been found!

Their instruments showed that the boat was submerged but had not sunk to the bottom of the ocean. The equipment measured that the boat was about one hundred feet below the surface. There was no sign of life. The two mariners that had been on the boat when the storm began were missing and assumed dead. That was a total of three sailors lost during the adventure. Ash marked and recorded the location while Reggie radioed Igor that the boat had been discovered.

The two I.N.C.I.S.O.R. founders turned Aurora II back toward Saipan to land at Francisco Ada Airport. It was time to set up their transmitter to spoof the Russians. But first they would enjoy an evening of fine food, good drinks and interesting narrative.

Reggie and Ash set up a dinner with Jeff Beach and Nicky Bells. The two wanted to learn more about the island that had been their recent home. Nicky had picked Casa Urashima for their restaurant the evening. The restaurant was in an old home and the small rooms each had a table and chairs for dining with some intimacy. Nicky was the best storyteller that Reggie had ever encountered, and tonight was no different. The four men all chose the set menu for one hundred dollars for two people. Drinks were ordered.

As the first appetizers came to the table, Nicky began to regale the table about his exploits at the Santa Fe hotel in Guam. The man that had brought Nicky to Saipan to help him start up a Sheraton hotel in the village of San Roque also had his eyes on hotel projects in Guam. The two developed a boutique-style hotel in Tamuning, Guam. The property boasted one hundred and five rooms, a small infinity pool and jacuzzi, and fabulous sunsets. Nicky, it turned out, was quite the ladies' man and he told stories about his conquests that lasted through the appetizers, salad and pasta dish.

By the time the steak was served, Jeff had taken over the conversation talking about a number of times that the land ownership laws on Saipan had messed up development opportunities of some major corporations and kept the island economy depressed. There exists something in the laws of the Commonwealth of the Northern Mariana Islands called Article XII. This law, titled the 'Alienation of Land' law allows only people of Northern Marianas descent to own land. The law was designed to protect the land interests of the local population. The law failed miserably.

The Chamorro and Carolinian people were "land rich and cash poor". This led to the exact abuse that Article XII was written to protect. Since only locals could own land, the ones that had money would lend to the poorer folks with their land as collateral. If and when the borrower defaulted on a loan, the land would be scooped up at extremely depressed values by the lender. There are now about forty wealthy and powerful indigenous families on the island from this type of activity. The forty families controlled the island. Many family members held government positions.

Had there been a market for the land, i.e., outside investment, the land value would have been much higher, and the poorer Chamorro and Carolinian people would have been treated more fairly.

"They probably would have still lost their land, but would have had more money," Jeff finished.

"These people thought nothing about screwing with completed transactions," Nicky took over the conversation. "It was common to have a land deal fall apart because the locals would try to resell already sold land for more money."

"What?" Ash replied.

"Amazing!" I added.

"I know of two brothers who were both in the legislature who approached a Japanese man who had purchased leasing rights to their land two years before. They wanted their land back so they could sell it for a higher price since the land had appreciated in value and was worth more. They did not expect to repay him for what he had paid for the land. He was to turn it over to them, lose everything…just so they could make more money! They even threatened to use their positions in the legislature to make his life miserable if he did not comply," Nicky continued.

"The land of thieves!" Ash exclaimed.

"What do you think about the Army Corps of Engineers being here to dig up unexploded ordinance?" Jeff asked Ash and me, switching gears.

"World War II stuff?" I asked.

"No, but they are still finding unexploded shells from seventy-five years ago. They even have a disposal site on the old narrow gauge railroad tracks," Jeff replied.

"I've been up there!" Nicky added. "It is the craziest thing…they have this chain link fence stretching for about one hundred feet along the old railroad bed marking the site with warning signs. The fence stops and does not enclose the area. You can walk around both ends of the fence and access the disposal site! Crazy!"

"There is another site where the old Christian radio station was. It is now being used by the Hope recovery center for recovering addicts and alcoholics. During the Cold War the United States stored munitions there to be used by the insurgents being trained on Saipan to infiltrate the Communist countries to the northwest," Jeff continued.

"Are they exploding that old stuff?" I asked.

"Digging it up and destroying it," Jeff said.

"Three times so far," Nicky added.

"Three explosions?" Ash queried and looked at me.

I smiled a knowing smile back at Ash and asked if they were done.

"Another month to go," Jeff replied.

My wheels were turning. Ash and I had been able to see this area from our perch at the Plumeria Resort. We could fly a drone with a mirror at the site. We could lure the Russians to the site with our fake signal. And then…who knows!

While Ash and I were talking with our two new friends from Saipan, a man in a military uniform came over to our table. He was dining in another room and overheard our conversation about the disposal of military ordinance.

"Good evening, gentlemen, I am Rear Admiral Dee Mewbourne," he announced.

I sat up a little straighter at his announcement and I noticed that the other men at the table had done the same.

"I am the commandant of the Maritime Prepositioning Ship Squadron Three," he continued.

"Wow, what a title!" I replied.

"It's a long name for those ships anchored just outside the lagoon," he said as he pointed toward the Philippine Sea.

"I have been really curious about those ships. They're bigger than warships," Ash added.

"And there are usually only five or six ships stationed here. The others sailed over so that I could meet them all," the Admiral said. "And you are…"

"Oh, sorry, Admiral," I replied and stood to shake his hand. "I am Reginald Nelson, and this is Ash Black."

Ash rose and shook his hand also.

"We are new to the island and visiting," I offered.

"We're on a mission from God," Ash joked, remembering the line from the Blues Brothers movie.

Jeff stood and introduced himself and Nicky.

"We've been here a long time, Admiral," Nicky said.

"What do you do here?" Admiral Mewbourne asked, to make conversation.

"We are both retired," Jeff answered. "I was with the Department of the Interior…"

"And I helped the Japanese with some of the development here on the island, over the years," Nicky added.

"I heard that the Japanese came here in a big way years ago," the Admiral offered, showing some of his knowledge of the island.

"Yes, they did…and then the bubble in Japan burst and a large part of their investment money dried up and blew away," Nicky said.

"That was back when Japan Airlines went bankrupt. When was it? 2010?" the Admiral replied.

"Exactly right! They were a major player here on the island with the Nikko hotel and La Fiesta," Nicky added.

The Admiral turned to Jeff Beach, "The Interior Department?"

"Yes, sir. I was the first person ever to be labelled, persona non grata, even before I arrived."

"The island was adjusting to its new role as a commonwealth from the Trust Territory days," Jeff said.

"They did not appreciate interference from the United States and saw me as the main interference!"

"You two have seen many, many changes here," the Admiral opined. "I wanted to say 'hello' and meet someone who knows about the ordinance disposal up in Marpi. Also, I wanted to invite you to tour one of our ships in the harbor and join us for a nice steak lunch."

"Ash and I would love to," I replied.

"Nicky and I have been on a tour," Jeff responded and then turned to Ash and me. "It's really cool the way they pack those ships with supplies, vehicles, and munitions."

"When would you like us to join you?" Ash asked.

"How about tomorrow?" the Admiral said.

"Sold!" I replied. "Where do we go?"

"The Port of Saipan…" the Admiral began.

"I've seen the sign on Middle Road!" Ash interrupted.

"Yes, turn there and park. A boat will pick you up and ferry you out to the Charlton," Admiral Mewbourne finished. "Eleven sharp!"

The Admiral left to rejoin his party in the next room. We completed our dinner and departed for the rental house.

"How the hell are we going to get off of this rock when we keep getting invited to new adventures?" Ash asked while we drove.

"I'm dying to see inside of one of those ships!" I added.

"So, what? We're going to mess with the Russians AND make this lunch meeting on a ship?" Ash argued.

"I don't think it will take long to spoof the Russians. All I want to do is confuse them. They should have had two days with no findings. Tomorrow we tease them!" I spoke.

Back at the house we enjoyed a cocktail on the porch listening to the waves lapping ashore.

CHAPTER 32

Guam, Mariana Islands

The twelve I.N.C.I.S.O.R. team members and Becky gathered in the Westin lobby. Becky had discovered the night before that the Starbucks in the lobby served a delicious white chocolate mocha coffee. She waited until all of the men had placed their orders, picked up her drink, and paid for the group. They moved to open seating on the back side of the deli counter. The rest of the section was empty.

"So, now that you have us all here, what are you going to do with us?" Lance joked.

The men had been briefed during their long journey into the western Pacific. Several of the team had paid for the internet on the long leg of the trip to Japan and studied what they could about Saipan. Most of the information focused on the Battle of Saipan in 1944. There were some travelogues and videos of tourist spots and locations on the island. There were also references to the Boonie Dog population on Saipan.

"Looks like a fun vacation spot! Is that why we're here?" Flex asked.

"You guys! Stop with the joking around. This is business," Becky replied.

"How about we get in some pickleball while we are here?" Duncan suggested.

"Pickleball? What is that?" Dale asked.

"New guys haven't played yet," Kurt added.

"Great game...fun...combination of tennis, badminton, and ping pong...lots of fun," Powers opined.

"Hey guys...stop it! I am serious! We are here to help Reggie and Ash," Becky interrupted.

"Then why are we here?" Gary asked.

"Gary, right? Nice to meet you," Becky replied.

This was the first time that Becky had personally met the three new I.N.C.I.S.O.R. men, Dale Denby, Gary Grayneck, and Dick Giles.

"Yes, Mrs. Nelson," Gary stood and shook Becky's hand. Dale joined him with the introduction.

"Nice to meet you," Becky stated and continued, "I am flying over to Saipan on the morning United flight. You twelve are to report to Brigadier General Jeremy Sloane at Andersen Air Force Base and prepare the supplies and load the transport for your flight over. I will let you know when to leave."

"Isn't he the commander of the base?" Magnus asked.

"Yes, and he has been apprised of the situation by President Marron," Becky added. "Andersen Air Base is ready to provide transport and bomber support, and the Guam National Guard is on standby if you get into trouble."

"Wow! POTUS?" Dick asked.

"What did Reggie and Ash do to involve the United States government?" Graham wondered.

"It is about Reggie's new invention. It has the Arab terrorists running scared after only three tests of the device in Baghdad and some of the Middle Eastern countries, but the Russians are onto them. There are Russians in Saipan right now trying to find your bosses! They have flown in sophisticated equipment and are trying to track them down as we speak." Becky continued.

"Reggie and Ash were ordered to get out of Saipan, but they are still there. Those two think that they can toy with the Russians, but this is serious! We are here to get Reginald and Ash off of that island, or if we are too late, to provide the manpower to stop whatever the Russians decide to throw their way," Becky stated.

The twelve men sat in silence, contemplating what Becky had said. What if they got into a firefight? Well, that was what they were trained for by the United States military!

Saipan, Northern Mariana Islands

"Okay, Ash, fire up the generator," I said to my good friend.

We had purchased a small portable gas-powered electric generator at the local ACE hardware store and carried it up into the Plumeria Resort to the room where the equipment had been prepared to spoof the Russians. Ash pulled once on the cord and the generator started right up and began a steady hum of a gas motor.

Soon, the green lights on the array of transmitters all came on and showed a solid green glow. The equipment was ready to transmit. I turned the tuning wheel until the desired frequency showed on the display.

"All set," I announced.

"The Russian van just passed by the Plumeria heading north on Middle Road," Ash said as he watched through a pair of binoculars.

I flicked the transmit switch for a five second burst.

"The van just skidded to a halt!" Ash whispered.

"Ash…you don't have to whisper! They can't hear us," I replied.

"I know, but this is exciting!" Ash countered.

The short emission was not enough for the Russians to get a fix on the source. They waited for a few minutes and then began to slowly continue to the north.

I held the transmit switch down for another five second burst. Again, the van screeched to a halt. This time the van performed an about face and headed south back toward the abandoned hotel.

Ash rushed down the stairs and raced to the Escalade. We had mounted a parabolic mirror in the trunk space of the car. He sped away from the abandoned resort parking lot and drove the car past the La Fiesta Mall and on to route 320. He parked the SUV at the blue million-gallon water tank. Ash pressed a button on the dash and the rear door of the Escalade raised up to expose the mirror.

He and I had made a test run and discovered that the location we picked was line of sight to the empty hotel room we had taken over. Ash called to let me know that he had arrived. I repositioned the equipment and pulsed the signal again. This time I gave it several longer pulses.

The Russian technicians must have been wildly confused. The signal was now coming from northeast of their van. The ambulance van made a U-turn on Middle Road and ventured to the north. I pulsed the signal once more and called Ash.

He closed the rear door and now moved the Escalade further up route 320. The road had turned to a dirt road with the jungle creeping into the road from both sides. Ash drove slowly on the rutted road past where the Crams had entertained us and on to the old FEBQ road that led down a ravine to the drug rehabilitation center which was now the site where the Army Corps of Engineers was exploding ordinance.

Ash parked the SUV outside the center's gate and raised the rear door again. Once again, he called me to let me know that he was in position. He also got the drones up in the air with extra mirrors to bolster the signal and improve the line of sight.

I aligned the transmission equipment to his new position and pulsed the signal. This time I held the transmit button down for fifteen seconds, allowing the Russians to get a good fix on Ash's position. I waited for five minutes and then pulsed the signal again. I then called Ash and told him to get his ass out of there!

Ash retraced his route with the Escalade. The road from the Hope Center out to Middle Road was much better maintained, but he surmised that the Russians would come up that road and he did not want to encounter them.

Soon he was back at the Plumeria Resort hotel. Ash climbed the stairs and joined me in the room. I had turned off the equipment and had killed the generator out on the room's patio. The room was eerily quiet without the hum from the machines.

"What do you know, Reggie?" Ash asked, a little out of breath.

"They took the bait. They are driving up to the center," I said.

"And what about the disposal guys?" Ash asked.

"The blast is scheduled for…" I looked at my watch. "Now!"

We both listened closely. I thought that I heard a low rumble but was not sure. Ash reacted to the same sound.

"Was that it?" I asked.

"Don't know…maybe," Ash replied.

We were far enough away from the detonation site not to have heard much. The Russians on the other hand had just reached the blast site when their van was rocked by a huge blast.

The blast area had been carefully cordoned off by the local police in preparation for the explosion. The road leading off of Middle Road and up to the Hope Center was also closed off. The one thing that the local police did not do was have armed constables at the barricade. The residents were usually good about respecting and honoring blockades when the police erected them. The Russians paid no heed to the blockade and sped the van around the warnings to pursue the signal that they had received from the Hope Center.

It made sense to the technicians in the van. An old radio station probably with equipment that was abandoned when the radio station left the site. The drug rehabilitation people would not have any use or need for the old radio equipment. It was a perfect site to conduct transmitting a signal from Saipan! Until they came upon the ordinance disposal site at the same moment that the explosion occurred.

The van was rocked into the air and knocked over on its side. The sensitive receiving equipment housed in the van was completely destroyed. Several of the electronic pieces actually caught fire and badly burned the technician watching over the equipment in the rear of the van. The driver was also hurt. When the van shot upwards and onto its side, his femur was fractured by the van's steering wheel.

The driver looked to the rear of the van and saw that it was on fire. He kicked out the front windshield with his good leg and limped his way to the rear doors. After much effort the driver got one of the doors to open and worked to free his burned comrade from the building fire. As he dragged the man free, the fire reached the van's gasoline tank and the vehicle exploded.

Ash and I were packing up our gear and making the numerous trips down the resort stairs to the Escalade. We heard and then saw an ambulance racing north on Middle Road followed by three police cars and the fire department. Figuring that something more had happened than what we had planned, Ash hopped into the passenger seat and powered up one of the drones. He directed it with the coordinates for the center and watched the screen in the SUV as the drone flew off to the northeast. The drone reached the scene before the emergency vehicles arrived and Ash and I looked at the burning van as the onboard camera autofocused on the devastation.

We could see two men lying fairly close to the van which was laying on its side and burning. Ash and I were not prepared for any of this!

"Oh shit!" Ash exclaimed for both of us.

We had hoped for and planned to scare the pants off the Russians by luring them close to the detonation site. Our assumption was that the blast would be well contained. Welcome to Saipan! The engineers had piled the ordinance above ground, poured gasoline on the munitions and detonated the pile by remote control not caring for anything around the site.

The ambulance arrived and the two men were administered to and moved inside the vehicle. We were able to see both of them moving and knew that they had not died…at least at the blast site! The ambulance left with lights and sirens blaring for the short trip to the Community Health Center. One of the police cars served as the ambulance's escort, while the other police began to move around the site working to secure the area. A firetruck arrived from Garapan, and the firefighters quickly extinguished the burning van. They then moved their hoses to spray water on the burning heap that used to be Cold War weaponry.

"Wow!" Ash exclaimed.

"What did we do?" I moaned.

"Well, Reggie…you got what you wanted! You…we…spoofed the Russians!" Ash joked trying to lighten the mood.

"Funny man," I said. "Call the drone back and let's get out of here," I ordered.

"Just go," Ash said. "The drone will find us and can land on the roof while we are moving."

"Really? That is so cool! I want one of these," I exclaimed.

"We have one," Ash retorted.

"You are right, my friend…but we have to get it off of Saipan," I said.

"They have containers for that," Ash countered. "And maybe we can get the CIA to deliver it somewhere…like Frankfurt! There's already two armed Escalades in Denver," Ash remembered.

"Can't hurt to ask," I finished.

We drove south to the Saipan Seaport. We would arrive just when we were told to present ourselves for the boat ride to one of the prepositioned ships.

"We'll have to wait to hear what the fallout was from our little escapade," I said.

I looked at the roof after we parked. The drone was back in its housing. I had not heard it arrive or felt it land on the vehicle. Smooth as silk.

The transport vessel had about a dozen seamen already seated on benches that lined both the port and starboard side of the craft for the journey out to their ships. Ash and I joined the men and the boat pulled away from the dock. It had two stops before we reached the Charlton.

Ash and I joined four others to climb up the ramp to the main deck. The Commadore was waiting for us and greeted us warmly.

"Welcome to your first tour of a prepositioned ship," the Commodore offered. "Let's begin belowdecks."

We entered an elevator that took us down to the lowest level. I noticed that there were thirteen levels in the elevator. I was amazed that there were so many levels to the ship…and most were below the water line! When the elevator door opened, Ash and I were open-mouthed as we looked out on all of the equipment that was displayed before us. Humvees, tanks, trucks and other vehicles were arrayed before us and packed so tightly that it looked like there were only inches between the vehicles.

"How…" I began to say.

"There are specialized merchant seamen whose job is to load and unload these ships every three years. They are skilled at maneuvering the vehicles within inches of each other and not a nick on any of the paint jobs," the Commodore opened.

"You telling us that they replace all of this equipment every three years?" Ash questioned.

"That's correct, Ash, every three years," the Commodore added.

"I wonder what they do with the old stuff?" Ash said.

"And all of the levels look like this?" I asked.

"Everything from generators to fresh water converters. All of the infrastructure that the Marines need to continue an action. Whether it is a defensive response or an aggressive maneuver," the Commodore continued.

"And when do you respond?" Ash wondered.

"If there is a conflict anywhere in the world, we can respond within seventy-two hours. A Marine is inserted with three days of supplies that he carries. We then respond to resupply the troops. We have enough equipment, supplies and ammunition to support a Marine Air-Ground Task Force for thirty days, the Commodore added.

"What is this task force?" I asked.

"There are four elements of a Marine air-ground task force," the Commodore said. "The command element or headquarters unit, the ground combat element made up of infantry units, the aviation combat element, and the logistics combat element for command and control. These four elements do not change…ever, but the size and number of troops change depending on the conflict. Hey, Reggie, you're a dentist, right?"

"Yes, sir," I replied.

"Advanced dental units fall under the logistics combat element of the Marine Air-Ground Task Force," the Commodore added.

"Wow!" I said and tried to imagine working out in a tent somewhere with people shooting at me! So much for a steady hand!

"And you have a bunch of these ships," Ash said.

"There are seventeen ships like this stationed in Diego Garcia and here in Guam and Saipan," the Commodore replied. "We can also respond to natural disasters. A good example was just a couple of years ago right here on Saipan. Typhoon Yutu devastated the southern half of the island. We set up a reverse osmosis plant on shore and provided fresh water for the residents. Come, let's go…lunch is waiting for us."

We were served fabulous grilled steaks and all the fixings. I did not expect a feast like this on a ship!

When lunch ended, the transport boat had returned to take Ash and me back to the Port of Saipan. The two of us were mostly speechless on the boat ride back to port. On the dock I looked back at the large ships anchored just beyond the lagoon. I had a new respect for those steel giants floating on the Philippine Sea.

CHAPTER 33

Vladivostok, Russia

Ivan and Vlad had finished reviewing the latest report from Saipan. Both of their investigators were in the hospital. One had a broken thigh bone, and the other was badly burned on his face and upper torso. The two technicians were not field operatives, and both had been hurt. The two comrades were in a foul mood.

"Now what?" Ivan said to Vlad.

"Yes, now what," Vlad began. "I have reviewed the data gathered during their stay on Saipan. I believe that Saipan is the source of the signal that was recorded in Iraq."

"So, what if that is true?" Ivan replied. "Let us agree that Saipan is the source. What do we do with that assumption?"

"I think it is time to meet with the terror cells in Baghdad, again," Vlad offered.

"And do what? Ivan argued. "Are we going to attack Saipan? A United States territory?"

"The terrorists are not going to be comfortable with utilizing their stores of C-4 explosives that they have until something is done to eliminate the signals from Saipan."

Langley, Virginia

The CIA Director was pacing in his office when there was a knock at the door.

"Enter!" he barked.

The door opened and an analyst sheepishly stuck their head into the room.

"Sir, there is news from Saipan," the analyst began.

"Those two still there? They have put the whole project at risk! They would be dogmeat if they worked for me!" the Director seethed.

"Becky Nelson and the I.N.C.I.S.O.R. teams are in Guam and ready to help," the analyst said. "And the Russians that were tracking Dr. Nelson and Mr. Black have been injured in an accident."

"I read about that," the Director continued. "The Russian van blew up?"

"Yes, sir. The van had ventured onto a bomb disposal site right when there was an ignition," the analyst spoke.

"And Reggie and Ash…er… Dr. Nelson and Mr. Black…are they still on the island?" the Director asked.

"Yes sir!" the analyst replied.

"Well, tell the teams to get over there and bodily remove the two of them! Hog tie them if they have to, but I want them off of that island, dammit!" the Director finished.

Washington, DC

"Things sound like they are heating up in our easternmost territory," the President surmised.

"Well, Mr. President, if you mean that the Russians are there and so are the I.N.C.I.S.O.R. leaders…you are right," the CIA Director agreed.

"Even though I have personally ordered them to get the hell out?" POTUS replied.

"President Marron, I have given the order for them to be removed from Saipan. It will happen soon!" the Director answered.

"And what about the rest of the world? Let's get on with the briefing,"

The Director changed his focus, and the Saipan issue was tabled for the moment.

Baghdad, Iraq

The various terror cells that operated in the Baghdad area had just finished a meeting with the two Russian advisors, Vlad and Ivan.

The terrorists knew now that the problems and destruction to the buildings in their city were caused by Signals from Saipan. The leaders did not understand how a radio signal could detonate their plastique explosives without any sort of primer or detonation cap. Plastique explosives were supposed to be safe! They also did not understand why Saipan was the source of their problems. A little island that nobody had heard of had nothing to do with the Middle East...or so they thought.

The leaders did not need to understand. They had chosen to accept the Russians' theory and act on faith. They had voted and the decision was to mount an attack on the tiny island. They would utilize their existing army of illiterate thugs and the remaining stores of munitions. But they would need transportation to the remote island.

It was time to approach their Russian advisors to see if transports could be made available to carry them southeast.

Damascus, Syria

Two of the Baghdad terrorist cell leaders had travelled to the capital city of Damascus to meet with the Russians there that were supporting Assad's failing government. Their mission was to secure the Russian's help with transporting a large number of terrorist fighters and their equipment to a tiny island in Micronesia.

Ivan and Vlad had been asked to provide the support that the terrorists requested. The two comrades had made the trip from Vladivostok to Damascus for the meeting. The four men met at the airfield that Russia was using outside Damascus to support Assad's military.

"Privet," one of the two terrorists opened. He had worked on the phrase for a long time. The Russian language did not come easily for him.

"Asalaamu alaikum," Ivan replied, showing deference to the Iraqi culture. When he was learning a proper greeting in Iraq, he had wondered why the Iraqis use 'hello' so much in their culture. Vlad explained to him that 'hello' in Iraq really meant goodbye! Ivan still wondered how an English word had crept into Arabic dialect.

"We are here to ask for you to support a mission we wish to commence against the perpetrators of the destruction in Baghdad," one of the terrorists opened after the pleasantries were finished and tea had been served.

"How may we help you?" Ivan asked.

"We wish to have two of your Antonov AN 12's to be placed at our disposal," the other terrorist leader said.

"And these cargo planes will be used for what purpose?" Vlad wondered.

"We will take fifty men to wipe out the facility that you discovered on the island of Saipan," Achmed replied.

The two Russians looked at each other, sensing that the Arabs did not have a clue. They had picked up signals from Saipan. They knew nothing about a facility or even how many were behind the emanations. They couldn't exactly be sure that it was Saipan! And yet these men were going off, halfcocked, thousands of miles…for what?

"You plan to just fly in to the international airport in Saipan with two planes full of terrorists and equipment? That is ludicrous!" Ivan opined.

"Do not assume that we are not prepared to complete our mission!" Achmed countered. "We will land at the Francisco Ada International Airport at night when the terminal is closed. No one will know that we have arrived on the island until it is too late."

"Do you fools know that the tower is manned twenty-four hours a day?" Vlad argued. "They will see you coming a long time before you get to the island. They will have enough time to warn Guam and they will respond with jet fighters against our turbo-prop transports! The

United States Air Force will blow you out of the sky before you get close to the island."

"Hey Vlad," Ivan thought. "What about flying into Pagan? We could land the transports there and load the fifty fighters for Islam onto a Russian trawler and spirit them, equipment and all, south to Saipan."

"A trawler would not be a problem in those waters?" Vlad asked, talking to Ivan as if the two Iraqis were not there.

"The Japanese and us have been fishing those waters for decades. We have oceanic charts and manuscripts that Russia occupied the island of Tinian, next to Saipan in the 1800's. Even the United States declaring the Marianas Trench as a marine preserve hasn't stopped us from fishing in those waters," Ivan answered.

"What about the runway? Was it not cut in half by lava when the volcano erupted in 1981?" Vlad continued to disagree, thinking this was a bad plan.

Ivan pulled out an aerial photo of an island that was labelled Pagan Air Strip. The image displayed a straight line that demarcated the runway and illustrated the lava flow that crossed the runway, shortening the runway length by half.

"That is what I am talking about!" Vlad exclaimed and pointed to the photograph. "What do we do about this?"

"First, two pieces of good news…the volcanic eruption in 1981 caused the evacuation of the island of Pagan and there have been no attempts to re-inhabit the island in thirty years," Ivan began. "There will not be any locals to contend with or to report our activities."

"And the second piece?" Vlad asked.

"Here is a report from 2006 addressing the repair of the runway. The Americans have already figured out how to restore the runway so that it can be used to get supplies to the northern islands of the Marianas," Ivan stated and plopped a copy of the report on the table.

"Did you read this?" Vlad questioned, leafing through the long report. Reading English was difficult for Vlad.

"Da, comrade, I did!" Ivan announced. "The Pagan airstrip is a grass field that is nineteen hundred feet long. I get a kick out of this part…" Ivan turned to a descriptive page. "Cattle and goats are commonly seen grazing on the airstrip, which keeps the grass somewhat under control." Ivan let out a chuckle.

Ivan continued reading, "the west end of the runway is an abrupt drop off to the beach, a drop of approximately twenty feet. The east end of the runway is interrupted by the lava flow, which abruptly rises to a height of approximately fifteen to twenty feet."

"And the takeoff and landing specifications for the Antonov AN-12?" Vlad questioned.

"Landing distance is sixteen hundred feet," Ivan began.

"So, we can fly in to the strip!" Vlad exclaimed.

"Da, comrade…the problem is leaving…the AN-12 needs twenty-three hundred feet!" Ivan concluded reading his notes.

"We cannot get the planes out unless we clear the lava flow at the end of the runway," Vlad announced. "We cannot abandon two cargo planes on a remote island in the Marianas!"

"I have thought about that," Ivan replied. "We include a bulldozer and road grader to clear the runway of the debris. Then the aircraft can depart."

"And fuel?" Vlad asked. "It is a long flight and the Antonov has a range of just over thirty-five hundred miles. Damascus to Saipan is over sixty-five hundred miles."

"Da, comrade, the transports must re-fuel in the air…twice each leg!" Ivan added.

"So, it can be done," Achmed interrupted.

The Russians were perturbed that their conversation had been stopped.

"Yes, sir…if you are serious about preparing an attack on the person or persons on the island of Saipan so you can seek vengeance for the material and men that you lost in the explosions, we are ready and able to provide the aircraft, fueling aircraft, fishing trawler, and logistics in transporting you to and from Saipan," Vlad surmised.

"We cannot provide men or materials for your mission. That would put us in direct conflict with the United States. The pilots of the aircraft are okay, but no men involved in the conflict. Russia is not ready to commit to that!" Ivan added.

"Fair enough! You get us there and we take care of everything else," the other terrorist leader interjected.

Achmed prayed, "Praise Allah, the Signals from Saipan will be stopped…forever!"

The Russians looked at each other and shrugged. It was so easy to meddle in the affairs of the Middle East and mess with the policies of the United States.

Saipan, Northern Mariana Islands

When Ash and I returned to the rental house on the beach I observed the Becky was sitting at the dining table on the patio. I was shocked to see her.

"Wow! What a great surprise!" I announced and went to kiss her.

"Great to see you, Becky." Ash said.

Becky pushed me away.

"This is not a 'for fun' visit!" She announced. "Why are you two still here? You were ordered off of this island by everyone…including the President of the United States! What do you two idiots think you are doing?"

Strong words from an angry woman. I knew that I had to tread lightly or be in real trouble with my wife. Ash sat down and acted like a mute. He was going to stay out of this tirade.

"I am so sorry, my love…? I began.

"Bullshit! Reggie you are once again doing what you want no matter what everybody else says!"

Becky was getting ready to really let me have it. I had nothing I could argue about. Ash and I had been told several times to get out of Saipan. It was only because I was not ready to leave that we were still here. All I could think about was how hot Becky was when she was like this…I wanted to get her into bed!

"Again, I am sorry," I tried again. Becky had taught me years ago that it was better to ask for forgiveness than it was to ask for permission. So far, it was not working.

"Have you even packed?" Becky looked at Ash.

"Hey, I never really unpacked," Ash said. "And just so you know, we stopped the Russians from finishing their reconnaissance mission."

"The whole point was to get you two off of the island before the Russians arrived. What if they had discovered anything that could lead them to I.N.C.I.S.O.R.? Did you think about that?" Becky's voice was rising.

Ash sensed that he was fighting a losing battle and turned back into a mute. He made sure not to make eye contact with Becky.

"What about you, Reggie?" Becky asked.

"I can be ready in a jiffy! Why? What is the hurry?" I countered.

"What if the Russians send others to help with the injuries? What if they believe that the accident was not coincidental? What if somebody pieces together that you two fools lured them by creating a similar signal as the Radio Free World signal? What if…"

"Okay! I give…lighten up!" I retorted. I knew those were the wrong words as soon as they left my mouth.

Becky glared at me for a moment that seemed to last forever, and then rose and went inside without saying a word. The glare was my sign that I had messed up big-time. I knew that I was in trouble.

Baghdad, Iraq

Each of the five terror cell leaders had agreed to make their ten top fighters available for the mission to Saipan. Fifty of the best desert fighters would be armed to the teeth with the best weaponry that the terrorists had.

The leaders did not know who they were going up against, but they would be ready to take on a small army if that was to be what they would encounter. A caravan of pickup trucks and SUVs left Baghdad for the journey to Damascus where the fighters would board two Russian transport aircraft that would take them to their next battle.

Guam, Mariana Islands

"Yes, ma'am!" Powers said into his phone as he scribbled down his marching orders from Becky Nelson.

The twelve men had just finished a workout in the gym at Andersen Air Force Base. Sweat was dripping off all of the men. Both teams were from much drier climates than the high humidity on Guam. The twelve were drinking heavily from the water machine trying to replace some of the water weight that had been lost.

"What's up?" Flex asked when Powers placed his phone on the table.

"Time to move!" Powers replied. "We are to get to Saipan ASAP, and we are to bring the Radio Free World transmitter with us."

"And where do we go once we are on Saipan?" Dale asked.

"Becky has put us up at the Hyatt," Powers answered. "But first we are to escort the RFW equipment out to the Charlton."

"All twelve of us?" Gary wondered.

"We are all expected to be the escort for the transmitter," Powers stated.

"Must be some valuable stuff!" Magnus opined.

"It is the stuff that can change the world," Powers ended, and headed off to arrange a military transport to take the I.N.C.I.S.O.R. teams to Saipan.

CHAPTER 34

Washington, DC

President Marron had just completed a briefing with the CIA Director and the NSA Director. He sat behind the Resolute desk in the Oval Office and placed both elbows on the desk with his head in his hands. He contemplated what had been explained to him as the next move...a defensive move at best which was not his strong suit. He liked being the leader of the free world. He liked being the protagonist and driving most of the world situations. The President did not like having to be in a reactive position, letting somebody else make the opening moves.

This time he was having to react to a number of Iraqi terrorist groups that the CIA learned were going to mount an attack against a United States territory! A P&C listening device that was the first of Dr. Reginal Nelson's inventions had picked up conversations among the terrorist leaders about the impending attack. The terrorists saw this attack as revenge against destruction that had occurred in Baghdad.

Saipan was the target of this terrorist plot. President Marron had never been to Saipan, but remembered stories told by his father of the Battle of Saipan in World War II. His father was among the marines that hit the western beach of Saipan on the first day of the conflict with the Japanese. His father had considered himself very lucky because almost a third of that first wave of marines were killed during the attack.

His father also loved to tell the story of being involved in two major campaigns in the Pacific theater. He fought bravely and was awarded the purple heart for an injury he suffered during a battle. He returned to his home state of Texas only to find that he was too young to have alcohol! The President's dad laughed every time he told that story to his son.

Saipan had become part of America after that battle. The island functioned as a trust territory for many years after the war. The local people voted to become a commonwealth over forty years ago. The United States still believed that the island held strategic importance for them in the Western Pacific due to its close proximity to Asia.

On top of that, once again it was confirmed that the Russians were behind this next move by the Arab terrorists. He had grown up during the Cold War when America and the Soviet Union were the world's two superpowers. The two nations faced off numerous times during that period. The rest of the world players took back seats to the two.

President Marron had been a student of history and studied how the two different socio-economic systems had fared against one another. Quite simply, a previous Republican President pitted Capitalism against Communism and the United States just outspent the Soviet Union into submission. Once the Communists could not keep up economically with Capitalism, the Soviet Union began to break apart and crumble.

The President remembered now one specific example of the Cold War. America came up with the strategy of having a defensive satellite network to stop any intercontinental missiles from the Soviet Union from piercing through the shield. It was named the Space Defense Initiative, and nicknamed Star Wars.

The theory may have been good, but the United States could not make it work with the state of technology at that time. But the Soviet Union did not know this! They had to spend billions of rubles that they did not have in an attempt to counter America's SDI program.

"We just outspent them," the President thought out loud.

Now America faced opponents that often had no statehood. There were many of these bad apples, and rogue nations willing to support the groups with money and infrastructure. Bad actors like Iran and North Korea were well known to aid and abet terrorism around the world.

"We are the only superpower left and everybody wants to attack the king of the hill," was President Marron's next spoken thought.

So many people in the world perceive America as the ultimate goal of prosperity made available to the masses that are willing to work for it. The United States has absorbed people from all countries, and they can call themselves 'American'. They may say, 'Mexican American, or Chinese American, or African American.'

"We are the only country that is willing to include all people as Americans," POTUS stated to the empty room.

The President understood obliquely that terrorists relied on mostly ignorant, uneducated, and unemployed individuals to fill their ranks. Smarter people would not blow themselves up! He also understood that terror groups claim that God is on their side. The killing done in God's name had always left President Marron baffled.

The President also had an understanding about why Russia chose to be so contrary and against the goals of the United States. He felt that the Russians were very short sighted. The terrorists would just as quickly turn against that country if they needed a new target…but America and its shining light gave the terror groups all the target that they needed for the time being.

These were people who had been at war with each other since the beginning of time. Then the world leaders plopped Israel down right in the middle of this hotbed and gave the Arabs a common enemy to war against. The Arab countries would still turn against each other like Iran and Iraq did in their war, but Israel gave them a common focus…a new enemy.

"The Kremlin should be much more cautious and walk carefully in their affairs with Arab states," President Marron said out loud.

POTUS also considered the Russian leader. He had been in power much longer the Russian constitution allowed. The Russian's laws were changed to placate that man. He was becoming more of a dictator than the leader of a fledgling democracy. This leader was extremely jealous of his power and went to great lengths to eliminate any person who chose a contrary position to his own.

There had also been rumors that the Russian president had been replaced by a look-alike, and a core group of Russian nationalists was really running the country. That rumor mill was fun to consider… that the Russian leader was a stand in…a puppet! The would be one bizarre twist on the world political stage if it was a fact.

"It would be awful for our country if this was true," POTUS mused, but then realized that much of Russia's actions that were so contrary to the United States were with this man at the helm.

The President also thought about what he knew about Dr. Reginald Nelson, Ash Black and I.N.C.I.S.O.R. He had decided to give Reggie and Ash a good scolding for not obeying when he ordered them out of Saipan. On top of that, Dr. Nelson and Ash Black had stuck around just to play tricks on a couple of Russian operatives. Had they not been there, and had they not played that silly game, the Russians may have found nothing! No evidence to bolster their claim that the Radio Free World emissions picked up by them had been signals from Saipan.

President Marron knew that his scolding of the two men would be mild at best. These two had done much to help the United States counter terrorism against America and against the world. He could not think of any two civilians who had given so much for their country in the war against terrorism.

"I'll be gentle," the President announced to the empty Oval Office.

Langley, Virginia

A group of analysts had gathered to review the latest reports from Baghdad. The men sat and watched on a large monitor as a drone's camera followed the movement of a caravan of vehicles departing Baghdad and heading for Damascus. The group at CIA headquarters knew of the caravan and its destination even before the trucks had departed from Baghdad. The CIA also knew that there were Russian transports being readied in Damascus to fly this group toward Saipan.

Dr. Nelson's listening device, which was first used in Project Loudmouth, had proven invaluable in providing voice transcripts of the terrorists' plans.

"Why don't we just use a couple of Mavericks and blow these idiots off the face of the planet?" one analyst wondered.

"Then the Arabs would know that we had inside information," another analyst offered.

"So?"

"We'd stop them in their tracks, that's for sure!" another said.

"We have another plan," the Director interrupted. "It will make the Russians look bad, also…if that's possible with them."

Damascus, Syria

The fifty men disembarked from their pickup truck caravan and milled around on the tarmac while the two aircraft taxied over to their location. Some of the men worked to unload all of their gear from the trucks, but most of the men just moved around trying to act tough. To an untrained eye it was a ragtag bunch, not worthy of provoking fear in the innocent population.

The bunch even practiced strutting around the pile of munitions to see who looked toughest among the group.

Inside the men knew they were cowards. In the past when they were confronted by a worthy opponent, the men threw down their weapons and hid among the innocent civilian population, hoping that their lives would be spared.

The rear doors opened on both planes. Ramps were positioned and the equipment was loaded into the bellies of the aircraft. The men split into two groups and marched into the planes. Seats lined the sides of the fuselages and the men settled in. Each terrorist held on to his rifle, pistol and knife. Extra ammunition, explosives, other munitions and food occupied the middle of both aircraft.

Achmed signaled to the pilots and the ramps were retracted and rear doors closed. The engine start sequence was begun and soon four loud turboprop turbines were running and spewing out black smoke. Achmed donned a headset that was hanging in the rear cargo hold of his plane. He heard the Russian pilots speaking in their native language to the men in the tower. He could not understand the language but assumed that the planes had been given permission to taxi when they began to move.

Both planes took the runway together with the trailing plane in formation behind and to the right of the lead plane. These were military transports and pilots. They did not follow civilian protocol for spacing three minutes apart for domestic flights. The planes lifted off smoothly and climbed into the sky. Gears and flaps were raised to clean up the airframes for the journey south. The lead pilot dialed in the GPS coordinates for the volcanic island of Pagan and turned the flying over to the autopilot.

Saipan, Northern Mariana Islands

The transport from Guam landed and the twelve I.N.C.I.S.O.R. men disembarked. Two vans had been hired to carry them to the Hyatt Regency hotel in Garapan. Ash, Becky and I drove to the Hyatt for a reunion of sorts.

The men checked into their rooms and quickly donned their swimsuits for a swim in the Hyatt pool. Ash and I ordered some of the pool bar's famous burgers and the team of fifteen gathered poolside around several round tables. Drinks were ordered. Most of the younger men were happy with their beer, but some of them experimented with some of the tropical-themed drinks that the bartenders whipped up in their blenders.

I ordered my double Crown Royal on the rocks with a twist, while Becky and Ash chose vodka tonics to quench their thirst.

The young team members wanted to bring up the recent past and understand why Ash and I didn't leave when we were ordered off of the island. But they were wise enough not to ask the question directly and wait patiently for the conversation to move toward addressing and hopefully answering their questions.

Most of the initial talk focused around the three newest team members, Dale, Gary, and Dick. After their introductions, each was given time to tell their bosses about themselves.

Then the conversation began to get heavy.

"Why are we here, Reggie?" Powers asked bluntly.

Becky cut me off and said, "We're here because my husband and his friend over there…" she pointed to Ash at another table. "…are idiots!"

"Awe, come on, Beck…that's not fair," Ash countered. "Reggie's the idiot…I'm just along for the ride."

"A perilous ride!" Becky answered.

I was smiling watching my two closest friends in the world banter with each other. Ash, I knew could end any life at these tables in a matter of seconds, but he was acting like a bad puppy being scolded their master.

"So, where are we with all that?" Flex asked.

"Our plan backfired a little bit," I began.

"A little bit?" Becky cut me off. "Your two Russians are in the hospital with some pretty severe injuries!"

"It is not our fault…we did not tell them to park so close to the blast," Ash ventured.

"But you led them up there on your little wild goose chase and you knew that the Army Corps of Engineers was exploding ordinance!" Becky replied in a louder and higher-pitched voice.

Ash looked at Becky and began to speak, but then thought that the wiser action was to stay quiet. Now it was my turn to get roasted.

"So, what we know is that the Russians have provided two transports and a bunch of Iraqi terrorists are heading this way. There is one report that they will attempt to land on the grass strip on Pagan…" I started.

"What is Pagan?" Kurt inquired.

"Pagan is an uninhabited island two hundred miles from here to the north. The United States military wants to use it for live fire training scenarios. The locals here are fighting that, but I expect that the military will win out and blow the shit out of that island. A volcano already did that years ago, which is why it is uninhabited," I continued.

"So, the Russians are coming, everybody to get from street?" Magnus joked.

"You are too young to remember that movie!" I argued.

"You're right, Reggie…I have never seen it, but my father loved that line from the movie. He said it all the time," Magnus replied.

"Good man, your father," I added.

"The only Russians we know of are flying and will stay with the planes. But there are a bunch of Arab terrorists on their way armed to the teeth!" Ash added.

"The President has authorized the use of the prepositioned ships and has already ordered the Charlton to steam north toward Pagan. While you were seeing to your rooms here, the Air Force technicians transferred the equipment for Radio Free World to the Charlton. Clarence White and Billy Black are the two technicians working to set up the equipment as the ship sails north," Becky informed the group.

"I remember those two…they helped get us and the equipment here when we began this journey," I said.

"Journey? Is that what you call this? You two are something else!" Becky interrupted.

"Why have they loaded that equipment onto the Charlton?" Dale wondered.

"Good question, new guy," Ash replied. "Langley thinks that the emissions from RFW may be effective in disrupting the navigation systems on board the Russian planes."

"Kinda like what the terrorists did to the planes in Die Hard 2?" Gary asked.

"You guys are all too young to remember these movies," Ash countered.

"It's been on Netflix," Gary retorted. "Also, the idea was used in a James Bond movie against the North Koreans!"

"So, what do we do now that we are here?" Aaron asked.

"Ash and I thought…" I began.

"There's the blind leading the blind," Becky interjected.

I was wishing that Becky would lighten up a bit. The younger men were visibly concerned about her rhetoric. And now she was openly questioning our leadership skills!

I held up my hand, gesturing for Becky to be quiet.

"The plan right now is to move our base of operations to Alamagan. It is also an uninhabited island in the Marianas chain and only seventy miles from Pagan. We will use seaplanes to get us there. I have lined up two of them out of Guam. They will land at the seaport. There is a ramp just off Lower Base Road that they can taxi onto. We will move all of this gear down to that ramp and load up the planes. It will take several trips," I continued.

"I didn't see any floatplanes," Dick commented.

"There aren't any here probably since Larry Hillblom died in a seaplane crash. Reggie just said that they are being flown over from Guam," Ash said.

"Hillblom! He's the guy in that movie, also on Netflix…Billionaire, I think it was called," Magnus interrupted.

"The movie name is right, but it was Amazon that carried it," Aaron replied. "I saw it when I was looking for stuff about Saipan. He's the 'H' in DHL."

"And a billionaire? What happened?" Dick asked.

"Made his money and moved to this island in the '80's and died in '95 when his seaplane went down on a trip from Pagan to Saipan. His body was never recovered," Magnus added.

"A heavy lift helicopter is also on its way to transport the Escalade to the north end of that island," I added.

"You said it is uninhabited…are there roads? What good is the Escalade?" Graham asked.

"We think that the drones may be useful against the terrorists, and the controls for the drones are built into the Escalade. Kind of like a command post. We are just going to park in on the beach on the northern end of Alamagan and run the drones from there," Ash said.

"So, settle in and enjoy your afternoon. All this happens tomorrow!" I ordered.

CHAPTER 35

Alamagan, Northern Mariana Islands

The men worked to set up a temporary camp and perimeter safety zone. They also worked to clear an area just off the beach as a landing zone for the heavy lift helicopter to lower the Escalade onto the island.

Once the camp was ready, the men saw to their weapons and made sure that all the equipment was in good working order. There were twelve young men of I.N.C.I.S.O.R. present, the two Air Force techies, and Reggie and Ash. The two float plane pilots also asked to stay for the show. So, the island of Alamagan was now home to eighteen men. Eighteen more guests than the island had experienced in a long time.

Reggie and Ash got word from the two technicians that the Radio Free World transmission equipment had been set up and was operational. They walked over to the location. The same small generator that Reggie and Ash had used in the Plumeria Resort was humming next to the equipment surrounded by several five-gallon cans of fuel. A quick glance at the equipment showed all green lights. They were ready to go!

Pagan, Northern Mariana Islands

"We're one hundred miles out," the lead pilot announced. "Beginning our approach to Pagan Island."

The Arabs lining the sides of the fuselage heard the Russian words and waited for the translator to inform them about what the pilot had just communicated. Once they understood, the tension in the back of the transport plane was noticeable. Most of the men had extremely little experience with planes and there had been much tension throughout the flight. Now they knew they were close to their destination. The flight was almost over.

One of the terrorists aboard the lead aircraft noticed a buzzing coming from the pile of munitions in the middle of the fuselage. The buzzing became louder as it grew in intensity.

He stood up and began to sound an alarm. He began to scream. The scream was stifled by a series of small explosions that ignited the whole pile of munitions. The middle of the plane exploded taking out the sides of the aircraft. The fuel tank in the belly of the craft ignited next and the explosion was immense.

The wounded plane began to fall out of the sky. As it spiraled down the wings failed and detached from the body. The fuel bladders in each wing also ignited and the separated wings began to burn.

The tail separated from the fuselage and men and equipment flew into the sky. The human and inanimate debris were all on fire as they fell out of the plane's open belly. Some of the debris exploded behind the aircraft.

All of the failed pieces of the flying machine fell into the ocean below. It did not take long for the falling parts and men to be extinguished as contact was made with the water. Some of the plane's parts floated for a brief period. Most sank immediately. The plane and all of its contents fell into a watery grave, never to be seen again.

The pilots in the trailing plane watched in horror as the lead plane literally disintegrated before their eyes. They stayed silent and motionless for a moment and then their military training took over.

"Mark the site…latitude and longitude…mark the GPS!" the pilot ordered. The first officer did as he was told and marked their location.

"Comrade, do we search for survivors?" the first officer asked.

The two pilots looked out of their windows to the ocean below. They looked for any sign of life. They were amazed how little of the plane was on the surface. No survivors were seen.

"No, comrade…we continue our approach. Get Achmed up here to the cockpit!" the pilot ordered.

Vladivostok, Russia

Vlad and Ivan were watching Russia's own version of spy satellite footage on a flat screen monitor in their office. It showed the two Russian transports as burning white dots. The geographic overlay showed the northern islands of the Mariana Archipelago as the white dots moved in a southerly direction.

"What the f…" Ivan started.

"And then there was one," Vlad whispered in awe as one of the white dots on the screen disappeared.

"We lost a plane," Ivan began and picked up the phone. "We have a downed aircraft! Launch a rescue mission!"

Vlad continued to be glued to the screen. His mind was having difficulty accepting what his eyes were communicating. Two dots had become one. Had they lost half their force? How could this have happened? No warning? No distress call over the radio.

Suddenly the receiver on the desk became active. Vlad snapped out of his stupor and answered the call on the radio. It was the first officer of the trailing plane. What the crew saw was related over the air waves. Small explosions became a giant explosion and the aircraft disintegrated before their eyes and they watched burning pieces of the wreckage fall into the ocean. No telltale missile trail was seen, and their missile threat radar onboard had not gone off. No warning whatsoever!

The first officer asked for instructions…proceed or abandon the mission. Vlad told him that he would have to call back after consultation with his comrade. Just a few minutes. The first officer let him know that they had begun their approach to the island of Pagan. They would hold short of the final approach, but the crew needed a response quickly.

Langley, Virginia

"Did you see that?" an analyst stood up and exclaimed while pointing to the big screen on the wall of their cavernous room filled with cubicles, desks, and computers.

"Woah!"

"My God"

"The plane is gone"

"What happened?"

"No idea! A bright flash and the lead plane disappeared!"

The analysts took their seats and began to punch on the keyboards in front of them. Much work had to be done to figure out what had just occurred. The Director of the CIA saw the activity and came out of his office.

"What is the hubbub?" he asked.

"Director, the two-plane formation that we were following on their attack path to Saipan is now just one plane. It looks like the lead plane has crashed…or rather…blew up! And fell into the ocean!" an analyst offered.

"Did this have anything to do with I.N.C.I.S.O.R.? I heard that they were planning on disrupting that flight with their RFW equipment," the Director asked.

"We knew that they had moved to a northern island in the Marianas to deal with the attacking terrorists, and we knew they were going to use their invention to disrupt the flight paths of the incoming plane… but not that they were going to attack the planes. Those planes are Russian! That could mean war!" the analyst said.

"Stay on it…we need to know why that plane went down before the Russians do," the Director ordered and returned to his office.

Vladivostok, Russia

"Did the Iraqis have…what do the Americans call them…Claymores in their weaponry?" Vlad questioned.

"I do not know, comrade, but I will call Baghdad," Ivan responded and picked up the phone.

After a brief conversation he hung up the phone and turned to Vlad.

"Yes, they loaded a number of stolen Claymore mines in with their other munitions. Why do you ask? They are anti-personnel mines," Ivan replied.

"What do you think the propellant in those mines is, comrade?" Vlad asked.

"Oh! Damn! C-4! The same stuff that blew up in Baghdad!" Ivan exclaimed.

"Da, comrade…da!" Vlad exhaled.

Alamagan, Northern Mariana Islands

"Shut it down!" I yelled.

Clarence White flipped a switch and the equipment stopped transmitting.

"What's up?" he asked. "Why are we stopping?"

"One of the aircraft has disappeared!" I announced.

"How would that happen? We were just wanting to cause a course correction," Brock Black asked.

Ash stood up quickly. "What if they had some C-4 on board that plane?"

"It would go Ka Boom!" I exclaimed. "Would the terrorists be stupid enough to pack a plane full of the stuff that was exploding in Baghdad? That's not very bright."

"As far as I know, these are not smart men," Ash added.

"So, look on the bright side…one plane down and half of their force and supplies gone. I wonder if they will keep coming, or abort their ill-fated mission?" I asked.

"Time to phone Langley," Ash announced.

"I want to call Becky also," I said.

Clarence was studying the radar screen. He lifted up from the screen to let us all know that it looked to him like the terrorist mission was still a go. The other plane was still approaching Pagan. The men of I.N.C.I.S.O.R. gathered around the radar equipment to watch the progress of the men who were coming to hurt them.

"Turn on RFW now!" I ordered.

Washington, DC

The CIA Director entered into the Oval Office to meet with POTUS. The room had become very familiar to him. There were almost daily briefings that he participated in. Today he was alone with the President for a few minutes.

"Mr. President the Russian plane exploded because it was filled with C-4 munitions. The same plastique explosives that Dr. Nelson's invention set off in Baghdad," the Director began.

"And in the United States!" President Marron added.

"Yes, sir, that was the fourth phase of a very successful test," the Director replied.

"And they used that equipment against the Russian plane?" POTUS asked.

"Well, Mr. President, it looks like an oversight. The I.N.C.I.S.O.R. fellows were not expecting the Arabs to carry the same C-4 with them on this mission. They were using the equipment to see if they could interfere with the flight navigation equipment on board the two aircraft. It was not their intent to blow up the plane," the Director stated.

"So, can Russia tie us to their lost aircraft in any way?" President Marron wondered.

"Absolutely not, sir. We had nothing to do with it. But, sir, the Russians are going to be looking pretty bad that the Arabs lost half of their force. They cannot even transport people very safely!" the Director continued.

"So, we are in the clear…are the terrorists continuing their attack?" POTUS asked.

"It looks like we are, Mr. President," the Director answered.

"I'm calling Guam. I want their National Guard unit activated and moved to Saipan. Just in case the boys from Baghdad get by those I.N.C.I.S.O.R. fellows. Better safe than sorry," the President announced.

The CIA Director took this statement as his cue to leave the Oval Office and return to Virginia.

Pagan, Northern Mariana Islands

The Russian pilot knew that it was ultimately his call in a 'go' 'no go' scenario. He had listened to Achmed who claimed to be the leader of the ragtag bunch that sat in the belly of his plane. Achmed had a 'do or die' attitude toward the mission and would not be swayed from his desire to complete what they had begun. The pilot also knew that he played no bigger role than 'taxi driver' for this mob of terrorists.

The pilot looked to the first officer and announced, "We're landing! Let us go through the pre-flight checklist."

"A-O-K, skipper!" was the reply.

The two men also used the remaining time to review short takeoff and landing procedures for their aircraft. This landing could possibly be the hairiest landing the two had ever performed.

Alamagan, Northern Mariana Islands

"So, they are still coming!" Ash exclaimed as he watched the radar scope.

"Yes they are!" I replied as I hung up the satellite phone. "Langley said there was no break in the approach even though the lead plane disintegrated. They did not even circle to look for survivors."

"We still have not tested RFW to see if we can interrupt the autopilot and inertial guidance systems on a Russian plane," Ash continued.

"We took out one of their planes…I'm okay messing with the other," I answered.

"Fire up the equipment!" Ash announced to Clarence.

"Already on…Dr. Nelson ordered it activated earlier," Clarence replied.

"So, what do we want to accomplish?" I asked Ash.

"There are no navigation aids on the island of Pagan, so they won't be flying any type of instrument approach," Ash began. He then looked upwards into the sky. "It is also a beautiful day so the pilots will be flying their final approach into Pagan by visual flight rules."

"Wouldn't it be fun if they thought the runway was twenty feet lower than the actual altitude of the landing strip? The height of the beach before the field," I asked deviously.

"Oh, so fun…we could end this excursion even before it began!" Ash agreed.

As we watched the scope, Clarence punched up a computer overlay of the projected approach to Pagan, and we saw that the plane had taken up an approach that was well below the glideslope that the computer had created.

"Wow! We've affected their approach," Ash observed.

"Yeah, nice addition to Radio Free World!" I stated.

"Clarence, let's keep the equipment on for a little longer," Ash ordered.

"Yes, sir!" was Clarence's reply.

Pagan, Northern Mariana Islands

The pilots looked down upon the island and worked their eyes back and forth across the terrain so that the two men could make out the grass landing strip on the northern part of the island. They began a slow, gentle circle around the volcano to check out the island and line the aircraft up for its final approach.

Their eyes scanned the island for human activity. All the two pilots observed were some goats and a cow feeding on the grass on the strip. The animals would scatter as the plane approached. A couple of dilapidated buildings were seen, showing that there had been an attempt at occupying the island at an earlier time. It did not look to the pilots that there had been any kind of human activity happening here in years.

As the plane began a wide left bank to circle the volcano, the pilot noted that there was steam escaping from the mouth of the volcano. He remembered that they had checked their Russian sources and that no seismic activity had been noted. The volcano was not expected to react any time in the near future.

"That data must be wrong," the pilot thought.

He lined up for the approach to the grass strip. The landing strip was twenty feet above the sandy beach. The AGL instrument indicated that he was one hundred feet above ground level. That was just right for this approach he thought.

The first officer lowered the flaps and landing gear as the pilot directed him.

"Down and locked," he commented.

"Tell the men in the back to get ready and to grab hold of something. This will be a hard stop!" the pilot ordered.

"We are touching down shortly! Stow your gear and hold on!" the first officer announced into the intercom.

The pilot realized that there was something wrong with his approach just in the nick of time and pulled up on the yoke. The plane was on a course to fly directly into the soil bank between the beach and the runway. The plane barely cleared the cliff and bounced on the end of the grass strip. He knew that he was too far down the strip for his planned touchdown, but the plane was too heavy and slow to recover for a go around.

He committed to land and pushed downward on the yoke, willing the plane onto the ground. There were several more bounces along the grass strip, much like a porpoise on the surface of the ocean, before the plane made stable contact and the brakes could be applied. Both of the men in the cockpit jumped heavily on the foot pedals while the pilot reversed the thrust in the engines. A good part of the strip was already used up and the plane was still hurling toward the lava flow that interrupted the strip.

The plane slowed slowly, but not fast enough for the pilots. They were both sweating profusely as the nose of the aircraft neared the lava. There was a horrible scraping noise as the underneath aluminum skin on the nose hit the lava flow. Two large gashes were ripped into the airplane as it halted quickly once contact with the rock wall was made.

The pilots sat in silence waiting for a bad aftermath to occur. Nothing happened and they both reacted by jumping up and hitting the open lever to the back of the plane. Both men urged the terrorist passengers off the plane. Once all of the men were off the plane and milling around on the grass behind the aircraft, the two Russians ambled to the front of the plane to check the damage. Both men noticed the tears in the fuselage…it was worse than they had expected…the aluminum skin had been peeled back and curled up like the lid of a sardine tin and the electronic gear housed in the nose of the plane was exposed to the elements!

"It is good that we have the heavy equipment on the flight to deal with the lava flow," the pilot began. "We can use it to pull us off of these rocks!"

"Yes, comrade, but what was on our plane and what was on the other plane?" the first officer asked.

"Oh, God, I hadn't thought about that! What is here?" the pilot continued as they both ran to the back of the aircraft.

"The bulldozer is here," the co-pilot observed. "The road grader is no longer with us."

"So that is what was on the other plane," the pilot commented.

"The bulldozer will be able to pull us off of that rock," the first officer said.

"Yes…and?" the pilot retorted.

"We do not have materials to repair the airplane. We need to radio the trawler. You get pictures of the damaged nose compartment comrade, and I will go back on board and place a call to the ship we flew over on our approach," the pilot said.

The two Russian pilots and the captain and crew of the Russian trawler were definitely not the 'MacGyver' types who could fix anything with some household goods and duct tape. Once the boat captain thought he understood the issue with the damaged plane and loss of heavy equipment to repair the runway so that the plane could leave, he said that he would call Vladivostok for advice and orders. He would also forward the pictures of the damaged plane.

The Arabs were beginning to move their supplies to the shore. Many were beginning to move up and down the beach, kicking at the little crabs that scurried for the waves from their holes in the sand. The crabs had been undisturbed in their homes for years! They could not be happy with these intruders with big boots on.

"You tell those Arabs to stay on that beach!" the captain commanded to the pilot. "I will not pick them up until we have new instructions from the homeland!"

The pilot moved aft from the cockpit and walked down the rear ramp. Only a few men were seen at the back of the plane and all of the supplies had been offloaded. He found the first officer and told him to instruct the terrorists to stay in their location on the beach and that they would not be picked up by the boat's crew until the higher ups in Russia got back to them with new instructions.

Alamagan, Northern Mariana Islands

"Ash let's get the drones up and flying," I suggested.

"What is going on, Reggie?" Ash asked.

"Langley just checked in and the Russian plane landed on Pagan. There is a Russian fishing boat waiting to transport the terrorists from Pagan to Saipan," I related.

"What do you want with the drones?" Ash asked again.

"To get a bird's eye view of what is happening on the ground," I replied.

"Well, then we don't need them all! I'll go to the Escalade and get one of the drones on the way to Pagan. It will take about forty minutes to travel there, so come join me in the car in twenty," Ash said.

"Yes, sir!" I answered.

Langley, Virginia

People were gathered around the latest satellite image of Pagan which showed that a large Russian transport aircraft was parked on the island with its nose making contact with the lava flow that transected the island runway. Men and supplies were gathering on the beach and a fishing boat was offshore adjacent to the beach at the end of the runway.

"That plane looks like it is kissing the rocks!" an analyst commented.

"I bet the pilots are kissing the rocks too," another offered.

"We always thought that Russian pilots were not as good as our own, but that was one hell of a landing!" another opined.

"Absolutely correct!" the Director said. "That pilot did a great job getting the plane stopped. I understand that Dr. Nelson and Mr. Black tried to interfere with the plane's approach. We'll have to discover what they did."

"Sir, what do you think will happen now?" one of the analysts asked.

"Good question…I do not know…half of the terrorists are now lost at sea, and so is much of their ammo and all of their explosives," the Director said. "I think it is a coin toss as to whether they will continue south or turn that boat to the north once everybody is on board. Your guess is as good as mine!"

"We should start up a betting pool," an analyst suggested.

"None of that, now…let's focus on what is at hand," the Director ordered.

Vladivostok, Russia

Ivan and Vlad sat facing each other, feeling dejected at the latest news. This mission of the Iraqi terrorists was not going well. One plane lost…half of their men gone…and now the second plane badly damaged and unable to fly in its current state. The mission just seemed cursed from the beginning!

"See what we get for trying to help those idiots out!" Vlad cursed.

"And the plane…we cannot even land another rescue aircraft with that plane sitting on the runway," Ivan added.

"Well, let's think that through…they can use the bulldozer to pull the plane off of the runway. The two pilots can also use the bulldozer to attack that pile of lava so that the runway can be long enough to land another aircraft. We can load the rescue plane up with supplies and repair technicians to affect an immediate repair and get the damaged plane home. And also, the rescue plane can carry the lost road grader to make the runway operable after the lava is cleared," Vlad thought.

"We were attempting to keep a low profile and not make it really obvious that we were helping terrorists that have it as their mission to destroy the United States. A rescue attempt will make it really hard to keep this quiet," Ivan argued.

"So, comrade…what do we do?" Vlad asked.

Ivan shrugged his shoulders. "I think we have to go and get them!"

CHAPTER 36

Pagan, Northern Mariana Islands

Word came down from Russia that a rescue mission was planned. The trawler was to load up the remaining terrorists and steam for Saipan. The pilot and first officer were to stay on Pagan and work to drag the aircraft off of the grass runway and to make sure that the disabled plane was far enough removed from the runway edge so that the rescue plane was clear to land on the small Pagan airstrip.

Russia needed two days to compile the repair materials and men and then the rescue flight would commence.

Alamagan, Northern Mariana Islands

Ash and I were watching the screen in the Escalade as the camera in the drone was trained on the activity on the Pagan beach. We observed that small dinghies were being used to ferry men from the beach out to a fishing boat. The drone picked up that two lighter-skinned men were moving around a plane that was parked precariously on a grass runway.

"I bet those two are the Russian pilots," I suggested as I pointed to the two uniformed men near the outline of the plane on the television monitor. "What a great picture!"

The camera aboard the drone was broadcasting a very clean image for us from seventy miles away.

"Yep, and those are the Iraqi terrorists coming for us," Ash added.

"So, Reggie…what's the plan?" Ash continued.

"Okay, good friend…let's have some fun!" I spoke.

"Sure…what does that mean?" Ash asked.

"First, how long can that drone stay up and observe?" I questioned.

"The manual says it can stay up a good long time…many hours," Ash answered.

"Good…have it follow that trawler until it is close to our location and then recall it. I want to make sure that the trawler does not deviate from its course to Saipan. The Russians and the Arabs should not know that we are on Alamagan. If they change course then we know that something is up," I began.

"Am I right that we do not want that ship and the towelheads on board to reach Saipan?" Ash wondered.

"Absolutely!" I replied. "That is why we are here on this island. We are going to attack that ship from our current location."

"What are you thinking, Sir Reginald?" Ash queried.

"Stop it Ash!" I ordered. "Here's what I have planned…

Saipan, Northern Mariana Islands

Dr. Charles Cram and Igor had met to discuss a way to retrieve the sunken gold from the lost and sunken craft on its return to Saipan from the Philippines. They were enjoying a beer at Salty's after playing two hours of pickleball with two guys that had lived on Saipan for nearly thirty years. They both had won tennis tournaments on the island but had quickly become converts for the new sport that Dr. Cram had brought to the island…and they kicked Dr. Cram's and Igor's collective butts when they played!

Dr. Cram had his phone out and was using the calculator function.

"How much did you say the boat carried?" he asked.

Igor smiled and knew that Dr. Cram had the gold fever. "There are eight boxes on that boat. Each box has ten gold bars."

Charles punched frantically on his phone as Igor smiled. He checked and re-checked his numbers.

"That's sixty million dollars!" he exclaimed.

"That's what I came up with," Igor replied, grinning from ear to ear.

"I've never seen you smile like that," Dr. Cram observed.

"If we can figure out how to salvage that boat, my contact in the Philippines said that we can have it all!" Igor added. "And I have found a buyer."

"How far down do you figure the boat is?" Charles asked. He had spent very little time on the ocean. His father had taken Charles and his brothers deep sea fishing when he was in high school, and he got violently sea sick. But for this he was going to become a fast student of the sea and join Igor in this recovery mission.

"About one hundred and twenty feet," Igor answered.

"I've been to one hundred feet. I received my PADI deep diver certification doing that, but one hundred feet was the maximum depth. I remember that I couldn't stay down at that depth very long," Dr. Cram stated, "The air in my tank did not last long."

"That was standard scuba stuff, right? What about a mix of gases?" Igor questioned.

"I know nothing about that," Charles replied. "I'm sure there are divers here on Saipan that have done dives with helium and oxygen mixtures."

"Not that I can trust to keep quiet," Igor argued.

"What about a rig from the surface so I don't have to use tanks? Then I can stay down longer." Charles asked.

"I have a friend that has a surface diving air compressor for sale. I can pick it up pretty cheap," Igor replied.

"So that is solved," Dr. Cram said. "Now…how about a winch to get the boxes to the surface?"

"Been thinking about that, too. A winch to bring up a three-hundred-pound box needs to be pretty strong," Igor stated. "I just purchased a crane and winch that is rated for five hundred pounds. It can bring up one box, but not two at a time. Also, it is not about getting the boxes to the surface because the water neutralizes most of the weight. The crane only works hard on the final leg of the box's journey from the water surface into the boat. And the electric winch only has to make eight lifts."

"Sounds like you have it all worked out," Charles said.

"Yes, and just you and me…that is important! You know that loose lips sink ships…" Igor announced. "When is your next day off?"

"Day after tomorrow," Charles replied.

"Then that's our day!" Igor said. We will leave Smiling Cove at 0600."

Dr. Cram quickly converted Igor's military verbiage to his civilian twelve-hour clock.

"Okay…see you at 6am day after tomorrow," Charles said. "I'll bring my mask, snorkel and fins, right? No tanks."

Igor nodded in agreement and rose to pay the bill for their drinks and snacks. He still got a kick out of the islanders referring to the snacks as chasers. He knew that in many a bar that he had been in over the years that the term, chaser, meant the beer that followed a shot of whiskey. Here on Saipan, it was food.

Charles commented as they were leaving, "Tell me more about that 'cheap' compressor you found…"

Pacific Ocean South of Pagan

The Russian trawler with its load of terrorists was steaming south. The trailing drone was positioned high and somewhat behind the fishing boat. The drone received an electronic signal to return to base. As it banked to turn east, a brief reflection shone on the deck of the trawler.

One of the Iraqi terrorists was day dreaming on the deck of the boat. He noticed the glint. It was similar to flashes he had seen in Baghdad. A quadcopter was following them! He jumped to his feet and reached for his automatic weapon. He emptied the gun's clip toward the reflection. He watched the sky intently as other men gathered to see why he was firing into the air and wasting ammunition. The flash did not repeat. He saw nothing. The other men saw nothing and went back to wasting their time as the boat chugged south.

Alamagan, Northern Mariana Islands

"Ash! Did you see that?" I exclaimed as I pointed to the monitor.

The monitor was blank when Ash looked up.

"What was it? What did you see?" he wondered.

"There was a bright light and then there was nothing. The camera has stopped transmitting an image. Probably made in China! Ash, the camera is broken," I replied.

Ash was working some of the controls on the panel in front of him. He kept fingering a button that said 'reset' on it. When he was convinced, he lifted his head and turned to me in the back seat.

"It wasn't the camera, Reggie. The drone is gone! I think it was shot down by someone on that boat. Dammit! They know that we're following them. That will give them more urgency to complete their mission," Ash ranted.

Pacific Ocean Seventy Miles South of Pagan

Achmed told the captain of the boat about the sighting and the gunfire. If the captain was intrigued by the news he did not show it. In fact, Achmed was not sure he was being listened to. Then the captain spoke, "Which way did the drone turn? Did anybody see it?"

"I do not know...I will ask," Achmed replied and left the wheel house for a few minutes.

Upon his return he stated, "My man that saw it says that it was turning east."

"Are you sure?" the captain said as he studied his marine charts laying in front of him. He stabbed the chart with his finger. "There is an island here...Alamagan, it says. That drone could have come from there!"

The captain flung the wheel to the port side and the trawler veered to the east. "Make this your target!" he ordered to his first mate as he touched the island of Alamagan on the map.

"Aye aye, captain," the first mate answered and checked the boat's heading.

"We will be there in one hour," he stated to Achmed. "Ready your men!"

Philippine Sea West of Saipan

Igor and Charles had been working hard.

Charles had come up from the depths along with the fourth box for some breaths of fresh air. He pulled himself up onto the platform on the rear of Igor's boat and sat with his legs dangling in the water.

"This is harder, and it is going slower than I could have imagined!" Charles exclaimed to Igor who was struggling with getting the fourth box out of the water and secured on the deck of the boat.

"We are halfway there my friend," Igor replied. Igor was always the optimist, seeing life as full of opportunities and not full of obstacles.

Charles laid back on the platform.

"Man, this feels good," he stated as he clasped his hands behind his neck and looked up at the blue sky dotted with small cumulus clouds. "How about a swig of that Russian vodka you have on board?"

"Let us finish our task first," Igor countered.

"No! I want some now! And I want to see the gold…have you looked? What are you doing up here while I am acting like a fish? I bet you are rubbing the gold bars and drinking that vodka all by yourself!" Dr. Cram retorted.

"I have not looked, and I have not had any vodka. I have been working to pilot this boat and keep it positioned right above you," Igor pouted as if his feelings were hurt.

"Well, okay…let's have a look now!" Charles urged.

Igor gave in an pulled out a knife to pry open the box that he had just secured to the deck. Water was still draining from the box. With some effort he first got the lid to give way a small amount and the with a loud creak the first corner was pried open. Igor worked his knife around the wooden edge and the lid popped off of the box.

Charles reached into the box and removed the cloth covering from the top of their prize. The sun caught the metal bars. "Gold!" they both whispered out loud in unison.

The two men studied each other for a moment.

"I think it is a good time for that drink now," Igor agreed and headed below deck to retrieve the bottle and two glasses. He pulled the cork out of the bottle and filled the two vessels. Igor handed one to Charles.

"Na Zdorovie!" Igor urged and held his glass up high.

"To us!" Charles returned the toast. "But let's not get drunk…at least not yet."

"I agree…we must finish…why do you say that?" Igor asked.

"I thought that Nostrovia meant 'let's get drunk'," Charles replied.

"That's American slang! What I said was Na Zdorovie…which means 'cheers', Igor corrected Dr. Cram and spelled out the two words for him.

"Okay, lesson learned, back to work," Charles agreed and donned his diving mask and fins. He sat on the gunwale of the boat, pressed the mask to his face and fell backwards into the water. Igor moved the winch's gear to neutral and watched the cable play out as it headed downward with Charles.

Charles found the remaining four boxes on the sunken craft. He secured the cable around the next box and tugged on the cable to signal Igor to raise the box. The box lifted easily from the boat and moved upward. Charles grabbed hold of the cable and began his ride to the surface.

The box climbed to the surface without any problem. Igor switched the gears to a lower gear with extra lifting power and the box began to rise out of the water and banged against the side of his boat.

"I'll buy a new boat!" Igor thought. "Hell, I'll buy two boats!"

Just then the winch jammed, and the boom failed and bent rapidly down toward the water. A loud screeching of fatigued metal was heard. The box dropped into the water, hitting Charles on the head. He sank beneath the waves…

"Charles!" Igor yelled. "Dr. Cram…"

CHAPTER 37

Alamagan, Northern Mariana Islands

Brock Black ran to retrieve Reggie and Ash from the Escalade.

"Clarence and I have been watching the radar scope at the campsite. The trawler is now approaching this island. A minute ago, the boat changed course and is making a beeline for us! They will be on us in less than one hour," Brock opened.

"And just a few minutes ago we lost contact with the drone we sent to observe that ship," Ash said.

"We believe that they discovered the drone and shot it out of the sky," I added.

"And now they think it came from here?" Ash asked.

"No matter how they deduced that…we need to get ready! There is not much time," I opined.

"How do you want to do this, Reggie?" Ash wondered.

"You stay here in the Escalade and get the remaining drones ready. I'll go to the camp and get the men ready," I replied.

Brock and I headed back to the campsite where the men of I.N.C.I.S.O.R. were already busy cleaning and preparing their weapons for war.

"We are guessing that the Arab numbers are twenty-five, correct?" Magnus asked.

"And twelve of us…oops! We also have Reggie and Ash and Clarence and Brock," Flex added.

"Sounds like twelve of us!" Powers interrupted and the twelve young warriors laughed.

"We'll make sure to be right behind you!" I offered. "Now stop the joking around. That trawler's instruments are sensitive enough that within fifteen minutes they will be picking up our presence on this island. We need to prepare to defend ourselves against a force twice our size and who have been fighting in Iraq and Syria for years. They are hardened warriors!"

"So, what are we? Dogmeat?" Powers argued, obviously upset that I did not recognize their abilities and time spent in Iraq and Afghanistan. Our men were also seasoned warriors.

"I'm sorry, Powers…I was not implying that you are not capable," I apologized to the men. "But now we need to prepare for a battle. Let's talk about a defense strategy for the island."

Lance Everett had obviously been doing his homework. "The island is an oval that is three miles long north to south and two and a half miles wide. It is the tip of a volcano that hasn't made any noise in modern times."

"Great geography lesson Lance," Duncan interrupted.

"Then let me continue Duncan," Lance argued. "The eastern side has steep cliffs along the shoreline. An attack from there would be difficult. The western slope has very deep canyons and valleys with caves. That would be a logical place to mount an attack."

"And they will have spotted the Escalade and our camp on the northern shore," Aaron added.

"We should lure them into one of those canyons and take up positions above the canyon walls looking down into the canyon!" Dick suggested.

"Denver on one side and Frankfurt on the other," Kurt suggested.

"It'll be like shooting fish in a barrel!" Graham added. "By the way, anybody know where that saying came from?"

"Well men, it is a simile that is a form of a metaphor and it mea..." Flex began and then was cut off.

"What is this crap?" Dick interrupted.

"Yeah, I didn't do well in English when I was in school," Powers added.

Flex continued, "it means simple, or easy to do! You dolts!"

"If I were them I would land at the Patida camp in the northwest and use that area for my base camp. Then I would work inland from there," I suggested.

"Yeah, and we need to remember that these guys are desert warfare trained and battle tested. This is the jungle here. We could hide in the swordgrass, and they could literally tramp within inches of us and not see us," Powers said.

"Do we have to worry about any locals?" Lance asked.

"The island has been uninhabited since it was hit by a typhoon in 2009," I added.

"So, nobody to watch out for except the bad guys," Duncan finished.

"Finish your work here and then move out. Find a good ambush point and establish your lines of fire. I am going to see how Ash is getting along," I said to the young men. I looked around as they made their final preparations and I felt really proud to be a part of I.N.C.I.S.O.R. I left the men and walked toward the Escalade.

Ash had the other three drones up in the air and was watching intently at the screens in front of him. He looked up when he heard my approach.

"You know, Reggie, I could blow that ship out of the water with just one hellfire missile from a drone," Ash announced.

"What's the fun in that? No, seriously, I want to give the men a chance to show us what they've got," I replied.

"But somebody could get hurt...or worse! They could die!" Ash responded.

"I'm sure they are thinking that is what we pay them for," I answered.

"Well...isn't it?" Ash asked.

Alamagan Western Shore

The Russian trawler edged in as close as the captain dared to the northwestern shore of Alamagan island. His maps had shown him that this location would be the best for unloading the men and equipment he had transported from the island of Pagan. They had made this detour from their original course heading to Saipan to investigate a possible drone sighting and the chance that the quadcopter that had been shot down by one of the Iraqi terrorists on board had come from this island.

As the boat approached the island the radar picked up a large SUV on the northern shore of Alamagan. "How did that vehicle get there?" the captain asked of the other Russian seamen in the wheelhouse. "Well, it is damn sure that the car did not swim here!" He then went over in his mind the various options for transporting a car to this remote island. He chose a heavy lift helicopter as his pick for the most efficient method of transportation.

Next question was, "From where?" Saipan was his obvious choice for a couple of reasons. That island was inhabited, and his trawler was motoring there on a mission to ferret out the responsible party or parties that had caused the destruction in Iraq. There had been some signals from Saipan just before the technicians had been injured. The captain hoped that the intel from his homeland was accurate and that this was not another wild goose chase. The captain believed that the Russian intel was 'iffy' at best, but he would follow his orders like a good comrade.

Continuing to move closer to Alamagan island, the sensitive equipment on board was able to pick up the presence of over a dozen men. There was a camp just inland from the SUV planted on the shore. The captain sent out word for Achmed to join him in the wheelhouse.

"Look at that scope," the captain urged.

Achmed was not experienced at studying radar screens or the images that presented on them. He looked and nodded his head.

"What do you see?" the captain asked.

Achmed continued to nod and study the screen in front of him.

"Those blips close together and the bigger blip there!" Achmed said as he pointed to the radar.

The captain was nonplussed by the lack of understanding in this Iraqi leader.

"Those are men gathered at a camp and that is a large SUV on the shore. I do not know why that vehicle, or those men are here, but it cannot be good. You should get your men ready. We offload in ten minutes," the captain ordered.

Achmed felt his spine begin to tingle as he sensed the urgency in the Russian captain's voice. He and his men would get to do battle soon! That is why they had come this far and endured so much. He readied his men and they moved to the gunwales of the boat to observe the island ahead.

When the captain was satisfied with his boat's position the order was given. "All Iraqis disembark!"

The men from the desert scrambled over the side and dropped into the shallow water. They waded to the shoreline. Sand from the shore was sticking to their wet pantlegs and boots. Their shirts were drenched with their own sweat and salty water. The terrorists were not used to this environment and the conditions that they were forced to deal with. They were used to hot and dry with their sweat evaporating to cool them down. Here it was hot and moist, and the sweat-drenched clothing never dried and just added about five pounds to their weight which was already stressed by the weight of the packs on their backs.

Achmed gathered the men and split them into two exploratory parties. He chose to lead the group that headed around to the northeast hugging the shoreline as best they could. The other group headed inland to find a route to the camp they had observed. The assumption was that their landing on the western shore of Alamagan had not been detected. Little did they know…

I.N.C.I.S.O.R. Camp

"Two teams of equal size heading this way. The numbers look to be what we guessed. There are thirteen men in each group. All have large backpacks and are carrying automatic weapons," Ash called out to the other men. "Are we ready with our greeting party?"

"Like no other!" Flex answered affirmatively.

"It also looks like the Russians stayed on that trawler. They were wise not to set foot on American land! That would be an act of war!" Ash continued.

"That's too weird to hear you say American soil when we are on the other side of the planet from the States," I said.

"I know, Reggie, but this little island belongs to the U.S. of A.!" Ash countered.

"Well, let's go do some U.S. of A. ass kicking!" I ordered. "You guys, the Denver team…you are with me!"

"The German team is with me," Ash said and picked up his weapon.

The two groups marched out of the campsite to take up positions before the terrorists arrived at the ambush locations. Ash and I had talked about using the drones for observation and as a fail-safe if we had trouble, but Ash wanted in on this fight. The drones sat silently in their perches on the roof of the Escalade.

Ambush Sites on Alamagan Island

The team of terrorists that was marching inland had left the shoreline and was beginning to proceed inland. They encountered heavy vegetation that had been undisturbed in many years. There were no human or animal paths for the Iraqi men to follow. The two lead terrorists had pulled out their machetes and were hacking away at the swordgrass. Progress was extremely slow. One of the men in the middle of the pack reached out his hand to wave it through the grass.

"Ouch!" he cried and pulled his hand up to his face. He looked at his palm. It was bloody! The sharp swordgrass had cut a deep gash in his hand. He looked around to the other men close by and held up his hand. The others saw what had happened and noted in their memories not to play in this grass…it would hurt them.

The terrorist was tending to his wound with a rag pulled out of his backpack. As he applied pressure to the wound to staunch the flow of blood he looked up and saw that the walls on the sides of the path were rising and becoming quite steep. They now had to walk in single file as the Iraqi terrorists pushed ahead.

"This would be a great place for an amb…" his thought was interrupted by a single sharp sound!

His mind and the minds of the others registered that sound. It was the sound created when the hammer of a gun hits the explosive cap in the chambered bullet causing a small explosion that propels a bullet out of the gun's chamber. The bullet spins out of the rifled barrel of the gun and gains speed. It leaves the barrel of the gun on its way to a target chosen by the shooter.

"…ambush!" the terrorist's mind finished the thought as he watched the leader of his band of evil jump briefly into the air and fall backward…a growing red mark on his forehead as blood oozed from the new hole into his brain.

The remaining twelve crouched down and realized that there was no cover for them. No large rock or pieces of wrecked buildings to hide behind like they were accustomed to in the Middle East. They had marched into the perfect trap!

Other shots were echoing against the sides of the rocky walls.

The other men were falling as they fired their weapons wildly into the air. In typical terrorist fashion they sprayed their guns and aimed at nothing in particular as the guns were fired from their hips. Very inefficient, but the massive number of bullets sprayed into the air sometimes hit a target. Not this time!

The last word uttered from his mouth before he perished to join his fellow terrorists in the promised land with so many virgins was, "shit!"

The group of thirteen all died where they stood and crumpled to the ground. A lethal crossfire had been launched from the plateau above the two steep rocky sides. Ash's team had quickly and easily annihilated the enemy in this ambush.

The island of Alamagan is small enough that the gunfire was heard by the other group of terrorists working their way around to the northeast in search of targets. They had not yet reached the trap that Reggie and his team had set before they heard the sounds of gunfire.

The men in Achmed's group immediately crouched down and listened intently. They searched their surroundings looking for something… anything that looked out of place. All that they could see was jungle. And they could only see into the jungle a few feet! The vegetation and grasses were thick, overgrown, and wild.

The sounds told them of the familiar sound of their Russian-made weapons. That was comforting. But they also heard strange reports from weapons they did not recognize. The men were now anxious and every nerve in their bodies was focused on the surrounding environment.

Was the last sound of gunfire from their comrades' weapons or was it a new sound from weapons they did not recognize? It was hard to discern. The last sound would tell them if their comrades were successful, or whether they were all gone.

Achmed picked up his American made radio that had been stolen from the United States Army. He didn't much care for how his supplies, be it American, Chinese, or Russian, made it into his hands. He always thanked Allah for the provisions to fight his war against the Americans…the Infidels…and for all of his successes in battle. He now silently called on Allah to protect his comrades, but he feared the worst. His men should have been on the radio first, calling him. He was now having to make the call…

He spoke into the radio several times attempting to raise the men that led the other group. There was no response. He had to now assume the worst of his fears that his men had perished. How? Who was it that fired against them?

The captain of the Russian trawler had also heard the gunfire. He now listened to his radio in the wheelhouse, and he heard Achmed calling out. In the short while that the Russian captain had known the Iraqi that was called Achmed, he knew that it was his voice on the radio. The captain did not know Farsi, but he was able to discern that the conversation was one-sided. Nobody was responding to Achmed.

Achmed gave up attempting to raise the other raiding party and signaled his men to move forward and continue their search. The Iraqis moved slowly and stealthily, listening even closer to every jungle sound. They were used to being able to see for long distances, not just a few feet. The men were out of their element. They hated being here on this tiny island with no space to move and no protection!

The men of I.N.C.I.S.O.R. whispered between themselves and decided to venture out of their ambush positions to attack the Iraqis. They crept forward knowing that there were only a few yards separating them from their foe.

One of the terrorists heard a faint click…the sound of a rifle safety being switched off. He arose from his crouching position and gave out a holler, "Allah 'Akbar!" and sprayed the plant life in an arc of one hundred and twenty degrees until his weapon was empty.

The other Iraqi men who had become 'trigger happy' at not being able to see the enemy, also stood and fired their weapons spraying hot lead into the jungle.

I ordered into my headset, "Kneecap them!"

'Kneecapping' is a difficult art in the field of battle. The legs are usually moving, and the target is quite small. Shooting for the heart is an easier job because the chest is a large, usually immobile target. If you don't hit the heart, you will hit some other vital organ. The training of 'two in the chest and one to the brain' is useful because the chest presents such a large and opportune target.

The Denver team opened fire with short bursts aimed at the lower legs of the Iraqis. Anguished cries went out from the Arab men as the bullets found their mark and their legs were incapacitated. Several of the terrorists had been able to reload and now fired their weapons wildly into the air.

Luckily for the I.N.C.I.S.O.R. team, the random sprays of bullets had been ineffective. No Iraqi bullet found its mark, and all fell harmlessly away. So many American soldiers had fallen to this technique of random spraying. Not today!

During the exchange Achmed remained in a crouching position and did not present himself as a target for the Denver team. Seeing that his men were all injured, and their legs could not support them, he turned and crawled toward the shore. He was abandoning his men. As he crawled, he whispered into the radio that the captain should get the boat turned around and ready to depart. What Achmed did not know was that the trawler captain had already prepared his boat for a hasty retreat.

As Achmed whispered into the radio, Ash silently appeared over him and with a single upward pull of his arm the Arab's throat was slashed. Ash then moved among the downed Iraqi terrorists and quickly dispatched them all to join Allah. He performed the task so quickly and stealthily that the Denver team did not witness his brutal and lethal movements just feet away from them. He talked to the team members through his headset and urged them not to fire and stood up in the mangled swordgrass.

"All clear!" he called, and we all stood to join him. The team members moved to congratulate each other and there were many comments about how close the Arabs were to their location.

I called out to Ash over the headset, "Ash…any Arab survivors?"

"Not a one!" Ash replied.

"Well so much for interrogating them to get intel," I stated.

"What intel? These were bad men!" Ash argued.

I gave up the debate. The Arab terrorists were all gone.

The trawler departed as soon as Achmed ceased talking on the radio and began to hightail its way back toward Pagan. The captain and crew of the boat had heard the exchanges of gunfire but had been unable to see any of the action on the shore. They chose to run rather than confront the American men on the island and were well out to sea when the two I.N.C.I.S.O.R. teams met on the shoreline.

Vladivostok, Russia

"Ivan! The trawler just reported in…all of the terrorists are dead. The mission has failed!" Vlad announced when he completed his call with the Russian boat. "They are steaming back to Pagan. Should they pick up the pilots?"

"Ah comrade, this is horrible news! We should not have been involved. We should have made and completed our own investigation, and not involved the Iraqis like we did," Ivan lamented.

"Comrade," Vlad spoke with disgust. "This was your idea all along! You wanted to embarrass the United States! Remember?"

Ivan turned to Vlad and scowled, "We still have to rescue that aircraft!"

CHAPTER 38

Saipan, Northern Mariana Islands

Igor and Charles motored their boat back to Saipan and docked at Smiling Cove Marina. Upon reaching their mooring the two men were swamped by the other fishermen of the island. Most of the men had become wealthy because of their involvement transporting the gold from the Philippines to Saipan and some were mourning the loss of the two men who were on the ill-fated craft that went down off to the west. The other dead seaman had been buried with a glorious sendoff.

All eight boxes and Dr. Cram were on board. The others wanted to hear the story of rescuing the gold, but first they helped remove the two bodies from the fishing boat. The coroner's office had been called and they whisked the bodies away to the hospital for future autopsies.

The men on the pier could see that the boat's crane was damaged.

"What happened to your winch?" one of the men asked.

"It is part of a long story that I will tell you," Igor began. "But first I need some coffee! Let us meet at J's restaurant for some breakfast and I will tell you all our story."

Pagan, Northern Mariana Islands

The pilots of the damaged airplane sat in the shade playing cards and drinking vodka. They had done all they could for the aircraft. It was now sitting in the grass off to the side of the landing strip. The latest report the two had was that the Russian trawler was chugging north toward their position and that a transport was on the way with material to repair the damage to the nose of their plane. They were both anxious for other human contact than themselves and to get off of this volcanic rock of an island. Any remote, lush tropical island visions of this place had been lost over the previous days alone here. They wanted to go home!

Saipan, Northern Mariana Islands

The same seaplane that had picked up the men of I.N.C.I.S.O.R. to deliver them from Saipan to the island of Alamagan returned them to Saipan. The seaplane took three trips to ferry all of the men and equipment. The heavy lift helicopter had been ordered to the island of Alamagan from Guam to carry the Escalade back to Saipan, and transport the Radio Free World equipment back to Guam. The I.N.C.I.S.O.R. teams from Frankfurt and Denver, along with Becky, Ash and Reggie were all on the island of Saipan together. Clarence and Brock had hitched a ride on the seaplane when it returned to Guam.

"So, Dr. Nelson…" Dale Denby began.

I interrupted, "You can call me Reggie."

"Awe, Reggie, it was a long time before I was willing to address you by your first name," Powers spoke.

"Okay guys, I am making it official…you can all call me Reggie," I replied.

"So…Reggie, how do you think the mission went? How did we do?" Dale finished his sentence.

"Yeah, it is rare for us all to have the three chiefs all together with all of us, Indians" Flex added.

"So, let us have it!" Duncan said.

"First the good news…there are a couple of dozen less terrorists in the world today and at least one important leader is now with Allah," I began.

There was a brief discussion before leaving Alamagan about how to dispose of the bodies of the Arab terrorists. The terrorists were dragged out into the ocean for a swift burial at sea. The Iraqis joined the other men that had been lost in the plane crash. There was talk of leaving the terrorists to the small critters, bugs, and grubs that inhabited Alamagan, but burial at sea seemed cleaner. The terrorists were now fish food.

"On the 'bad news' side, Ash and I were wrong to play with the Russians. Becky, please forgive me, but my ego clearly got in the way of my better judgement," I continued.

"Forgiven but not forgotten," Becky replied.

"Aw…cummon Beck!" Ash interjected in his best Southern slang. "Just for me? How about a kiss?"

Becky gave Ash a big hug and planted a kiss on his lips. "I'm glad you guys are all okay. You had to be in harm's way because my husband was stupid. But you're all okay. Should we all be here…exposed… together? That sounds careless to me."

"Party pooper!" Ash argued.

"Once again, Becky, you are right," I said. "You guys all enjoy tonight, and we are outta here tomorrow!"

"What is next for us, if I may ask?" Gary asked.

"Get settled back on your home turf. I'm working on a couple of options for us. I still think that we can help out in Somalia, and there are some other crazy areas in Africa where terrorists are performing uncivilized and offensive acts against innocent civilians. Maybe it is time for a trip to the dark continent," I replied.

"Well, you decide, and we will be there…just let us know! Hey guys… beer! Where are the girls on this island?" Lance said and the men left in small groups to explore the island, enjoy the tropical climate, and discover where the young island girls were hiding.

Pagan, Northern Mariana Islands

All of the Russians were busy working on restoring the damage to the plane's nose. They worked in earnest so that they could leave this island and return to their homeland. Many tools and equipment and supplies lay scattered in the long grass around the damaged aircraft. Some of the men were hammering and shaping the thin metal so that it could be used to reskin the nose. Others were laboring over electronic gear that would replace damaged equipment inside the nose.

Deep within the earth a massive tectonic plate moved beneath an oceanic plate. The immense pressure caused the release of water captured within the rock. The lighter magma, caused by the loss of water weight, began to build up in the magma chamber. The chamber grew and moved toward the surface ready to burst at any moment.

Without warning there was a monstrous explosion just off to their north. The men dropped everything, jumped to their feet, and looked toward the explosion.

Inside the Pagan volcano there was a massive eruption. The top two-thirds of the mountain disintegrated and blew apart sending ash and molten lava out for miles into the surrounding sea.

The eruption measured greater than 8 on the VEI or Volcanic Eruptions Index. This was a supervolcano that may happen once every fifty-thousand years.

The men were frozen where they stood, as they were covered in the hot ash. Just like the citizens of Pompei in 79 AD, they all died instantly. Lava then slowly moved to completely cover the island of Pagan. The Russians were never to be seen of or heard from again. The lava became their tomb. There also was no evidence that the mission had ever occurred. The molten lava removed any traces of human interference on this tiny island. Vladivostok chose to take the easy way out and deny that a mission was planned and executed against an American island in the Western Pacific.

The island of Pagan had become what the United States military had wanted for years and the local Chamorros and Carolinians fought against for decades. Pagan had become a live fire exercise location. The American military could bomb the hell out of it, having little effect on the cooling lava that now encased the island.

Saipan, Northern Mariana Islands

"Did you see today's paper?" Becky asked as we sat on our patio enjoying some coffee for me and herbal tea for Becky.

"No, didn't look at the paper," I replied.

Ash sauntered onto the patio looking ready for a day at the beach. "Need to work on my tan!"

"You're black!" I argued.

"When did that happen?" he joked as he checked out his body. "Reggie just so you know…we can burn too!"

"Hey guys, the volcano on Pagan blew!" Becky urged, interrupting our repartee. "Should we be worried here?"

"Naw, Becky, Pagan is two hundred miles from us here," Ash replied.

"What's the paper say?" I asked.

"I just told you! Pagan blew up!" Becky exclaimed and acted frustrated.

"Hope those Russian dudes made it off the island," Ash said.

"I guess we'll never know…" I began.

Just then the phone chirped on the patio table.

"Reginald Nelson," I answered.

"Dr. Nelson…this is the president of Nigeria…have you heard of Boko Haram?" the man on the phone asked.

I stood up and Becky and Ash looked at me expectantly.

"Yes sir, I have!" I stated into the phone, probably a little too loudly.

"Your President Marron suggested that I call you. He told me that you have done much to help your country fight terrorism. What is your group called? I.N.C.I.S.O.R.?"

"Yes, sir. How may I help you?" I answered.

"It is just that…I need your help…

CPSIA information can be obtained
at www.ICGtesting.com
Printed in the USA
LVHW110917310822
727098LV00026B/17